I AM CHINA | 最蔚蓝的海

"A complex and fascinating political narrative. The lives of Jian and Mu, haunted by the turbulent history of Chinese politics (in particular, the Tiananmen Square massacre of 1989), read like a eulogy for a lost vision of China." —*The Observer* (London)

"Steeped in music, revolution, exile and romance, this is a story from the front lines of contemporary China." —*Houston Chronicle*

"With *I Am China*, Xiaolu Guo has completed her metamorphosis from an exile writing about displacement in a second language to a writer who seems to occupy two worlds at once, with a discerning eye cast on each and the myriad intersections between them." —*Toronto Star*

"A compelling read. . . . Vividly captures the mixed emotions of the youths of the 1980s about their home country and the impact on their lives decades after." —*The Asian Review of Books*

"A harrowing glimpse into post-Tiananmen repression in China. . . . A mix of dissident rhetoric and heartbreak that turns on one couple's story." —*Kirkus Reviews*

"Guo's bittersweet tale of love and politics with a soupçon of obsession plays out against the contrast between East and West. . . . This is truly a finely crafted novel whose characters will remain in memory long after reading the final page." —*Booklist*

XIAOLU GUO

I AM CHINA │ 最蔚蓝的海

Xiaolu Guo published six books in China before moving to London in 2002. The English translation of *Village of Stone* was shortlisted for the Independent Foreign Fiction Prize and nominated for the International IMPAC Dublin Literary Award. Her first novel written in English, *A Concise Chinese–English Dictionary for Lovers*, was shortlisted for the Orange Broadband Prize for Fiction, and *Twenty Fragments of a Ravenous Youth* was longlisted for the Man Asian Literary Prize. She is also a successful director of feature films, including *She, a Chinese* and *UFO in Her Eyes*, and documentaries; her work has premiered at the Venice Film Festival, the Toronto Film Festival, and other venues all over the world. She was named as one of *Granta*'s Best Young British Novelists.

www.guoxiaolu.com

Also by Xiaolu Guo

Village of Stone (translated from the Chinese)
A Concise Chinese–English Dictionary for Lovers
Twenty Fragments of a Ravenous Youth
UFO in Her Eyes
Lovers in the Age of Indifference

I AM CHINA | 最蔚蓝的海

A NOVEL

XIAOLU GUO

ANCHOR BOOKS

A Division of Penguin Random House LLC

New York

FIRST ANCHOR BOOKS EDITION, AUGUST 2015

This is a work of fiction. Names, characters, places, and incidents either are the
product of the author's imagination or are used fictitiously. Any resemblance to
actual persons, living or dead, events, or locales is entirely coincidental.

The Library of Congress has cataloged the Nan A. Talese /
Doubleday edition as follows:
Guo, Xiaolu.
I Am China : a novel / Xiaolu Guo. — First American Edition.
pages cm
1. Short stories, English.   I. Title.
PR9450.9.G86I26 2014   823'.92—dc23   2013049786

Anchor Books Trade Paperback ISBN: 978-0-8041-7047-5
eBook ISBN: 978-0-385-53872-5

www.vintagebooks.com

Printed in the United States of America
10   9   8   7   6   5   4   3   2   1

I'll love you, dear, I'll love you
Till China and Africa meet,
And the river jumps over the mountain
And the salmon sing in the street.

"AS I WALKED OUT ONE EVENING," W. H. AUDEN

CONTENTS

PRELUDE

Dearest Mu,

The sun is piercing, old bastard sky. I am feeling empty and bare. Nothing is in my soul, apart from the image of you.

I am writing to you from a place I cannot tell you about yet. Perhaps when I am safe I will be able to let you know where I am. I don't know what the plan is and what my future might hold. One thing is for sure: I will try to stay free and alive, for you. And whatever happens, these ideas I have stuck by all my life—the beliefs that landed me here in the first place—I cannot let them go. I must live for them. I know we'll see each other again, my love, but how long until that day I cannot tell.

When I look around at where I am now, it seems so obvious it should have come to this. Maybe this is where I was going the whole time, I just never saw it coming. Or never believed it. I've been headed here, I realise, ever since June 1989. I know we have talked about it so much, but tonight under this southern sky the images of that night are burning in my head. You were still in your southern home town. We hadn't even met. But I was there, and here I'll say it again: I wish I had been shot that day. I should have died there. Shot and crushed under the tanks.

I remember the night after the massacre. I went alone to Tiananmen Square. It was midnight. The troops of the People's Liberation Army had washed the blood off the pavement. The hunger strikers' tents had been pulled down and the square was deserted, but rubbish was scattered everywhere—blood-soaked shirts and ripped student scarves. If you looked closely you could see the blood had soaked into the gaps between the stones. I stood there and thought: this is our most glorious square. For hundreds of years people have celebrated, fought and marched on it. Every day hundreds of thousands of bicycles roll over it; hundreds of thousands of people walk on it. But now the people are defeated. I wished my blood was soaking into the earth between those stones: that would have been a worthy death. That would have been a worthy youth.

Dearest Mu, you know what I am saying. It repeats itself in my mind. It repeats itself because of this split in me, that's still there after all these eighteen years of us being together. I have loved you so long—you are my only family in this world. But you say you never really understand politics. You were not there in 1989. You could not understand.

I remember that May, a month before the massacre. It was the week when Chairman Hu Yaobang died, and I had just discovered the first Chinese translation of "Howl," that pocket edition we used to read together. All the students in Beijing's universities started to worry about the future. Hu was the last good leader of China. We sat and argued in cafes—somehow studying seemed so unimportant. Is there any hope? we wondered. And that same week the socialist Polish government held its first democratic election. Everyone in the West was talking about democracy vs. communism. But China was uninterested. Nothing would change. We knew that. I was only seventeen years old, but I felt like an old man already, sad and depressed. Where was my faith? And the balls and the belief to achieve something in politics? But then I thought: forget about the politics, there is only one good thing in all this. It was the band, of course. I had just formed my first band. That band

4

you came to like so much. And you know how it felt for me then—I was going to start the new century with music, the first real Chinese rock 'n' roll band. And this is what it came down to: I would rather burst eardrums with my guitar than fight with it at the barricades.

So that June, when the student demonstration started in the square, I was feverishly in love with rock 'n' roll. I reckon I had already decided that a musical revolution was better than direct action while all my classmates were out protesting and on hunger strike. On 3 June, after spending two hours in the square and raising banners and flags, I have to confess, a weariness overcame me. Mu, did I ever talk about this weariness? I returned to the campus alone. I should have stayed. It should really have been my event. It's like my defining life moment happened without me.

On the night of that fateful day I stayed in the empty dormitory listening to the Sex Pistols and thinking about music, my music. The building was utterly deserted. There was this unruly wind going crazy, back and forth along the long empty corridors, and sending shivers up my spine. I sat on my bed and began fiddling with my old guitar. It needed new strings. The tuning was fucked and my amp had lost two valves. But still, with that crazy wind running up my spine, I wrote the first lines of "Long March into the Night": "Hey, little sister, let me take you down the street, the long march is waiting . . ."

I must go now, my dearest woman. The plane is waiting to take me away. I believe we will be soon in each other's arms again.

Your love,
Jian

ONE | IONA

谁谓河广，一叶杭之。
谁谓宋远，趾予望之。

shui wei he guang, yi ye hang zi.
shui wei song yuan, zhi yu wang zhi.

Who says that the river is wide?
With a bundle of reeds I can cross it.
Who says that the Kingdom of Song is distant?
On my tiptoes I can view it.

THE BOOK OF ODES (1000–700 BC)

1 LONDON, APRIL 2013

London is a roar, a slow explosion, scattering every living and dead thing and never letting them rest. Every corner hums, or echoes with a hum, which both repels and attracts. Even the colours and smells seem to roar. Even in the seemingly serene corners of green-grey Hackney parks, with their steel-trap ornate fences, this savage sound reverberates. The City is drowned, infected by the ooze of its energy, and out east along the waterways, Docklands and Limehouse, with their fake Venetian-Lido-style living, are stained by the intensity of sound. And further and further outward to New Cross, Shepherd's Bush, Kilburn, Kensal Rise, with its black faces and ghost-white youth leading pig-eyed surly dogs, all humming, all electrified by a single slow shout.

In a poky two-room flat not far from Islington, the ripples of the roar still resound. Here the middle class has found a cosy corner, and a young woman called Iona Kirkpatrick has made herself a home, if only temporarily.

Iona is jet-black-haired and blue-eyed. As another London day is breaking she is getting up from her bed. She places two bare feet on her wooden floor. Naked, she puts on her black bra. Moving towards the window, she opens it, lets out last night's stale air. She takes a deep breath, tracking the skid of an aeroplane in the morning sky.

Behind her in the background gloom of her flat, a nameless man finishes dressing, putting on his shirt and trousers. He gazes at Iona's bare back, her boyish bottom, her bony and compact features. He betrays a certain awkwardness. Iona doesn't ask him to stay for breakfast, or make the simple offer of a morning coffee. Since they woke up she has offered him nothing. Yet last night she had been so receptive, the way she had opened her body for him.

"Shall we have a coffee together somewhere?" he asks, and then leaves the sentence hanging, as if he were going to say more, but doesn't.

"No." Iona shakes her head, not turning to look at him. "Too much to do."

Watching her slip into the black silk panties, he remembers how he had pulled them off last night as she stood by her desk. Like a soldier surrendering, she had raised both arms above her head as he undressed her. She had been submissive. But now she is cold. As she puts on her pyjama top, she doesn't look at him at all.

"So, you know where you are," she says, polite but distant. "I don't need to come down with you, do I?" She buttons up her pyjama top but leaves her legs bare.

"I'll be fine," he answers. A pause. "When can we see each other again?"

She turns to him now, refusal in her eyes. She shrugs her shoulders in a gentle gesture of "no."

The nameless man kisses her goodbye and leaves. She hears the soft press of his feet on the carpet grow steadily fainter until the door shuts behind him.

Up above the morning traffic Iona stands by the window, watching him disappear into the throng of the cobbled street. The scent of sex still lingers in the room, and seems to surprise her. It's on the sheets, and on her body. She sees a scattering of hairs on the pillow, and an odour, not hers, leaves a cloying warmth in the bed. She strips off the sheets and stuffs the knotted mass into the washing machine. In less than an hour, she says to herself, she won't remember his smell. And before long the recollection of his face will also have been washed from her memory.

In the bathroom she removes her pyjama top and underwear. Standing under the shower head, she lets the water pour down on her hair. A familiar sense of relief floods over her. The lust and dirt of last night, staining her pale skin, are rinsed off and washed down the drain, mingling with other waste, to begin their journey through London's numberless sewers and then ultimately out into the muddy Thames.

2 LONDON, APRIL 2013

For Iona, there are two modes of expression that bring her to life. One is the sexual act. All it takes to rekindle her sense of being alive is that small breath of a decision. The decision to leave a pub with an unknown man and go back with him. She takes pleasure in entering a totally new world in the pitch black of night. The next day she can live with ease.

Her other world is through words. To delve into words, to live with them circling in her mind, allows her to regain something of her life. Perhaps this, most of all, is what enables her to connect. As a teenager, driven crazy by the boredom of living on a small Scottish island inhabited largely by sheep, she found herself longing for foreign words: the alien sound, the unknown syllable, the mysterious sign. Learning languages consumed her. She stuffed herself full with them, and went to university for more. Perhaps a foreign language would offer her an escape. At school everyone had teased her about acting because of her striking resemblance to Hollywood actress Winona Ryder, but shy Iona never saw herself as an actress. She retreated into words.

As the noise of morning from the street below surges up to her at the window, she shakes off her lethargy and the memory of the man's touch only a few hours ago. Iona makes herself a strong cup of tea and sits down at her desk. On the table, beside a bulky English–Chinese Dictionary, sits a stack of photocopied Chinese documents. She leafs through the papers. Some appear to be letters; others are diary entries of hardly legible Chinese characters. She randomly picks one of the pages from the stack. Almost a scrawl, she thinks. This may be harder than I thought. She starts to read the first letter on the top of the pile.

Dearest Mu,

The sun is piercing, old bastard sky. I am feeling empty and bare. Nothing is in my soul, apart from the image of you.

I am writing to you from a place I cannot tell you about yet. Perhaps when I am safe I will be able to let you know where I am . . .

A few weeks earlier Iona had received an email from a publisher she hadn't worked with before. They were interested in translating some Chinese letters and diaries—this motley heap on her desk. The pay wasn't bad; most of the other translation jobs she took up were deeply boring: business or legal documents. Iona didn't demand anything more: no information, no context. She remembered that lull after graduation where she seemed to live only moment to moment, with no plan, no future and five thousand Chinese characters lodged in her mind struggling to get out.

With long fine fingers she picks up a pencil and is ready to begin her work. But the pages look very confusing. Some pages don't have dates on them, some are only half legible due to the deep black stain of the photocopier. The person who photocopied the original documents clearly didn't speak Chinese as the pages are completely muddled and in no particular order. As she flicks through the folder, she begins to wonder where the publisher got hold of them. It looks like some of the letters and diaries are from a long time ago, some more recent. They span nearly twenty years—there are dark spots from greasy fingers, smudges and ink stains and, in a few places, blurry characters as if someone had spilt something or cried onto the page. The editor at Applegate Books had sent her the heavy folder through the post with only a cursory note, saying the material related to a famous Chinese musician. "We need a bit of an idea of what we've got here," she had written. "We think there could be something very interesting, but it's hard to know without some sort of translation." At a rare appearance at a publishing party recently, where she had stayed for two quick drinks and lingered mostly on the edges of the crowd—her skirt was too long, her conversation too intense—Iona had overheard this editor declaiming, "We used to publish eminent people's biographies, like the Dalai Lama's, but no one cares about 'eminent figures' any more. We're more interested in marginal characters, especially if they're connected to something big."

There's an officious-looking letterhead on the first letter. It reads "*Beijing 1540 Civil Crime Detention Centre,*" and there's an address— somewhere she doesn't recognise. She looks it up on Google maps. The pin lands in an empty grey landscape of main roads in the dark hinterland outside Beijing. She tries to imagine the desolation of a place like that—grey buildings, grey roads. She looks back at the messy script and starts to read.

11 November 2011

Dear Mu,

I can't bear this. My days are going by agonisingly slowly. There's so little light from the window and I'm only accompanied by the stark and cold prison walls. How do I distract myself from going completely mad? I'm building the walls of our little flat inside the dark cave of this cell—our little home, where there is hot afternoon light and droopy plants, and we stand on our balcony facing the distant Xiang Mountain listening to those pirated foreign CDs we used to buy at the market—it soothes me when I think of all this.

I know you cannot visit me, but I wish you would write to me. Your silence since I showed you my manifesto is just unbearable. How can you say you don't believe in what I've written? Does it sound extreme to say that if you don't believe in my manifesto, you don't believe in me? Not to me it doesn't, though you may laugh and call me naive, call me too idealistic. For me art, politics and love are all connected. You have seen how I lived for all these years—this is nothing new. It's been nearly twenty years since I wrote my very first song, Mu! Twenty years is half a life! Half our lives, and all the time I've known you. And all that time you knew me. You lived with me. You accepted me by loving me. So what's different now?

What manifesto? Iona wonders. She puts down her pencil and rereads what she's translated. The voice on the page is angry. Even his handwriting is angry: the pen is pressed deep into the page; there are crossings-out and repetitions. And who is this Mu? Iona looks out of the window. The sky has whitened still further, as if it's sucking all the energy out of the busying crowds below.

I'm going to say it again, even if you might not want to hear it. I know you, and I know you understand. There is no art without political commitment. All art is political expression. You know that—please, Mu, you know these things, why do you continue to block me out? We've talked about this. You knew I was going to distribute the statement at my concert. I felt stifled. We knew this might happen. Even as I miss you, I still think it was worth it.

Imagine my arms around you in our bed. My woman, you know I love you.

Your Peking Man,
Jian

3 LINCOLNSHIRE, JANUARY 2012

The Chinese man sits at a table, holding a broken ballpoint pen. The surface of the table is heavily scratched, marked by the handwriting of every man who has sat there before him. Opening his diary, the pages all falling out, he tries to record the last few weeks. But he feels weary. Perhaps he is still jet-lagged, or disorientated. He stares at an oak tree outside the window whose twisted branches seem to stretch into the cloud laden sky like his thoughts. An old garden under an old sky. Old skin on an old body. Old, England is old, he murmurs to himself. His only reminder of China are two small cherry trees sheltering under the canopy of the huge oak. In this overheated room his eyes feel tired and his head congested. Maybe it's the sleeping pills he's been given to take. Or the words, words, words that the nurses fling at him in a language he can't fully understand, despite what he learned at university. Their exasperated faces grimacing as he looks back at them blank and mournful.

He wonders about the unit he is in—the Florence Nightingale Unit—as he watches the strange people around him. All in matching striped pyjamas, either agonised or oblivious, but all hurting in some way. Why don't they just call it what it is: "Mad People's Reform Hospital," exactly as the Chinese would do? He cannot understand the layers of confusion around him.

He looks back at the desk in front of him, his thoughts awash with recent events. The white-greyness around him is numbing. The humiliation, some days ago, when the doctor told him about his "borderline personality." The words wouldn't come. He felt totally inert and unable to argue back or explain what was really wrong.

Each night he stares at his battered guitar, which he brought all the way from China; he has barely touched its metal strings since he got here. There's a new dent on the body from the scuffle and fight at the concert. The rough hot hands which grabbed him and pulled him off the stage as the spotlights were burning his face. He hasn't let that day into his thoughts for weeks. The guitar stands there, almost in judgement against him. But he can't look at it without seeing the face of a Chinese girl, gazing up at him from the front of the crowd, her face open, full and light—the one still point in that underground den of mania.

Then he thinks of those rare days he tried to set aside and spend alone, away from his musician friends, trying to write a song in memory of his long-dead mother. He remembers he wept as a little child, in rage and utter confusion, standing before his mother's gravestone. Now the days of being alone seem to be the normal pattern of his life.

Suddenly a shattering sound cuts through the air, like the frantic squawk of a bird trapped inside a room. Jian is startled out of sleep. He finds himself in the patients' library. His fellow inmates are absorbed in Sudoku puzzles and blotted crossword grids. He's awake, but tiredness clings to his limbs. His mind is possessed by hallucinatory impressions of his favourite "mala" beef-and-hog noodle soup with extra Sichuan peppers. The soup is steaming with heat right in front of his face. China is still alive for him. It has not been too long; he can still taste it. Smell the dank, sharp tang of the backstreets of Beijing and the tickle in his nose of the chilli in the air as he passes market stalls. He waits. His body dull and heavy.

It's late evening. He looks up at the darkening sky, searching for familiar stars. He can see the Big Dipper, only a little obscured by clouds. Swathes of empty blank sky. And then he spots a comet, speeding fast towards the dark horizon. It zips along. Barely seen. As his eyes follow the trail of the comet's burning dust, it feels like his body has been a comet zooming through the dark blue, from his birth in the leap year of 1972, when China was still in the throes of the Cultural

Revolution. There he was, landed in a half-Mongol, half-Beijing family. And now the comet has landed here, in some backwater of a sodden suburb of a second-rate town in a country long since descended from glory. It must have been something about his origins, he thinks, in the Year of the Rat, that has led him here, along an inscrutable path. The rat was running as he burst out of his mother's womb. According to his grandparents, when he came out, a screaming brat in Beijing's No. 8 Women's Hospital, with the umbilical cord almost strangling his cries, his family was in the midst of Mao's madness, the Chairman's very last ideological war against the bogeyman of imperialism and the bourgeois infection of the people's revolution. The rat was hissing, for sure, when his grandmother took him to an old palm-reader in Beijing's Heavenly Gate Park. The white-bearded man opened the child's palm, studied it for a few seconds, then announced: "There are dark clouds floating in his destiny; but his energy is stronger than the clouds. He will prevail if he avoids his wilfulness." Jian's grandmother didn't fully understand those words as the child's hand escaped from her grip and tried to flee from the palm-reader into the steamy Beijing streets. But the rat-child grew up in a time of indoctrination. He was fed on the milk of ideology: Marxism plus Leninism, interpreted through Maoism. And when he was eight he was spouting the slogans of the party, a robust, fierce, cherry-faced child, on a flag-hung stage, with a wooden gun and a red kerchief around his neck, as if bursting from a socialist-realist canvas. But his allegiance didn't last long: his teenage years blew his spirit to the opposite shore.

Now, in the cool night, beneath a low English sky and distant Midland traffic, Jian's past seems to him like dying embers, like a theatre of bright shadows playing quietly in his mind. A nurse passes, muttering words in a still-unfamiliar tongue; he remembers where he is. It is late, ten thirty at night. Slowly, he walks back to the bedroom he shares with other patients. He swallows a sleeping pill left for him in a small plastic cup on his bedside table. He sits on his bed, picks up his battered guitar and strokes the fretboard. The guitar has a line of characters written on its side. Although it is very scratched, Jian can still read it:

资本主义清道夫—This Machine Kills Capitalists

His fingers find the familiar chords that still resonate with his energetic rat's heart inside. He plucks a string. The sound stretches out in the silent night. One of his room-mates suddenly wakes up, turning his neck and staring at Jian blankly until he sighs and puts his guitar down. Laying his head on the cold pillow, he gazes up at the grey ceiling and feels the darkness around him. Until dawn, sleep does not come. He wakes up with a single burning thought: I have to get out of here, any way I can. So he starts at the top.

4 LINCOLNSHIRE, FEBRUARY 2012

Kublai Jian
Lincolnshire Psychiatric Hospital
2 Brocklehurst Crescent
Grantham NG31

The Queen
Buckingham Palace
London SW1A 1AA

Dearest Queen,

My name is Kublai Jian, but they usually call me Jian—it means strong and vigorous. I'm writing to you from a madhouse in Lincolnshire. I'm sure you know your English towns as well as you know how many toes you have and how many nails are attached to your toes, and that Lincolnshire is where your Lady Thatcher comes from. You may think I am not sober, like the people in this madhouse. But I promise you that at this very moment, I am more sober and steady than anyone else here.

I believe you understand the justice of this world. I think a powerful person like you can really help me out. In China we say if you can talk to the boss then don't talk to the boss's secretary, and if you can talk to the boss's wife then no need to talk to the boss. So, dear Queen, you are that boss lady, you are the top one!

I lived all my life in China. Well, up until a few weeks ago. I arrived in London at the end of December, and ended up in a wet and poky flat near Mile End station. It was quite depressing to live on a rotten carpet all day, but that was nothing compared with what came afterwards. One morning I was downstairs eating two oily sausages, and I found a letter from the UK Home Office and they had turned down my asylum application. I swallowed the second sausage and decided to fight back. I needed to gather £2,000 for an appeal, plus many extra documents which I don't have. That day I went crazy and began to scream at everyone who was trying to talk to me. Then during the night my stomach declared a war on me, sharp pains in my intestines. Dear Queen, maybe this is not your business but I have had a very troubled bowel since I was a child, which is exactly what Fidel Castro has suffered from all his life. Bad intestine, knotted and throbbed and bubbled. I thought I was going to die that very night.

But I did not die. Next morning someone took me to a hospital. And after an overall check-up with one doctor, he said there was nothing wrong with my bowel but possibly something wrong with my head. I cursed the man's mother and grandmother and his great-great-uncle. He then immediately sent me to another doctor who specialises on brain but not body. I was so angry and impatient that I hit the brain doctor on his face and smashed his glasses.

Right after that three security guards seized me and put me in a van. Two hours later I found myself in some ugly suburb with sheep walking in the fields. I arrived in a very lonely town that looked like an old people's retirement village, and only several hours later I find out this is psychiatric hospital! They asked me to remove my own clothes and to change into regulation striped pyjamas, they said I should rest on a bed in a windowless room. "Rest? Rest for what?" I shouted to them, but they didn't bother to answer me. Next morning a "Consultant Psychiatrist" called me into an office and told me that I wasn't well enough to leave. "It would be best for you to stay here," he said. I argued with him and told him they got me wrong: I was being thrown on a truck blindly and driven to a madhouse like a pig being sent to a slaughterhouse. But he said all patients claimed such things when they first arrived. "Soon you'll get used to being here." He patted on my shoulder like I was one of his distant cousins.

Now, dearest Queen, let me be direct—why I'm writing to you? I need your help in this country. You may think I am a troublemaker. But I am not. I grew up in Beijing. An ideology-rigid city. That's where my struggle began. In Beijing I was a punk musician. But I must explain, being Chinese punk is very different from your country's youth. You may think we are not decent boys, swearing and spitting, burning our guitars or taking out our genitals from our jeans on the stage. No, we are not like that at all. We are disciplined, well educated, and sing about politics and art. But it is not always easy to rage against the government. I think you might like my music so I'm enclosing our most famous album with the leading song: "Long March into the Night."

Excuse me being wordy, but I do hope you can get me out of here!

Yours sincerely,
Kublai Jian

5 LONDON, APRIL 2013

Iona is on her third coffee of the day. As usual, she has barely eaten anything all day, but she likes the spare feeling in her stomach of "running on empty." She often forgets to eat. Her sister said once that she had an eating disorder. Certainly food, like men, has a certain problematic position in her life.

For now, it's the pleasure of reading these Chinese texts that is sustaining her. Like a nun in her cell, with precious illuminated manuscripts set out before her, Iona works on a photocopied diary entry. The handwriting looks similar to the letters she translated a few days ago—messy, masculine, with big strokes and a sort of urgent calligraphy. The diary must be written by the same man, Iona thinks to herself. Slowly she types out her translation.

It's eight thirty in the morning and I'm not going to lectures today. A few hours ago I met again that moon-faced girl. I feel as if I now have a clearer picture of her. She has a nervous energy, like a little canary standing at the mouth of a hot-vapoured volcano. There is something tough about her that draws me in, but at the same time, she is as delicate as a fragile young bird. It sounds foolish—I hardly know her!—but I feel as if I can sense her moods, like waves of the sea pressing into my chest as I look at her dark eyes hidden beneath her fringe. I wanted to ask her out a few weeks ago when we met for the first time at the volleyball match, but I've been practising with the band so much I just haven't had a chance. I see her in class and at lectures, half looking at me and then quickly glancing away—fresh, small, biting her lower lip, not looking me in the eye, like a lonely flower fearful of the wind.

But last night we talked in a new way. It was at the concert our band had been building up to. My fingers are still sore. My ears still ringing. I don't feel like I've slept properly or eaten properly in weeks. But I don't give a fuck! I'm on a rush, like I'm on a runaway train and I won't be getting off soon.

We were in Cafe Proletarian in Wudaokou. It's small but it felt like a big deal for me and the band. There were at least two hundred fans even though the space could only fit in eighty, and the sound system was lousy but we played as loud as we could. We just went with the flow, and it all seemed to come together so well. Suddenly she seemed like the focus of it all.

Now I divide my life between Before-Her and After-Her. She's dug herself into me. She's a heat inside me, churning me up. Tonight she told me she has only been kissed once before, when she was just fifteen, by a boy she knew back home in the village where she grew up. And now the second one is me! The first grown man in her life. Tonight she became my fire, and I hers. The band were playing under the tacky, eighties spinning disco lights, and the spotlights were zinging in my eyes. She was standing and jumping right at the front of the stage. The colours of the neon lights were bouncing off her white dress. I was singing hard and fast, sweat pouring from my face and my fingers melding with my guitar and the music, and then I looked down and she was looking up at me with her big black button eyes. Her eyes were the brightest eyes in that field of eyes before me. I thought I could see them glistening in the centre of the smoky haze. It's a rock cliché but no one would refuse it. I stood in the middle of the stage with Raohao playing his bass on my right side, Yanwu his guitar on my left, and Sunxin hitting his drums behind my head. I was screaming and howling. And she was right at the front singing along with the mass, swishing her shiny dark hair. I even thought I could hear her high and girlish voice in the cloud of noise. It was one ripple in the churned-up sea, and I was the eye of the storm.

Suddenly a sharp sound breaks Iona's quiet. She looks around; her phone is ringing loudly on her desk and the vibrating motion against the wood makes it hum insistently. Still holding the photocopied pages of the Chinese man's diary, Iona turns back to the page and tries to ignore it. But the sound is persistent and after the caller hangs up they try again straight away.

"Yes?"

"Iona? Is this a bad time?" Her mother's voice sounds hesitant.

"Mum, I'm working."

"Oh, that's surprising! Yes, very good, darling."

"What's up? Are you all right?" Iona speaks impatiently.

"Yes, all good, darling. But the milking machine isn't working properly, and one of last year's calves died yesterday. I've been in the garden, but it's so cold I came back into the kitchen to warm up. So I just thought I'd call you while I wait for the kettle to boil."

"Oh dear. I'm so sorry." Iona is hasty and distracted. "Listen, Mum, can I call you back in a bit? I'm just in the middle of something." She pauses and there's silence on the other end. "I'm sorry, Mum, I'm sorry, it's just—"

"It's fine, darling. Bye dear." And she puts the phone down.

Iona sits down again and picks up her pencil. She resumes where she left off, and starts translating the rest of the passage, this time with a more urgent energy. The words are spilling out of her onto the page.

. . . It was one ripple in the churned-up sea, and I was the eye of the storm. Through the smoky air, the vortex of turning lights, I could see some students had lit candles and lighters to match the lines from my song. The disco lights dimmed. We could feel this wave of sound, all of us connected by our music. It was unforgettable! Perfection! And her right in the middle of it! Then all of a sudden the electric power was cut and the double doors at the back of the hall swung open. Police. Now there was just screaming in the dark. And all the lights went out. I felt someone lunge for me in the dark. Mu's skinny arms had found me in the blackness and her soft cheeks were next to my face, her cold hands tight around my waist. And among the sirens and the mess in the darkness, she screamed into my ear: "Jian, I will come with you if the police take you. I won't let you be arrested alone!" I found her lips with mine. She, the most delicate girl, the bravest of all, stood there waiting to go under with me. We were very still, in all the noise and movement around us. Then after what seemed like forever, the lights were back on, the venue was quiet and the police were gone. There weren't many people left and the cafe manager totally freaked out but we didn't give a fuck. We started playing again. Gradually, more and more

people returned to the cafe. We played until this morning, more
fervent than before. We came back to my studio (luckily I'd made
the bed). And she has only just left for class. I can't get enough
of her.

Iona puts down her pencil and looks towards the darkening distant skyline. She can hear vans loading unsold vegetables from the market stalls down below, dealers continuing to holler and roar to the crowds before the day ends, and pots and pans banging in the restaurants for dinner. But all she can really see and hear is a Chinese band on an illuminated stage waving their dark hair and revving the crowd with each dramatic lunge and each twang of the electric guitars, then a girl in a white dress squeezing herself into the front row, chanting and crying . . . And after the concert, what then? Perhaps the silhouettes of two young lovers, their hair damp with sweat, their skin still glowing with the acid neon colours of the disco lights. Shy together, excited together. Iona's vision curdles. Music and romance—that's what youth is all about! Suddenly she feels restless, she can't stand to sit still on her chair. She feels as if her body has been poured like wet concrete into a mould—she has been stuck in her comfortable little prison for too long. Iona closes her computer. Best to get out of here.

6 LONDON, APRIL 2013

Iona zigzags through the crowds on White Lion Street, crossing Upper Street, passing Angel Tube station, heading towards her favourite park—Duncan Terrace Garden. The sparks from Kublai Jian's words flare within her as if she too were walking around with a teenage body and teenage spirit. She has just turned thirty-one, but she looks younger. One couldn't tell from just a glance that she was a child of the spring of 1982, when Britain and Argentina went to war over the Falkland Islands and Ronald Reagan became president of the United States. She was born, she still thinks improbably, to Michael and Bethan Kirkpatrick on the Isle of Mull in Scotland. She was the second girl in the family, her parents hoping against hope for a boy. The day after Iona was born, war broke out. As the young mother bathed their new baby, fed her and cuddled her, the father held his ear to the ancient radio in the sitting room and listened to Margaret Thatcher's speeches. He was convinced with rabid certainty that Britain was on the verge of a Third World War. He collected tins of beans and pulses, tomatoes and peas. The cupboards were filled with packets of pasta and cartons of long-life milk. He was worried. And he was prepared. But no world war came and Iona grew up. Instead of melting in the fires of Armageddon she became a skinny child with knock knees and tousled hair.

Her childhood was all about waiting, wondering, and the promise of what lay beyond the sea. She would stand on the beach on the Isle of Mull and look across the blackened-purple channel to the hilly shape of the island opposite—the Isle of Iona, looming as a hazy silhouette in the distance. The Isle of Mull that her feet trod every day held no secrets for Iona Kirkpatrick, but the bluish islet in the distance enchanted her. The place that gave Iona her name was still an unknown place. Islanders would talk in whispers; "magical," they would say, a place to dream about, to yearn for. But she had never set foot there. In the winter it seemed further away, as if it were a blurred brown ship beyond the spray; in the summer it glowed green against the rare blue sky.

Her parents had honeymooned on the Isle of Iona, and constantly talked of going back. But they were always too busy. As the years passed, the story of the island became a kind of fable in Iona's mind. It seemed to change with each retelling, as her father embroidered and exaggerated, and the truth—whatever that may be—was submerged in a swirl of youthful images, as turbid as the sea itself. Perhaps they had seen dolphins from their hotel window one night, and perhaps they might even eke out their retirement there. But Iona could never be sure what to believe, and her mother would always give her at best an enigmatic smile.

Her teenage years went by on the island pretty quietly, until the day she left with two large suitcases. That year she was seventeen. She still remembers the morning in late August, she was taking a ferry, leaving the Isle of Mull for her college study. Her mother was standing by the bank waving a hand and smiling, and her father, as always, was standing further back, without any gesture. He never liked to show emotion in front of women, at least on the surface. And her sister Nell, far away in Russia, had already left the family for ten good months. As the ferry was leaving, a gust of wind started to blow. Suddenly Iona heard her father's shout in the blasting wind: "Send me postcards, Iona, will you?!" She looked straight to her grey-haired father and her small-built mother. Her father's face was reddened—had he been drinking into the early hours the night before? Or perhaps he had always been like that. His skinny arms were now raised in the air, and his body seemed to quiver and tremble in the invisible wind. He looked sad and weak. Suddenly, her throat snagged on itself. Instinctively, she gripped her hands on the railing, set her jaw and twisted her face into a smile. She didn't want to show any sign of anguish to her parents. It would be weak, a sign of indecision, and failure to be adult. After all, she had always wanted to leave the place. And hadn't she outgrown it? The ferry headed towards Oban, the biggest town near their island, where she could take the train. But as she glanced at the ever smaller and smaller figures of her parents by the shore, she found her tears were flowing. The waves slithered past like white-backed green lizards coiling under each other. She turned back and saw the mainland coming monotonously closer to her with each surge of the ferry. Her tears soon turning joyful, sliding down her cheeks, then dried by the wind.

Years later, when Iona thinks of her father, the image of the man standing by the shore shouting to her through the blasting wind sticks in her mind. It's an image of a man, aged in body yet still with a youthful energy and sinewy masculinity, but broken by the coarseness and isolation of island life. His mouth is open as he shouts, but she cannot hear the sound of his voice. It's like a still from a silent black and white film, and makes her shudder. It's hard to believe there was ever any spark of love between her parents, looking at them now. Perhaps when her elder sister, Nell, was born. But it seems like it had already exhausted itself by the time they had her—the mistake, the interloper. She had felt so free as the boat pulled away from the harbour, and she left her complicated feelings about her parents behind. And now, she still feels free despite these echoes from her past. Free and open to a world of possibility. A world beyond the confines of a dark sea-ringed island, combed by raw winds.

7 LINCOLNSHIRE, FEBRUARY 2012

The nurse's morning visit wakes Jian. He opens his eyes, sees his diary lying open beside his pillow. His pen is still held loosely in his right hand. He hears the rain. Another rainy Midland morning in Lincolnshire Psychiatric Hospital. But there is a surprise today. His nurse not only brings pills and water for him, she also hands Jian a letter.

This is the only thing that's arrived from the outside world since he's been here: an immaculate white envelope in heavy white vellum with a raised golden Buckingham Palace emblem in the top left corner, and his address leaving little indentations into the paper. This is truly noble. He hadn't thought calligraphy was so developed in this part of the world. His heart beats with anticipation as he tears open the envelope. How strange: he finds his own letter to the Queen inside, and a little card. It reads:

BUCKINGHAM PALACE

Please take note: anyone who wishes to communicate with
Her Majesty should address their correspondence to
Her Lady-in-Waiting at Windsor Castle, Berkshire SL4 1NJ,
and affix a Royal Mail stamp.

Jian frowns. Why can't someone in Buckingham Palace just forward his letter to an official "Lady-in-Waiting"? What's the point of sending a tired, staggering Nigerian postman all the way to this Thatcher town just to give him instructions in how to address the Queen? No efficiency, bureaucratic bullshit. Nevertheless, Jian stops cursing and requests two sheets of paper from his nurse. He drafts his second letter to the Queen.

To: Lady-in-Waiting
Windsor Castle
Berkshire SL4 1NJ

Your Majesty,

I wrote you a letter earlier this month dated 1 February which has returned, presumably unread by you. But I will not give up, I need you to hear my story and I need your help urgently.

Now, Your Majesty, because I write to you from a madhouse, you might think I am not worthy of your time and patience. But I am sober and steady. I have managed not to take those mad pills. You may not know about those pills, but I tell you, dear Queen, if you ever have problems, I advise you never to take "spredee" or "darvon." They tell me this shit can provide anxiety relief to calm me down. But I don't want to be calm, Your Majesty! I feel very uncalm! I am writing to you with a serious heart. Please read my first letter.

No time left, you excellent Queen! My visa will be expired tomorrow and they've decided that they don't believe I'm suffering from a mental disorder, but they're planning on handing me to the Border Control Police! And I plead to them if they send me back to China I will be yet another imprisoned artist. So Your Majesty must lift your finger! You are now my Nüwa, our ancient Chinese goddess who repaired the ceiling of heaven and rescued all humanity. Woman is always greater than man, I know it.

Last but not least, one thing more, dearest Queen, you actually met my father once, on your 1986 China visit. I have a photograph he gave me when I was little. He was sitting behind Deng Xiaoping but I'm sure you don't remember his face. Anyway, my telephone number here is 01498 67803, it is the reception number but if they know it is Your Majesty calling they will have to take it serious.

Yours,

Kublai Jian

PS If you already decided not to help me, can you return my CD? My album is the only proof of my achievement in a foreign country.

8 LINCOLNSHIRE, FEBRUARY 2012

In the midst of grappling with written English, Jian befriends his nurse. Beth is in her mid-thirties, chubby and warm with soft blonde hair. She tells him that she has her own Chinese connection—her father works for a pharmaceutical company that exports most of their products to China. She's barely been outside Lincolnshire, she tells him, but one day she will visit China, "walk on the Great Wall, learn to practise tai chi," but Jian isn't convinced.

Today she greets him with questions.

"Good morning, Kublai Jian, why don't you tell me a little about yourself? How about your family? Do you have a wife back in China?" She leans a little closer. "Kublai Jian?"

"A wife?" he repeats blankly.

She looks at him enquiringly, just a light tilt of her head as if to say, yes, tell me more.

Jian is bewildered. Wife? He shakes his head dully.

"Not married? Did you have a girlfriend?" She hesitates. Jian smiles and shakes his head again. Not any more, he thinks.

It was the beginning of his third year in college, twenty-one years away from this odd Lincolnshire life. The university had organised a volleyball match to welcome the students to the new term. They were sitting on the thin concrete kerb by the court, watching the match and sucking sugared ice sticks. The girl sitting beside him was thin and small, but she wore a large man's shirt, light blue in colour, with a huge pocket on her left breast. When the wind blew, her shirt billowed as if she were about to fly away in a blue balloon.

"Where did you get this shirt?" Jian said.

"From my father," the girl answered. "I like to wear men's shirts." She smiled, revealing a row of perfect yet gappy front teeth, like small pillars of pearl.

Maybe it was that first impression of the girl's gappy teeth, so pretty and dear to Jian's eyes, maybe it was her billowing shirt that revealed so little, but whatever it was he began to like her. There was a break in the game and together in silence they watched the players walk off court to the changing rooms. Then she turned to Jian, looked at him curiously for a second and said:

"You know, you look like Peking Man." She laughed. "Peking Man who lived in caves half a million years ago!" She turned at a noise from across the court and asked, "Which department are you in?"

"History," Jian answered, awkwardly.

When the girl heard this, she laughed even louder. "How fitting!" She coughed, in between fits of shaking laughter.

Jian was taken aback. He wasn't thrilled to hear that he looked like Peking Man. "I'm not that ugly! Peking Man wasn't even a man, he wasn't even a *Homo sapiens!*"

"But look." The girl traced Jian's jaw with a soft finger and he shivered. "Look, your jawline and bone structure *are* exactly like the fossilised head I saw in a museum once. I remember it so well—he had a very big jaw just like yours, and his forehead was as steep as yours!" All Jian could do was smile at her insistence; being compared to the supposed original ancestor of all Chinese men couldn't be a bad thing.

"Which department are you in?" Jian gazed at the girl's front teeth.

"Literature," she answered, suddenly more serious, "Western Literature."

Jian remembered well those few days after the volleyball game—he had looked out for her in lectures and around the campus, and even spied her looking at him from across the room. She told him of her mild obsession with Peking Man since her middle-school days. Like other students in her history class she had to recite facts about the ancient apes, especially Peking Man: ". . . he lived 750,000 years ago, but as primitive as he was, he already knew how to use fire and tools in his cave." She told Jian about her trip to the museum in Beijing's Zhoukoudian—the original cave where they discovered the fossils of Peking Man—and how she had stood in a large and empty exhibition hall and looked at the skull. It was like the head of a modern human, except its teeth looked oversized and fierce. "And now I get to meet a real Peking Man. Alive!" Her moon-shaped face glowed as she talked and she tugged the billowing shirt over her knees and coiled her small body up inside it like butterfly in a cocoon.

9 LONDON, MAY 2013

Standing in front of a mirror in her bathroom, Iona brushes her hair; black strands glisten under a battered art deco lamp, and her face looms beneath, familiar, inescapably her. There is a tug of entangled hair at the back; she tries to comb it straight, but it won't behave. Her phone rings in the kitchen. She continues to brush her hair. The phone rings again. No, I should not go out tonight, or even this weekend. I must work. Lots to do. She talks to herself in the mirror, and her hand cuts down through the black fall of her hair.

She returns to the kitchen and leans against the table where the laid-out pages wait. Leafing through the heavy pile of documents, she draws out a page which begins with a pencil drawing:

A girl with a messy fringe obscuring her eyes, and a mouth smeared below, with eyes drooping like tears. The line has a certain fluency, like a shape-changing snake moving across the page. Is this Mu? Or some other girl, caught on paper one morning, after a long night? Is it Jian's drawing? It must be, judging from the handwriting beneath. The shape-changing line makes her think of a lean, fluent body, in a dark-coloured jacket. Iona begins to read the writing below.

13 October 1993

I met that girl again from the volleyball match. She still seems to be finding her way around the university. I was in the reading room trying to finish that Trotsky book and she walked over and took the chair next to me. We sat beside each other for about an hour; at one point she opened her palm and showed me her fingers. "Do you see anything abnormal?" she asked, looking straight into my eyes as if she were a hypnotist.

I pored over her hand. It felt cool and fragile. "What am I meant to be looking for?" I felt a little ridiculous and I let out an awkward half-laugh, but when I looked up she was curiously serious. I rubbed her palm gently, "Well, perhaps your index finger is a little bent."

"My father made me practise calligraphy every day from when I was very little, and this is the result of holding the brush! And what a worthless effort!" She has this excited, childish tone whenever she tries to describe something bad or disturbing, like a child in love with horror stories. "I've never managed to use my calligraphy skills. But I'll be stuck with a bent finger forever!"

She laughed and her animated voice was like a string of bells in a windy valley. Her front teeth stuck out slightly, showing a glimpse of that cute gap between them. I wanted to kiss her badly. But instead I said:

"Then you must hate your father!"

"No, no, I don't! I love my father. How could anyone hate their parents?"

"Oh, I certainly do," I said, quietly. "I hate my father."

She looked very surprised by what I had said, but she didn't ask me why. A brief cool silence fell in the air between us.

Then I glanced at a map spread out on the desk in front of her and asked her what she was looking at.

"I'm looking at these small islands in the middle of the sea." She pointed at an expanse of turquoise blue in the centre of the world map. "Wouldn't it be amazing if one day we could visit these islands?"

Her slightly bent index finger pointed out a few yellow dots in the blue sea. She pronounced their names haltingly as she placed her finger on each island. "Easter Island, Pitcairn, Majorca, Corsica, Sardinia, Crete."

"Where would you go, if you could choose just one island?" she asked me.

"I don't know," I shrugged. "How are we to know anything if we have never been outside of China?"

"Come on . . . just imagine. Imagine that one day you wake up and find yourself on a quiet and beautiful island in the middle of a very blue sea. Where would it be?" She nudged me.

Then she covered my eyes with her palm, lifted my hand and let my finger land at random on the map. Then she removed her hand from my eyes and in an excited voice said: "Here it is. Crete." A Greek island in the middle of the Mediterranean. That's where my finger had found its place.

10 LONDON, MAY 2013

Crete. Iona has never been to Greece, though she would love to travel to those sunny islands, smell the ancient earth's smell. She has led a strange still life. Iona reads the date on some of the diary entries: *February 1989, September 1991, March 1992*. In 1992 she was only ten years old, Iona thinks, scampering around her Scottish island, shuttling back and forth on a ferry from her school to her home. She didn't know then that she would study Chinese and end up as a translator. She thought she would become a writer, or a primary-school teacher. Perhaps her first fascination with China was triggered in her primary school—she remembers asking one of the other kids in a serious manner, "If we dug through the earth, would we find Eskimos on the other side?" The other child replied with total conviction, "No, Iona, we'd find a Chinaman with his pet dragon of course." Iona thought of the books she read at home, of Jules Verne, and the dark, pitch-black tunnels sinking deeper and deeper into the earth. For days, fear clenching her chest, in her imagination she would clamber through the tunnels, and then, finally, by some topsy-turvy logic she would be led up to daylight. She might hear sounds from the world above as she was tunnelling upwards—honking horns on the street and sing-song voices. Then suddenly she would pop out under the Forbidden City. Chinese faces would crowd around to gawk at the fabulous foreign girl, perhaps a little grimy, breaking out of the earth's membrane, like a bird cracking an egg. China! She would make a Chinese friend like Tintin does in his Tibet journey. How wonderful it had seemed. Fifteen years later, still remembering that feeling, she travelled to China for two months as part of her degree. She found China fascinating but impossible to grasp, and the people she met scarred by their traumatic pasts. Now, in the sunniest corner of her London flat, scrutinising the dancing, jagged, handwriting of a mysterious Chinese man, Iona feels again that intense emotion, building up from within, firing up her eyes.

She types out a very short diary entry trying to decipher Kublai Jian's messy and large handwriting.

Haidian Music Store, 4 July 1995

A celebration with a bunch of university poets and a few young journalists! But most importantly, it was the debut of Kublai Jian and the Wild Sprouts—and the release of my first proper album. This is it! We have arrived! After two bootleg CDs in three years! The whole band was there and we really feel a bond between us now, like warriors or adventurers. Beijing's sky had turned red and purple, putting on a show for us, and we drank. We drank so much! Mu says this never would have happened if I hadn't met Li Hua Dong. But she is so naive. A peasant girl with rice grains still hidden in her hair. Kublai Jian has learned how to write better songs—that's what this success is about, and nothing to do with a bloody manager! Having a manager is just like having an accountant wearing an ironed suit. It's a necessity, but it's nothing to do with our music, old bastard sky!

Iona types "Kublai Jian and the Wild Sprouts" into Google. She waits a few seconds, the timer spins, the laptop whirrs and a blank window pops up. The great Chinese firewall, it seems. Iona tries a few more options but she just gets the same result. All that comes up is an album cover for *Yuan vs. Dollars* in Google images. She can only presume it's Jian's most well-known album, or the latest perhaps. It's a powerful picture: a headshot of a young man with a blindfolded face. It has punch, she thinks. There are no articles about him. She sighs. She really knows so little about Chinese cyber-policing and Internet censorship. They're clearly doing a great job. And when she searches again just for images of "Kublai Jian," millions of pictures of Chinese- and Mongolian-looking men with the name "Kublai" or "Jian" come up—either standing by some tacky tourist spot or smiling a plastic smile with the backdrop of fake Mongol people in a yurt, or here again among a line-up of fat bureaucrats wearing ridiculous Khalkha Mongol hats . . . Nothing about his family or his hated father. And none of them remotely matches her idea of a young and vigorous musician who writes angry manifestos.

TWO | WELCOME TO DOVER

水能载舟，亦能覆舟.

shui neng zai zhou, ye neng fu zhou.

Water can float a boat, it can also sink it.

XUN ZI (PHILOSOPHER, WARRING STATES PERIOD, 475–221 BC)

1 DOVER, APRIL 2012

Cafe-on-the-Channel is located on the west side of Dover's busy port. It is only a mile from the Dover Immigration Removal Centre. This is where Kublai Jian has been held since he was dragged out from Lincolnshire by two policemen. Jian has never been to the cafe; his life is charted by locked doors and high walls. But Iona went there once. Some years ago Iona visited Dover with a man for a weekend. "Romantic getaway," he'd said, "cheaper than a city break, babe, but it'll be great, really it will." They had stayed in a B&B where the bed had sagged and the sex had been only OK. She had tried not to care. Then they had walked down the road to find a spot for lunch and ended up in the Cafe-on-the-Channel. It was a terrace cafe, with old wooden tables and rustic-looking benches against the backdrop of the grey sea. There was a TV showing a tourist promotion on a loop. As Iona and her boyfriend ate a lukewarm omelette, a well-known actress came on the TV to talk about the sights, her encouraging voice just loud enough to disrupt conversation.

> *Dover is a major ferry port on the English Channel. Facing France, the area has always been a focus for people entering and leaving Britain. It also served as a bastion against various attackers: notably the French during the Napoleonic Wars and Germany during the Second World War. And nowadays the port is the busiest shipping lane in the world. Dear visitors, why not take a lovely walk along the beach and enjoy some fresh seafood? We hope you have a pleasant stay in Dover!*

A visitor sitting in the Cafe-on-the-Channel can just see the wavy sea, and flotilla of boats. Birds scavenging for scraps of food and dead fish.

If you had been sitting there on 4 April 2012, around midday, you would have seen a white van driving past with "Dover Immigration Removal Centre" printed in blue letters on the side. It stopped at the cafe for a few moments while the driver picked up a takeaway coffee and soggy sandwich. Inside the van were several individuals, including a slight Chinese man with a hungry look in his eyes. He, too, from the small window at the back, saw the birds swooping, and the grey mist on the sea.

2 DOVER, APRIL 2012

In a grey, nearly empty room lit by a white fluorescent tube, Jian is writing a serious letter to the Home Office concerning his future.

As he writes and rewrites his sentences, he imagines an immigration officer in the Border Control HQ opening a pile of letters. Probably, this tired and over-routinised officer will simply glance at the applicant's nationality and the address of each letter, then throw it into a second pile of papers which he will take to another immigration officer; then another officer in another office will open these letters and read them again and put them in another pile, and then this officer will take the papers to another officer . . . like a crazed man crawling up an Escher staircase, unable to reach the top.

Jian sits back and looks round at his two room-mates in this, his second grey-white box in this strange country. During the day, the quietly chattering wardens and the silently bored refugees in the Dover Immigration Removal Centre are little different from the quietly murmuring nurses and the numbed patients in Lincolnshire. Nothing much has changed. Even his dank cell in Beijing felt pulsing and alive in comparison to this. As he tries to put words down, straining to remember the right English phrase, he feels a machine-like throbbing in his head. It is a dreadfully familiar sensation—he remembers that feeling from being hit by an electric baton at his final concert. His body becomes stiff, his pen is frozen in his hands. Now the throbbing sound interrupts the quiet around him and he sees his childhood family house—a house surrounded by acacia trees hidden in a hutong beside Hou Hai Lake in central Beijing.

A brief, blurred memory of his mother comes to him. Perhaps it is the very first memory Jian has of her, he was only two or three. She is in the kitchen, standing in front of a small mirror. She uses a heated iron poker to curl her hair. The burning smell floats into his nostrils. Then his father's image sneaks in, like a black crow in a bright garden, squawking. The squawking man-bird sticks in his mind. In this foreign, in-between space, Jian chooses to confront it rather than shoo it away.

The day he last saw his father now returns to him as a sequence of pictures. Can this really be him, this smiling ten-year-old boy running down the narrow alleyways of Beijing? The summer sun hits hard, seeming to singe the poplar trees and melt the asphalt roads. Dogs are sleeping in the shadows of the trees, as are elderly people from the hutong quarter, sitting there like sacks of rice. It's a relentless August, the summer of 1982. Jian's mother had died a few years before, and his grandparents are visiting relatives out of town. He is left at home alone throughout the summer.

On the day of the annual conference of the Beijing People's Representatives Congress, for which Jian's father was an Administration Secretary, he decides to take his son into the office with him. As the chime tolls from the Dongcheng Bell Tower behind his father's office, hundreds of delegates start arriving in the conference hall with their dark shiny suits and their hot shiny faces. Jian's father orders him to keep quiet and stay in the kitchen, where the chefs are clattering about preparing tea and food. It is a scorching day and Jian's cotton shorts cling to the backs of his thighs. He does his homework and he waits. And he waits. Two hours later, though, Jian is already bored to death. He sneaks past the guard tasked to keep an eye on him, and escapes through the Congress gate. Wandering in the sleepy hutong, the ten-year-old boy feels the freedom and aimlessness of a stray dog. He sees a gang of older boys riding their bikes, and longs to join them. They welcome him into their game. It's the usual war story kids played out so often on the streets of Beijing: Chinese soldiers versus American soldiers in the Korean War. Jian enters the game a bit late, so he is told to be a Korean peasant standing on the sidelines. But he refuses.

He's bored and hot and wants to take a side in the conflict. He asks if he can join the group of Chinese soldiers. But in order to be assigned to a unit, he has to be given a rank and, most importantly, to recite the "Soldier Oath." Jian is never good at reciting anything, but he is eager to try. Raising the clenched right fist, he speaks aloud like a real soldier: "*I am a member of the People's Liberation Army. I promise that I will follow the leadership of the Chinese Communist Party, serve the people wholeheartedly, obey orders, fight heroically; under no circumstances will I . . .*" Then Jian can't remember the next two lines, the crucial lines about betraying one's motherland. Everybody laughs at him. Smeared with humiliation, he has to take on the role of an American soldier and the boys turn on him: he becomes everybody's target. This game of war becomes violent, and Jian is badly beaten up, punched in the face so hard that he bleeds. Someone holding a branch hits him across his face—he escapes the sharp end, but gets a deep cut into his skin and forever after he will wear a scar under his eye like a sickle moon.

After dark, with his clothes torn and his face bloody, young Jian stumbles back to his father's office to find him in a rage. Silently he puts Jian on the back of his bike and rides home without a word. His father enters the house, places the keys with deliberate care on the kitchen table and, still saying nothing, with his back to Jian picks up a steel ruler. Suddenly he turns, grabs his son and shouts: "You want another cut under your eye? Do you? Do you? Here it is!" His father raises the weapon and seems about to bring it down upon the cringing boy. But instead of the expected blow, nothing happens. A look comes over his father's face: a fixed stare, like a frozen image from a Communist banner, with a cruel coldness in his eyes. Grasping his son, he takes Jian to his bedroom, shoves him towards the bed and closes the door. He locks it and leaves him inside. Jian is locked in all night and most of the next day. Twenty hours later, when the door is unlocked again, the boy has passed out on the floor from exhaustion and hunger. His lips are blue and swollen, his cut is dark and encrusted, his eyes red from constant crying. Perhaps those twenty hours were the worst hours his body had suffered.

A week later, Jian remembers clearly, his grandparents returned and resumed their role in looking after him, and his father left Beijing. He was posted to the south and rarely came back to the city. After the episode with the steel ruler Jian lived with his grandparents and barely saw his father, or received any letters from him; he had regular nightmares about his father returning home. It wasn't the threat of his father's violence. It was the threat behind his father's face that day. At school a year or so later, when Jian hadn't seen his father for nearly nine months, a wave of gossip spread through his school about his father having a new wife and starting a new family elsewhere. He never came home to see his son after that. The boy was now a young man. He was locked in a dark room once again, only this time it was permanent: it was a larger room, from city to city, with occasional people to hold on to; a world in which the father he knew would never feature. His father had sent him into exile.

Suddenly Jian hears someone snoring loudly beside him. No, there are now two people snoring. He shares the room with two refugees from somewhere in Africa. His room-mates' snores blast into white space, their heads on sunken pillows, upturned slack-lipped faces breathing heavily like two buffalo in a backwood swamp. Good sleepers. They are sleeping in Dover with me. Jian's head is heavy, his eyes are closing. His last wakeful sensation is the feeling of his toes touching the strings of his guitar which rests against his bed.

3 LONDON, MAY 2013

It's after midnight; London oozes into the soundscape of late-night television dramas and the passing wail of sirens. The streets are saturated with shadows and lights. A flat above Chapel Market is still brightly lit. Iona is buried in a sea of papers. She has added two more dictionaries as well as a book about dialects in northern China to the pile on her desk. While she is sorting through the papers, trying to make sense of them, she finds a stray undated letter.

At first glance she thinks it's a letter from the 1990s, but the tone is angry and hurt like the first few letters Jian seems to have sent Mu after he left China in 2011. She's been muddling at these translations for a few weeks and she still hasn't managed to get a sense of the story. What went wrong in their relationship? They seemed so happy, so full of promise and excitement. There are nods and clues to a manifesto which changed everything, but she has no background information at all, and her Internet searches are fruitless.

She glances at the letter again—it's pretty vehement. Iona wonders if it was ever sent. No address, no sentiment, just straight in.

I can't understand why you're behaving like this, Mu. How could you say you hate my manifesto? I mean, you know I believe that what we do, the action we take, is the most essential expression of art and therefore the most essential expression of a political view. For us, the most basic action is to say No to the reactionary and raise our fist. I don't think I am asking too much, Mu. I just want you to understand me. I thought you did.

For years you have been telling me you want to live an apolitical life. You disagree with whatever I do. You know I think that to take no action is a political gesture, too. To take no action, to be ignorant and passive. Isn't that the worst? Didn't we always say that? The same goes for love—there is no simple love between one and another to the exclusion of the rest. I can only love . . .

The characters have blurred and Iona struggles to read what comes next. There is one more illegible phrase and then the letter comes abruptly to a halt.

4 DOVER, APRIL 2012

Another Dover night. Jian tries to sleep. But his mind is racing, like an express train from Shanghai to Nanjing with totally blurred scenes outside the window. He vaguely sees a small gap-toothed girl in the dim light, and he stretches out his arms. Wait, wait until tomorrow morning, someone will help me, someone will reach down and draw me out of this place. He thinks and thinks. A flood of faces rush past, then the flood stops with the calm, slightly pink complexion of his caseworker, Brandon.

Brandon is a law student who works as a volunteer for immigrants with problematic cases. Jian finds him incredibly kind, but it's as if his voice is wrapped in bed sheets, obscuring all meaning and clarity. He had said the other day, "Schjaaaan, an seen a wee hope, a wee hope!" Jian had looked at Brandon expectantly. It took a lot for Jian to finally understand Brandon's Glaswegian brogue—repetitions and gesticulations like actors in the Beijing Opera. Jian feels his own Mongol blood shares something with Brandon's wild-man ancestors, and this voice from a land of ice and whisky calls out to his past, his desire to rage and defy.

But now, enveloped in the dark, Jian twists under the damp bedcovers. The scenery of his past life is a silent river flowing through his blood. It's been like this for some days now. In the daytime he's numbed, he's fine, but when he lays his head down, he feels his skull is cracking open; he feels headless. He is sitting on a bench with Mu on a bright Beijing afternoon, under the shadow of a half-built flyover trying to write songs while watching a group of construction workers busy with a crane in the near distance. If you have to try to write a song, he has always said, it will never work. The struggle you have with one song is

53

only preparation for the real song that will come later in a rush, perfected at birth. It is this one which will be Your Song, not the one you struggle over.

And now, in the mind of this older Jian cradled by a moonless Dover night, he is rushing around Beijing's underground bars trying to replace the drummer in his band—drummers are always crazy and unreliable—and arguing with the Neighbourhood Police who control the noise levels in the street. Showing them the power cords to reassure them, while getting them to drink with him! The police are not natural rockers, so he buys them hard liquor and lambs' ribs as bribes. Waking up at midday, after a hard gig and midnight crab-eating with Yan, and non-stop drinking of er guo tou, and shambling under the street lamps along the avenues, and shocking the neighbourhood surveillance ladies. There he sees the loud-laughing migrants' faces, selling him steamed buns and a glass of warm soy drink, the lousy taxi rides through flag-waving Long-Peace Street, heading for some new venue, to plug in instruments and send out charged sound, and so on, and so on. In the morning he wakes up beside Mu, who has already prepared congee and pickles for their breakfast, and his head is a foggy blur, and aches like a torn drum.

Another month sinks into the sand that borders the English Channel. Jian's routine meetings with his caseworker Brandon frustrate him. The conversation moves through a thick treacle of accents. Nothing seems to cut through.

Brandon conciliatory in his Glasgow brogue:

"Ya must be patient, Schjiaan! Et's not in one day we can sor'oot yer application. We hav' ta wait for the leegal process . . ."

Jian desperate in his Chinese accent:

" 'Be pay-shon' doesn't bring immigration officer atten-shon, neither their respect-ah!"

"Whoa, laddie?"

Jian eventually understands what Brandon is trying to tell him:

since his visa is no longer valid until he's been registered as a refugee, he now has no status. He is a "non-person." A "non-person"? "You don't belong to any country; you are not a citizen of anywhere," the immigration officer explained.

Non-person, he thinks. It's so absurd it sounds almost Chinese to him.

10 November 1993

The desert wind from Mongolia sweeps through the capital; our hair is tangled and dusty. They've said Beijing is undergoing the worst sandstorms in its history. Perhaps within a few years, Beijing will turn into a desert, become a part of the Gobi Desert. But nothing can stop us. All day long, we race around on our bikes cutting through the wind and searching desperately for copies of Western novels and records we've heard of in the hidden bars downtown. Foreign CDs are hard to find. But I have gathered a lot of them. Stuff is happening, I can feel it. Perhaps 1989 did force the door open wider, but at the cost of so much blood. And while I'm working my way through all the English punk bands, Mu is going through this phase of being madly in love with Misty Poetry. I quite like it too, because of its obscure but sensuous language, so different from the sloganeering style of Mao's Little Red Book . . .

Iona is bemused. Misty Poetry? She sharpens her pencil and underlines *Misty Poetry* in Jian's diary. Scratching her head, she vaguely remembers her Tang-dynasty poetry study at university, but it seems a long time ago right now. Opening her computer, Iona instantly starts googling. The names Bei Dao, Duo Duo, Yang Lian, Shu Ting, Gu Cheng spring from the screen. A poetry movement writing about ideas of freedom which began in the early eighties, right after the Cultural Revolution, she reads. Poems address both individual and political freedom but ideas are expressed through descriptions of landscape, agriculture and the use of imagery like the blurred indeterminacy of hills in mist. Right, got it. She looks up from the screen. How fitting, she thinks, that the key year for this movement was 1989. Issues with freedom all right. She returns to Jian's diary, and reads on.

20 January 1994

I've been worried about Mu for some time now. I was afraid to tell her, I hoped that she'd move on, find a different literary movement to obsess over, but she still talks about the damn Misty Poets all the time, and her fanaticism about Hai Zi is so overpowering. It's exactly like the time she discovered Sylvia Plath, the first foreign poet she had ever read. It's all too sad, too weak for my taste. It feels morbid, perhaps. It seems to be about looking back, not advancing forward. I mean, Hai Zi committed suicide just a few years before Mu came here.

But today things took an even weirder turn. Mu bullied me into taking her to the railway bridge where Hai Zi killed himself just before his twenty-fifth birthday. She stood there and recited the lines of that poem she's got framed on her wall—"Facing the Sea, with Spring Blossoms behind Me." Old heaven knows how romantic and naive she was! Just a peasant girl still carrying around the soil under her shoes from her southern province. Old bastard sky, it took us twelve hours on our chain-broken bikes to get to Shanhaiguan railway path! (We had to sleep under the freezing cold Great Wall for the night and get back on our bikes at sunrise.) When we arrived at the railway track where the poet's body had supposedly been found there was nothing. No fucking sign, no tombstone, and not a single drop of dried blood on those tracks. The only thing there was a dead sheep, its guts spilling out, still fresh and ripe red. Mu was searching for anything Hai Zi might have left before he lay down to die. Like a detective she took hundreds of photographs, using up precious film, pictures of any object that might be linked to his death: the broken trunk of a pear tree beside the track, the crushed end of a pencil buried under the earth, an old scarf muddied with dirt. She was driven mad by her fascination. Perhaps one day she may be able to understand my madness, like why I skip classes to write songs in my dorm room. Oh, old sky, she will understand me, I know she will, in the end.

Iona returns to the Internet with a sense of dissatisfaction. She gathers information, thinking it might lead somewhere, give her a clue, unveil a personality, unlock a mysery. Hai Zi was a leading member of the Misty Poetry movement. Born in 1964 and committed suicide in March 1989. So before Tiananmen Square, she thinks. She then reads about Bei Dao, forced into exile after the student massacre. And Duo Duo, who left the square on the day of the demonstration, jumped on a plane to the West and never returned. And then Gu Cheng whose escape took him to an isolated village on Waiheke Island in New Zealand. The article quotes a famous two-line poem, "A Generation," from Gu Cheng: 黑夜给了我黑色的眼睛，而我却用它寻找光明。

Translating poetry is quite a challenge, but Iona has a go:

> *Dark night gives me dark eyes.*
> *I, however, use them to search for the light.*

She sits back and reads what she's typed. It's strained, forced. She holds down the delete button and tries again:

> *Dark night dims my vision.*
> *But I will still look for the brightness.*

Better, definitely better. Then she has a thought, moves down the page and starts rapidly typing yet another version:

> *Even with these dark eyes,*
> *I go to seek the shining light.*

It is hard to tell which version is more accurate. But what Iona can't make sense of is why a poet from revolutionary China would go from the heart of Beijing to such a remote corner of the globe like New Zealand? Was freedom so very hard to find? Iona returns to the page on the Misty Poets and reads how Gu Cheng built himself a bamboo forest as a barrier around his house on the island, that he lived simply with his wife and child and with almost no contact with the outside world. Iona scans the article. There are more excerpts from poems, more analytical commentary. She feels tired and her eyes haze over. She skips to the last paragraph and gets a shock: on 8 October 1993 Gu Cheng killed his wife and child with an axe that he used to chop wood, and then hanged himself. The article states it bluntly, no explanation, no reason. Despite the minimal information the images that come to Iona are so strikingly vivid. She imagines the young poet's last day. The sound of his bamboo barriers creaking in the wind. Perhaps there was a deep chill in the air. She knows what that feels like. The blue mist that lifts from the water to envelop you and makes space icy and lonesome, the violent bite of the wind eating into your skin.

Iona leaves the local GP surgery and walks away slowly. She admitted she often misses meals, sometimes she worries about putting on weight. And recently she's begun to feel exhaustion and dizziness. Occasionally she vomits. "It could be an anxiety disorder, or stress from your work or difficult family relations, and it can be related to low self-esteem," her GP suggested to her almost casually while scrolling through her medical records on the computer. She's been given a prescription for antidepressants, but she feels uneasy about taking them. As she passes a pharmacy she holds the piece of paper, as if dirty, a little away from her.

Low self-esteem. She could just about agree with all the other conditions, but she has never considered herself someone with "low self-esteem." It's true, though, that she isn't able to think of herself romantically. Although she feels at ease with the satisfaction of her body, she doesn't have the language to connect with a man emotionally. Her father often said she was a perfectionist, a "silly" idealist. For Iona, there are certain things in life that are just not *beautiful*, many things in this world are too ugly, and she is not going to give in just like that. The same goes with men: she is not going to commit herself to any old man. She always finds something not right, imperfect, attached to a man after she has seen him once or twice. And the more she knows that person, the less she wants to entangle herself with him. To stay away is to protect her vision of the perfect man, even if it is a knowing act of self-deception.

It is a cloudy afternoon; Iona feels like shaking off the grey energy around her body. She walks to the British Library, heading along the canal, and coming up behind King's Cross station, enjoying the view of the constantly shifting building works, the cranes and semi-industrial landscape. She finds herself drawn to this library every now and again. Working in a quiet reading room with strangers is a way of feeling less lonely: an abstract community, sharing their minutes and hours in silent acts. Today, as usual, she settles herself in a corner by the window, and continues to work on Kublai Jian's documents. To her left, in a corner, she sees a familiar figure. A bearded man, maybe fifty odd, with scraggly hair and foggy glasses, and an intense look, mumbling silently as he reads. He's always there and never acknowledges her. She likes that, in a way. Opening her laptop and laying out the Chinese photocopies, Iona pulls her focus back to the page, and begins to translate a new diary entry.

Beijing, 1 August 1997

Our graduation ceremony was held at ten this morning. All the boys got themselves shaved last night, except for the smooth hairless ones, and some even got new haircuts. By ten o'clock, with cicadas screaming in the poplar trees across campus, our new shirts were already soaked in sweat. We had to listen to all sorts of tedious speeches from deans and professors for hours. This is your final day here and your most glorious day at the college . . . blah blah. But today's accomplishment is just the beginning of a new tomorrow . . . blah blah. Everyone had their parents around, and even some old grannies stood at the back blubbering. For me, of course, there were no blubbering grannies or anxious parents. I had no one there apart from Mu. She sat beside me, half reading her favourite Latin American poet Neruda, half worrying about her upcoming term examination paper.

At midday the dean of our department handed me a piece of paper with a golden stamp on it. It read: "On the 1st of August 1997, Beijing University grants Kublai Jian the Degree of Master of Arts in Chinese History." Underneath it was the signature of our university chancellor in his mad Mao-style scrawl.

Mu tapped the certificate with a wicked smile and teased me. "Congratulations, Jian. It's not entirely useless. One day when your music no longer earns you a living, this piece of paper might help."

"With a degree in Chinese history? I doubt it."

"You never know, my Peking Man."

She squinted at me, and took a photo—a gangly long-haired hungry young man, holding a certificate, with a warped smile on his face, surrounded by sweat-soaked classmates greeting their parents.

And then the mad evening drinking began. Yanjing beers were gulped down with spicy beef. Mu didn't stay for the banquet, she was never a part of the drinking scene. Instead she waited for me in the library. She said she was reading this huge Russian novel: "serious literature, like War and Peace." Her usual rave. But of course I didn't give a shit about any damn book that night. And before long the table was lined with empty bottles and no more cold beers could be supplied from the canteen. We drank the warm ones. We screamed to each other and hugged each other and some students even cried like babies. No one said the words "Tiananmen" or "1989" or mentioned the class-mates who were no longer with them. Perhaps it was the fear of being reported, or perhaps it was the fear that even one word, one look might tear open our deep scars. Then all the Tsingtao beers were gone as well, and we began to drink warm Haerbin beer, the cheapest kind. We were smashed. Everyone sang "La Marseillaise" tunelessly, drunkenly, while finishing a glass: "Arise, children of the fatherland! The day of glory has arrived. Against us tyranny's bloody flag is raised . . ." We sang together with a howling crying tone: "Good Lord! By chained hands, Our brows would yield under the yoke, The vile despots would have them-selves be the masters of our destiny . . ." And we cried like a group of stupid idiots.

7 DOVER, MAY 2012

Brandon walks through the gate of the Removal Centre with his pepperoni pizza and his watery coffee. Today he has bad news for Jian. He passes two blue-uniformed workers perched on a ladder, taking down the sign that says *Dover Immigration Removal Centre.* Up the ladder again and *Removal Centre* becomes *Detention Centre.* Brandon raises his eyes; heavy dark clouds drift across the sky. Rain is falling, instantly drenching the sign the workers have just put up.

One of the workers turns to his companion. "Detention or Removal—isn't it the same thing? Most of the foreigners in this place are gonna be sent back. Right?"

Brandon walks on as raindrops pelt down, exploding in his hair and eyes, like gobs of pigeon shit. He scoots into the building for shelter.

Rain is battering the windows next to Jian. As Brandon breaks the news he hunches further over his world map, trying to dissolve into it. The UK authorities are closing the door to immigrants; nearly 90 per cent of applications will be refused, according to the new points-based system.

"Jian, you gotta understand, there's nai more space for people in this country. This is not China!"

"How many people you got then?" Jian asks.

"Sixty million. That's a laat for a wee island. It's not like Switzerland, only got sieven million!"

It's not like Switzerland, only got sieven million. Like a breeze gently murmuring in Jian's ears, the thought occurs to him that maybe it wouldn't be so bad to live like a goat on the side of a Swiss mountain.

A mountain would be good enough, for a while at least. And this is what inspires Jian to write to Switzerland, a country that might be kinder than the Queen's Land to someone like him.

"Do you know the address of the immigration office in Switzerland?" he asks eagerly.

The pile of letters before Iona seems to be a never-ending mystery—haphazardly organised, some dated, some not. Iona had assumed all the material was from Kublai Jian and it's rather a surprise to find the letter she is reading now is written in a totally different style.

亲爱的伊建：

总算，我收到了你的一封信！现在我知道你在哪里！我一直在担心你。给伦敦的人权协会组织还有其他的避难组织打过电话。但他们都说没有你的消息。你只发给我一张"我没事"的明信片，你觉得我就放心了吗？多写信给我吧。

我还是没法接受你"消失"的事实。这已经有一个多月了。家里空空荡荡的，我还是觉得慌恐

Unlike Jian's letters and diary entries, messy to the point of indecipherable, the handwriting on the page in front of Iona is neat and clear, with elegant flourishes, touches of calligraphy even. A feminine hand; a woman's voice. Indeed, it is "Mu's voice," as Iona guesses from reading the first paragraph. Perhaps translating is another kind of storytelling: finding the writer's voice, unravelling the narrator. Yet Iona's storytelling is frustrated by the muddle in this new job—she still feels she knows so little about where their story started, how it ended here, where they are now.

It is a long letter. The dusk is falling quietly at Iona's window. She reads on until she reaches the end of the letter and goes back to the beginning again. Slowly she types out the text, consulting her dictionaries when an unfamiliar word crops up.

20 January 2012

Dear Jian,

A letter at last! Finally I now know where you are! I've been so worried. I've been ringing Amnesty in London and every other refugee agency I can think of, but they didn't know anything about you. And only one small postcard with the words "I am safe" isn't enough. Tell me more. I am still in shock about your disappearance. It's been over a month now, our home is bare without you, and I feel exhausted and angry. Please. Just tell me what's going on. How can politics really be worth all this?

There's so much I want to tell you. Without you, my sense of stability disappears.

Right now I cannot even begin to countenance your ideas about art and politics. Even if you are right in what you believe in and what you fight for, argument and revolution seem so unimportant right now. All I can do is separate you from your manifesto and think about what it was like before all this.

I hope this letter reaches you. I am sitting in a corridor in the People's Liberation Army Hospital in Shanghai. My father has been diagnosed with terminal throat cancer. And all I can think is: why aren't you here with me?

This feels like a place for the nearly dead. There are people here for all kinds of radiation treatment—cancer, leukaemia, diabetes, kidney diseases. But most are terminal cancer patients like my father. My father, Jian. You know. My father! I have one, even though you like to pretend we have no families and you have no father at all.

The last two lines are entirely cryptic for Iona. Why would he pretend he has no family? She reads on.

I wish you were here with me in this strange antiseptic place. I wouldn't have to explain it, I wouldn't have to describe it. But I want you to know, Jian, what my reality is right now. Even if I can't know yours. It's the closest we can get to being in the same room. This is what's going on, bear it if you can. My father is being transferred to the intensive care ward at the back of the hospital—each room has six patients alongside their relatives on camp beds. There is nothing to do here but wait: we lie on our beds, hot in the sordid air. The wives tend to their husbands, feeding them, watching them. The windows are closed, the fans turned off. They don't want anyone to catch cold so the air is thick with heat despite the cold outside and the frost making patterns on the windows. My mother is sitting beside my father, watching the vitamin drip connected to his vein, feeling the pulse on his wrist. A big sign—SILENCE—is on the wall. Silence is all we have. No one reads books or listens to the radio. Sometimes one of the relatives, an uncle, mother or sister, falls asleep during the night on the camp bed by the side of each hospital bed, their head leaning over against the patient's feet, body stiff from being in the same position for so long. This endurance leaves us stiff and numb—unable to think or feel much further than the aches in our own bodies.

After midnight the nurses stop coming. A cleaner will come to distribute hot-water bottles and clean up everyone's discharges. The toilet is located at the end of the passageway, but none of us use it. It looks like hell—God knows what's floating on the floor, from dead or near-dead people. This is a corridor of death— you would not want to be here.

My corridor is lined with late-stage patients waiting to enter

the radiation room, wrapped in striped uniforms ready for this
advanced Western machine to kill the evil cells in their bodies.
My father meditates while he waits. He looks calmer than the
rest of us. He says it's the only way he can endure the wait. My
mother is sitting next to me, staring at the letter I am writing
to you. And what a good thing she is illiterate! Otherwise I
would never cope with her! And you know what she says, Jian?
"I only have one regret in my life, I wish I had learned to read
and write." Then she sighs. And it makes me think of you and
me. What has all our reading and writing given us?

A shrieking siren is flying down a nearby road and wakes Iona from
her focus. A high-pitched voice is speaking through a megaphone, and
now a group of voices follow rhythmically. There is a protest going on
somewhere close by, Iona realises. As she listens more carefully, she
can almost make out the sound of anti-capitalism protest slogans. She
stands up, closes the window. She can't quite face the relentless bad
news that's sweeping round Britain; her ears have grown weary of it.

I've been making an effort to talk to my father, ever since I came
here. It scares me, but I don't know when there will be another
chance. I talk to him about anything and everything, especially
his past. And he answers me in writing, since he can no longer
speak because of the throat operation he's had.

So I asked him, "Father, what do you believe in?" Silly
question, I told myself. My father is a crazy man, nearly as crazy
as you! But he has a pure, uncorrupted nature; he has dedicated
his whole life to the party and he believes in it all.

So my father answers me, and I can feel his anger as he
writes, "Oh, Mu, you should know by now!"

"So tell me again," I say, calmer, as if I've never met this old
man. My father puts down his pen and stares at me in disap-
proval. "Even now, do you still really believe in communism?"

He picks up his pen and writes each word on his notepad with intensity, pressing the biro into the page with deliberate force. "Like everything, communism has its faults, but it's our only hope."

I can feel his unwavering strength even as he lies sick and weak. He uses such force to write these words that the sharp tip of the pen rips through the paper.

You know, you and my father are made of similar stuff. I know it seems mad, but in his case he believes in communism; and you, you believe in freedom of expression through confrontation, even if it involves confronting the state and your own father. Years of life separate the two of you, but what I want to say is this: my father wanted to be a free person but rigid Communist ideology has been killing him little by little over the years. I think that's why he has this cancer. He has been fighting like mad throughout his life, but the disease is swallowing him, he cannot win. You are still young, Jian. Is it worth it? Think about it.

Your Mu

It's early afternoon. Iona has retreated to her bathroom and to a warm bath. Reclining in the steamy water, she reads a letter. Often when a certain frustration colours her mind, slipping into a hot bath seems the only way forward. There's a delicate, musical drip from the tap, and the paint is peeling away from the ceiling in orange-peel curls. The flat needs serious work but her landlord is dismissive at best. The page she is holding with one dry hand is covered with doodles, black ink mixed with blue. Large characters. She recognises Kublai Jian's scrawl. Here and there the words have been furiously crossed out.

It's a difficult text. Iona strains to understand. Jian seems very angry, and she doesn't totally comprehend some of the idiom he uses. She feels stressed. The Chinese seem to love using old, formal idiom, even when a young person is writing. But there is also masses of text written in a very colloquial way, as if it were a blog or an email dashed off in a rush. Nightmare if you're trying to produce some sort of stylistic coherence in the translation! Modern Chinese colloquial idiom is the worst, she thinks. Her dictionaries are no help in deciphering many of Jian's expressions. There are so many basic difficulties in translating Chinese into English, Iona thinks. No tense differentiation; no conjugation of verbs; no articles, no inversion in questions—and I have to invent all this and add it to fit the translation. She gets out of the bath, the water having lost its reviving quality, puts on her dressing gown and wraps her hair in a towel.

People say that islanders and mainlanders have very different ways of thinking. There is some truth in this. Islanders contemplate the distant shore, and want to communicate with the rest of the world, but mainlanders often don't feel the need. That seems to be the case when it comes to Jian—he seems to think he's the mainlander and the rest mere islanders. His writing is much more difficult to grasp than that of the Chinese girl writing from Shanghai.

There's no curtain in Iona's south-facing window and the afternoon sun cooks her head. She lurches unsteadily into the kitchen and turns on the tap. Letting the unfiltered Thames water run for fifteen seconds, she drinks a mouthful of the cold liquid. She stretches, puts on a Debussy CD and sits back down. As the piano music flows she types out a rough translation of Jian's letter.

March 2012

Dearest Mu,

Your letter reached me, but from Shanghai, old bastard sky! Someone with a kind soul transferred it from my old Lincolnshire address. Try to send another one to my Dover address—and soon! I don't know how long I will be here, but send another one anyway. The more you send, the better chance I have of receiving them. It's a ping-pong game!

OK, I will try to be sensible: no manifesto or ideology for now. But in exchange, you are not allowed to mention my "father" again. NO MORE. I have no father. I have said that a thousand times. For me, he is long dead.

So, my first question to you: how long are you going to stay in Shanghai before you return to Beijing? Second question: how is your father now? Better or worse? Don't tell me he is dying—I don't believe he will die. He will last longer than you think—he may even last longer than me, you will see! And now: my situation.

Thinking of you makes me "zhou—轴." [Translator's note: not sure what this means. It's a new colloquial expression I've not heard before.] It's hard thinking about you and our life together, with me here in this brown-brick world. Despite everything that's happened, despite all our time apart, the image I carry of you is of us sitting on our windy balcony looking down into Dongsi Hutong; or you on the sofa in the living room and me in the broken rattan chair where I used to play my guitar; the red paper lamp you made with film posters; those insane cockroaches wrecking the kitchen cardboards (oh how they loved your instant noodles!). And how could I ever forget the view through the window to distant blue-green Xiang Mountain, and beneath it the capital circled by the ringroads and choked with people and traffic. I miss it all badly. Here in this wet and gloomy country I'm a man of nothing. Merely a registration number: UK66034–GH568. I've even learned to recite it.

I still know so little about this country. The only thing here worth mentioning is that I found an English edition of Karl Marx's Das Kapital on one of the dusty shelves in the Detention Centre library. I tried to make out the English by picturing that Chinese translation we read at school. What a different book it is in English! Now I feel like I never understood Marx, and maybe all of China doesn't understood what Das Kapital is really about.

Some light stuff for you—a poor man's sightseeing! I rode their underground train twice (they call it "Tube," like in a sausage factory) and it was utterly depressing to be in their sausage tubes. Everyone looked like they had tax problems or couldn't afford their electricity bills. Graveyard faces. Old bastard sky! If I could choose, I would prefer to be punished in a different place. Somewhere like . . . a Siberian forest. Sometimes I wonder, would it be better to be sent to the Gulag, like those Soviet convicts were? To lay a railway line along the Arctic Ocean, or fell trees in forests of snow? At least in those conditions a man feels he is a man and he is using his body and his hands. Or am I being stupid again?

And this Dover camp is crammed with lost souls—from the Middle East, from Africa—all seeking protection under the British flag. But I doubt they really want to live on this rainy, windy, gloomy island. It's like being a dog that sits where his master tells him to sit. That's how it is here. But I should not make you worry about me. At least I'm still fit and I eat three meals a day. (The problem is they don't have chillies; each meal comes with a different form of potato, but you know potatoes are potatoes: even if you treat them like chicken legs they still taste of potato. So I told them that they should get this clear: either potato or no potato but definitely not potato-pretending-to-be-something-else.) Apart from that, my mind is still working, busy and restless, just like those words we used to recite from Frankenstein: *"My courage and my resolution are firm, but my hopes fluctuate and my spirits are often depressed." These are the perfect lines to describe my mood.*

爱—"love" is the most simple and complicated word I can say to you now. I shall write more to you tomorrow.

Your Peking Man,

Jian

10 LONDON, MAY 2013

It's deep into the night. Through the open window the purple sky is illuminated by the stark fluorescent light of office blocks and council flats. Iona finds herself alone on her bed. Perhaps work is the compensation for her unsatisfying sexual life, she mocks herself while tidying a mass of muddled pages spread on top of her duvet. She has been trying to establish some sort of chronology in her translation. But some of the letters are undated and often the diary pages seem to launch straight in without any indication of date or location. A two-page letter, in Mu's neat handwriting, rises to the top of the pile. It seems to be sent soon after Jian's letter from Dover.

My Peking Man,

No father talk, no manifesto discussion. It's a deal.

Tell me firstly: how are your stomach pains? How are your bowels doing with no familiar meals of noodles and rice every day? It's all the mundane daily silliness of living together that I miss so much. I can't understand where you are now—what's this Immigration Removal Centre? What does it mean? You're going to be "removed"? Are you allowed to walk in the street freely? I don't understand the legal issue—I thought you had a special UK visa. Why do they have to detain you there?

Tell me more, even if it's depressing!

It's been raining today, Shanghai is muddy and foggy. The air smells sour and sweaty, like soy sauce. 11 a.m., I just got up to start my day but my parents were already clamouring for lunch. We put my father in a wheelchair and went to a nearby restaurant. "Your father needs nutrition," Mother said, and ordered an enormous bowl of chicken soup. Then she drank most of it herself. Father tried to bite into the chicken feet floating in the broth with his pathetic fake teeth, but he has no strength any more and just gave up. I find it so hard to watch. Mother told the restaurant to put the bony soup to one side and save it for us to come back and finish off tonight. "And how should we do that?" the waitress asked in a dismissive tone.

"How? Just put the chicken bones back into the pan and boil them with new water and add some greenery—and don't forget to add a bit of ginger." The waitress listened in silence, taken aback.

"We can't do that. You need to pay the cooking fee. That's at least five yuan," she said sulkily.

My mother laughed at her attitude and said firmly, "Of course, sister! Now also add three or four pieces of tofu. We will finish it for dinner." She stood up and paid from her fake-leather wallet.

My father has been in intensive care for nearly three months now, Jian. I'm so accustomed to the routine: Father has one injection in the morning and one dose of radiotherapy every two days. But yesterday after his most recent bout of treatment my weak, pale, reduced father refused to stay in the ward any longer. He says he can't stand another minute of watching the patient next to him dying. When one of the other patients dies we seem to sit there watching the body for what feels like forever, until finally a harassed nurse or relative comes and discovers the dead man. Sometimes there are tears, there is shock, or resignation. The nurses barely respond at all. We sit there and watch the body being lifted from the bed and wrapped like a dumpling in the bed sheets the body's former owner slept in. Then we stare at the empty bed, for what can seem like hours, remembering vividly the dead man's cough, his particular way of speaking to his daughter and fussing around his wife, how he would always spill his tea or drop his book. The worst of the worst is when, on the following day, a new patient is laid out on that very same bed. He'll turn to us, a room full of drawn and tired faces, try to smile in a friendly way, but he must wonder why we all stare at him as if he were a ghost. No one dares tell him anything. My father believes if he stays in this room he will definitely go before his time. He'll become the bandaged body, and we the weeping figures. And I'm sure he's right. So we've decided to rent a room at a hostel nearby. Although the room at the hostel is bare and tacky, at least my mother has a TV to watch, and a private bathroom for us to use whenever we want. And there's only one more week of radiotherapy to go, so perhaps we'll be out of here soon.

I have been thinking about your manifesto, dear Jian, though I can't see that it's of any use right now.

I've got to run, I have to get my father's medicine from the pharmacy before it closes.

Your very own Mu

11 LONDON, MAY 2013

Words, symbols, verbal gestures. Sometimes clear, sometimes obscure. Iona struggles, unable to gauge their depth in the parallel world of Mu and Jian. But she tries, and at the same time she shuffles around the pages, trying to arrange them in the right order.

Dear Mu,

I'm sitting in this foul-smelling little library writing to you like a Mongol who has lost his horse! How pathetic, old bastard sky! But I've no army gearing up for battle, and there are no hills surrounding my room, just a whole pile of legal files and the sound of seagulls screeching somewhere nearby.

I try to be USEFUL even when I cannot be used here. I study European history like I did at school, but I am too old to be re-educated! But yes, TO BE USEFUL, that's what I must strive for. Someone has taken the only copy of Das Kapital *the library holds, so I don't have anything sensible to read—I didn't know Marx was as popular in the West as he is in China. You may ask why I don't read the Russian book you gave me all those months ago. It sits by my bed most days and the words on the front feel like some kind of warning: Life and Fate. Right now I am not in the mood to read about Russian soldiers being shot in their millions and dying in the freezing winter— don't we Chinese have enough stories like that already? . . .* [Translator's note: Jian's handwriting in this passage on *Life and Fate* is illegible.]

I have no idea how people have reacted to my manifesto since I left China and whether they continue to discuss my ideas in the underground bars. Have you heard anything since the concert? I know you prefer not to mention these things again. I know you'll find it hard to believe, but it is as upsetting to me as it is to you, but I can't just let my work or my beliefs go like that. I need to know more, since I've been cut off from my world.

Dearest Mu, tell me, when are you leaving Shanghai for Beijing? Has your magazine job given you more time off? It seems so unlike them. I remember you saying you couldn't work for them any more. That the cheesy poetry they published was just to pass the censorship laws, and it got you down. You're wasting time with them, you should move on. Don't let them eat up your beliefs. Don't wait around. Maybe you shouldn't wait for me either. Keep yourself inspired if you can.

Your Jian, the Peking Man

Iona has an image of two rebels in love. Their strong emotions colour her mind with shades of red and shimmering blue. Mu and Jian, separated by their beliefs, and now separated by space, dropped on different alien planets. Both of them grappling with their own reality. Both of them trying to build a bridge on which to meet. And it's like Iona is building this bridge again, through her reading, her translation. Building a bridge of meaning from their letters, and she has to choose the right words to keep the structure standing. And it is so hard. The Roman letters of English and the oriental characters of Chinese are not natural bedfellows. Take expressions like "niu bi"—牛逼, "cao dan"—操蛋, "ta da ye de"—他大爷的, "zhou"—轴. How can she find the right translation for these swear words in English? If she had spent more time in Beijing's streets and markets and noodle stores on her year in China at university perhaps she would now grasp much more. One day, she thinks, she will master the language and understand the culture perfectly. Iona imagines herself eventually settling down in China—and perhaps one morning, say, on the Fifth Ring Road of

Beijing's Haidian District, as she is trying to cross the massive junction, squeezed between thousands of cyclists, she might overhear the exact curse that appears in one of Jian's letters. But right now she can only sense Jian's world from the remote isolation of her Islington flat. She has to work with what she has in her islander's head. It's like alchemy, but in reverse. She has to transform their gold into her lead. If she translated "*niu bi, cao dan, ta da ye de, zhou*" literally, it would read "cow's cunt, wank the balls, fuck his father-in-law" or something like that. Western readers would think she was writing cheap porn. The crudeness would repel them. And she would have failed. The bridge she is trying to build between Mu and Jian would fall into the river that separates the lovers. But if she translates blandly and drily, their revolutionary love story will grow cold and stagnant. And Iona is not about to give up, having hardly begun. She knows too well the struggle of the imagination. On her island home, as a solitary child, she used to imagine faraway places. So here she is now, in her tiny London flat, imagining faraway cities and smells, the sensations of China, and faraway minds.

Still, she feels the need to rest. Her body is like a large, sluggish octopus, reminding her of its human form only through the aches in her shoulders and neck. She also has worries. She finds herself worrying about her mother. Why now, she isn't sure. But like her shoulder pain, it's there, weighing down on her. When her imagination drifts towards the north, this worrying pain about the woman who gave birth to her gives her a stomach cramp. With a certain sadness she thinks of their infrequent telephone conversations.

"You OK, Mum? What are you up to?"

"Oh dear, is that you, Iona? I can't hear you very well . . . it must be the rain." Her mother's voice is frail on the end of the line. "Toby is being very noisy today. Toby! Toby! Stop messing around, come and sit here!" Toby is a Siberian Husky, her sister's last Christmas present to her mother.

The rest of the conversation is loose: the weather forecast and making strawberry jam and fixing the generator and one of the cows is about to give birth . . . Then there is always some problem with the hired workers on the farm—lazy or irresponsible or both. Everything is sort of interesting but not really interesting, nothing is unfamiliar, and there's never a turning point. Her mother has bad rheumatism; every rainy or even cloudy day she suffers severe joint pain and muscle inflammation. On the worst days she can't even make the trip between the bedroom and the bathroom. More and more she stays inside, listening to the radio and baking cakes that no one will eat. Her father is either out on the farm or working in the basement, where they produce and store their cheeses. When he's not on the farm, Iona's father will sit and drink tumblers of Scotch or several pints in their local pub down the valley, staggering back late. He is, and has always been, a good drinker.

She doesn't quite know why—perhaps it's reading about so strange a place as a Shanghai hospital—but today is a day of images of home: wearing green wellies, the pungent sting of cowshit-soaked earth in her nostrils, the squish of the rain-sodden land. For Iona, the only beautiful time on the island is summertime. In the summer the temperature is just warm enough to remove coats and boots; the tall grass in the valleys is lush, and wild blue daisies bloom in blankets that cover the hillside; they eat all their meals in the garden and read books in the meadow. It is lovely, as her mother would say, but the loveliness is always so brief. Summer on the island "only lasts seven and a half days," Iona would tell you. The rest is the winter, the ever-familiar cold, damp, windy, mossy, long, long winter.

Iona sinks back into her chair. Her body feels lonely, although her mind is full. A longing, a need, a swoon is rising between her loins and mounting to her chest. She can't help but lower her hand. Her fingers find their way into her underwear—it's warm and damp there. She presses her pubic region. Her body begins to recede into a realm of pure sensation, delicate and enticing. She rests her head on the back of the chair. For a while she remains in that position, as if lying back on a man's chest, her head resting on the warm skin covering a pulsing heart. Away, away . . . in some drowsy mix of pleasure and sunlight, she falls slowly, and sinks into oblivion.

By the end of the next day Iona is racing through the letters. She's barely even getting up to make tea and stretch her legs any more. Her flat dissolves at the edges of her consciousness. All she can feel around her are the blank faceless rooms of the letters: one lined with dying cancer patients, the other with immigrant refugees in limbo.

Kublai Jian
Dover Immigration Removal Centre
Dover 2ER 4GS
UK

Dear Jian,
So you are detained. Do you think they might send you home?
I am also waiting. I am waiting to leave the hospital. I feel desperate. This morning I played the ukulele in the corridor, just to break the silence. Or perhaps to avoid looking into the ghostly eyes that follow me—Father, Mother, and all the dying souls here that envy me my energy. It's that same electric ukulele we bought together. I played the smallest sound I could make, but still the nurse approached with her head tilted on one side, a stern disapproving look on her face. They prefer the sound of death here. They prefer the sound of a sigh. Death is respected, but not the living. All the nearly dead patients do is look at the TVs the hospital has put in every room. It's as if the TV has replaced the figurines of Buddha or posters of Mao. I can't see how the news—a stream of propaganda as ever!—will help with

these poor sick people's hallucinatory ends. Our General Secretary of State paid a visit to the mineworkers and praised their hard work; the Shanghai Education Bureau said education is the key to the future; a Fujian tea farmer praised the Open Door Policy, said it changed his life entirely . . . How tedious! These can't be the highlights of reality, nor serve as the spiritual hallucinations of the dying. We have become so practical with our ideologies that we no longer have any imagination. Maybe that's why I don't agree with your manifesto. Not all art must be political, Jian. Some artists strive to go beyond the political—though I know that's hard for you to imagine.

You know, I really wish you had met my father, I wish you'd met just once, that's all. You know that I've wanted you to meet him for years, and now it's too late. As he endures each coming hour on his bed I can feel his end within reach. Perhaps he doesn't feel that he is merely enduring, perhaps I'm the one doing the enduring. I think perhaps it's only me who's desperate to leave this diseased place of endings. The tracheotomy has done a great deal of damage to his neck and now he's got an open hole in his throat so that when he coughs his saliva trickles out of the hole down his neck. All we can do is mop it up with endless tissues. The doctors say it's astonishing, even magical, that he is still alive. But I don't think so. To me it feels like the last fight before death.

I keep thinking of that proverb, "Zhi zhe gua yan"—"He who knows doesn't talk." You know my father respected you but he always worried about the impact of protest. And I wonder now that maybe that's a better way to think about my father's voiceless hole.

Room 415. The cancer ward. My experience of Shanghai boils down to just this one room. It's all I will remember. It's like I can almost hear the silent sound of cancer cells dividing. Bodies are rotting away—my father's, and next to my father's,

83

mine. A single molecule produces more molecules, then other
molecules die at the same time, joints grow stiff, bones get brittle,
organs shrink inside the dark flesh, blood vessels slowly pump,
skin flakes off, cells die on the hospital sheets, on the crushed
pillows and the sunken duvets. I'm full of melancholy, Jian. Please
come home.

I love you as much as I love my father.
Your Mu

Iona feels a knot in her throat. Suddenly she thinks of death. Death
rarely visits her mind. But Mu's letter has invited it in. It lolls there
coldly in a corner along with distant memories from her past, and it
makes her feel sad. But she has been lucky. Iona has never had to face
anything too traumatic. Her only experience of death was her grandmother, sitting slumped in an old armchair in her home in the
highlands. It was Boxing Day, her mother was downstairs, heating up
leftover turkey, and eight-year-old Iona had been wandering about the
house, bored and listless, and had gone upstairs, following the silent
old carpet. At first she had thought the old lady was asleep. But as she
moved closer a coldness seemed to be coming from the figure. It was
a horrifying moment, her grandmother's eyes were still wide open; her
face was directed towards the window which overlooked the valley.
And that day the valley was grey and empty, no single living being
could be seen. She heard the door open and her sister Nell crept up
to stand beside her. The two little girls stood in front of the dead lady
with the tremble of fear about them. Still, no tears. For Iona, her
grandmother had lived in a family photo album. Death felt linked to
the immobility, a frozen image.

13 SHANGHAI, APRIL 2012

The south wind carries the humidity from the East China Sea between the monumental skyscrapers of Shanghai. Every household opens their windows wide, as the walls are mouldy with winter damp. Inside Fuxing Park the cherry blossoms are fully bloomed, their petals falling like snow in the wind; the willow trees and maples turn deep green with their fast-spreading shoots. Spring cannot wait to arrive; it rushes in on the tide of the Yangtze River, making everyone sluggish and restless, as if one had drunk too much hot Oolong tea.

In the patients' canteen, over fried tilapia fish, Mu breaks the news of her departure.

"I'm leaving tomorrow. Flying back to Beijing." She speaks in a neutral tone, as if she is just taking a trip between her father's room and the doctor's office.

"Tomorrow? So sudden!" her mother responds. "What have we done to make you so miserable here? Eh? Can't you see your father is dying? We haven't seen you for two years, you come back for two minutes and now you want to leave us again!"

Swallowing a piece of fish, Mu keeps her head cast down at her rice bowl.

Her father is saddened, but he says nothing. He puts down his chopsticks.

There is no good excuse the daughter can offer her family. She has been a determined person since she was small. She was born in the year in which the Vietnam War ended, 1975. Although her mother desperately wanted another child—a son, or two or three more sons if possible—her exhausted womb wouldn't produce any siblings for Mu.

She tried swallowing kilos of ginseng and oyster powder but to no avail. So the "Lonely Only" girl grew up in a tea-producing southern village accompanied by her mother's discontent. Her father was the one who showed love and affection for Mu. It was also him who taught her the first poem she ever heard, "Farewell to the Grassland," from a Tang-dynasty poet, Bai Juyi. "The grass on the vast plain, one season it dies, another season it grows; wild fire cannot bring it scorching death, spring wind draws it into new life." Her father would recite it slowly to his young, eager daughter, lingering over the words, drawing out each character with his ink brush.

When Mu was very young she kept falling ill from sunstroke. Her nose would often bleed in the summer. Her father took her out of school or the Young Pioneers' Palace, where she would study at weekends, and put her in a clinic. And the child with her burning red cheeks would swear to her father: "One day I will leave this hot oven and I will live in the north. I'll find a snowy town, I'll live in Haerbin or Beijing." It was as if she was never meant to be in the south, as if by pure accident she had been placed there, a child who really belonged to snow and crisp blue skies. And one day she did run away. A four-day train ride took her to what had always been the home town of her heart: Beijing. Her first year in the city was a mix of loneliness and exhilaration. She loved the ice skating and the heavy snows, the broad streets, the urban ugliness, the vast sports stadium and the secret underground bars. She would cycle around the enormous city, in spring through sandstorms, in winter through blizzards. She hardly slept. It was here that she discovered her people, her friends and comrades. The ones with whom she could live the life of ideas, with whom she could create a new world of literature and freedom.

In Mu's heart, her father is the person she cares for most, but she tells herself that she can do nothing more to change his situation. "I cannot bury my life with his cancer cells, and I am not going to just wait here for him to die! I cannot repeat my mother's life!" Mu feels like it's all very clear for her suddenly: "And when I grow old, I will not mind dying alone. Goddamnit! I can die alone without demanding that anyone die with me. And I am not going to make my children sit beside my deathbed watching me wither away." She remembers conversations with Jian on their balcony looking out over the hectic ringroads below, foodstall sellers, businessmen, peasants and students all walking fast on the same pavement.

It is the last day of Mu's stay in Shanghai. A train ticket to Beijing is in her pocket and it is a one-way pass. After her last lunch with her parents, there are a few hours to go before her departure. She writes in her diary:

Father and Mother laid their skeletal bodies on the bed for their afternoon nap. I lay beside them, flipping through the local newspaper which only publishes adverts. Slowly, I felt the anguish growing with each passing second. I looked at them, as they lay there. For the last decade the only life my parents have been allowed is one of eating and sleeping. Like animals—like cows or pigs. I gazed into their faces, half covered by a bed sheet. It felt strange, like I was invading their skin. Their bodies moved only very slightly, their breath coming between long pauses. It was as if a slow cyclic sigh was escaping from their half-open quivering mouths. It was a collective sigh, the only act that they now truly perform together. They are my parents, who once held me up as a baby, and helped me walk, and fed me, now lying together in their exhaustion. I could see the sigh that travelled through their bodies, back and forth between the walls, with no release, no escape.

THREE | INTERIM ZONE

东张西望.

dong zhang xi wang.

To look east and west; to look all around.

TRADITIONAL CHINESE PROVERB

1 LONDON, MAY 2013

It is Tuesday morning. After paying her overdue gas bill and her council tax, Iona sits down and types an email.

From: Iona1982@gmail.com
To: Jonathan.Barker@applegate.co.uk
Subject: Regarding the translation

Dear Jonathan,

My name is Iona Kirkpatrick. We haven't met yet, but I've been in contact with Maria Chambers regarding the translation of documents from a Chinese musician she asked me to take a look at. As Maria is now on maternity leave, I understand you are overseeing things. I thought you should know that there might be a delay in the completion of my translation. Huge apologies about this, and I hope it doesn't set back your publication plans, but judging by the time it's taken me to translate the letters and diary entries this last week I imagine I'm going to need a bit more time.

I'm ploughing through the material, trying to comb out some real coherence, to find a central narrative thread, but I have to say I don't think I have enough background information to do justice to the translation as things stand. Maria told me very little. Do you have any further information? The most important issue seems to me the identity of Kublai Jian himself. There are lots of oblique references to his background and family, his music and something he and his girlfriend refer to as his "manifesto" in the text, but I haven't come across anything on Weibo clips or Boku archives—the Chinese equivalent of YouTube and Wikipedia—to fill in the details. I presume he changed his name long ago (standard musician behaviour, surely?) or perhaps the Chinese censors have managed to clean up everything relating to him. It seems he was imprisoned in China—presumably related to this manifesto (do you know anything more about it?)—and then ended up in the UK. But this was some months ago, and obviously I've still got much more to translate, but I can't yet work out how he left China and where he is now. I hope you'll excuse my curiosity! I'd say I need six or eight more weeks. I hope you understand that I want to do the best possible job! Do let me know whether that is going to work for you.

All best wishes,
Iona Kirkpatrick

In no time Iona receives an automatic reply.

From: Jonathan.Barker@applegate.co.uk
To: Iona1982@gmail.com
Subject: Regarding the translation

Thanks for your email. I am out of the office this week with no access to email, back in the office on Monday 20th. If your query is urgent, please contact my assistant Suzy Warbuton on Suzy.Warbuton@applegate.co.uk

All best wishes,
Jonathan Barker

Iona stares at the reply. It astounds her; apparently when you have an office job you are always out of the office. With no set hours to subscribe to, she finds herself at her desk from morning till night. It rankles her, working so hard with others seemingly off on holiday all the time. She knows there is something about this "case" that has got under her skin. Something in her wants to leap out of its box and crack open the mysterious riddle.

2 LONDON, MAY 2013

Wearing a new lilac dress, Iona walks through Camden Passage, turns left, and comes to an old narrow street called Baker's Close. It is a Wednesday, rubbish-collection day. Piles of plastic bags are gathered on the pavement. Pigeons peck scraps of bread that spill from the bags and litter the ground. Iona normally feels so at home in these backstreets around the Angel, but today she doesn't know where exactly she is, and feels a little out of control.

She stands in front of a house, number 126, looking at its neglected garden: a rusty fence, a few dead plants, a dried-out sunflower stem are all that suggest this might once have been a lively household. She presses the doorbell and waits. A postman passes her, carrying a large shoulder bag of mail. He gives her a long look and walks on. He doesn't stop at the house. She presses the bell again—there's no ring. It must be broken. She peers into the frosted-glass panes on the door, and sees just darkness behind the door. She knocks loudly. A few seconds later a man in his late thirties opens the door. According to his Internet name, this should be Tony.

They barely speak to each other. She has come here for one simple reason: the unsaid sex in their brief but obvious Internet communication. Tony is muscular and tall, not at all unattractive. She feels her loins becoming wet as he is unzipping her lilac dress. He tries to kiss her, from her cheeks to her neck, then on the mouth, but Iona feels disgusted when his lips get close to hers. She can't do it. There's something repulsive about the idea of their lips and tongues colliding. Instead, she commands him: "Lick me."

The man is a bit surprised, but he obeys. He strips off her tights. She bought this semi-erotic lingerie with transparent lace patterns. It takes him a while to remove it. When her lower body is completely exposed before him, he is on his knees, his jeans already unzipped at the flies and loose on his thighs. At first he kisses her pubic area, then he sucks her lower lips. She takes pride in her position, opening her legs wider. As he passes his tongue over her clit, his other hand reaches inside his pants. He takes his penis out and rubs it. Iona watches him swelling. His erect penis juts forward with a fleshy madness that she finds hypnotic. She watches his cock hardening almost to the point of bursting against her.

Then he stops rubbing himself. He takes her nipple into his mouth and sucks on it really hard. Iona feels a slight ache in his squeeze, almost sore. He buries his face in her breasts; his soft brown hair tickles her chin, a soapy, newly washed smell. She wants to caress it, but her hands are stiff, clenching her upper body against his face. She wants to submit herself completely, yet at the same time she doesn't want to offer him any tenderness.

He takes her upstairs and pushes her gently onto the bed. He fumbles with a condom and she feels him enter her. A slight pain flickers through her body. She gasps with the welcome sensation of intrusion. The hollowness is momentarily filled. But it isn't absolute. She's in a zone between losing herself and remaining with herself. At the moment of climax, after his own thrashing groans, she feels a certain completeness, so brief, so ungraspable; it's like the farthest reach of a wave upon a shore. No sooner has it conquered the sand than it recedes, leaving wet sand bubbling under the sun; and she is left alone as the tide goes out.

When they finish, they both feel slightly embarrassed. The man goes to the kitchen to make her some tea. She looks around the empty room, almost devoid of furniture. There's a bookshelf in the corner but it's rammed with files and folders, and she can only see one book, a large hardback, *Great Railways of Britain*. An engineer? She gets out of bed and looks out of the window. The back garden is overgrown and seems utterly abandoned.

"Do you live here?" Iona asks, trying not to show her curiosity.

"Sort of." He's come back with two cups of tea. "We're selling it. Divorce, you know . . ." He smiles at her, ever so slightly.

Iona reaches for her shoes and zips up her dress. A tiny piece of material gets caught in the zip. She doesn't want to force it. She thanks him for the tea and leaves the house, with the side of her dress half open.

Hearing her heels knock on the cobbled street, she leaves Baker's Close. As she walks up the crowded high street Iona feels a sad urge for love, an urge for something substantial and lasting, something beyond the excitations of her pubic area. Perhaps I should never see a man of my own age again, she thinks to herself. They are too young, the way they embrace me lacks warmth and patience. Iona longs for something that can take her into a world of sun and earth, like a warm tropical island where people can grow their own vegetables and rest on their own land.

3 LONDON, MAY 2013

From: Iona1982@gmail.com
To: Jonathan.Barker@applegate.co.uk
Subject: Regarding the translation

Dear Jonathan,

Excuse my writing to you again. I did contact your assistant Suzy, but she said she didn't know much about this project and promised she would speak to you first, before she got back to me. But I don't seem to have received any further news. Please forgive my impatience; I'm eager for any advice or information you can offer. I would be very grateful if you could get back to me when you have a chance.

Yours,
Iona

From: Jonathan.barker@applegate.co.uk
To: Iona1982@gmail.com
Subject: Regarding the translation

Dear Iona,

Thanks for your email. So sorry about the wait—things are manic, as ever, so I'm afraid your email got lost in my inbox. Very pleased to hear you are immersed in the work. Needless to say we're all very curious to read your translation as soon as you finish a draft.

To answer your question about "the book"—well, I can only say that I'm equally curious about what to make from these files. I guess you might have been wondering where these documents come from. Well, it's all rather mysterious, to be honest. A few months ago, I was in Beijing for an international literature festival. In a talk about the publication history of post-Soviet literature, I mentioned the importance of certain banned books, including Grossman's *Life and Fate*. Afterwards, a woman came up to me. She introduced herself as Deng Mu and told me that *Life and Fate* was one of her favourite books. She appeared very agitated. She then gave me a package of photocopied Chinese letters and diaries. She told me her boyfriend was missing in Europe and they had lost contact two months ago. She asked if I could give this package to the London office of Amnesty International. Surely she could just send the documents, I said, but she was really insistent. She said in a quiet voice that it would be too dangerous for her to deal with this situation in person. She even said that if Amnesty couldn't find him, then perhaps I should read these documents, to find a way to help him. She gave me her Beijing phone number and walked off. It all happened rather quickly—I was whisked off to dinner with the other speakers and then had to rush to get my flight. To be honest, I didn't take it very seriously. What am I supposed to do with a package of documents written in Chinese? I can barely get around in Beijing!

I returned to London and phoned Amnesty. They said they didn't know anything about the case, had never heard of Deng Mu or this Kublai Jian person, and they would need someone to translate the documents before they could take any action. I tried a few times to find this woman again. The number she gave to me is no longer valid. And that's about the size of it. There's no obligation to translate this material or even do anything with it, but I'm a sucker for a mystery and this grain of a story has sort of got its hooks into me. Once I've read your rough translations, I'll have a clearer idea of the kind of story we're looking at.

This is pretty much all I know so far, but I'm happy to meet up for a proper chat once I've had a read. Can you send me what you've translated so far?

With all best wishes,
Jonathan

Iona reads the line again: "*She told me her boyfriend was missing in Europe and they had lost contact two months ago.*" She reads Jonathan's email for a second time, and writes down the title of the Russian novel that has cropped up in Jian's letters, *Life and Fate*, in her notebook. One for bedside reading perhaps?

She moves around the flat and finds herself examining the little bookshelf by her bed. There are a few books she has kept with her since her schooldays: Céline and Milan Kundera, Wu Cheng'en and Eileen Chang. Lots of fiction in translation. Then a few academic tomes on China and Chinese language, written by her professors at SOAS. These are the kinds of books that filled her years of study at school and university. She preferred Kundera to Céline. And she liked Eileen Chang more than Wu Cheng'en. "History" is too big a subject for someone like her, growing up marooned on a Scottish island, chilled by an arctic ocean. Oddly, she thinks, for all she gorged herself on books as a teenager, she has remained untouched by Russian literature: not much Tolstoy, certainly no Grossman. But there seems to be no excuse now. Iona goes online at once, and orders herself a copy of *Life and Fate*. The book will arrive within a week, it tells her. A week, she thinks, in her urgent impatient state. She cannot wait that long!

She has an idea and calls her sister. "Nell? Hi. What are you doing?" Iona can hear the kids screaming in the background. Her sister has twin boys of three years old.

"Oh God . . . I'm just about to collapse . . . hold on—" Nell's voice is interrupted by crying. Lots of noise on the other side of the line, water running, chairs banging, Nell's scolding . . .

"Is everything OK? Are the boys fighting? I can call back later if that's better." Iona's words vibrate through the noisy echoing phone line but fail to catch her sister's attention.

No answer, only Nell's bustling and busy motherhood muffling the shrill voices. It sounds like the twins are in the bath, making mayhem in their watery playpen.

"They were going nuts with their new water pistols, the whole floor's wet, and I've no dry towels left . . ."

Iona hasn't much patience for her sister's warm domestic anarchy. She imagines the steamy press of the young milk-fed pink bodies, and the mother enclosing them both. With a shiver, she feels her own distance, and a vision of the solitary night ahead suddenly flashes in her head.

"Listen, is Volodymyr around?"

"No, he's still at work . . . Can I help?" Her sister switches off the tap. Now her voice is clearer, although still breathy and puffed.

"No, I don't think so. I just want to ask him if he knows about a Russian novel."

"Oh, right, which one's that then? He's been foisting lots of long Russian novels on me recently."

"*Life and Fate*? I thought Vlods might know—"

But before she can say anything else the water war breaks out again, and a bursting, keening scream comes down the phone. "Stop, will you?!" Nell shouts to one of the twins. "Iona, look, sorry. Call again later when Vlods gets back, will you?"

"OK." Iona hangs up the phone, feeling a bit disheartened.

The sun is sending golden beams onto Iona's desk and her fake-Persian carpet. She can see motes of dust dancing in the light. Outside it's a beautiful spring day. She misses her bench in the shadowy spot where she often sits and ponders. It's an old wooden bench in Duncan Terrace Garden, but in her mind it's her own private shelter. It is sometimes occupied by homeless men; most of the time, though, it's hers. She'll happily sit there, even on a rainy day, camped out under her umbrella, watching the squirrels jumping in and out between the bushes, and listening to the sound of the wisteria whispering in the urban breeze. It's thinking time.

Iona puts on a jacket and slips her feet into a pair of trainers. Closing the door behind her, she walks down the bright street.

4 LONDON, MAY 2013

The publishing house is very close to Hyde Park. Iona comes out of Queensway Tube station and walks along the edge of the park. She notices the bright-yellow daffodils are blooming. From time to time, here and there, her leather boots encounter tiny buds of blue irises on the soil. She hasn't noticed spring flowering in her part of London. The sky above the Bayswater Road seems bluer and brighter. This is west London, not her north-east messy bohemian hangout, she grins to herself.

She gives her name to the receptionist and looks around. The publishing house has obviously been recently refurbished: it looks newly painted and immaculate, like they have been running a good business. Iona still remembers the time she came here for an interview, right after she had received her MA degree. "No, I don't think you're quite right for the position. You know, we get so many applications, and some of them even have PhDs." Iona had failed immediately, yet at the time, newly graduated and without much sense of direction, she had only wanted to become one of their PR staff, or even a receptionist, picking up the phone to say, "Hello, Applegate Books, how can I help you?"

She waits for Jonathan in the staff cafe. The cafe has the same white, clean, fresh design as the lobby, with white tables and white chairs, an extremely bright white ceiling and white walls dazzling to an eye accustomed to the modulated lamplight of her small flat. As she sits there alone, she watches a tall, handsome man crossing the room. His smile is generously directed towards her.

"Hello, I'm Jonathan." He puts out his right hand. "You must be Iona."

"Yes. Good to finally meet you," Iona says as she stands up and extends her hand, feeling his strong grip.

"I don't have much time, I'm afraid, something urgent has just come up. Can I get you something to drink—a coffee? Tea?" He talks in a quick, practical businesslike tone, laced with charm, which makes Iona suddenly unsettled.

"Yes, a white coffee would be great, if it's no bother."

As Jonathan orders the coffee, Iona discreetly observes him. He is lean, wearing a close-fitting black suit and a pair of polished shoes that tap on the wooden floor as he waits for the coffees. His wavy, dark hair betrays hints of the dandy and bounces gently on his shoulders while he leans on the counter and turns to Iona. His voice is a warm, smoky baritone.

"Sorry we couldn't meet earlier. I was travelling in Asia until last week."

"Right. Do you travel a lot for work?" asks Iona, slightly nervous.

"I go to India often. We seem to have so much business with them these days—their publishing industry is really starting to take off, especially English language. And I'm sometimes in Russia." He smiles—he's warm, but professional. My time is short, his face seems to say, as he brings the coffees to the table. "So, how's the translation coming along? I've read those few pages you sent over. I know you said they were still draft, but it seems very intriguing."

"Indeed, intriguing is the word." She holds the coffee in both her hands and takes a tentative sip; it's too hot and her tongue stings with the burn.

Iona feels his eyes on her breasts. She is wearing a low-cut pink blouse. "I'm quite bewildered by the absence of any background information. As I said in my email, there are hints of all sorts of mysteries—there's the prison, then this manifesto thing, and Kublai Jian seems to have serious issues with his father, who sounds like an official of some kind. Hard to know what this could be about. I wondered whether Jian's father was someone important but every search I do is completely fruitless. I know there's a really stringent Internet filter in China, but I sense this is somehow more suspicious. Have you found anything?"

"Well, not much. I can only infer, of course, as we have almost no information. I'm hoping we can unravel this somehow and—if this doesn't sound too horribly commercial—that we find something big. Obviously the story, the writing, et cetera, is interesting regardless, but I have this feeling there's something big lurking underneath that we haven't got at yet."

As he talks the professional screen slips away and something more organic takes its place. She begins to understand why his publishing house has been so successful.

He picks up his coffee, drinks quickly and continues. "We've not been able to find anything online about him at all, which seems odd if he was a famous musician. The only reference we could find was for this album, *Yuan vs. Dollars*. You must have had the same experience." He looks straight at her—it's unnerving—and Iona nods as she looks down into the coffee. "I also wondered whether Kublai Jian was a stage name. If he's banned and censored, then we've got a great story here—a big story, what's more—about the suppression of artistic freedom, the state of China today, you know, all that jazz. So little gets out about real censorship in China. We take it for granted but what do we know, really?" He sits back and smiles. "Anyway, it's all in your hands, Iona. It's very exciting. Potentially."

Feeling her cheeks burn, Iona is almost flushed. She's one to stumble into things, accidentally, lightly, casually. She's never felt such a sense of responsibility. She hears her slightly trembling voice: "Yes, Jonathan, it's exciting. I'll be sure to let you know how I get on."

His phone rings, and he quickly glances at it.

"Do let us know if you need further assistance. I look forward to hearing more about your progress, Iona." He stands up, stretching his hand out again.

"OK . . ." Iona says, still clutching onto her coffee.

As he turns to leave, Jonathan gazes at Iona for a brief moment. "By the way, has anyone ever told you that you look like that actress? Oh, what was her name? Eighties stuff. Dark, petite. Um . . ."

"Winona Ryder?" Iona is nearly embarrassed.

Nodding his head, Jonathan smiles ambiguously.

5 ZENTRUM FÜR DEN SCHUTZ VON ASYL, SWITZERLAND, MAY 2012

Everything happens in time. They say time is like a great valley stretching into the distance; our lives are the great valley's lakes and rivers, each with high and low points, depressions and hilltops. Iona doesn't know it yet, as she walks along Regent's Canal in Camden Town, but just a year and three days ago, Jian was caught up in his own waterway. He felt black-hearted and out of control, like he was being carried by a rushing river towards some sinkhole of oblivion within it. A police van was driving him down a winding road, away from an anonymous immigration office to—Jian didn't quite know yet. The office had been stuck in the foothills of the Alps. Strange that he had ended up in the most glaciated area in Western Europe, the Aletsch Glacier region. To be surrounded by mountains, grey-green, clenched by icy fingers, only sharpened the pain inside, the cold fall of his stomach through a void.

Jian walks around his new home and experiences a surreal feeling of déjà vu: bare white walls, small square desk, plastic chairs, a vending machine, and a fridge containing nothing but half a pint of milk. He can't help feeling he's been here before. He knows he was in England before, and before England, China. And before China it was still China. So when was he here? Or did this place once come to him in a dream? For a moment he cannot locate himself. The sunlight penetrates the dormitory windows; the town outside seems like a dream town that the sleeping mountains themselves have imagined. The distant street lamps, the neon signs of occasional cafes, the quiet and lonely streets . . . he has seen all this before.

A week ago Jian arrived here with his old guitar and a few personal belongings. All of himself bundled up into one small suitcase. Perhaps he is lucky, whether he likes to believe it or not: he is one of a few refugees granted a transfer to a Third Country, owing to uncommon political status. Right now, all this movement, processing, and transfer from one jurisdiction to the next, have brought him here, standing in front of a stove, in a communal kitchen, making a cup of tea. *This is Switzerland, I am in Berne*, Jian tells himself in English. Then he realises it's not English he should be speaking, and repeats it in German exactly as he has been taught, like a child in a primary school: *Das ist die Schweiz, Ich bin in Bern.* He wanders around the quiet building while serious-looking staff discuss their work in German with the occasional French word or sentence thrown in. I am in a kind country, he thinks, as he picks up his tea and walks outside into the fresh, bright day. The courtyard is surrounded by tall, solemn pine trees. He speaks to himself: this is the basketball court where they have said I should do some exercise. He walks on, and this is the laundry room with washing machines for everyone; and this is the shower room with hot water provided every day; and this is the canteen where the refugees can eat for free—the white plates are for tasteless pastas and the green plastic cups for tap water. It is good though, definitely an improvement on Dover and Lincolnshire. But still you have to report to the reception each time you go out and sign a form, say where you're going, and you can only go out at most three hours a day. The sign on the front says this is an asylum protection centre—what does that mean? Protection from whom? How long can he live here, with the protection of free food and free bed and three free hours a day?

6 ZENTRUM FÜR DEN SCHUTZ VON ASYL, SWITZERLAND, MAY 2012

In the afternoon, Jian sits in the canteen "Imbisshalle" with his new room-mate, Mahmud, a loud bearded man from the Libyan Desert. Mahmud teaches Jian all kinds of things about the desert: its oases and depressions, its wind and dryness. Mahmud's speech is a blend of Arabic and English.

"You know, Kublai Khan, there are eight depressions and oases in the eastern Libyan Desert. Eight! Can you believe that?"

Mahmud has called him Kublai Khan since the first time Jian introduced himself, and Jian doesn't bother to correct him.

"Hmm, oasis." Hearing the faint music coming from next door's German-speaking radio, Jian recalls oases in films he has seen: a king sits under a white tent with grapes and slices of melon on a platter in front of him as his many mistresses dance to lilting music.

"But the oases now are all fucked up, you know, they have no water."

Jian nods in agreement, thinking of the Taklamakan Desert in western China. He had gone there with his band for a gig many years ago. It was for the annual Silk Road Music Festival, and nearly all of the underground Beijing punk bands went there, because of the loose censorship in the more remote provinces. They stayed in tents, overheated in the day and frozen to death at night. When their time to perform finally came they played on a makeshift stage to a few camels patiently nudging the sand and watching them scream. Culture and nature don't go together, as was once again proved. The highlight of the trip for the band was watching the locals killing and skinning a sheep and cooking it for them. They waited ravenously for hours for the meat to be boiled—one sheep for four hungry men! This wasn't the greatest trip the band had ever had. It felt utterly uninhabitable on the hopeless sand. It had been wise of Mu to stay at home, he later realised. Better to be a Mongol on a horse than a desert man on a camel.

"You know, Kublai Khan, water is what we need the most, even more than food, more than oil." Mahmud speaks like a cultural ambassador. "Water could bring peace to the whole country, you know. C'est simple, we've got nothing to drink!"

"But what about wells?" Jian asks. He thinks of how the Chinese had to dig wells to irrigate the agricultural land of the plains. In his childhood he even saw a team of professional well diggers come to their hutong to make a well. He was standing nearby with a bunch of kids, watching the loud digging and banging. It lasted for two days. On the third day the neighbours arrived with ropes and buckets to fetch water. But his father wouldn't participate in the event. He told Jian's grandparents that water pipes would soon be installed and they would have running water from the taps in their kitchen within a few days. To everyone's surprise, his promise came true. And as he grew up, Jian started to notice that his father's predictions on government policies were invariably accurate.

"Wells? It is just not possible in the desert, man. You've got to find subterranean water, you can't see what's under the sand. You know, you don't want to dig a hole for nothing, Kublai Khan."

Jian likes this Mahmud. In this city of lakes and mountains, he wants to talk to the desert man about the Yangtze River and the Yellow River and even the dirty wash outside the window in Dover. But he doesn't know where to start. Time has passed; perhaps his Chinese rivers are now muddy and dry. Eventually the rivers and plains will be transformed into another desert, another Taklamakan, another Sahara.

7 ZENTRUM FÜR DEN SCHUTZ VON ASYL, SWITZERLAND, MAY 2012

When Mahmud of the Libyan Desert is not talking loudly or making a mess in their room, Jian lies on his bed and kills time reading. He's finally turned to Grossman's *Life and Fate*, immersing himself in a world of Russian Communists and Nazi spirits.

The Chinese translation of *Life and Fate* is in three volumes, 989 pages long in total. Unlike most translated literature in Chinese, which is unreadable and makes almost no sense, this book reads fluently to Jian. He feels a certain affinity with these Soviet wartime stories, apart from the long, unmemorable Russian names. Curious, he turns to the back cover, reading the praise on the blurb once again: "*an epic saga against Fascism; a masterpiece of socialist-realism—a must-read for all Chinese citizens!*" Then he turns to the front page:

China Workers' Publishing House
Translated by Yan Yongxing
This edition published in 1989

No wonder, he thinks, published in 1989! That was the year everything burst—the year of the Tiananmen Square student demonstration and the fall of the Berlin Wall. That was the year when suddenly the phrase "Anti-Spiritual Pollution Campaign" was being reused by the authorities. The translation of *Life and Fate* could only have been published before June 1989. And after 4 June Jian remembers seeing the foreign-literature shelves of his local bookshop half empty. Punk music and beat poetry are perfect examples of "Spiritual Pollution" from the West, he thinks.

Jian is on page 64. Nadya, the daughter of Viktor and Lyudmila, is unhappily drinking condensed milk and the physicist is trying to get on with his work, as the Germans and Russians hunker down in the trenches. Science against violence. I must read slowly, very slowly, Jian tells himself, I don't want the war in Stalingrad to end. It would be better for me if neither Germany nor Russia could win the war! Although, in his heart, he knows that no one really does win a war like that. Everyone will die, from the commissars to the horses. Only the ruined city will remain.

8 LONDON, MAY 2013

There was rain last night, and Duncan Terrace Garden is wet and quiet today. Floating clouds pass by above a giant pine tree towering above Iona. The pine is at least four hundred years old, as the sign attached to the tree trunk states. It reminds her of a tall pine tree in front of the house she grew up in, which she often climbed as a little girl. And here, by City Road and Upper Street in the midst of this urban wind, the pine grows as strong as it would in a wild forest. She gazes at its clusters of sharp needles, strong roots, and smells the rich scent of the forest it exudes.

As she walks by the tree, Iona inhales the ever-familiar moisture of London spring air—a little rain, a little sun. She has brought yesterday's newspaper with her. Laying the paper down on her wet bench, she sits and opens her work folder.

April 2012

Dear Kublai Jian,

You say you might not be in Dover for long, so I really hope this reaches you.

You'll never guess where I will be THE DAY AFTER TOMORROW! I will be in that place I always dreamed about going to: America! Yes, you won't believe it, and neither do I. But I am going to go to America! You remember how desperate I was to get out? Dreamed for years and now it comes true. This is the last letter I'm sending you from China before I leave!

Perhaps you are wondering why I have left it until the last moment to tell you this. The truth is, Jian, I have been trying to make a life here without you. This must be hard for you to hear. But I don't know if you are coming back to China. Without you I am lost. I need to become someone new. When we got back together a year ago our relationship wasn't the same. I am changing. So, I quit my job. No more wasting time in the printing room checking typos and punctuation on those cheesy poems written by sentimental businessmen moaning for their lost youth. I really need to get back to my own writing. Secondly, we have been busy forming a collective band—Underground Slam Poetry Group. I'm sure you're wondering what I am talking about. Ha! Well, it's simple. It's my band. I am one of the vocalists, although I am only doing poetry. The boys sing. We were "discovered" or "created" just a few weeks ago. And I think we are brilliant, Jian.

I had to get out of Shanghai. The dying was sapping my bones. And then Beijing was no better: our flat was cold and empty and a hollow shell of what it had been and what we had shared. I was so used to seeing you sit in that rattan chair playing your guitar, now I couldn't bear that there was no one around, nor any sound. I had to get out of miserable Beijing, wasting my day looking at tea leaves and kicking about in bars waiting for news of you, waiting for you to come home.

I met this "artist scouting manager" (that's what was written on his card) a couple of months ago at our favourite cafe round the corner. His name is Bruce and he's one of these scummy Americans with half-Chinese blood. You know, the ones we hate. He speaks a little crap Chinese that he got from his mother. (And he was wearing this expensive Vivienne Westwood checked suit.) He had been listening to bands in cafes in the hutong and then tumbled into our place. He said he'd been into that bar near Qing Hua University—you know the one—Mute Trumpet. I was doing a reading of some cut-up pieces and strumming my silly ukulele. I was so angry, Jian, that I decided to do something a little different this time. I found an amplifier and plugged in my uke. I got this really sharp sound, squeaky but heavy, with an acid echo behind it. It was discordant, but I liked it. When I smashed out a few chords, I could see foreigners in the audience raising their eyebrows and some even gathered their stuff and walked out. The half-Chinese guy, Bruce, though, seemed to like it. He came up to me afterwards, and that's how it all began. He wanted to put me with a band—Beijing Manic—do you know them? They're new. Strictly underground, your style. Why me? I asked him, a little peasant poet who can't really sing a song (or entertain people in public), with this hot sweaty punk band? Bruce had this kind of Andy Warhol idea. (Like he thought I was a kind of naive Communist version of Nico.) He said my anti-style screaming delivery, along with my electronic uke squeaks, would really work with Beijing Manic's heavy punk. He said I would fit right in with the acts on the tour he was organising anyway. So two weeks later we were in Bruce's super-expensive office in Jianwai Soho, and we signed on the dotted line. We came up with the name China Underground Slam Poetry Group. And that's it! I know, it's crazy. And feels strange, and sort of fitting, to be making music and punk with you gone—almost like I'm doing what you cannot.

And because you're not here, everything is different.

The three boys from Beijing Manic—do you know Lutao, the vocalist and guitarist?—and I had to get passports. We kept quiet about it. Didn't tell anyone. It was like we were on some secret mission. I didn't even tell my parents. I think Bruce had to really work hard at getting our U.S. visas. I will only really believe the whole thing once we are on the other side of the planet.

It's hard to know what will come in the next weeks, my ape man, but I'm all inspired. I hope your situation gets better soon.

Love from the bravest woman you ever knew,

Your Mu

PS From now on, in the next two months, you can write to me at this address (my manager's): PO Box 2121, Boston, MA 02215, USA

It has started to rain again. Iona bundles the photocopies back into the folder and slips it inside her coat, hugging it to her chest as she buttons up. Back at her flat she puts the kettle on, towel-dries her dripping hair and opens her laptop. She types "Beijing Manic China" into Google. A flood of information comes up on the screen. In an interview with the band a headline reads NEW CHINESE BAND HEIRS TO JOY DIVISION? after a claim by frontman Lutao that the English band is their main inspiration. Iona finds another article on the fashion and sense style favoured by the band. There are two photos—although blurred, clearly taken at a concert, she can make out the figures. They are very young. All leather jackets and the familiar attitude of punk—a metallic youth, she thinks, and the phrase comes to her in Chinese and in English.

Iona finishes the latest translation feeling totally energised and exhausted. Mu writes fluently and vigorously; she is a natural writer, compared with Jian's fragmented and unfocussed style. Still, she doesn't feel quite ready to embark on a brand-new journey with this Chinese woman yet. Instead, she returns to an early part of Jian's diary, where she discovers a loose fragment on a floating photocopy.

Beijing, July 1999

Typical situation: I was inside the History Museum looking at documents from the Opium War time while she waited outside in the cafe reading some suicidal poet—Sylvia Plath, it turns out. And when I came out we started to quarrel. I want to record this argument—it's troubling me, I keep playing it over and over and I can't find a way out. She fascinates me and I can't seem to function without her but, Old Sky, I can't bear the fact that on the surface she acts like a rebel but deep down she is a conformist for anything fashionable. I can't take her blind acceptance of anything Western. (Isn't it a perfect example of our difference that she studies Western literature and I am reading Chinese history?) I know she hasn't had to fight like me, she hasn't had a father like mine, but she needs to find her own ground to stand upon, not some second-hand interpretation of Western culture.

So I said I thought it was ridiculous that all our syllabus told us to read were these Western novels. That we knew the lives of the Americans and the British better than our own artists, better than our own parents, even. She just shrugged and said she kind of liked these books, and why was it such a big deal anyway. She laughed as if it was no big deal—lighten up, Jian, stop taking everything so damn seriously! And that just made it worse. This is China and we live in China, I said. Why would we abandon our own history and allow ourselves to be totally swallowed by Western culture? She said she thought it was good to learn about the West and then I just lost it. I know I kind of got things out of proportion, but she brought up my father and turned to me and said seriously: Look, Jian, the way you sound now is just like how your father speaks on TV! If you care so much and disagree so violently, then do something about it! Playing your guitar is not going to change this society! I don't know, but maybe she has a point. I can't think straight when she brings up my father but I've got to do something. Hasn't there got to be a way of shaking things up without being like my father? It terrifies me to think I'm more like him than I want to admit. It just depends whose side you're on, doesn't it?

10 BEIJING, MILLENNIUM EVE, 1999

. . . Everyone is talking about the Y2K bug and is petrified that their precious computers will die at the last stroke of midnight of this millennium. Personally, I think this might be the best thing that could happen. If all the computers of the world were to die as the clock tolled for 2000, we could happily go back to the Bronze Age, hiding ourselves in caves, making tools and singing poetry under the stars. Ha! What a caveman's paradise! But in just a few hours, we will be stepping into a new millennium. We are waiting restlessly for the click of the clock to take us into the new century. But into what? Everyone hopes for the big change, the big renewal. They want to cast off their old selves like snakes shedding their skins. But when midnight passes, nothing will have changed.

Jian scribbled these words in his diary in the last remaining hours of 1999. It was a year of important events. That summer, just before most of Beijing craned their necks to see a total solar eclipse in the sky, Mu received her MA in Western Literature. In the following weeks, as Jian scribbled songs and prepared his second album, she managed to find her first ever job, with a poetry magazine called *Tomorrow*. She told Jian the magazine had been introducing and translating Western poetry to a Chinese readership for a few years, printing works from Keats and Byron to Ginsberg and Bukowski. The job was titled assistant editor but in fact she didn't get the chance to do any editing. "I will look at commas with the fullest concentration," she told the editor-in-chief during her interview, when he told her it was mostly proofreading. Jian couldn't believe that he'd been out of college for three years already. It all still seemed so new. The band were doing well, playing in different venues almost every weekend. Until a strange day in December when all performances were banned in the capital. There was no information about why or when they might be able to perform again but Jian and Mu assumed it had something to do with Cambodia. They had recently learned from a journalist friend about the official dissolving of the Khmer Rouge and they guessed the Chinese government would be fearful of infection from the south, as they would always be whenever there was an international disturbance.

On the eve of the year 2000, Mu, Kublai Jian and his band gathered in the super-congested hangout, Cafe Proletarian, to celebrate the new millennium, and also for another exciting reason. There had been gossip around Beijing that the punk godfather himself, Johnny Rotten, was in town and would be coming to this bar with his friends that evening. Already, one could see a bunch of youths clutching pirate copies of Sex Pistols albums and looking around anxiously through the ever-thickening Camel and Zhonghua smoke haze for glimpses of their idol.

Just a quarter of an hour before the chimes of the new millennium, Jian and his pals heard a collective scream erupt from their midst. They looked to the entrance, and saw three white men walk through the door—in the centre of the trio was a rather tall man with red hair wearing an oversized pyjama-like suit. It was the godfather of punk royalty. The crowd's screams grew louder still: "This is the Sex Pistol man!" or "You're so behind the times, his band is Public Image Ltd now!" or "Whatever monkey they are, don't tell me that's not Johnny Rotten!"

As the white foreigners, acting as one, squeezed themselves through the crowd to find a place to sit, the assembled Chinese youth swarmed over them with CDs and posters for signatures. Kublai Jian and his band moved forward, while Mu stayed behind, shielding herself from the crazed throng.

In the midst of undifferentiated Chinese yelling and shouting, Jian heard the white man's distinguished English:

"If you Chinese really want to be polite, then don't call me bloody Mr. Rotten. I'm not some fucking comedy-show character unless you pay me. Call me Mr. Lydon if you can't bear to call a man by his first name."

Before any sensible conversation, the crowd suddenly began to scream the countdown, each number resounding like great gongs in an empty tower: Nine! Eight! Seven! Six! Five! Four! Three! Two! One! Hooray!! Everyone hugged each other, patting backs, grabbing shoulders and waists, and squeezing limbs, crying and smiling into the blurred forest of tangled bodies. Beer bottles opened, voices were raised, fireworks shot out in the street like a war had started.

Amid the general cheer, a conversation sparked into life between Kublai Jian and Johnny Rotten.

Jian, with all sincerity, stammering, dry-throated: "I've never been to the West. But can you tell me, Mr. Lydon, is there any positive punk scene in the West? I mean, good punk that does practical good for society?"

"Nah, there's only negative punk, man."

"Only negative?"

"Absolutely. Punks are useless, or worse, by definition!"

"But I don't believe that."

"Well, then you've been born in the wrong time!"

"But I know one, for sure, a positive punk. Here in China."

Johnny began to twitch his lips again, almost laughing sarcastically. "Who is this positive Chinese punk? Eh?"

"Have you heard of Kublai Jian, a Beijing musician?"

Johnny shrugged his shoulders, unimpressed by the name. "What's he done?"

"A new album is coming out soon, called *Yuan vs. Dollars.*"

Johnny shook his head. "*Yuan vs. Dollars*—not a bad name at least."

Mu was now too impatient to stand behind and watch, and she cut in with her better English.

"But, Mr. Lydon, why didn't punk bring anything good to society?"

"Good? Didn't bring any good?! It brought good all right. Think of an enema, girl. You know what an enema is? That's what punk was. Flushed it all out!"

Mu murmurs, "Enema?"

"Yeah, colonic irrigation of society!"

Jian didn't understand Johnny's words and just went on, almost angrily. "But shouldn't they do something good to help society?"

Before the white man could answer with even more enigmatic riddles, a wave of fans pressed onto the star their notebooks and CDs, grabbing the demigod's shoulders and hands, desperate for his mark. Outside the bar, the midnight sky was lit by a vast cascade of fireworks, illuminating the solemn and dark Long Peace Avenue, the featureless Heavenly Gate Park, the foreboding Forbidden City, the drumming Bell Tower, and finally creating a fake light of day in Tiananmen Square. A new century of amnesia had arrived on China's earth.

FOUR | ON THE ROAD

读万卷书不如行万里路.

Du wan juan shu buru xing wanli lu.

Reading ten thousand books is not as useful as travelling ten thousand miles.

LIU YI (WRITER, SONG DYNASTY, 11TH CENTURY)

1 PHILADELPHIA, MAY 2012

A fully loaded American Airlines flight carries 332 passengers cutting through the clouds above the Pacific Ocean. Inside the plane, most of the passengers look like business people, either reading the *Financial Times* or furiously typing on their laptops. In the back of the plane there is a loud group of Chinese passengers, all young and long-haired, taking photos and laughing at each other like overexcited first-time travellers. Beside them, a half-Chinese half-American man in a dark Vivienne Westwood checked suit studies a tour schedule on his computer.

A brand-new world. And a brand-new me. I'm no longer Deng Mu, according to our manager Bruce. He said no one was going to be interested in a poet whose name was Mu, I needed a stage name, something that fitted with the band name Beijing Manic. So he came up with a new one for me. This is what I have just read on the newly printed leaflet: "Slam Poetry from Sabotage Sister, a poet from Post-Mao China." Is that me? I feel like I am wearing a disguise—underneath I am still a hundred per cent Chinese daughter of the countryside, and unconfident in front of a Western audience. I don't feel true to myself; it's as if I'm pretending to be someone else—a fake, a vain attention seeker, something I hate when I see it in others. Sabotage Sister is really Bruce's invention, a new package of me.

All of a sudden the spotlight trains on Mu and the house lights dim. The audience quietens, the band are ready with their instruments. Even seconds before she starts performing she is still racked with anguish, and feels unprepared and vulnerable. She plugs in her ukulele, turns up the reverb and sets the tone buttons low. Nervously, she hits a series of D chords. It sounds like a screeching cat on heat, and two middle-aged women in the audience cringe and move towards the exit with trembling fingers in their ears. She belts out her verses above the roar of Beijing Manic's driving rhythms, her uke adding a whining, tortured drone to the pounding noise of the band. She doesn't really know what she is doing, just follows the howling in her ears, laying down a chant in half-Chinese and half-English. Two elderly men who look like veterans from an ancient trench war seem shell-shocked by the barrage; they stagger after the women to the exit. Mu sees this from the corner of her eye, and gulps back her disappointment. Her mouth speaks and her fingers move up and down her instrument. All she can see as she looks out into the crowd and the lights burn on her forehead is another stage, long ago, in a faraway place, where the lights danced and the music roared and she is in her white dress dancing and crying and screaming among the Beijing crowd.

2 LONDON, MAY 2013

The photocopied diary pages of Mu's America tour are neat, well organised, each entry dated. It is a recent tour, only last year, according to the dates. Iona has a feeling that some secret hand has been putting these documents together properly, and it seems from April of 2012 onwards there is barely any correspondence between Mu and Jian. Most of the photocopies are from their diaries.

West 22nd Street, Manhattan, 28 May 2012

A budget hotel beside the Chelsea. We storm into the lobby with tons of luggage. At reception we were asked these strange questions: "How are you today, sweetheart?" or "You enjoy your chocolate brownie, sister?" or, even more bizarre, "I heard you Chinese still believe in communism, s'at right?" Americans don't seem to really believe that there are other people in the world, and so, when they see you in their country, it's like you've stepped straight out of a television set.

This is New York City, the great model that Beijing and Shanghai are desperately trying to ape. But now I think China could never match the USA because we have no black people in our country, and no foreigner can become a Chinese citizen. It's amazing what you see when you leave a place. It makes me realise how we Chinese have the worst prejudice against "others." I look around and I imagine that I will be an immigrant here one day. Everybody I pass on the street has a confident look about them, like they're going somewhere and accomplishing something. Only two slight disappointments—Times Square is much smaller than I imagined, not even half the size of our Tiananmen Square. It's just a big lurid billboard. And Broadway— Broadway isn't broad at all, it's narrow. It's just a load of street blocks all squeezed in like tubes of toothpaste. The boys from the band seem to be oblivious of their new surroundings, but they all protest about the food. They've threatened to quit the tour if there are no pork ribs or mala beef with rice on the table from now on. So Bruce takes us to Chinatown. Big fat noodles with fried pigs' trotters and stewed intestines and sour cabbage blood soup. There we don't have to force down weird eggy cheesy sandwiches. Actually the mere sight of a sandwich is depressing enough. "It sucks." Lutao has just learned this expression, and he uses it all the time. "It sucks, man."

Thinking of Jian. My heart aches as I see a succession of young Chinese men pass with a melancholy look on their faces. Have I just missed him? Where is he now? Did he walk by half an hour ago while we were having lunch? Would he see the posters in front of a Brooklyn club advertising my poetry perfor- mance tonight? If there was only one person in this part of the world who would recognise my voice in the crowd, that would be Jian . . .

West 22nd Street, Manhattan, Iona murmurs, and stops reading Mu's diary. She thinks of her Uncle David. Three years younger than her father, David has lived in Manhattan since he left the farm on Mull in the seventies. Now a very successful businessman, David runs an accounting firm in New York City. When Iona visited him with her father a few years ago, they went to his office near West 21st Street. In the front window she remembered an advertisement for the business: *We Help Small Biz Owners Minimize Audit Risk While Lowering Their Tax Bill!!* Whenever a potential client dropped in, her uncle would give the visitor a "free thirty-minute consultation" and a cup of filtered coffee with two sugars and the offer of soya milk. It was savvy business sense. Damn sight more savvy than his Guinness-drinking brother. Iona often wonders what it would have been like if she had moved to New York. Would she still have worked as a translator? Would she ever have encountered Jian and Mu's story? Perhaps she would have become one of those successful members of the immigrant American business community, with her Scottish accent, a plush apartment in town and a large place upstate. Iona gazes at the Islington human zoo below her, jostling in the street, and nearly laughs at herself—if only life could be lived simultaneously in parallel spaces and times!

3 CHICAGO, MAY 2012

Chicago. The city looks hard, like it's carved out of sheer granite. What would Walt Whitman think if he woke up in downtown Chicago, on a park bench, say, like so many of the "bums"? This bum Walt would find himself looking on an unrecognisable world. He might even start uttering one of his own poems to himself, like the one that begins "O Captain, my Captain." There would be no leaves of grass for his spirit to merge with, except for the grass of the cold city park he would be lying in. He would shrivel up in the air conditioning, and shrink from the smiling hotel staff waiting for a tip.

And this is the city of lakes! Lake Michigan squats here by the concrete bank. Motionless. No wind at all. What would an old Chinese fisherman think of it? Maybe all American fish live in Third World seas and are caught by nets pulled up by Third World hands. So the Americans can design Apple Macs or smoke marijuana in their spare time.

Bruce is always hanging around. There's an odd tension between us; although my head is still obsessed by Peking Man, I feel a certain attraction to him. This troubles me; I feel like I'm a soldier's wife, trying to make a new life after my husband has gone missing in action. Then I hear Bruce's voice in his East Coast accent: "Don't be so miserable, Sabota. In America a poet has to be a salesman too. You gotta learn self-promotion and dress like a pop star, not some sad boring intellectual." Bruce. A banana with yellow skin. "That's awesome"—he says it ten times a day. Could someone like that really understand me?

Chicago's Athletic Club Hotel, where Sabotage Sister and Beijing Manic are staying, is a sportsman's weekend hangout, with a lobby playing Sinatra's music all day long—*Songs for Swingin' Lovers* on a loop. The walls of the club are adorned with stills from the film *The Man with the Golden Arm*, claiming a scene was shot on the street outside, though it was cut from the original film so the connection is hazy to say the least. In the Cigar Room, Bruce is forced to smoke whenever the Chinese men smoke. They hand him a cigarette whenever they light up, having told him: "If you don't smoke with us then you are *zhuang-ya-de*"—a wanker, a ponce. As the tour wears on, he is the one who's responsible for Camel supply. The boys smoke Camel No. 9. "It gives you a throat kick," Lutao, the singer and guitarist, claims. Lutao offers one to the girl. Sabotage Sister takes a few puffs, but already her mouth is bitter, and a pain goes shooting through her lungs. Camel No. 9. Not so good for a cancer patient's daughter.

Instead of messing around like a tourist, our Chinese daughter spends her days writing. Maybe I will become a real writer in America, she says to herself. Because I can do nothing here apart from write. In her limbo state, she writes new poems. She feels her Peking Man's spirit in her pen, as if he is softly whispering anarchic lyrics into her ear, his breath on the back of her neck, his fingers stroking her bare shoulders. Her new poem subverts an Allen Ginsberg piece. She has replaced the key word "America" with "China," and "Russia" with "America." Who knows how it will go down here, but she has almost stopped worrying about reception. They can all go jump in the lake, she says, somewhat nervously. I should do what I want to do, I am no longer a proofreader for a state magazine in China. This is America after all.

> *China I've given you all and now I'm nothing.*
> *China two dollars and twenty-seven cents*
> *I can't stand my own mind.*

China when will we end the human war?
Go fuck yourself with your atom bomb.
I don't feel good don't bother me.
I won't write my poem till I'm in my right mind.

China when will you be angelic?
When will you take off your clothes?
When will you look at yourself through the grave?
When will you be worthy of your million Trotskyites?
China why are your libraries full of tears?
China when will you send your eggs to India?

4 LONDON, MAY 2013

The garden is very quiet today. Nobody around. Just one or two nervous squirrels in the bushes. Since the day Iona started this translation job, she's been feeling that her own life has abandoned her. What is it, this subject called "life"? Is there some kind of qualitative scale? She thinks the life of Jian and Mu is worthy of being called a life: from the little she's gathered so far, Kublai Jian seems to have lived dramatically and confrontationally. Yet her own life seems an insubstantial, almost colourless timeline dotted with trivial details.

Then she thinks of her publisher Jonathan, the man she knows as little about as she does about Kublai Jian. It turns out Jonathan went to the same university as she did, but a few years before. She wonders if they were taught by the same professors, perhaps they sat on the same seat in the library and borrowed exactly the same books, or perhaps he too got into the habit of having a coffee at the British Museum while writing his graduation thesis. She assembles the landmarks of his life, not quite at ease with her own uncontrollable curiosity about him. His biography on the company website tells her all she needs to know, but she wants more. Degree at SOAS, then into journalism briefly, then publishing. The facts about Jonathan begin to assemble themselves. He seems to be very involved in the project, perhaps rare for someone so senior. For Iona Kirkpatrick, though, Jonathan is still just a stepping stone to the story of Kublai Jian and Deng Mu.

She stops herself. She is nearly drowning in her work, or, rather, in Jian and Mu's world. She needs to swim further, deeper, to test how deep it goes, and what islands it might take her to.

Buried in her thoughts, Iona leaves her bench and walks out from the Duncan Terrace Garden. The evening light is soft, the May wind pleasant. She finds herself walking along the Regent's Canal, wending her way home as the ducks squawk alongside her. The section of the canal she favours most is overgrown and strangely dead-looking, with lines of narrowboats eager to discharge their detritus into the water's dank stillness. Staring down into the canal, she thinks to herself: maybe I should go and live abroad. Go to America or China, indeed, some vast country in a new world. Britain feels old, narrow, made stale by history. Perhaps all she needs at the moment is to do what Mu does in her own life: leave the protective space of her own culture and embark on a brand-new journey into a brand-new world. The ducks swim away. The dim water with its reflected trees remains inert, and keeps the secret of its depths.

Iona's sister Nell and her husband Volodymyr live in Shepherd's Bush Green, just behind Europe's so-called largest mega shopping centre, Westfield. Before she even steps into the house, Iona hears a wave of loud screaming. Not only is there the familiar noise of her sister's twins—she recognises a particular squawk as belonging to Otto—but chirpings and shouts from alien toddlers, perhaps a whole crowd of them, are mixed in with the sound of motherly reassurance.

As soon as Iona takes out her gift, the twins tear open the package. Plastic aeroplanes are smashed against the wall and new wails and tears join the general din. Nell is exhausted as usual, but somehow seems unflappable and exercises command over her progeny. The three-year-old twins writhe like monkeys in her grip. Then there are the other mums and children Iona has never met. They chatter noisily in Russian, and Iona feels inadequate with her minimal hello and goodbye. She is caught up in vapid sociability, her head and smiling face in a nodding blur. Volodymyr remains calm as ever, and hangs around in the background of the baby bedlam. She wishes he would rescue her from this.

After kisses and a few words with her sister and the children, Iona follows Volodymyr into the kitchen, where she stays. Her brother-in-law is in charge of food for the party and he's already started getting the ingredients together for pancakes. He's assembling golden syrup, honey, sugar, lemon juice and a bowl of whipped cream. Iona feels a little queasy.

"Can I help at all, Vlods?" Iona looks with trepidation at the sink, brimming with colourful plastic spoons, twisted soiled bibs, and some gunk that looks like regurgitated porridge.

"I'm fine, thanks, Iona. I'm used to it," quips the Ukrainian professor. Clearly he likes being a house husband too. "Just making some extra pancakes for us adults. The kids have already eaten. You hungry?"

Iona laughs and shakes her head. Her first laugh for a week, she thinks. Mu and Jian's story doesn't exactly inspire much mirth. She likes Volodymyr a lot, perhaps a little too much. He's busy with his cloud of flour, as he mixes up more batter in a large bowl, and glances back warmly at his wife's younger sister as she laughs.

"So how's work at the moment?"

"OK, . . . got a new translation going now . . . this one is complicated . . . I think it might be an important book, but so far I don't quite understand what's going on, or how to approach it."

"Well, anything to do with China is always complicated, as far as I can see! Nell told me you'd called about a Russian novel. What was it you were after?"

"Oh, yes, thanks, *Life and Fate*, by Vasily Grossman. I've actually just bought it but I'm only a few pages in."

"Ah, that's a great book!"

"Yes, but the size of it! My God!"

"So, since when have you been interested in Russian literature, Iona. Are you switching sides now?" Volodymyr teases her, as he pours a ladle-full of the buttery-milky batter into the heated pan. It splatters and bubbles.

"Er, no, not exactly. I actually want to read Grossman so I can understand what I'm translating." Iona sighs and looks out of the kitchen window onto another wall, the yellow-and-greyish afternoon light making her restless and anxious.

"Grossman is deadly serious—it's heavy stuff, you know. Nearly Solzhenitsyn, but not quite Solzhenitsyn yet . . . to read Grossman is like taking a Soviet history lesson . . ."

Iona can feel the excitement growing in her brother-in-law's voice. Nell once told her that Volodymyr had supported a capitalist agenda in Ukraine, then when he arrived in London his views veered more radically left-wing.

"You know, most books were just banned for publication in the Soviet Union, but *Life and Fate* was the only book which was actually confiscated while Grossman was writing it. KGB men came to his flat, took his manuscript and removed all the carbon paper he had bought and even the ribbon from his typewriter. The poor man died four years later."

"So how did the book get published then?"

"It didn't. In fact there were another twenty-five years of silence after Grossman died until in the eighties the first published version appeared in France. A dissident Soviet writer confessed he had secretly smuggled a microfilm copy to Europe—that was how the book survived."

As Volodymyr speaks, his eyes are focusing on Iona in that way they often do with her. She wonders if he would like to have her, along with his wife, in his own urban harem. There's always been a spark between them. Cutting off Volodymyr in the middle of a long sentence describing the post-Leninist world of Stalin's cultural spring comes the desperate plea of Iona's sister from the front room.

"Vlods! Vlods! What the hell are you doing in there? Come and give me a hand. Otto has cut his finger!"

Volodymyr runs out, leaving his pancake sizzling in the hot pan, handing Iona a wet spatula with an order to "flip it" when it begins to smell good. A few minutes later, she appears in the main room with three burnt pancakes.

On the train from Milwaukee to Minneapolis, the band are teaching Bruce how to swear in Chinese. Having grown up in Boston, his Mandarin vocabulary is poor, especially his slang and street talk. He's a poor fit for this all-cursing Beijing punk gang, but he starts having fun with the new insults he's learning. "You stupid cunt, don't be zhuang-ya-de!" Mu uses a small dictaphone to record all the conversation and street sounds around her.

"What is the recording for, Mu?" her Chinese buddies ask.

"Some people take photos, others record sounds. I choose sound," answers Mu, as she records the train's clunking rhythm mixing with the loudspeaker's announcement. "You never know, maybe one day I will transcribe all these sounds and conversations into a book."

In a bar, Mu records her very first English conversation with a local man. The man, easily over eighty judging by the folds and wrinkles on his skin, has a sunburnt face and muddy eyes. But his eyes begin to shine as the evening wears on and he works his way through beer after beer. When she's home Mu sits down with her machine and transcribes the recording, making comments on the conversation as she goes along, remembering how she felt only hours ago in the sweaty dim bar.

"Are you local?" I asked him.

"Well, I'm local enough to be local." Local enough to be local. I didn't really understand what he meant. "I came over from England." He took a big gulp of beer. "A long, very long time ago now."

"England? You mean, real England? Not New England?" I stuttered in my bad English.

"Yes, that very England. Queen and country and all that."

I suddenly thought of Jian. He went to the land where this old man comes from.

"Which part of England you came from?"

"I'm from Hull, you know. Ever heard of Hull?"

"Hell?"

"Ha! No, not Hell. Hull. Though might as well have been, you know."

"OK, Hull. So when you were in England what did you do?" I asked, feeling like a journalist from the China Daily.

"Well, I moved around a bit, had lots of different jobs, anything I could get, wasn't fussy. A bit of fruit-picking, vegetable-selling, street-cleaning, even worked in a slaughterhouse for a while. Then I got into truck-driving. Drove up and down motor-ways just as they were starting to build them."

I was only able to understand about half of what he said, and just when I wanted to ask if he knew a town called Dover, he kept on. "So one day I just thought to myself: what the hell am I doing here? It's bloody gloomy and cold, and I was beginning to hate the truck. I knew other people who'd done it, so I just went out and bought myself a ticket, got on a boat and arrived here. Been here over forty years. And Milwaukee's all right, it's one of the most decent places I've ever been. And I've been to a few. I just thought: bugger England. All because I came from Hull."

Then he finished his drink and ordered another bottle. He shouted down the bar, "Hey, boy, gimme another forty-ounce Colt 45, will yer?!"

"What is a Colt?" I asked.

"It's a revolver."

"A revolver? You mean, like, a gun? A beer named after a gun—is that allowed by the government?"

"Ha, everything is allowed here as long as you can talk like a lawyer! That Obama was a lawyer, you know. Anyway, in England a colt is a young horse. But here it's a kind of gun. And this kind of beer is named after that kind of gun. Both can do you some damage! Ha! Watch out, girl!" The old man laughed loudly and the table and chair trembled with the vibrations. I set the empty beer bottle down on the table before me and wondered if I would ever visit his home country.

The old man snorted into the mouth of his Colt, and gave me a beery, rheumy eyeball, and a cracked-smile look.

"If you ever visit England, then send my regards to that old hag of a town, London, though I'm sure she's tarted up well enough now."

"Tarted up?"

I didn't understand what he meant, but he ignored my question and went on talking to himself.

"You won't know about this. Too young. But places and people, old and dead, get under your skin, when age weighs you down . . . You get an urge to return, like haunted by a ghost. And you want to see for the last time what you left and lost . . ."

The old man suddenly stopped speaking. In his silence, I think I understood what he was talking about. Perhaps one day I will get to England.

7 LONDON, MAY 2013

As Sabotage Sister and the band leave Wisconsin, heading for Minnesota, on the other side of the Atlantic, Jian is writing to his lost lover.

Dearest Mu,

I received your letter finally—the one about you going to America! America! Old Hell! I don't know how it made it to me, across seas and continents, but somehow it did. But that was two months ago, so who knows where you are now. I'm going to try this Boston address, but I don't hold out much hope—on tour means on the road, surely. What a surreal concept; my world is in stasis. I don't know what it is to explore any longer. I am quarrying inside myself; that's all there is left.

I am still in an in-between state. I'm waiting for my asylum application to be granted. That is all. No news, no change—or at least that's how I feel after days in this grey box. I can't see what there is beyond this right now, I can't even see you here with me, or us together in Beijing any more. Even my memories of our flat are hazy and dissolving. I hope you're having a good time, wherever you are. And I hope you can lead the life you've always wanted to live. America must be better than China, whatever I think of it.

You should start a new life, a brand-new life without me. Good luck, Mu.

Jian

Iona is reading the letter in the fifth-floor cafe of Tate Modern. She repeats the line: *You should start a new life, a brand-new life without me.* As she repeats the phrase in Chinese she rises, then leaves the cafe and briefly visits the current exhibition, a retrospective of the American artist Roy Lichtenstein. Standing in front of a comic strip called *Drowning Girl*, Iona thinks of Mu; somehow the drowning girl becomes Mu's face. Mu, an individual, struggles for her voice in the sea of multiple American voices. Iona decides to go out for some fresh air.

She is on the Millennium Bridge, swaying in the faintly fetid wind above the grey currents of the Thames. The steel floor vibrates and echoes with hundreds of footsteps. She stops at the central point, sees the city crouching on both sides of the great gash of river whose waves spread wide the legs of the capital. The tide is strong. She imagines people drowning in the stench-coloured water, the opaque liquid ready to consume any living thing. She remembers she heard on the radio the other day that each year there are about forty-five people drowned in the Thames. She can almost see their drowning limbs struggling, grey mud painting out the humanity of their faces before they sink forever. And in the distance the buildings of empire are indifferent to it all. Iona is shaken out of her vision by the feel of a hand touching her left arm. She turns. It's an old tramp, stump-like limb outstretched, she assumes for money, mouth gurgling something. Automatically, Iona draws out a few coins from her pocket and drops them in the open palm. But she does not linger to confront the eyes upon her.

Proceeding along the bridge she again feels a tug. On the brink of annoyance, Iona turns her head and automatically speaks:

"Yes, what now?"

At first all Iona notices is a traditional full-sized umbrella with a wooden handle hanging in the crook of a man's arm. Then she notices the familiar big brown coat the man wears. Iona looks up; it is her old professor from the Chinese department at SOAS.

"God, Charles!"

"God indeed." He laughs. "I thought to myself: who is this slim creature lingering on the bridge, with that devilishly stylish black hair, très Louise Brooks, wandering alone? It could only be Iona Kirkpatrick!"

"Oh, Charles!" Iona almost laughs. "You look exactly the same. I recognised your umbrella first!"

"Oh yes, my gentleman's umbrella! It ensures my hair is just so in even the worst London downpour." The professor gestures to his hair— he is completely bald, and has always been, apparently. But his boyish, bright-eyed face is still there, smooth and almost unlined.

"My star pupil. What are you doing nowadays, Iona?"

Professor Handfield's eyes are full of humorous affection for her. Charles, a well-known sinologist in his mid-sixties, is still bursting with vigorous energy. She knows that she was one of his favourite students, and she got the highest marks on her final dissertation. He had hoped she might continue studying, do a Ph.D. on Chinese history, or work for some important cross-governmental organisation. But she didn't. Instead she disappeared from the academic scene.

"Well, I'm still freelance, working on translations." Iona feels a bit embarrassed. "Most of the jobs are not very interesting, to be honest . . ." Her voice peters out as the professor looks at her intently. "But there is a job I've been working on recently which is getting me really fired up . . ."

"Oh really? What is it? Do tell me. I'm intrigued! Landscape poets from the Ming dynasty? The travel writings of Bai Juyi?" He shifts his umbrella onto his other arm and walks with her over the bridge.

"Actually, something more contemporary. A publisher sent me a pile of Chinese letters and diaries in April, asking me to translate them. All a bit of a mystery, as they didn't really know what they were or whether they were even publishable. But I'm uncovering more and more as I go. So far I know that the letter writer is a banned punk musician who used to live in Beijing, but is now in exile in the West."

"Excellent. I knew you would do something interesting. But this musician—would I know his songs?" Her professor speaks with what can only be a glint of sarcasm, though with Charles it's always difficult to tell if he is being serious or not. "You know, I'm not as much of a fuddy-duddy as I look. I'm quite partial to second-generation Beijing punk. Do you know Cold Blooded Animal—Leng Xue Dong Wu?"

"No, Charles, I don't. And I'm not entirely sure you do, either." They laugh together. "My musician's name is Kublai Jian. It's probably his stage name, though I can't find anything about him online. I think the most famous album was called *Yuan vs. Dollars—Renminbi Huan Mei Yuan*. And that wasn't all that long ago. Only a couple of years. I can't find his music online at all. I think everything's probably been cleaned away by Chinese cyber police."

"Hmm, that title sounds suspiciously euphemistic, don't you think? Well, the cyber police in China are the best in the world. If this musician is banned, he's probably someone who's done something important, said something dangerous, incited crowds to rebel—the list is endless! We know all about Ai Weiwei, and the familiar list of dissident writers. They are not nobodies. Often they're connected to the elite. That's why they're watched even more closely."

Iona nods vigorously. "Yes, exactly. I've been thinking that, too. But I have to get further with the translation, delve further into the letters. I still have mountains to get through."

"Well, Iona, you know where to find me if you ever need an expert opinion. I realise I'm more at home with the Boxer Rebellion on the whole, but contemporary resistance has also started to interest me intensely." Here Charles's hypnotic brown eyes, with their laser-like lustre, momentarily arrest her. "You know, we really miss you at SOAS," Charles says with a great show of sincerity. "If you ever reconsider academia, do let me know . . ." He checks his watch quickly. "I must rush—meeting a friend at the South Bank. We're seeing Khachaturian's *Spartacus*. Lots of nude muscular young men under the Roman lash." He raises his eyebrows suggestively. "Remember, do come and find me any time in July. I'll be in Nangking until the end of next month. Zai-jian!"

Charles and Iona hug and move on. As they walk in opposite directions over the bridge, Iona's university days come vividly to life. She studied language mainly with Charles—prerevolutionary Chinese idiom in particular. But she also dipped a toe in history. She did a course with Charles on Chinese secret societies like the Boxers at the end of the nineteenth century. What would he make of her mysterious punk musician? she wondered. He might translate him better than her, since didn't he teach her all she knows about translating? She feels cheered by his presence. As she crosses the street, the roar of the city returns to her: traffic, church bells, buses, gulls, sirens. The weak spring sun momentarily flashes and she suddenly feels a rush: she is alive! Yes, she is still young—I have hardly begun my life! And, she tells herself, feeling she has declared something solemn and serious, I will not live a trivial life.

8 IDAHO, MAY 2012

This is the twelfth hotel we have stayed at in the U.S. The twelfth bed I have lain in since we arrived in this country. So far the band's American trip has always taken place inside: in hotel rooms, in concert halls, in waiting rooms, in trains, in bars, in planes. There is always a curtain and a window to separate us from the world. Nature is out there, like a perfect postcard, but we haven't managed to put ourselves in the picture.

We arrived in Idaho yesterday. Lying on my bed looking at a straight road outside the window, I see a scene from the film My Own Private Idaho: *a young man standing on an Idaho highway, trying to decide which way he should go. Why am I thinking about this? Is it just that travelling through America feels like travelling through a film set? Everywhere you go, the mythology of cinema has left its trace. I remember reading the Chinese translation of the novel the film was based on. An extract was published in a Chinese state magazine called* Western Classics. *In Chinese the title was modified to* Idaho in My Heart. *Using the word "private" was not thought a good idea in a state magazine, while "heart" is more a positive word. But having never been to the West, it was hard for me to imagine the sandy desert roads and cheap motels, the neon signs and greasy food. And I really don't remember the gay story from the book at all—censored like everything else.*

My stomach is all I care about in the West. Our first meal in Idaho was in a Mexican restaurant called La Pasadita Drive-In. Pancakes stuffed with red kidney beans, served with an enormous flat fish. All for $9.99, the waitress said with a big smile. Everyone smiles here. In America you can eat exotic foods *at bargain prices. There's a lot to get used to. A television on the wall in the restaurant was showing* Top Gun *with the sound down low; everything in the film was lit to make it look gorgeous: the planes, the pilots, the hero, the heroine. It was a bright and golden day outside, the sunlight flooding into the restaurant, making the whole place look like part of an afternoon dream, bright and unreal. Only the mountains of red kidney beans heaped with guacamole tell me that I am not in a* Top Gun *fantasy but a regular cowboy state of America.*

Jian, I hear your voice inside my head. You're asking: is America as we always imagined? Well, there is everything you would expect from America. All the clichés about this land of living clichés are true. But perhaps that's because people want them to be true. It's like ideology, you are told to believe some stuff and you are never supposed to give it up! It feels like you can become important here if you dedicate your life to fulfilling your goals. Maybe that's the difference with China. We struggle like buffalo all our lives and we still don't become someone.

The next day, as Beijing Manic and Sabotage Sister march back to the same restaurant, *Top Gun* is playing again on the big screen in the corner, as if it is on loop eternally. The band's front man, Lutao, says he has some important news to announce. He speaks as he eats, his words coming out as a muffled hiss as he chomps down his three-and-half-inch sirloin steak. After he finishes the steak, he takes a mouthful of Coke, and repeats his announcement.

"I will stay in America, whatever the cost."

Everyone raises their head from their plates, and stares.

"Brother, what do you mean 'stay in America'? Illegally? With an expired visa?" Dongdong, the drummer, asks.

Then the bassist, Liuwei, speaks up. "Man! What about us? Tell us what your plans are. Quickly, before Bruce comes in." He turns his head towards Mu.

When Bruce's name is mentioned, everyone turns to look at Mu, their eyes intent with suspicion.

"Don't look at me, guys!"

"You know why we're looking at you, Mu!"

"What? You assume I'm sleeping with Bruce, and now I've gone over to the side of the enemy?" She is furious suddenly. "Don't you go thinking I'm Bruce's dog just because we're sleeping together. And I'm not saying we are!"

Lutao continues with a steady tone. "You guys can go back to China or on to somewhere else or go wherever you want. I'm going to find my own way." He pauses and looks at his empty plate, then looks up at them and adds, "I'm gonna go solo."

Everybody is silent.

America is better than China. The band are in demand here, receiving hard cash and eating three-and-a-half-inch sirloin steaks any time they want.

"But what are you going to do in America?" asks Dongdong. "You can't speak more than five words in English!"

"I'll learn! I'm going to start a business. A Chinese takeout joint first. Isn't that what everyone does? I've saved some money. I have plans. I'm not an idiot."

At that moment Bruce enters the restaurant and the band go back to sipping their Coca-Colas, pretending nothing has happened.

9 LONDON, MAY 2013

The annual reunion of the Chinese Study Department is held in the usual bar near Bloomsbury. Iona plans to go only for a bit, just to say hello to her professor, Charles, and a few fellow students she used to hang out with. She needs to go back to work, and there are one or two ex-boyfriends she doesn't particularly feel like seeing.

Two beers later, Iona is beginning to feel restless. The usual catching-up and photo-taking with her old friends somehow doesn't inspire her, she wants something more, something fun to happen. Iona is bored; she's surprised her professor hasn't made it. Across the room she watches a bunch of young men playing pool. As she stands at the bar to buy another drink she gets into a conversation with one of them, a man of thirty-something with ginger hair. He buys them two Belgian Leffes and says he is a veterinary surgeon. She's always found vets creepy; for her they're kind of like undertakers. But she is curious about the animals, and tells him about her family's farm in Scotland, and of the few times she tried to milk the cows with her hands. It's all mechanised now, though. Hand-milking is only to draw the tourists. As the reunion gradually breaks up, the ginger-haired man orders two more Leffes while they talk about castrated dogs and sick cats, accompanied by the background throb of tinny pub music. He says he has castrated about 250 dogs. Iona is impressed, but doesn't quite know how to respond. After the call for last orders they leave the pub and walk into the evening rain. Their body language has been working on each other all evening, with a secret but clear code, and both sides have received the message perfectly. She follows him into a taxi, and they go back to his flat. He seems an experienced sexual partner—clear and confident about what he wants. He is very tall and thin, matching the size and shape of his cock. When he is inside her, she feels her lower body filling up so much it is about to burst. His hand forcefully holds her hip. It is good sex, from a technical point of view, but she can't seem to ignore the sharp antiseptic tang that pervades his flat. During sex, she feels at one point as if she were a dog being manipulated for an unknown operation. As their bodies tangle, the image of herself as a bitch lying on his surgical table, waiting for her womb to be removed, plays in her mind with lurid vividness. She does not orgasm. After he comes on her, she can't wait to leave. There she is, in the cold midnight dew in the dead zone again, a neutered dog released from sexual need. She finds herself in a cab in Clapton, where sirens are still blaring and drunken multitudes stumbling out of pubs onto the pavement. As the taxi pulls up at her flat, she cannot wait for a hot bath.

An hour later, after her bath, she drinks a mug of peppermint tea. She doesn't feel like going to sleep immediately, so instead she reads a page of Mu's diary.

The day before yesterday, Bruce and I passed by a wedding party in a park somewhere. We stopped our car and peered through the trees at the bride and groom—they were both fair, young and healthy; their smiles were as perfect as the smiles in a television commercial. They seemed to have big families and plenty of friends. There was even an orchestra playing. I watched Bruce walking towards the young couple to congratulate them. He then came back and handed me a glass of champagne. It had never occurred to me, but suddenly I thought: what if Bruce and I get together and even get married? It seems a ludicrous idea. I wonder whether Bruce has had a similar idea, although the Peking Man has been lurking around the back of my mind.

Even though we lived together for so many years, Jian and I never thought about getting married. No, it's more than that: we have always rejected the idea of marriage. We saw marriage as a trap and we didn't want to enter that trap like everyone else. But now. Now I don't know any more. This foreign soil makes me rethink everything, and I am becoming more and more practical. Perhaps one day I will no longer know how to write a single line of poetry. This practicality will rob me of all my words. And perhaps then I might even welcome this obscene act of robbery.

FIVE | THE SECOND SEX

不闻不若闻之，闻之不若见之。
见之不若知之，知之不若行之。

bu wen bu rou wen zi, wen zi bu ruo jian zhi.
jian zhi bu ruo zhi zi, zhi zi bu ruo xing zi.

**Tell me and I will forget. Show me and I will
remember.
But involve me, I will understand.**

XUN ZI (PHILOSOPHER, WARRING STATES PERIOD,
475–221 BC)

1 CENTRE D'ASSISTANCE EUROPÉEN POUR REQUÉRANTS D'ASILE, SWITZERLAND, JUNE 2012

In the beginning there was nothing in the universe. The sky and the earth were glued together and the whole world was a hot and bubbling pool. For twenty thousand years nothing changed, until one day there appeared a cosmic egg. Inside this cosmic egg, yin and yang slowly found their balance, and a half-man half-dragon was shaped inside the egg. His name was Pangu . . .

Jian writes this on the first page of his new diary, a slender notebook he found lying around on a staff table the other day. It is early summer, but in this part of the world he still feels cold. He is in a camp in Lausanne, after being transferred from Berne with several other asylum seekers. In this new setting he starts to have strange dreams at night. Somehow the ancient god Pangu, the first creature of ancient China, has infiltrated his mind in the last few days. Jian sees the great creature vividly. Pangu seems to fit well into this alien space, like a vine winding through a lush rainforest, or a fungus growing on a mouldy carpet. He hears people around him speaking in French or German and he feels even more mute and deafened. His own Chinese world has come to an end, so why not think of the origins of things, the beginning of China, the mythic world, before emperors or the cultivation of rice? Before laws, or the worship of gods; before human feet left their footprints on the muddy shores of the first lakes . . .

Suddenly everyone is gathering for breakfast and he stands, bored, in a queue in the canteen. The other inmates sit or stand around in the boxy white room with sullen expressions, skinny creatures on stick legs. Jian laughs to himself occasionally, hunched over in his corner of the canteen, as he contemplates his plate of bread, cheese, coffee on the table in front of him, and pictures his ancient ancestor.

After breakfast the canteen transforms into a classroom for their French-language class. Sitting among the Muslim women wrapped tightly in their scarves, Jian peeks at their naked eyes, wondering what they are hiding. "Don't stare at me!" He can almost hear the women cursing in Arabic under their veils! They don't seem to want to be in Europe at all. They sit on the hard benches of grey Switzerland; perhaps they are thinking of nothing, have nothing but fragmentary images of their previous life looping around in their heads: a shady corner of a clay house, hens pecking in the dirt, an old plum tree on the dusty road, fish bones thrown towards a stray cat, the afternoon sun blazing down . . .

The French class is the only thing Jian likes about being here. The teacher, Monsieur Georges Godard, is someone who has admirable patience for the elder foreign students and the mentally disarranged. A useful sentence Jian has learned to speak this week: "Asile de réfugié, je suis venu de Chine."

Monsieur Godard asks everybody in the class to change the last word according to their origin and to say the sentence out loud.

"Requérant d'asile, je suis venu de Somalie."

"Requérant d'asile, je suis venu d'Angola."

"Requérant d'asile, je suis venu de Libye."

"Requérant d'asile, je suis venu d'Égypte."

"Requérant d'asile, je suis venu de Syrie."

2 CENTRE D'ASSISTANCE EUROPÉEN POUR REQUÉRANTS D'ASILE, SWITZERLAND, JUNE 2012

In the library that evening, Jian reads his Russian novel, looking up now and then at the scrawny Africans reading their Qurans, which they flip through with grimy fingers, snot dripping from their noses. They look like they are crying, he thinks, as they mumble their prayers. Their god is not his god Pangu. Man makes gods in his own image, and in his case the gods had Mongol faces. They were there from his early childhood, the years he spent with his maternal grandparents before they passed away.

Then all of a sudden there's a ringing in his ear, sharp and persistent. His head is throbbing again. He feels he is somewhere underneath the earth. Like an infinitely deep pit with cogs, wheels and pistons whirring, the stink of oil in churning water. The water of the Yangtze River. He remembers his first ferry trip across the river; he was eleven years old. He had heard that exact same throbbing sound coming from the engine room. He ran to the front of boat and leaned over the railing, trying to see where the pulsing sound came from. Clunk! He fell. He was nearly swallowed up in grinding gears and flying sparks. A blinding flash in his eye, and he touched his broken skin on the sharp wheel. He was crying. His grandparents ran to pull him out. They wrapped his broken forehead with someone's handkerchief. It was an unforgettable trip, not only because his head throbbed from the injury, but because of what happened when they finally arrived. His grandparents had brought him all the way from Beijing to Jiangsu Province, trying to get the son to meet his father. Jian's father had left fourteen months before and hadn't returned home since. They only knew he had a post as an industry delegate in the Communist Party Head Office in the province. There were occasional messages sent back home from the south saying the father was too busy to return home. But the rumour was quite different, something which the child Jian didn't entirely understand. When they got off the ferry and arrived in Nanjing's newly built town hall, they were told his father was in a meeting and couldn't see them right away. So Jian and his grandparents stayed in the father's office waiting—they were given sunflower seeds to eat and tea to drink. But the waiting took forever and the father didn't turn up. The child was bored and looked around the room. Before his grandmother could stop him, young Jian saw a framed picture sitting on the corner of the table, squeezed in between official photographs taken of his father at conferences and local events. In this picture his father is sitting upright before a fake mythical mountain landscape beside a young woman in red whom Jian had never seen before. The woman had glasses and very short hair. They were both smiling at the camera, holding each other's hands. Young Jian stared at the photo in utter bewilderment. His grandmother pulled him away from the table quickly and fussed the photograph away into a drawer. Half an hour later, someone came in. It was the woman from the photo, with the exact same short haircut and the exact same glasses. She carried a little baby in one arm and a lunch box in another. As she entered the room she stared at the three strangers and didn't say a word. Silently, she laid the lunch box on the father's table and went away. As her footsteps subsided in the corridor outside, Jian heard the baby's plaintive cry. Now, nearly three decades later, in a white room in Lausanne, Jian can still recall every detail of that trip. It comes back to him as if in Technicolor, so he writes it down, as if the process of recording might transfer the pain from inside his body onto the page.

The very next day my grandparents and I took the same ferry back. My forehead was still wrapped in a bandage and it ached and throbbed for the entire journey home. In the middle of the Yangtze River I went to the edge of the deck and looked down at the water surging behind the boat. As I watched the churning water I felt my eyes sting as if bursting. Hot tears streamed down my cheeks and my mouth quivered, my breath choked. No one heard my cry, covered by the throbbing mechanical sound of the engine and the wash of waves filling the river air. I swore I would never return to Nanjing. And I've kept my oath. I've never been back there, not even for concerts, just like my father never returned to our family house in Beijing.

The pen held tightly between Jian's fingers is running out of ink. He doodles on the edge of his diary page, pressing hard. Nothing comes out. He throws the pen across the room in the direction of the rubbish bin. Now I can never go back. He thinks to himself: Nanjing is a city full of shame and sorrow, as they say. But perhaps nothing is more shameful than staying in a refugee camp in Switzerland. Jian stands up, picking up his diary from the table, and walks back to his room. He needs his guitar.

3 LONDON, JUNE 2013

Iona is sitting working in a Dongbei restaurant in the middle of Chinatown, alone, while eating slowly. She is drinking a bowl of blood-red soup. The restaurant is decorated with scrolls of kitsch mountain paintings. Seventies Maoist propaganda music plays in the background.

Her red bowl is no ordinary soup: it's pig's blood and sour cabbage soup, and it's the soup Mu often writes about. Iona wants to taste what it has to offer a disconsolate mind. Besides this, she has ordered some mala tofu and a chive pancake. She likes the sour cabbage because it reminds her of Nell's sauerkraut which Vlod is so keen on. She is not so sure about the pig's blood, though. Jelly-like, it has a bitter taste and a smell of rusty iron, as if it's come from a rancid wok. The soup is sour-sharp, and "nutritious," as the Dongbei peasants might say. Iona makes one last effort, chewing another piece of the gelatinous blood. She finds it hard to believe that this is the delicacy Mu and Jian ate every week in one of the Beijing food stores. Pushing the soup bowl slightly away from her notebook, she takes a mouthful of tea and continues working on one of Jian's diary entries.

May 2012

Dreamed of my father last night. Since I left China he seems to be present again in my life. Surreal, since I'm now further from him, and more disconnected, than I've ever been before.

The figure in the dream was not fully recognisable, but it was definitely him. I could tell by the sound of his breathing, the stench of cigarette smoke and the hard rattled cough. Why does he come back to me now? When I think of my childhood, I cannot see him, except as a kind of shadow in the corner of my eye, something that disturbs my peripheral vision. These days all I remember is that summer day when he threatened me with the steel ruler and locked me up. Even before he left the family I have almost no memories of him reading a story to me, or picking me up from school, or playing ping-pong with me. But I remember him telling me about his father, an anecdote he repeated frequently. He would tell it in a strained, choked voice and never looked at me as he talked. It was for him, this story, and the telling of it was agonising and painful, but he wanted to live and relive it countless times.

He would tell of his parents—both had died during the Long March in 1934, only a few months after he was born. When the Long March ended, my baby father was left with a band of female soldiers. Then he would relate in excruciating detail— details he can only have heard from those women who looked after him or other ex-soldiers on the road—those days of Red Army soldiers eating grass and boiling leather belts in soup for protein. Starvation and gun wounds. That's how over a hundred thousand soldiers died on the 8,000-mile journey. Each time my father told the story he would wince as he related how his father had died from a gun wound and his mother from infections she sustained from his birth. He knew exactly how to make me feel guilty, as if my easy life was a little drop of spit on the ground, a weightless existence, a nothingness in history. Or worse still, my existence was a crime, and it almost felt like my father was trying to tell me this, that my life was built on millions of corpses. I am a "qian-gu-zui-ren"—a man born with debt and guilt, a man beyond redemption. Perhaps my indignation towards my father has diluted a bit after all this time living with Mu. But for so many years, as soon as his image slipped into my mind, my fear of him would grow and rise like a poisonous wave.

If you spend enough time reading someone else's thoughts, after a while their thoughts begin to infect you. Your grasp on yourself becomes tenuous. Or you begin to see that you never were the essential you in the first place, Iona thinks to herself as she takes the bus back to Angel. To be a person is to imagine being someone, and the someone you imagine most of the time is what people call "you." How strange to be in time and space with something called a "character." Jian is separated from Iona by time and space. But there is something about his sadness, his strength, that emboldens her. It makes her long for some other self, some ability to reach outside herself and be brave. The dream about Jian's father haunts her and she can't help but keep coming back to that image of him holding the steel ruler over his son's head. So far Jian has barely mentioned his mother, she's noticed. It is as if there's a whole section of his life that's absent from her translation.

Iona feels her body is like an oyster, in its dark, cold sealed shell. In the first year of its life, a young oyster spills its sperm into the water. During the next two years it grows larger and then releases eggs. Then the water surrounding it does the rest of the work. An oyster shifts from being male to female. It plays both roles. That's how Iona feels as she walks around, confined to her oyster-shell flat—sometimes like Jian, sometimes like Mu, sometimes both. Sometimes like a hooligan in a Beijing hutong, shouting out: "*Ta ma de, ta da ye de*—Down on his uncle, bugger his grandma." She seems to relive the lives of others in strange, unsatisfactory fragments.

She hears the rumble of the street outside—her own Islington hutong with its rough market lads, buying and selling, its own particular odours and sounds. As she stretches and gets up to walk around her flat, waiting for the day to end and night to begin, she thinks of Liang and Zhu in *The Butterfly Lovers*, an ancient Chinese legend set two thousand years ago. Two lovers are tragically separated by their elders. After the young man's death his lover throws herself into his grave and before long their spirits emerge from the grave as two butterflies. Iona feels an urge to leap into the past. To grasp Mu and Jian before they become butterflies and bring them back together. She wants to talk to them, to guide them, to help them to unite.

4 CENTRE D'ASSISTANCE EUROPÉEN POUR REQUÉRANTS D'ASILE, SWITZERLAND, JUNE 2012

Most refugees leave the Lausanne asylum centre after two weeks. Some are granted asylum by the authorities; others are rejected. Jian's fate is suspended in a limbo space between arrival and departure, waiting to hear his destiny.

Jian's only friend, Mahmud of the Libya Desert, transferred from Berne with him, is finally denied asylum. The reports say he's an ex-terrorist, and is not entitled to remain in Switzerland. Jian cannot believe it. They claim Mahmud was a mercenary fighting for Gaddafi's dying regime against the rebelling populace. He also overhears gossip about how his African friend first arrived in Europe—a tale of violence and brutality, and totally different from the story Mahmud told him. The rumours said that Mahmud was a member of a mercenary group, soldiers paid by Gaddafi to fight. The group was armed with guns and grenades. Formed in the desert to the south of Libya, they paraded into rebel cities hoping to scare the people into surrender. The first thing they did when they arrived in a place was to rob the banks, loot shops for food and set fire to public buildings. In each new city they would kill a few men to set an example for the locals. They would carve up the corpses and hang them in public squares, even in places children would regularly pass to and from school. Jian heard that Mahmud had been involved with one of these groups but had not been a willing participant. He hadn't wanted to be involved in the killings and had escaped. The other mercenaries had pursued him as traitor. He too was to be slain and his body displayed in public as a threat to all those who dared to quit the cause. His only way out was to flee. He had managed to get on a boat from Libya to the coast of southern Italy, and then after interminable days in the back of a windowless truck, hot, exhausted and thin, he arrived in Switzerland, presenting himself as a refugee fleeing the horrors of war.

There's the real story, Jian thinks. So he asks, "And did you kill people, like they're saying?"

"Yes, I did." Mahmud looks honestly at the Chinese man.

"How many?"

"Many." There is a brittle silence. "Perhaps around twenty, or thirty, or fifty people."

Another pause. "What's it like to kill someone?"

"It's not a big deal, brother," Mahmud shrugs. "If you can kill one man, you can kill many. If you had been in my position, you would have done the same."

Jian nods his head, vaguely. He is thinking about those numbers: twenty, thirty, fifty. Mahmud's casual indifference to numbers. Each number is a man. And it's all so very familiar to him. Mao's famous comment on the mass death was simply: It is just numbers.

"I didn't want to kill, believe me. But I am a poor man. The only thing I learned how to do was fight. If you grow up learning to shoot a gun and to kill, then you become a mercenary. There are no other options. Of course there is this voice that demands all the time why you do it. I had this voice. But I pushed it away. I did not listen to it. Until one day, I felt I had died. It was like *I* was the ghost. A ghost killer. A ghost with a gun, and I watched the power of my gun waste everything around me. Except at night. At night the ghost killer was haunted by the people he had killed. Then one night my dead brother appeared to me in a dream and said, 'I will turn away from you, since you have killed me.' I woke up screaming, with the peaceful bodies of my fellow soldiers around me in the dark. That's when I began to listen to the voice in my head. I had to stop."

Jian wonders if this is just another story. It sounds too neat to be true.

* * *

Before Mahmud is taken away by two officers, he gives Jian a hug and a big smile.

"Thanks for listening to me, Kublai Khan. You are my last friend, for the road will be short once I leave here."

Jian sits alone in the canteen where he and Mahmud had been accustomed to sit and read, and wonders gloomily: can someone still be a kind person if he has killed fifty people? Mahmud was not a killer to Jian. Maybe the angry ghost of one of his ancestors made him kill. Or maybe we all have these ghosts in us. The Chinese are as good as any other race when it comes to the subject of killing. Jian chews on these bitter thoughts as the afternoon drags to a close.

5 LONDON, JUNE 2013

It has been a strange day for Iona. In the morning, the sun is shining brightly so she changes into a summer dress and sandals. As she leaves her flat for the British Library, clouds begin to gather and the sky turns dark. With an eerie colour in the atmosphere, as if a great grey pigeon wing had enveloped the earth, hail suddenly hammers on her head. Pearls of ice clatter onto the roofs and the pavement, making the whole world like a teeth-gnashing skeleton. Everyone is running to escape the sheets of icy shards. Iona runs into a greasy spoon near King's Cross. Inside, sheltering with a few supersized regulars, she shakes the rain out of her hair as she listens to the mad rat-a-tat of the hail, and the billowing demented haze of the storm. The famous British summer strikes again, she thinks. Only a malevolent higher power can explain this weather. She orders a pot of tea and takes out a page at random from a bundle of diary entries.

Beijing, 2 May 2006

I am finished. I am cursed, forever. So is Jian. We couldn't even speak to each other afterwards or utter a word about this. No. We don't even have the strength to look into each other's eyes. This place is a hell now. I should simply pack my bags and go away, disappear to somewhere far away. I don't think I can bear one more hour of living in this flat, the "home" which is no longer a home for three of us.

What's happened? Three? Iona reads these lines in total confusion. This is clearly from Mu's diary, judging from the handwriting. Outside, the hail subsides, but she has now forgotten what she came out to do. This is her focus now, this is her day's work. She doesn't understand what Mu means when she says she is "cursed, forever." She stumbles on the "three of us"—this is new, she thinks, this isn't something she's said before. Iona goes back through the photocopies of diary entries but there's nothing to explain what's just happened. She tries a new tack and goes forward— 3 May, 4, 5, 6 May. Nothing. Then she finds an entry for 7 May and grips the page. She lays it down in front of her and starts reading.

Beijing, 7 May 2006

I saw Little Shu, his beautiful small face, small crinkled lips, and his tiny hands, so delicate like soft clasping flowers. His eyes were still, resting on mine. I reached out to hold him. But I couldn't get to him. I was too tired, I didn't have the strength to pick him up and hold him to my breast. He kept on receding into a tunnel that lay dark behind him, until he seemed to disappear. Then I woke up. It was the middle of the night. I burst into tears. It's been like this every night since it happened. The same dream. I can't get even a few hours' sleep without slipping down into that tunnel. I sat up and Jian hugged me close. When I couldn't stop weeping, he got up and went to the balcony. He stood in the cold air on the balcony alone, for nearly an hour . . . I think he didn't want to see me crying, or felt powerless. Unable to shift this weight dragging us down.

The next entry she can find is a couple of weeks later.

Beijing, 20 May 2006

It has already been three weeks. It doesn't feel possible. I thought perhaps there would be a calmer time beyond the real sorrow, but there's no respite from this bottomless place. I can no longer think, eat or sleep. I am finished. Our son, Little Shu, is dead.

He only lived six and a half months in this world. He had just learned to smile and laugh, and began to garble a few sounds to make his needs clear, he had learned to sit up and already knew how to turn on his back and play with toys. But Little Shu will no longer learn anything. He no longer sees anything or hears the voices of his parents. All the tears and screams since he was born led to a void, a dark grave where his own memory is so brief and blurred.

We no longer know how to talk. We can no longer love each other like we used to do. We have slept with our backs to each other for the last three weeks. Embracing in the dark is even sadder, I think. That day, when our son died, we came back home from the morgue, and Jian lay down on the bed. His mourning is totally silent. He is buried in depression.

First we thought Little Shu's fever had calmed. But then his skin flushed from red to blue, his breathing was shallow, and his hands and feet were cold and shivery. I burst into tears in the ambulance taking us to hospital. Jian was shaking the baby's body madly and hoping he would wake up to his voice. But the baby was already dead. The doctors said it wasn't unusual for a new baby to die instantly from meningitis. Why this punishment?

Jian has cancelled the tour. The band have gone silent. What could they possibly say?

Iona urgently turns the page. The following entry is only three lines long.

Beijing, 1 June 2006

Jian and I live in the same space but we don't talk. We only eat together, but silently, we lie in the same bed together, but facing opposite directions. Is there any point now being together?

Outside the hail has long passed and the sun appears, brightening the world outside—the canal, the run-down Georgian terrace houses, the passing families. Iona feels bewildered in a disorientating geography: her world, their world and the page in front of her. So Jian and Mu had a child, Little Shu, who lived for just six and a half months! Did they separate after their baby died? It's hard to work out exactly, and there are no entries for several weeks until she finds a page from a month later.

Beijing, 3 July 2006

Waking up alone, making myself some breakfast, taking the bus to the office, having lunch with the colleagues from the magazine but not uttering a word about my baby, then always returning home late, having supper then going straight to bed—this has been my life for the last four weeks. Since our decision that I would move out of the flat, I have not returned. I haven't called Jian. I haven't taken his calls either. Yesterday he rang again, and left a message. He wanted to come over and visit me. But I don't want him around. It is still too painful. My woman's body still remembers that I was a mother, and I am still a mother even though my little child is no longer in this world. I don't want to see Jian right now. We have not said for how long this separation would be. But he agreed to my moving out. At the moment, living alone in this newly rented flat suits me. It is almost empty: white walls, no furniture, no books—no memories. This is my way of separating from the past. Perhaps it will be for three months, or for three years, or forever. I can't know.

6 CALIFORNIA, MAY 2012

A four-star desert hotel, the Palm Oasis, not mentioned in any Michelin guide. White, hacienda-style buildings like the ones you might see on the cover of an Eagles album. From an upstairs room, the endless highway vanishing sharply on the horizon. It's thirty-seven degrees and dry. Death Valley is sixty miles south on Highway 64, the Grand Canyon is three hundred miles north-east, and the sun is ninety-three million miles above. A large garden lies behind the hotel building, dotted with newly planted palm trees. A pool, with blue water reflecting the drifting desert clouds. A dark-haired woman floats in the pool on an orange blow-up mattress. The water is still and flat, with the occasional errant ripple blown by the wind.

Mu is half asleep on the mattress. Strands of wet hair cover her face behind her sunglasses. Her bathing suit is a two-piece, satin-black garment. Her mouth moves slightly; from a certain distance she seems to be humming a song. Her hands are folded symmetrically over her belly. She is not aware of anyone around her; she is sinking deep into a dream, beneath the hot sun.

Under a palm tree by the pool, Bruce is on a chair, half naked, watching his current favourite Chinese woman from behind dark sunglasses. Well, at least, his favourite on this trip. The hotel is deserted, no one else is around.

Bruce drinks his Pepsi. But he feels unsettled; something pulls him over to the water. He takes off his sunglasses and steps gingerly into the pool. Moving towards her, he sinks deeper into the water. Bubbles pop on the surface. Somehow, Bruce always feels confident, especially with native Chinese girls. Maybe because of his half-American, half-Chinese background and his Harvard education. With these two assets, he feels automatically superior to his yellow cousins. And the natives in return look up at him. At least that's how he feels when he is in China. And even now, in the warmed turquoise water, he has this image of himself in mind, and it sends a little thrill of excitement through his body. He is in no hurry, he knows that he is engaged in a delicate operation.

He approaches the floating mattress and hesitates. He stares at her slim, feminine body for a moment. The floating woman does not react. Is she dreaming of someone? All he can hear is the sound of distant cars passing the hotel, sending up a mist of dust into the palm leaves.

He speaks, a little too loudly. "You're gonna get burnt."

Silence.

"Your performance the other night was . . . crap."

Still nothing.

Then he says in bad Chinese: "*Ni shui jiao ma?*"

Still nothing.

He tries another tactic. He lifts one hand, cupping a palmful of water, and pours it on her left thigh. There's a reaction: a shiver from the inert woman.

"You like that?" Still no response. Then another palmful of liquid and more shivering.

"I see you like that."

He moves closer to her head and now pours it onto her shoulders, eliciting a gentle spasm. Under the scorching sun, her wet brown skin dries almost immediately. She moves her head, turns towards the shadow by her side. Then she takes off her glasses. She speaks.

"Don't bother me, I am sleeping."

Despite her words, he thinks he hears a kind of invitation in her voice.

He touches her hair, slips his hand onto her neck. He then massages her head, gently. He hears the low feminine groan and another sound, a half-breath, half-reverberation. Something tells him to proceed, and his hands press deeper, with a slow motion, feeling the shape of her breasts.

Grasping her, he slips her body off the mattress and into the water. He holds her tightly against him in the corner of the pool. She struggles. Confused. It feels like he is teasing her, playing with her, but his grip is almost violent. He holds her shoulders and turns her hips round. He is behind her, his hands around her waist now. Still she doesn't believe he will force her, even though his mouth now presses down on her shoulder, his teeth clasping the nape of her neck, printing red welts on her skin. He is breathing more heavily now, growing feverish, uttering incomprehensible words. Swollen beneath the water, he finds a way in, entering her with full force. She cries out. A heat-filled dizzy shock leaves her blind and dumb to what's happening. Then there is a surging, a disturbance, in the water. The bodies seem to writhe under the surface. His thrusts are rapid, unrelenting. She releases another jagged cry, and the man instinctively puts his hand over her mouth. There is more pained sound, but it's muffled by the wet, gripping hand.

Then, suddenly, there is a bursting apart, and Mu's scream is louder. She moves rapidly away from Bruce into shallower water, clasping and shielding herself. He's left gurgling apologetic words that are eaten by his own twisted mouth. She climbs up the steps, and then blasts out of the water, grabs a towel, flicks it around her, and runs wordlessly, leaving a trail of wet footprints.

7 CALIFORNIA, MAY 2012

In her room above the pool, curtains drawn, Mu lies in a crumpled mess of sheets. Her body is still damp and she is shivering. Her bowels ache. Her lips are mouthing something, but she cannot quite hear what she's saying. For a few moments it's as if she is not in her body. When the evening arrives, she sits up on her bed, rests her diary on her damp, bare knees and writes.

Better not to inhabit your body at all. Bodies let you down, bodies are vulnerable. Lying in my darkened room I remembered how that sense of vulnerability first came to me. An image pierces me now, twisting the knife already in my gut. It's an old image that always seems to be lurking in the back row of the theatre of my mind, an image from years ago, from when I was nine or ten years old in my home town. A big, rough hand creeping up my skirt in the dark. I could not cry out, nor run away: the large man, with his dumb face, had me cornered in the village cinema. I trembled in the dark while the screen flickered with sound and pictures. I managed to escape momentarily, hiding myself in the space behind the stage curtains. And just when I thought I would be safe, he found me and trapped me again. His groping hand snatched me to him and found my lower body. I never dared tell my parents and I thought I had forgotten it, but now it's all come back to me here in America.

Fuck me. Even in the Palm Oasis Hotel. How could I let that animal-fool take me in that way? The pain in my bowels shoots up to fizzle and crackle in my jaw. That cockroach man, that machine with a cock, made me feel like a worthless hole.

When all is said and done, when I look beneath the smooth exterior, the charming manners, the good looks, the well-dressed ease, the Harvard degrees, you just get fucked. Taken. The fucking-machine takes over.

What can I do here? I am an alien in an alien land, and now it's made me alien to myself. My body isn't even mine either. My body makes me feel disgusted.

The band and their manager are squeezed into a jeep—an old Grand Cherokee—zigzagging through Colorado. In the near distance the Rocky Mountains look blank and indifferent, like Mu's expression. The boys drink can after can of American pale lager and eat takeout beef burgers. They burp, stink and fart. Bruce sits in the front and doesn't talk. They halt at a gas station. The boys get out to buy hot dogs and drinks. Bruce fills the jeep with petrol and takes cash from an ATM. When he returns to the driver's seat, he takes a quick glance at Mu. Her face turns to the window, looking into the distance. They breathe the same air for a few moments, and then he opens his mouth as if to speak but the boys are already returning.

Later, at the arts centre in Denver, waiting for her show to start, Mu sits at the back of the green room, away from the band, and writes.

Silence from Jian. I don't want to send letters into the void—what's the use? My diary is a solitary ear, a patient presence. So what would you say about my politics now, Jian? And about me? I'm not sure you would recognise me now. You once said I was a little housewife, a conformist; well, I think you got me wrong. Since our baby's death, since that four-year separation, I am no longer that conformist. I am no longer the little house-wife. I have become someone else. A mother without a child. A wife without a husband. A poet without words. I'm not sure I recognise myself any more.

憤青—Fen Qing, Disenchanted Youth. That is what our generation has been called. Fen Qing are these angry intellectuals who were born in the sixties and seventies. Fen Qing, the Chinese punk. Punks are supposed to be cultural revolutionaries, aren't they? That's what you wanted to be, wasn't it? I could not be that person. You saw it: there is always the repressed, dutiful daughter in me, struggling to fulfil other people's desires, the desire of continuing the tradition, and the weight of carrying history. You are not here to speak to me and to hold me. You are not here at all.

9 ATLANTA, MAY 2012

In a bookshop in the state of Georgia, Mu is in a daze. She's browsing the shelves aimlessly, killing time while Bruce checks out a new venue, until she spies a book called *Peking Man: Evidence for Archaic Asian Ancestry in the Human X Chromosome*. The band is bewildered when she buys the book. She hugs the paper bag to her chest, wrapping her arms tightly around it.

"What are you doing? You want to become a scientist in America?" Lutao asks, his mouth agape.

"Kind of weird thing to be interested in, Mu," Dongdong laughs.

"Peking Man? He's not even a real man," Liuwei says.

Mu doesn't bother to reply.

How can she tell them the real story? She doesn't want to read the book, not really, but it's a talisman, it's all she has of him. It's something in her destiny she cannot explain. All those four years apart from her Peking Man she pushed away any sign, any memory, anything that reminded her of her past life. And it worked, for a while. And then little by little the resurrection, the coming together until she lost him again, only a year later.

I found a book in the middle of America and it's all about Peking Man. I don't need to read the book, but I want to hold it close. The picture on the front is striking. Jian has the same facial structure, although he would never admit it, and the same broad forehead and strong square jaw. I know the pictures in this kind of book are always drawn so to make our ancestors look dumber than us. It suits our vanity, to think we have made progress. I'm sure that our ancestors were wiser than we are. I know they lived in a world in which things were intact, unlike our world, where things are crumbling fast.

I remember those first few weeks with Jian. I was alive to his ideas: we talked about time, about inheritance, and even then he was anxious about the idea of family. He gave me a tour of his philosophical cave and showed me his stone tools, heavy and crude but honest and simple. He cut through all the daily bullshit with them. He amazed me. I remember him talking about how deep time was—I couldn't understand, but he explained the Big Bang to me for the first time. I was only nineteen and I felt he was some hero of the past, born of ancient times. After so many years, I still have this admiration, this wonder, although so many other things have happened that might have undermined it. Now my world has nothing to do with Jian's world. We have known each other for so long. I cannot imagine not knowing Jian. But I cannot imagine now how we could be together. There is no way of fixing us, to make us be in one world together again. I feel him now. It's like the ghost of Little Shu. I carry his shade with me, like a dark cloud around me. Little Shu tries to speak to me, but cannot. He never learned how. Jian too is now like a ghost, an angry and sad ghost, carried along with me. When can I let my ghosts go?

As a part of their shambolic journey across the USA, China Underground Slam Poetry Group arrives in Atlanta. No one knows where they are or which direction the wind is blowing.

Seeing that everyone is disorientated, Bruce organises some local sightseeing. An hour later, the boys find themselves being driven up to a massive factory with an enormous Coca-Cola sign on top of the main building.

"Why are we here?" Dongdong asks when he sees the huge logo overhead, just like a Communist Central Party office in China.

"It's the headquarters of Coca-Cola," Bruce explains.

"No kidding!" Dongdong screams. He is the youngest in the band, born in 1990, and he has drunk Coca-Cola since he was in nappies. In fact, he claims he has only ever drunk two types of liquid since he was born—Coca-Cola and Yanjing beer.

"Why here? In Atlanta?" Lutao is still in a marijuana-induced daze.

"Why not?" says Bruce.

"But I mean, why do we have to visit a bubble-sugar factory?"

"Because we're performing in their club tomorrow. The tour is sponsored by them—to be more precise, our Atlanta trip is being paid for by the Coca-Cola Company." Bruce eyes Mu, but she does not react.

This is a worthy sightseeing trip for Chinese artists, given their natural poetic affinity with industrialised sugary water. The following day at the Coca-Cola Family Club the band perform one of their last shows. Mu reads a new poem—a piece no one has heard before. The band helps Sabotage Sister to build the atmosphere: the bassist, Liuwei, slides a glass bottleneck up and down the strings, Ry Cooder–style, and Dongdong hits the drums with Chinese opera's fighting rhythms; Lutao meanwhile plucks away at a harp he has borrowed from somewhere, as if they are presenting a new diva who has just arrived on the modern opera scene. Mu doesn't perform right away, instead she decides to tell the audience a little bit about herself first in her stuttering English.

"I just finished writing poem last night. It's called 'The Second Sex, Or Not?' Thanks to your country, outside of China makes me think more about what woman is. I want to mention my family here, my mother had seven sisters and brother. But none of women in her family had education. Eight sisters worked very hard, help raising family and support only brother for higher education. So my uncle is only man in her family can read and write. This makes me think about myself—I am only child for my mother, because I was born in one-child policy period. But even then, my mother still preferred to have baby boy instead of me."

The audience falls silent as Mu chants her poetry with a building wall of music surrounding her.

10 LONDON, JUNE 2013

"*The Second Sex, Or Not?*" These words are spoken by another woman, thousands of miles away in London, some time after Mu declaimed them in Atlanta. Iona is googling "Sabotage Sister" as well as "The Second Sex, Or Not." It doesn't take very long for her to discover a blog about feminism by a student at Atlanta University, and someone has posted the whole poem online.

> *The Second Sex, Or Not?*
> Sabotage Sister aka Mu
>
> *De Beauvoir published* The Second Sex *in 1949,*
> *Mao Zedong announced the birth of*
> *the People's Republic of China in 1949.*
> *And my mother was born in 1949*
> *in a house with seven sisters and one brother.*
> *Seven sisters formed an army*
> *assisting one brother to become educated.*
>
> *But I want to know:*
> *what is "the second sex"?*
> *what is "the feminine"?*
> *what is "domestic science"?*
>
> *In a suburban bungalow,*
> *A man chews his beef boiled,*
> *A woman cooks her soup slow*
> *sitting before the TV's glow.*

Sound and visuals each other swallow.
Lack, hollow, void, black hole giving birth to the universe.

Haunted by femininity, I scream:
Transplant the womb!
Grow it in men, in every boy-child's bowel!
In drone, in bull, in rooster, in ram,
in buck, stag, dog, in Chairman and President!
In every creature grown, the womb.

The poem is sending off sparks in a different mind now. Iona chews on the words, gets tangled up in their meaning until she cannot tell what is her meaning and what is Mu's. She feels an intimacy with this woman she has never met. Iona remembers arguing over de Beauvoir's work at university. Sitting in someone's room late at night: the bad decor, the heap of patchwork cushions on the floor and Ikea cupboards, the empty wine bottles and full glasses, the bulging ashtrays, and the heated debates about motherhood and work. They were just nineteen, they knew nothing about what it was to be a woman, about the trap of motherhood or the liberation of work. Iona isn't entirely sure she knows much more now, though, eleven years later. She hasn't thought about it for years.

Iona feels woken up by the poem. It's undeniable. Mu's poem sends a strange jolt through her body and her mind like the tingle of an electric field. For a long time, she has seen love as a form of night-life—an after-hours activity in which she will give herself over to random encounters. These ultimately impersonal sexual exchanges have been her "personal life." She has barely built any friendships with men of her age. This compulsive pattern seems to be the only form of encounter she has between herself and men. Amid these unsettling reflections, she thinks about her mother, and how she has been raised under this "second sex" unconsciousness.

Staring at her keyboard and the screen, Iona sits back and thinks.

The screensaver takes over and photographs flash up in a random order. Home: the house she grew up in on the Isle of Mull, the tall lone pine tree standing guard over the house, her mother in the kitchen making an apricot pie, a sheep giving birth, her sister Nell playing with their cat on the bed, a deer moving up the hillside at the back of their house. A deer! Yes, she remembers that moment when the deer passed.

In the north they say if you see a wild deer passing, it means your love has betrayed you. Iona's mother once told her that "women will always be betrayed by their men, but you have to be light about it." Now, looking at that blurred photograph of an escaping deer, she remembers a scene. She was probably about fourteen or fifteen, a pale-looking girl stuck on a Scottish island, unhappy at school and uninspired at home. One day she felt sick so she left school much earlier than usual. As she was passing her parents' bedroom she heard two voices inside. One was her father's, but the other was not her mother's, nor her sister's. Her mother had left on the morning ferry for town to see friends. Everyone knew she would only be back on the next morning's ferry. Meanwhile, young Iona lay in bed listening to the loud lovemaking coming from her parents' bedroom. Her father's groans sounded disgusting to her. She never remembered her father making such noises when he had been with her mother. Shamefully, she left the house with the sound of her father's groans sticking in her head. A feeling of nausea began to build in her as she walked up the hill and a paralysing vertigo gripped her head, causing the trees around her to swirl. Suddenly she found herself vomiting. She remembers looking indifferently at the warm slush from her stomach on the grass by her feet.

At her age, sex was still very alien to her. Now she thought it like the muck before her on the ground. She felt terrible and awfully lonely on the hill. Then suddenly she saw this little deer, a skinny deer passing, scampering up their hill. She was beautiful and magical. Iona watched the deer until it disappeared. She forgot about her father's groans, and the unknown woman in his bed. She wandered on over the hill, looking for that wild deer until the night soaked her into the darkness. The next morning when she woke, through her bedroom window with a view of the hill, she was astonished to see the deer passing in the distance, a silhouette on the brow of the hill. Moments later, she heard her mother turn the key in the lock and come through the front door. As she walked into the kitchen, her first words to Iona's father were, "I wish I could have stayed away a bit longer." Iona came out from her bedroom and looked straight at her father. It was a look of knowledge. He was shocked and turned his back on her, going out in silence to pull weeds in the back garden. Years later, the memory of her sickness and the beautiful little wild deer came back to her. "You have to be light about it," her mother's words often echo in Iona's head. She understood that her mother knew very well that her father was having an affair—a long affair, it turned out. It carried on until only recently when his lover died of cancer. It seemed the whole island knew of the affair, and had been gossiping about it for years. It is strange to Iona that her parents never acknowledged that anything had happened, neither to each other, nor to her, even on the day the other woman died.

11 LONDON, JUNE 2013

Iona has been thinking about revolution. She has read a hundred pages of Grossman's *Life and Fate*, but its weight, nine hundred pages of fine print, is intimidating. How much time can she invest in research for this translation project that is taking her over? Real lives, Mu's and Jian's, have replaced fictional ones for her right now: they have their own revolution. Iona has started reading about it in Mu's diary.

Beijing, 28 February 2011

Nervous atmosphere above Beijing's sky. It's ridiculous! The press aren't allowed to mention a word of what's going on in the Arab world right now. It's going mad in Tunisia and Egypt and we're not supposed to know.

It has been three days since I've seen Jian. Yesterday I went out looking for him all day and came back alone at night. Still he is not here. Today, the same. I've become desperate, pacing up and down in the flat waiting for news of him. He told me he might need to bed down somewhere else, wherever they ended up that first night, and might even go into the suburbs too as they "stroll" along. But still, I have the worst fear. The protest has been going on in Beijing for nearly a week now, in a quiet form—Strolling Revolution, as Jian and the other organisers called it. No banners or posters, but they do have slogans. Yesterday I saw the police begin to arrest the strollers—but they could not tell who were the protesters and who were normal people out walking, since the secret protesters have conducted their "strolling" in the park and on local streets. I don't know how many people have been arrested but I fear for Jian. He has no sense of proportion, no second thoughts. He's like a naive schoolboy sometimes, and it keeps him believing himself invincible. I know he just believes he is right: total conviction. The strolling was Jian's idea, and it was supposed to be a clever idea. But has he ever thought about his own safety? Or mine? Didn't Little Shu's death teach him anything? Isn't life fragile enough and family so easy to break apart?

Iona hurriedly gets down the basics, fiddles with a few passages, and then flicks to the next photocopied page.

Beijing, 1 March 2011

I fell asleep in total exhaustion, then in the early morning I woke up in a panic. The bed is still empty. This is now the fourth day since I've seen Jian. The streets below are quiet as I stand on our balcony where we normally drink in the evening together, looking out. The rallying cry for protest seems to be posted everywhere online: "We want work, we want housing, we want justice and fairness, we want free press!" I'm amazed the cyber police haven't shut it down yet. And then I read a blog Jian sometimes looks at which quoted a government source: "From today the government is banning the selling of jasmine flowers. All the window displays in hotels, restaurants and shops with jasmine flowers have been stripped bare. Most flower shops in Beijing will be closed indefinitely." As I walked down to the streets, strangely nobody was "strolling," just office workers hurrying to their work with nervous expressions on their faces, and then undercover policemen with telltale snake-like eyes. I pretended to be out food shopping, casually wandering along, looking in shops, and bought two buns from a street seller, then walked a U-turn to get to the crossroad flower shop while eating my buns. Far off in the distance I saw a troop of community policemen burning a sea of colourful flowers on the hard, black tarmac, right in front of the shop. There were not only jasmine flowers flaming, but also other plants—roses, bamboo, sunflowers, lilies . . . Damn, I couldn't believe this! They used to burn books, now they've started burning flowers! What's the next thing they're going to burn? The owner, Xu Wei, from the same province as me, stood in front of her shop, blank-faced and dead-eyed, watching her flowers flaming in the fire . . .

The bell rings and Iona runs down the stairs in bare feet. A delivery man stands on the pavement holding a huge bunch of white roses which obscure his face. All Iona can see are white flowers. A voice comes out of the bouquet:

"So, hang on . . ." There's a rustle and then, "I'm after Mrs. Nasreen Akin. Is that you?"

Iona shakes her head, points next door and heads silently back upstairs.

Beijing, 2 March 2011

Thank you, Old Sky! Jian came back, totally worn out and covered in dirt but at least he is still alive and here with me! "Don't be stupid, girl. I'm not going to die just like that. We walked for three days towards the suburbs. Slept a bit in the streets at night. Then we stayed in some local peasant's house for the night at Changping County, moved on the next day and took a bus and strolled in Hebei Province. Now I'm sure that every peasant in Hebei Province knows exactly what the Jasmine Revolution is all about!" He hugged me warmly, but he was so dismissive of my worry. "We were fine. We were smart and discreet enough so the cops couldn't follow us! It's the strategy of guerrilla warfare, you know that!"

I was still angry with him, but I lost all my fury as I watched him open the fridge and devour the leftover cold noodles like a ravenous dog. He seemed utterly indifferent to the consequences of his actions. Doesn't he realise that no other woman would be able to stand a boyfriend like him? And no matter what he says, he hasn't changed, even after our four years apart. I think he might have even got worse. He's out of control like a lone wolf. He told me that the 1989 student revolution didn't work. And he was right. But now it seems the excitement of the fight has got into his blood. This can go nowhere. But he won't see that. Has he some kind of suicidal wish? Does he want to destroy us? It makes all those conversations about trying to get pregnant again absurd! I can't bring another child into this mad life with Jian. Perhaps we are destined to be childless.

Good Lord. Iona sighs. She researches China's Jasmine Revolution in 2011. Then she finds a *New York Times* report that confirms everything she has just read—the rallying cry, the strolling, even the absurd burning of jasmine flowers. Then she comes to a quote from a government official, Li Chengde, Minister of State Security.

. . . *the probability of China having a Jasmine Revolution is absurd and unrealistic. I can give you every confidence that the government is combating these problems with extensive state measures. We are strong and have full public support. We will move forward successfully.*

All this politics is beyond Iona's knowledge. Things are heating up; she wants to share her excitement with someone and get a second opinion. She has an urge to talk to Jonathan. She finds the number for Applegate Books and phones him straight away.

12 LONDON, JUNE 2013

When Iona arrives at the Hayward Gallery, she checks her watch and realises she is twenty minutes late. She spies Jonathan leaving a queue with what look like tickets in his hand. He smiles when he spots her.

"Sorry, the bus took forever; I should have taken the Tube," Iona apologises.

"No worries. I had to queue for the tickets anyway. I didn't expect there to be so many people wanting to see an exhibition on the Cultural Revolution!" Jonathan kisses her on the cheek.

"Maybe they're here for my professor." Iona looks around, hoping to see Charles in the crowd. "He really is one of the most important historians on China, you know. I'm not exaggerating."

On the poster in front of the gallery a big banner reads, "The legacy of the Cultural Revolution—exhibition talk by Professor Charles Handfield, SOAS, University of London."

They walk slowly round the exhibition together after Charles's talk, occasionally pointing out pictures, mentioning something that seems to trigger a memory from Jian's and Mu's texts. Jonathan is deeply impressed by the wall of photographs from Chinese archives. Frenetic images of Red Guards marching through Beijing's streets; Mao greeting adoring young supporters; intellectuals being punished on a stage. Iona learned about the Cultural Revolution when she was at university, but still, some of these photos shock her into silence. Her professor's lecture perfectly complements the images in the exhibition, and Iona is struck by a wave of nostalgia for university. Perhaps she should have stayed longer and absorbed more from Charles's encyclopedic mind.

When the lecture ends, Charles is instantly surrounded by his audience. Iona waves at him from a distance, but he's hidden by a growing crowd. She follows Jonathan out of the gallery and along the South Bank.

She slows down. "Time for a drink? What about here?"

"Yes, OK, a quick one." He nods as he speaks.

"By the way, did you manage to contact Mu? I wonder if she is still in China, or in the States, perhaps."

"No information whatsoever, I'm afraid. Her telephone number doesn't seem to work. I've tried it many times."

"Maybe she doesn't want to be contacted—some political reason we don't know about perhaps," Iona speculates.

"I hadn't considered that . . . it's an interesting thought."

They head towards a nearby bar. Before they've even made it through the door Iona hears his phone ring. He turns away from her as he answers it, his voice taking on a terse and clipped manner, piercing the noise of the crowd. He hangs up and turns to Iona apologising.

"I am so sorry, Iona, it's my wife . . ." He looks uneasy. "I'm afraid I don't even have time for a quick drink. I'm going to have to head off right now."

She looks at him, slightly surprised.

"I don't want to be rude. It's just . . . family issues. I need to get back home immediately."

You're not explaining anything, Iona thinks, but she says, "Don't worry. I hope it's nothing serious. We can call or email tomorrow about plans for the translation. Thanks for coming along anyway."

As she wonders about what his wife might have said to him on the phone that was quite so urgent, he is already kissing her goodbye and striding quickly away.

Alone, Iona walks along the South Bank, buffeted by the night wind. A certain desolation wraps itself around her. She feels very cold, a chill climbing up her spine and tickling the back of her head. Looking down at her shadow under the lamps on the pavement, at her hands and the slim shape of her arms, she feels dazed. She walks up to the railing along the river walkway and gazes down at the dark Thames. Below the concrete bank, driftwood is washed onto the narrow mudflats and she makes out a pink plastic shoe among the rubbish. A tourist barge passes, illuminated by the strings of fairy lights. The passengers leaning out wave at the people on the bank and on the bridges, as characters do in films—big smiles and nostalgic sentiments. Iona watches them with indifference and walks away.

She turns and walks up onto the Millennium Bridge, heading in the direction of St. Paul's Cathedral where she can catch her bus home. Halfway across, she finds herself pausing and leaning over the rail to watch the scene below. The water is dark under the pale moon, the tide subsiding now. She contemplates the waves, thinking how fast the tide runs out. Then, from nowhere, she hears a voice beside her speaking.

"Old Thames, such an ancient bitch river, pouring herself into the old muddy Channel."

She turns her head, sees a figure, standing quite close to her, breathing roughly, leaning over and watching the same scene. It's an old man, rough coat on to protect him from the keen chill in the air and the wind that spins up from the surface of the river; unshaven face with a multitude of protuberances and folds. When the man catches her eye, he continues.

"I know you," he says in a rusty, rasping voice projected from oily lungs.

"Sorry? Sorry?" She's a little startled.

"You heard. I know you! Seen you here before. Seen you look into the river. You ain't gonna jump, are you?" He gives a kind of laughing grunt.

All Iona can do is stare, and retreat, stammering, "I'm sorry. No. I'm sorry."

"Nuffing to be sorry about, love. You ain't gonna jump. Ain't nuffing down there, my girl. Nuffing at all. Just shitty cold, it is. And worse, too. I got my eye on ya, you know!"

The old man seems like an apparition from another world. Her throat dry, unable to speak clearly, all she can do is mumble, "Sorry, I have to go. Bye."

She hears the old man start humming to himself as she hurries over the bridge. Then suddenly she remembers the old Englishman in Milwaukee from Mu's diary. Now his voice descends from the sky above the water: "*If you ever visit England, then send my regards to that old hag of a town, London, though I'm sure she's tarted up well enough now.*"

13 MEMPHIS, TENNESSEE, MAY 2012

The show is over. It's the day after the last performance and the band are having their longest lie-in of the entire trip—apart from Bruce, who is up early and on the phone, making calls and negotiating contracts with other musicians in God knows which country.

At noon, Dongdong wakes up. After drinking a mouthful of chilled water from the fridge, he discovers that Lutao is not in his bed. At first he thinks the singer might be in the bathroom, a long morning discharge after that spicy Mexican food and all those beers last night; but fifteen minutes pass and no one comes out. He checks the bathroom, but there is nothing—no vomiting, no blood, no dead body. Then Dongdong realises something is missing from their room—the blue suitcase covered with star stickers which belonged to Lutao. Gone with his clothes and his newly bought leather shoes and Elvis Presley T-shirts!

Dongdong knocks on Bruce's door and their manager's face drains of colour when he hears the news.

"I should have taken everyone's passports," he says regretfully. And now it's too late.

After lunch, they hang about watching the comings and goings on the street outside in silence. Mu is still wearing her pyjamas, sitting on Lutao's empty bed eating an apple, as if what has happened means very little to her. It is Monday, cars are flooding onto freeways, pedestrians are milling in the streets. Even in a city like Memphis, the Monday traffic is not light. The boys stare at the people passing by, vaguely hoping they might catch sight of a Chinese man with a blue suitcase crossing the street. But there are no Chinese men, no Japanese men, no Korean men in sight.

"Well, good luck to him." Bruce curses bitterly.

During the band's remaining days, Bruce wants to show his hospitality, and invites everyone to stay for a few days at his family home near Boston. "Now it's holiday relaxation time, you guys must come and have some chill out time with my parents. Free food! No more tipping and hotel service charges!"

There are cheers, from all except Mu.

Bruce shows them a photo of his family home. A roomy three-storey house with a garden.

"A great house, and good feng shui too," Liuwei praises with a twinge of envy. He is the other member of the band who would have loved to disappear and remain in America.

"That's why the American president has the loudest voice! They are paid better and live better than the president of any other continent!" cries Dongdong.

Bruce shrugs. "Well, if you grew up here you wouldn't find it so interesting. That's why I went to China." He turns to Mu. "Listen, Sister, I can try to organise a reading for you at a Harvard student club. I think those young intellectuals will like your style."

"Fine. Whatever," Mu responds tersely. She's stopped speaking in full sentences to Bruce now.

14 LONDON, JULY 2013

Iona is googling "Harvard University + Sabotage Sister" and it takes her instantly to a blog on the student forum of the Harvard website. The blog is a report about a performance Mu did at Harvard in May 2012, just over a year ago.

The Friday night poetry reading at the Student Club turned out to be a real disappointment. The advertisement said that the poet—Sabotage Sister, as per her nom de plume—is "A Brand New Voice from the Underground Chinese Poetry Scene." So we (three Chinese Ph.D.s as well as several M.A. graduates) went along, hoping for a chance to feel a bit nostalgic, a bit patriotic perhaps. But she turned out to be a total cultural prostitute. As soon as she announced she was going to read a Chinese cover version of an Allen Ginsberg poem, "America" it was called, I knew she (and that pretentious band) were Western-ass-kissing people. Let me share with you the beginning of her poem and you can see for yourself:

> China when will you be angelic?
> When will you take off your clothes?
> When will you look at yourself through the grave?
> When will you be worthy of your million Trotskyites?
> China why are your libraries full of tears?

How ridiculous is that? She would be jailed if she said something like that in China. As I said, a serious disappointment at the very least, and a despicable trashing of Chinese heritage and form at the worst. I find the idea of Sabotage Sister calling herself a poet downright insulting.

Posted on May 23, 2012. Read Alison Wang Blog **here**.

How interesting, Iona thinks, what a difficult end to the tour. The Chinese with their hard ideology don't seem to evolve much even outside of China. It seems they judge each other as harshly whether they're at home or abroad. She scrolls down and reads the comments section posted under the article.

Roosterinboston:

I don't agree. She is an honest poet. Just with a pretentious pen name. But she shouldn't be slapped. That was really rude.

Xiaotian:

She deserved the slapping. The security guards should have used catapults and shot stones at her every time she opened her mouth.

Keeion082:

Stop being so hypocritical, brothers and sisters. To have a few more sabotage sisters might help reduce the West's prejudice of China.

Qingyuan99:

I am sure that Sabotage Sister is taught and backed up by some Western dude. I bet she still eats rice with chopsticks. But she has forgotten her roots.

Iona then finds two pages from Mu's diary, dated 23 May 2012:

It was the most terrible experience. I wondered what Jian would do if he had faced such an abusive situation. The audiences at Harvard were mainly Chinese students from prestigious government-family backgrounds. Obviously all very corrupt. They got their rich daddies to pay for them to study overseas. I smelt the distinct whiff of strong nationalism the moment I entered the room. As I went onstage, I took a quick glance at those kids—mostly twenty-somethings, cheeks still plump with baby fat, their ignorant but confident faces shining with huge ambition, their eagerness for power radiating from behind their thick glasses. I didn't feel good at all in a room full of overfed goldfish.

As I announced I was going to read an Allen Ginsberg cover version of "America," their faces fell. I started to read, and from the corner of my eye I could see a few Chinese students beginning to shuffle and talk in their seats. Then the room became uncomfortably quiet. I read another two verses . . . I knew something terrible was going to happen. I was waiting for a bullet, bang, right in my forehead from somewhere in the corner of the room. Or perhaps they would wait until I had left the Student Club and just as I stepped onto the stairs the sniper would fire. But there was no bullet; instead, two big fat Chinese boys jumped onstage and grabbed me. They grabbed my arms exactly like the Red Guards had done to protesters during the Cultural Revolution. The only difference was that these little Red Guards were educated at Harvard, not in the rice fields of home. One of them was screaming at me and spitting all over my face. "Stop licking Western ass. Who do you think you are? Eh? This is Harvard, not some shitty Chinese restaurant where you can spit whatever you want to spit!" Another one spoke in a Beijing accent. "Don't you love your country? Eh? What kind of image do you want to show the West, eh? Our five thousand years of dignity have been ruined by you!"

There was a commotion in the hall. As I was being pushed and pulled by these plump bullies, students were gathering their belongings, murmuring in excited whispers to each other and leaving the room. I suddenly didn't care about the humiliation or the farce of the whole situation: I just wished I could have looked out into that sea of unkind faces and seen the only face I wanted to see. I know he would have smiled up at me, listened intently, listened deeply, applauded loudly.

In the frenzy I looked around for Bruce. I felt panic swell up all the way from the floor to my neck, hoping the young nationalists wouldn't chase after me and beat me up. But they couldn't be bothered to beat up a woman and just hissed at me instead, "Get out of our club! You shameful prostitute!"

More students followed me as I jumped down from the stage and tried to make a quick exit. They were less aggressive than the fat ones but their words were no less hurtful.

"Why would you want to read such a pretentious poem?"

"How dare you change Ginsberg's America to China? You and he are from totally different backgrounds, what you're doing is twisting reality!"

"What is your real intention in coming to Harvard?"

More accusations. More attacks. Before long my face and hair were soaked with the these rich boys' venomous spit.

I cried out: "Can't you see that what our government is doing is exactly like what the Americans did? They say it's in the name of people, when they're only interested in money and power?"

But my voice was drowned out in the rage of patriotism. Someone slapped my face and screamed at me to shut up. Thanks, old bastard sky!

I looked up and thought of you, Jian, my darling revolutionary. How you must have felt, all those months ago. I felt a burning sensation in my right cheek; it must have been red with the mark of his five fingers. One against all. Ugly. Disgusting. Not for them, but for me. You used to be punished in that way. I remember when your first manifesto was published two years *ago in "New Thoughts," thousands of young intellectuals read it and applauded, but many more thousands of people were instantly enraged. They wanted to shut you up. They wanted you to deny corruption in the Communist Party, deny corruption in the arts. But you just carried on, until they silenced your voice. And now it's my turn, my Peking Man. Perhaps in fact I'm really just fighting for you, after all. But it is one against all, and we cannot win. I can find nowhere to escape. Not even in America.*

I walked out of the Student Club alone, still with the burn of the slap on my cheek. In the distance I saw Bruce and the band, smoking and laughing by a fountain. I avoided them. I stood behind a tree and burst into tears.

So this was New England. This was Harvard, and our future—the Chinese Ph.D.s. The highest education for the highest stupidity. Nothing but brown shit stuck in those heads. Nothing but bad ideologies. How much money did those high-ranking government daddies pay for their ignorant sons to be at that school? Twenty-five thousand dollars a year? Plus another thirty-five thousand dollars for bed and board? If their sons and daughters are fed that way, no wonder they end up as idiots.

15 BOSTON, MAY 2012

The free holiday begins in Boston, the final week before the band return to China. Mu doesn't like having to stay at Bruce's house, although she is given her own bedroom upstairs while the boys have to share a lounge room. She mainly spends her time shopping for pork dumplings and tofu in Newton's gigantic Chinese supermarket, and cooks Chinese meals for everyone.

"I want to get away from Boston as soon as possible," Mu tells her manager at the breakfast table.

Bruce is surfing the Internet, wearing a Che Guevara T-shirt. And he is surprised, even offended, by Sabotage Sister's request.

Bruce's parents are preparing coffee and toast, unaware of their son's relationship with his Chinese poet. They choose to keep quiet, not to show too much curiosity. His father, a doctor in a downtown clinic, leafs through the *Boston Globe*, clearing his throat and occasionally mumbling something to his wife as she prepares breakfast.

"You know the crime rates are going up on the east side. It's migrant groups. Just won't assimilate."

Mu is stunned to hear this. A pause. "I want to take a train to the north, just for three days, then I'll be back."

"With the band?" Bruce asks cautiously.

"No. I want to be alone." She glances at the world cities calendar on the kitchen wall; this month is Shanghai. "We'll be going back to China together, anyway."

Bruce hesitates for a moment; he looks worried.

"I can come with you and show you around if you like."

Now Bruce's mother is sitting down with a plate of toast and jam. His mother is a Chinese Cantonese, and speaks in heavily-accented

English. "What did you just say, Mu? You would like to travel alone? That's how our young people like to do it here. Alone on the road!" She smiles warmly at Mu.

Bruce's father says, "But maybe you shouldn't hitchhike. Just take trains. And you should book your hotels online before you go."

Bruce is worrying about something else. Mu glances at his knitted frown and cuts the discussion short. "I know what you're worried about. You're afraid I'll become a second Lutao and run away with my passport, never to return. No, I don't think I want to live in America."

"You don't want to live in America?" Bruce's mother stops midmouthful.

Mu shakes her head. "No. I don't have a reason to live here."

The family looks at her, surprised.

"But you know, most Chinese want to live in America as soon as they get here," Bruce's mother says.

"Is that why you ended up here?"

"Well, it's a long story . . ." She sighs. "My parents left Hong Kong in the sixties and came here to start a business. I didn't get a chance to choose. If I could I would have prefered to live in Shanghai, the best city in the world!"

"And instead you married me, and never went back to your country!" Bruce's father says lightly and puts down his newspaper.

"Well, I'm a woman, aren't I? I must look after my husband and children first!" She speaks defensively.

Bruce listens in silence and turns to Mu, about to speak, but she gets in first.

"Now, Bruce, give me my passport." Mu reaches out her hand to him.

Several hours later she is on a train heading towards the state of Maine. No more Bruce, no more band members. Mu takes out her diary.

The cities were behind me. Only roadside petrol stations and drive-in restaurants here. The train passed a few small towns.

Lines of shabby houses, old caravans, small motels . . . I saw a sign in front of a town hall called Denmark; the next town I saw was called Finland, and the next one China! Ridiculous! It must be so desolate to live in a town called China in the state of Maine!

The train propelled itself onwards, aimlessly, with me, like a worm in a falling apple. The horizon offered no destination, only armies of cars moving on endless highways. I thought of the last time Jian and I broke up. This break-up had really little to do with his being forced out of China last winter. Our split began long ago, in fact, even before Little Shu died. I think our break-up perhaps began several years ago when he started to get famous. I always remembered his words after his very successful Shanghai concert in 2007. He was received in Shanghai Peace Hotel by representatives from the Cultural Bureau. At that time officials still had a neutral attitude to him. As he drank beer after beer, surrounded by cameramen and young female journalists, he said, "Mu, you know the mundanity of women and daily reality doesn't concern me, only power concerns me." I asked what he meant by this and he said, "What men value is their power and place in society. Men are political animals first and foremost. And men are easily seduced by it. But maybe it's our nature to be taken in by all this. Maybe that's what men really want." I listened in silence and watched him being grabbed by journalists. I wondered then whether we would make it. And after all these years where is my place in his life? If his mind is set like this, what about our vow to be together FOREVER? When the tour ended we came back to Beijing. A month later, I found out I was pregnant. My doubts of our life together were pushed away. I was excited by the future of a new person joining us and our nearly militant life. But then . . .

It is a moonless night. 11.40 p.m. Mu arrives at a roadside motel. All she wants as she enters the small room she's paid for in cash is a long dreamless sleep.

16 MAINE, MAY 2012

Took bus to Bar Harbor. I am on the edge of the Atlantic Ocean.
There is no more road for me to go on. And on the other side is
another foreign land where the ideological Peking Man shelters.
Peking Man, where in Europe are you? I wish you had been at
my Harvard reading to see how they treated me. Would it not
make you disillusioned for good, and fed up with politics? Well,
I'm fed up. Enough is enough. Too much ideology for a brief life.
I do not want to bear all this.

I've slept a lot since I've been here. I hear the sea roaring,
the waves from the other side of the ocean calling me, but I don't
even have the energy to step out of the room. Curtains are heavily
drawn. I don't even bother to get up to eat.

I feel hollow. Inside me is total hollowness. My heart holds
nothing. There is no one in this country I am willing to devote
my life to, nor could I dedicate myself to this culture. The fact
of my being here is the fact of being singular: there is no longer
a collective self within me. That's where I am now.

Drifting in America is like drifting without weight, like
drifting without carrying an ID card or a key. Yet I am so used
to walking around with my ID card and my key, like I do at
home in Beijing. Now that I am in a lifeless brand-new motel
room, nothing is required except money. That's how it is. If you
want to fill the empty closet you must buy stuff.

Perhaps America is a place one has to discover for oneself
and to live for oneself. Westerners believe in individuality—"Be
yourself and live for yourself"—whereas in China we are taught
to live for others and for the state but not for ourselves. And

even if it is good and valid to "live for yourself," the problem is, what if one hasn't got oneself? What if one is born with the mission of not living for oneself? In America they don't understand that not every person is an individual. Most of the time I feel we are just a tiny particle within a collective body. You have to go with the collective. With it, you are everything. Against it, you don't exist. Like Jian: he is non-existent now, a non-person person.

And me? I feel reduced to nothing here. Perhaps it is possible to live without yourself in China, but not in the West. Unless one invents oneself.

Yes, unless one invents oneself!

SIX | TALKING TO SATIE

远水救不了近火。

yuan shui jiu bu liao jin huo.

Distant water won't help extinguish the nearby fire.

HAN FEI ZI (PHILOSOPHER, 281–233 BC)

1 LONDON, AUGUST 2013

From: Iona1982@gmail.com
To: Jonathan.Barker@applegate.co.uk
Subject: Translation update

Dear Jonathan,

I hope this email finds you well, and that you received the tranche of translation I sent you. I'd love to know what you think.

I heard from your assistant that you have collected more information about Kublai Jian in the last few weeks. That's great to hear, as there seem to be lots of gaps. I've already translated a fair amount from Mu's diaries, but I don't yet see how her material can connect tightly to Jian's. It would be great to know more about him—do you know anything about his music?

I'd also love to know how you envisage using this material for a future publication. If you've got time, it would be great to meet up for a coffee and a bit of an update. I feel like we have a lot to talk about.

My best wishes,
Iona

A few hours later an email pops up on Iona's computer:

From: Jonathan.Barker@applegate.co.uk
To: Iona1982@gmail.com
Subject: RE: Translation update

Dear Iona,

Great to hear from you. Let's definitely meet up.

I've attached a scan of a letter from Switzerland which came my
way. It might illuminate a few things, perhaps. It was written in
French but one of my colleagues has done a rough translation.
Let me know when would suit you to meet up.

All best wishes,
Jonathan

Iona clicks open the attachment on Jonathan's email. The scan is of an
official letter printed on headed paper, and hurriedly signed.

> *Visa Office of the Department of Political Asylum*
> *Federal Office for Migration*
> *Berne 3402, Switzerland*

12 May 2012

Department for Political Asylum
Home Office
Dover
UK

Dear Officer,

 We're writing this letter from FOFM in Berne regarding the
case of applicant Kublai Jian (registration number: 867800RFUK;
original nationality: Chinese; DOB: 10 November 1972; CPS:
Dover Detention Centre Non-person Hold). After a considerable
investigation on the applicant's particular background, we are

pleased to inform you that we are willing to receive Mr. Kublai Jian from UK Border to Switzerland with the Safe Third Country Agreement. According to section 253 of the Geneva Convention this applicant will be allowed to stay in the Berne Asylum Aid Centre for a maximum of 45 days before a final decision on his application is taken. The applicant then can apply for further protection as long as the threat of persecution continues from his native country.

Please arrange the border transit with Berne Border Police Sector 12 within 99 days. If you have any questions please do not hesitate to contact us.

Yours,

Philip Dupont

Deputy Officer of Political Asylum Department of FFOM, Berne

In her local cafe, the Breakfast Club, Iona sits with the photocopies spread out before her. Kublai Jian. Half-Mongol, half-Chinese.
Kublai is an ancient Mongol name, she knows that much. Perhaps his
ancestors came from the great plains of central Asia. Or perhaps his
family descends from Kublai Khan, the grandson of Genghis Khan.
But Jian is an urban punk musician, a Beijing boy. A man with Mongol blood in the world of the Han Chinese. Blood and culture don't
always mix. Iona suddenly thinks of her own case, and feels a twinge
of melancholy. The source of her name—the Isle of Iona—is a place
she has never visited even though it's always there in the back room
of her life. That's how it is for all of us, she thinks to herself. We come
from somewhere we don't have any clue about.

The windows of the Breakfast Club are steamed up. There is a
familiar sour smell, like the odour of a windowless pub in Belfast or
any of the small, dismal Irish towns Iona's father used to frequent.
Iona feels agitated. Something isn't right. Something she is barely
aware of. What is it? She looks up from her work and watches the
world outside the cafe, as if looking for it. She used to think that as
long as she could lead a sexually active life, and be able to carry on
working, she would be fine. But now she feels depressed, unmoored
and even unhinged. She is ashamed to admit it. She feels like a flying
figure in a surrealist painting, without ground beneath her feet to
steady her. And she seems unable to see the problems in her life, as
if everything is hidden behind a heavy leaden curtain too heavy to
draw back. Iona sips more coffee, and tries to shake the pressure out
of her head. She rubs her eyes, sets her jaw, and pulls her attention
back to the sheet before her. Work, I need to work. And then her

hand moves across the page, making markings. She opens her laptop and begins to type.

Something is deeply wrong in our family, the famous Hu family, at least it has been wrong for the last three generations. My father has no memory of his own father. My grandfather, one of the original members of Mao's Jiangxi Soviet in the early thirties, died when my father was only three months old. According to the party's record, he was hailed as a war hero and received the Medal of the First of August. He used to train the new soldiers in the three basic infantry skills: shooting, throwing grenades and swimming with weapons. He was a regimental commander and married to one of the female soldiers in the Propaganda Unit in his regiment. A typical "Revolutionary Couple" as they said. But the Revolutionary Couple barely spent any time together and certainly had no spare time to raise children. Is this why my father ended up as such a selfish career-driven dictator? And me an aggressive kid hungry for love? First the war hero died and then his wife followed two months later. So my father was raised by female soldiers in the Welfare Unit. In 1949, after the revolution took the whole of China, the regiment commander's name was engraved on the People's Hero Memorial in Tiananmen Square; his photo was placed in the History Museum, and his name was even recorded in our school textbook. No one in my school knew that the cerebrated hero was my grandfather. I have always kept it quiet. Until today. I don't want to live under anyone's shadow. I often wondered whether my war-hero grandfather was the only reason my father was promoted so quickly in the party. Yes, my father's career was everything to him. My mother and I were nothing compared to the party. With Mother dead, our house became an orphanage, children without parents showing them love. The women in our family were sacrificed for these men, like those terracotta warriors buried along with their emperor under the earth: mute, lifeless, and dead forever.

Who is Jian's grandfather? Iona types "Medal of the First of August + China's Long March" into Google. It comes out with a few names: Peng Dehuai—the marshal of the People's Republic of China, Lieutenant General of the Liberation Army. Then Zhu De comes up—perhaps the most famous professional Chinese soldier, who later achieved the highest rank in the Chinese army. Even Iona has heard of him. Then mention of previous "Paramount Leader" Deng Xiaoping, who once served as the Secretary of Mao's Jiangxi Soviet in 1931 and also made the epic Long March. Then Liu Shaoqi, who was Mao's very first supporter as he rose to power, but was purged by Mao later during the Cultural Revolution and tragically died as a "state traitor" in the sixties.

There are many more names, male Chinese names, populating the Google search results, but none of them seems to have an obvious connection with Kublai Jian. She reads more, and is lost in the vast sea of Chinese civil war records. The untold story that lies behind Jian's background is a total enigma, cast in a secret stone, lying in a frozen past, and beyond all recovery.

3 CENTRE D'ASSISTANCE EUROPÉEN POUR REQUÉRANTS D'ASILE, SWITZERLAND, JUNE 2012

One otherwise ordinary summer morning, Jian is called to the centre's head office. As he steps through the door there is a ringing cry: "Congratulations, Kublai Jian!" The office erupts with raised voices. Members of staff approach to pat him on the back and hug him. He's been there so much longer than anyone else—he's become an institution. Then Mr. Battista, the director of the centre, hands him a stack of documents with official stamps here and there. Jian flips through the papers, sees the red and black marks almost on every single page, like Chinese artists' signature stamps on ink paintings. His head is whirling.

Mr. Battista explains, "It says you are granted 'Leave to Remain' in Switzerland. And your legal residence period in the country is one year. After one year you must apply for an extension and the Swiss authorities will reassess your case and decide on your new status. But for now, congratulations!"

He pours Jian a glass of wine and hands him a packet of salted nuts. "Now you are entitled to be a part of our country! But don't forget you must register your address with the police within eight days." Mr. Battista wags his finger at Jian, and then adds with his peculiar brand of sincerity: "I wish you all the best in the future and hope you will be able to make a living in Europe."

Jian receives five hundred Swiss francs from the organisation, as well as a clean T-shirt as a souvenir, with the asylum centre's logo on the back. It's not quite his *Never Mind the Bollocks* T-shirt, nor his Ming-dynasty black singlet. He won't wear it if he busks on the street with his guitar.

Slowly and heavy-headed, Jian walks back towards his room. Between the two buildings there is a basketball court, but today nobody is in the yard. The broken net swings weightlessly in the wind. Standing under the hoop, Jian's ears echo with sounds from the past. Suddenly he remembers his years playing basketball at high school; he was once a very good player, the best "shooting guard" on his team! In the school's annual basketball championship he would glue the ball to his hands and zigzag his way through the human wall in front of him, and lob the ball in the net! There would be yelling and clapping from the crowd, mingled with the sound of bodies jostling each other. Jian was always the kid who could run faster than the others, until one day he disappeared from the play-ground—that was the day he discovered music and songwriting. Now Jian stands on a basketball court once more, in this foreign land, looking up into a blue Swiss sky. The white vapour trails of jets transect the blue field. The morning's crispness is just beginning to slink off and let in the warmer rays of sunshine. He recalls the last game here, a week ago. There were eight people on each team, all from different countries, and four substitutes standing by—including a group of veiled Muslim girls wearing colourful trainers from places in the Middle East. It was like the Eight Nation Alliance, Jian thought, those military forces from eight countries who came to China to beat the Boxer Uprising in 1900. And perhaps I was the rebellious Boxer, he laughed at himself bitterly, eventually beheaded by the Eight Nation forces and the Qing emperor. After that "colourful" match, everyone slapped each other on the back and said that one day they would meet again out in the world and have a big party to celebrate their freedom. A big party, one day! The Freedom Anniversary party! No one has a permanent address. Everyone's freedom is the freedom of the naked road: none of them has a roof over their head nor belongs to the country. They don't even have telephone numbers. Only an email address scribbled on a cigarette paper. An email address, that's where their future will be written. Better than nowhere. Jian readies himself for a new taste. The taste of strange forms of life. The new place always seems arbitrary. Your body cannot fit into it. Then it becomes familiar, as if it had always been there, like the back of your hand.

4 LONDON, AUGUST 2013

On a hot summer day, at around teatime, Iona arrives at a cafe near Bloomsbury. As she waits for her professor to turn up, she takes out her notebook and laptop, as well as her dictionary and documents, and continues her translation.

As she works away, she hears a familiar laughing voice.

"I can see you're working on serious stuff! Look at all the paraphernalia you need!" Charles Handfield glances at Iona's papers, his left eyebrow rising with a familiar nervous spasm.

After buying himself a cup of tea, Charles sits down, picks up the photocopied page Iona is working from. "What handwriting! It may seem a cliché, but in my experience, it's the rebellious Chinese who often write with these sort of wild strokes. It tends to be true, you know." He pours his tea from a small white pot. "So, tell me about him."

"Right, so this is Kublai Jian. And what I'm struggling with is his colloquial style. It's fascinating, and I can manage some of it, but it's the precision I'm lacking—or maybe it's the spirit I find hard. At any rate there are a lot of expressions I'm not familiar with. Hopefully you can help."

"Ha!" Charles chuckles. "You know what, Iona? There is one thing from all your classes with me that you never wanted to learn: untranslatability."

"Untranslatability?"

"Yes, it's something I think it's important to teach students. It always got pushed to the end of the term and I never managed to fit it in alongside the scheduled syllabus."

Iona looks bemused.

"Untranslatability? Surely it's just to do with facing the lack of one-to-one equivalence between the word or phrase in the source language and in the target language. Nothing very mysterious about that."

"Yes, my dear, but what do you do with that problem?" Charles doesn't look at her, and is instead scanning the menu while gesticulating to a young waiter. As the waiter comes to him, he orders a scone with jam and butter to go with his tea. "Do you want another cup, Iona?"

"No, I'm fine. Thanks." Iona continues, undeflected. "I suppose there are the technical devices, the tricks of language—metaphors, paraphrase, adaptation, as you used to demonstrate to us. But I still have a problem."

"Yes, like Tintin's little canine friend 'Milou' becomes 'Snowy' in English. So now, tell me, what are your Milous, and what are the Snowys you are proposing on this page?"

Iona is silent as Charles butters his warm scone. He surveys her pale face and heavy brow.

"I see you don't want to follow up the matter with Milous and Snowys in your text."

"No. Perhaps not." She seems to confess with a sigh, "I think it's more to do with making people intelligible. You know, Charles, translations only work because we get inside a person's inner culture. And how does one do that? How does one get inside someone?"

Charles has his beaming, kindly eye upon her. "You have to imagine. Allow yourself to be opened up. The great translator, now and then, has to go beyond what they know. You have to go beyond translation and its techniques and tricks, and be absolutely human."

But Iona is still not at ease. Maybe it is something about this knowing but kindly man's gaze, like a better, kinder father looking at her. "Yes. I get all that. But it's just not working. There's something I'm completely missing."

"So what is it then, Iona? It's not translation, not intelligibility?"

"I seem to be failing here. I spend my days grappling with the real people, trying to get them to come out. But I feel like I'm not making contact with them. It's like, despite all my efforts to make them speak, they remain silent. Or won't speak to me. What can I do? What am I doing? What's the point without that connection?"

Charles draws towards Iona and rests his hand on hers. "I think, my dear, you're talking about something else here. I don't think it's about translation at all. I think it's more about you."

5 ANNECY, FRANCE, JULY 2012

"Take me to the French border, please," Jian tells the taxi driver as he throws his old guitar case onto the back seat. The driver is surprised, turns his head and looks at this strange Chinese man with a large shoulder bag and big round eyes ringed with shadowy circles. The Chinese face does not waver; indeed, it seems to have no expression at all.

"A French border?" the driver questions doubtfully in English, and then says, "*Il n'y a pas de frontière française, monsieur.*"

"Then take me to the nearest French city, I have had enough of Switzerland!"

After a few seconds of silence, the North African–looking driver doesn't bother to prevaricate. Maybe he realises that this man is not a tourist, is on no sightseeing trip. A little grumpily, he gets out and picks Jian's guitar case up off his clean back seat and puts it in the boot—he doesn't want his leather upholstery scratched. He starts the engine and they move off.

In no time at all the taxi takes Jian across into French Annecy. To Jian's surprise, there is no discernible border, no wires, no soldiers, no sign, no announcement, just a motorway connecting the two countries. So this is Europe! I am in Europe! And Europe has no borders.

The driver halts in Annecy's city centre, in front of a large Carrefour supermarket, and turns his head to announce: "*Voilà, monsieur. Vous êtes en France.*"

France! Getting out of the car, Jian pays the man the meter fee plus another ten euros as thanks. Carrying his shoulder bag and his old guitar, he speaks to himself, as if in a rap: "Now I am a FREE man.

No address, no bank account, no money, no family, no friends, no more persecution, no more protection. Absolutely free. Nothing to lose, nothing to gain, as I am a free man!" He laughs out loud.

For a few days he wanders around Annecy getting his bearings. He takes his guitar and sits in a square off one of the main streets and begins to play. He sings in a low voice, an old song. But soon a gendarme appears and asks him to move on. Jian doesn't protest. He moves through the cobbled streets. Everywhere feels like a suburb. Everywhere feels provincial, everywhere feels like hell for a Beijinger who is used to life in a lively city of twenty million. Mont Blanc and the Alps are always in view. It gives his day-to-day life a surreal penumbra, like the city is surrounded by an infinite sea of mountains. Nights pass on a bench in a park; days arrive with new hope. Then he walks into a local restaurant and finds himself a job. Labour should help him, he thinks; help both his wallet and his mind. The Chinese takeaway will be his re-education camp in the West.

6 ANNECY, FRANCE, JUNE 2012

In the Blue Lotus, there are two chefs working in the basement kitchen, both from Canton Province. They are long-married, with grown-up children. The two girls upstairs serving the customers are of course their daughters or some relative's daughters. Perhaps, for Chinese people, all social life starts with the kitchen, and everything else takes its course from there. But even so, in Jian's eyes, they don't seem to be very good cooks. In fact, the Blue Lotus has a terrible reputation. They use loads of MSG and recycle the oil from old dishes; their bok choi are refrigerated for nearly six months; their instant noodles expired three years before; they'll use any old rot to cook with as long as it has a bit of grease in it. The first time Jian sits with the other workers and eats a potato dish on the menu, he is shocked. This is a typical yi-ku-si-tian dish—忆苦思甜饭—a dish from the famine time, a dish that reminds him of all the miserable days he has had in his life. Not a dish of freedom. He thinks of England and the wretched pie and mash he ate when he first arrived in London, staying in a poky flat near Mile End station, and the tasteless jacket potatoes topped with greasy butter he ate in Lincolnshire. It's strange that his food fantasies take him in this direction. He can't help hating these overseas attempts at making Chinese dishes. Obviously, the chefs have had their hearts eaten by money, foreign money.

But it's not the food that makes the customers vomit in Blue Lotus. It's the stale tinny music that's played all day long: romantic Hong Kong ballads, second- or even third-hand imitations of Western pop rubbish: *huan huan xi xi, huan you xi*. And so on and so on. It all curdles in his head as Jian chops dried cabbage and frozen cucumbers mercilessly into pieces, and splits carrots into twos and fours, and strips spring onions of their souls. He casts it all into a never-washed wok or a boiling cauldron, to be melded into shapeless, flavourless oblivion. No wonder business has been so bad, with music like that.

But despite the irritations of the Blue Lotus, Jian is grateful to be there, and indebted to one of the chefs in particular—Chang Linyuan.

"I have had enough here, Jian, enough." Chef Chang opens his bearded oily mouth in his smoke-damaged face and tries to persuade Jian to go back to China. "Zhong Guo—that's the only place in the world you can live with some dignity and speak like a sensible man." Jian hasn't told his new workmates the whole story, Chef Chang doesn't know Jian can't just go back.

He carries on. "Jian, one day you will grow as old as a pickled egg, like me. And let me tell you—Europe is not for old men!" Chang shakes his head in desolation. "There is no more reason for me to stick around here waiting for the Buddha to turn up one day. And my children are all grown up and have their own lives."

No wonder, if the chef himself eats so badly every day—there is indeed no reason to stick around in the West waiting for the Buddha to perform some miracle. Jian swears silently with aching teeth and a pained stomach. In the last few days he has eaten nothing but rice with soy sauce.

There is a TV in the Blue Lotus which receives a Hong Kong news channel. That is the only entertainment the Chang family have for their leisure hours. The Alps stand proudly in the European wind only one and a half miles away, but it seems that the snowy peaks and cosy chalets have nothing to do with these yellow people. Nor have they ever climbed even the most modest foothill, let alone the most famous European mountain. "Not fun there, too lonely." It's as simple as Chang says.

Chang Linyuan has been preparing his return to China for a few months, and he has successfully transferred his savings to a Chinese bank in his province so he can buy a piece of land. One night, after the clients are gone and half a bottle of rice vodka swills in his stomach, Chef Chang starts treating Jian like a younger brother. He opens his wallet and takes out a plastic card with a string of numbers printed on it. He speaks as Confucius might.

"Young man, I know you don't have papers. I too had nothing for years, in the beginning. You see this piece of plastic? Keep it! It's my French health insurance card—it will help you!"

Jian doesn't say a word; he brings the plastic card up to his face and looks closely at the letters written on it.

"A leaf is bound to return to its roots; a man is bound to his homeland! When I return to China I'll buy a little house in Guangzhou and I will brew my tea and feed the sparrows in my garden, go fishing, play chess and grow my own vegetables." The chef speaks drunkenly, in a snaking Cantonese accent, appealing to Jian with his muddy little eyes.

Jian nods his head to show his respect for the old man, still studying the name printed on the card:

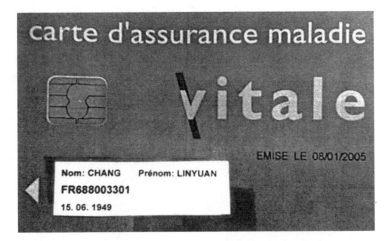

From that night on, Jian carries Mr. Chang's health insurance card with him wherever he goes—he has even made two photocopies. Surely this is going to be useful, he thinks. He recites his new name like he's accepting his personal karma—*Chang Linyuan, aka William Chang. Numéro de carte d'assurance maladie: FR688003301.*

William Chang is going to make a living in Paris, that's it. Like Picasso used to do, like Van Gogh, like Jim Morrison. Paris, that's where Kublai Jian, aka William Chang, is headed.

Number 141 rue Saint-Julien-le-Pauvre, a windowless basement room under the Hotel Esmeralda. It's not really part of the hotel, it's where they store the extra bedding, toilet products and all kinds of cleaning equipment. The corners are piled with old curtains, old mattresses and old carpets. The air is stagnant, and a strong smell of ammonia lurks everywhere. Remembering something he learned in a high-school science lesson, Jian fetches a basin of water, and puts it right in the middle of the room, to test the alkaline reaction. But there are barely more than four or five bubbles as the pH dissolves. Probably this type of gas prefers to stay in Jian's head rather than enter the water.

A fly has been stuck in my room for more than a week now. There are no windows in my basement, just a dark narrow staircase leading up to the ground floor and entrance.

Rain is pouring down outside. Water is dripping everywhere, from the Parisian roofs to the sewage flowing in pipes under my floorboards. But how did this little fly manage to live here for weeks without seeing any light at all? Perhaps it was born from the sewage under my feet. She's large, with a dark, heavy head between two transparent wings, and is always making this buzzing noise. Twenty-four hours a day. I think of that William Blake poem I read once at college:

> *Little Fly,*
> *Thy summer's play*
> *My thoughtless hand*
> *Has brushed away.*

Am not I
A fly like thee?
Or art not thou
A man like me?"

Later that night . . . I looked for the fly. I've decided that I'll either kill her or let her out through the doorway. But she is nowhere to be found and I realise I miss her low hum.

This morning when I woke up, the first thing I did was to look out for her, my large-headed one. There is absolutely no trace of her. Not in the toilet, not buzzing around the kitchen sink, not on the ceiling, not on the floor. Where did she go? Did she starve to death? Was she exhausted from being imprisoned here? She must be dead. I walk around the room, open the garbage bag, bring out a rotten banana. I expose the drooping banana on the floor. A fly would understand this, old bastard sky.

Are you a fly, or a butterfly? A fly likes rotten substances, but a butterfly prefers flowers. You say politics are rotten; you say art lives outside the rotten political sphere. Your antenna is drawn to something beyond the stench of politics. Maybe you are right in your own way. You'll have to convince me.

Iona finishes translating the diary entry and finds herself searching for insects on her geranium plants by the kitchen window. There is neither fly nor butterfly on her small red flowers. Instead, a sharp ringing pierces her ears. She feels a slight cramp in her head. The sounds from the street below, the all-day buzz of Chapel Market, are echoing in the chill gloom of a wet London evening.

What a peculiar thing to translate, she murmurs to herself. What's the meaning of these strange diary fragments? Are those lonely words supposed to be Jian's expressions of love to Mu? Or is it just me overinterpreting? Would they still think of themselves as lovers? Where are they now? Do they still deny their love? Or have they become the tragic spirit of the Butterfly Lovers of the ancient Chinese legend? Jian and Mu have now transformed into Liang Shanbo and Zhu Yingtai, the two star-crossed lovers of the 2,000-year-old myth.

Then Iona remembers her time in Beijing, and the Chinese boy she met in the foreign students' club, who had desired her and sent her a poorly written English love letter, quoting lengthy lines from traditional Beijing operas, lines like "you are the falling blossoms obscuring the moon." To a Western woman, his passion appeared naive. But at the same time he was so constrained and shy in the daylight, like a bat shrinking from the light. A young man totally of the head, not of the body. A young man very different from the Western ones she had met before. When she left China and returned to college in London, she still didn't understand that Chinese boy's protestations of love and, not knowing quite how to respond, she never replied to the letter.

But Jian isn't like that, in Iona's head at least. Or *wasn't* like that. But maybe that's because she has been allowed inside, into this private place, his journal. Jian is an angry monk. A hungry beggar with a knife, maybe holding it to his own chest. Ready to strike, with a single cut, and split everything in two. Maybe that's how he played the guitar, or gave out one of these cries—a bit theatrical, but haunted at the same time.

The street lamp gleams in her room. Iona sees herself drawn to the light like a moth. Like she is drawn to those men-boys that she has known, picked up in pubs or on the Internet, and then used. What would she have done with Jian, if she were Mu? She writes his name with a ballpoint pen: 健.

Under the acid-green light, the characters seem to shimmer and move. They are etched and yet alive-seeming. Maybe it's just her stiff, unpractised Chinese writing. She tries to imitate his writing style. His hand, there, on top of her paper. Her mind mingles with his image and seems to touch him, maybe, with these signs, half-pictures, half-words. Did he carry this image 健 inside his head while he lived outside of China, like an inner stamp?

And now she writes Mu's name: 木.

It looks more stable to her. The strokes are like arms reaching down, wanting to embrace someone.

It's all too much, Iona thinks. Her own life has been totally consumed. Still, there is something ungraspable about her anti-heroes, especially Jian, that inspires in her such a rampant curiosity and longing to know more. Iona almost feels that she needs to find Jian, to talk to him. She needs her Jian. She needs to think of his skin, his habits, his way of walking, his way of talking, laughing, singing and sleeping.

8 PARIS, JUNE 2012

Standing in front of a Turkish grocery. Suddenly lost the sense of where I was. I felt like I was Comrade Krymov in Life and Fate *being put in a solitary cell and losing all sense of my humanity. He was no longer Krymov and his soul was no longer corresponding with his body. "I need a piss, open the door!" I heard myself shouting, "Open the door! And I will remain pure to my belief!" Then the door opened, I ran out, and some rude impatient shoulders pushed and cursed me in French, and suddenly I realised I was in a queue in front of the grocery. Everyone stared at me in disgust. In embarrassment I bought two apples. Two polished waxy shiny green globes: immaculate as plastic. "One-fifty, please." The shopkeeper flapped his eyes up like a dead fish. One euro and fifty cents for two plastic apples I didn't even want to buy. 操他大爷的. I bit into one of the vitamin bundles anyway, right through the plastic leather jacket. Fuck me. It was absolutely tasteless. Eating a lump of cardboard.*

Rue Saint-Denis. Jian has wasted hours on the pavement, up and down, absent-mindedly looking at the glitzy shops, the beautifully lit cafes and occasional prostitutes standing about in their fur coats. He catches sight of a Chinese woman. She is probably forty-something, not young for someone who does this kind of job. Her red cheek suggests that she might have left her field just a few months ago, taken an illegal boat, a train, a coach and got herself here. Despite her fishnet tights and her fake leather coat, she reminds Jian of his mother. His mother, with her dark brown eyes, her lips full of unspoken words. He was four when his mother died. And her image remains forever young in his blurred memory.

As Jian zooms up and down rue Saint-Denis, he decides to go into a record shop to find out what the CD covers of Erik Satie recordings are like in this country. In fact, he's after a cover of the recording his mother had. Satie was the composer who indirectly killed her. He walks straight to the classical piano section and in no time finds a Satie CD. The cover design is not fashionable; he recognises the same smiley photo of the bearded man wearing the same suit he knows from a Chinese cassette, an image he remembers from his childhood.

It looks neither provocative nor decadent—how could anyone imagine that in a faraway country a mother would be classified as an enemy of the state for listening to this?

In the midst of loud pop music blaring across the shop floor, he slots the CD into a test-listening machine. Instantly a flow of melancholy piano notes seep into his ears. It's his mother's favourite, Gnossienne No. 4. So familiar, and deeply sad. Now Jian's stomach begins to ache. His guts knot together each time his mind fills with heavy thoughts.

He hangs up the headphones. With the pain still in his stomach, he takes the CD to the counter.

"Do you like Satie?" the cashier asks.

"Yes," Jian answers and pays. "But actually it's for my mother."

"That's nice. Hope she enjoys it."

A kind man, a regular nice guy, just like those innocent people who never stop to imagine that shit can fall from the sky in an instant, as they walk down the street. Jian murmurs to himself, and puts Satie in his green army bag.

9 PARIS, JUNE 2012

Marie, an old French prostitute, looks about fifty, or perhaps fifty-eight or sixty-two. She refuses to say. Whatever her age, she looks worn and drawn. One can't help but stare at her thickly powdered face, and the eyes, like those of a silent-movie actor, heavily outlined and glimmering up from a soup of dusty make-up. What a mouth! A labouring mouth. A hard-working mouth. How many men has that mouth taken? It must have been young once, a flower, an animated jewel. Marie! As her image starts to blur in Jian's head, he enters a Wenzhou restaurant in rue de Belleville. He is hungry, despite being unable to remove the image of that twilight creature from his mind. As he eats his pork dumpling soup, his stomach feels less miserable and those images return: Marie's leopard-skin skirt, the intricate lace around her neck, her breasts like semi-sunken ships but surprisingly white and soft beneath her black nylon dress. This is the first European woman he has slept with. It felt more like sleeping with a mother than a girlfriend.

People come into Jian's life the way maple leaves blow down the streets of Paris. It seems so random and futureless. He met Marie about two weeks ago, in the street where she works. The negotiation was fast. She asked for three hundred euros; he shook his head and said he couldn't afford even half of that. They settled on eighty. They went to a nearby hotel room. The room was so small that it could only fit the single bed. When they were inside, she stripped off her clothes right away. Jian felt awkward. She wore a bodysuit, a sort of body-shaping corset with wires to lift her breasts. Jian still remembers the red mark the wire made under her chest. He didn't ask how painful or constrained it felt in that costume. When she removed it and emerged from her cage, her sunken bottom looked like a large deformed pear. She told Jian she had been working the area for the last two decades. And before that she was in Marseilles—she used to hang out with the sailors. She said she would carry on working until the day she couldn't get up or didn't have the strength to open her legs any more. "C'est vrai, Jian, sometimes my legs are too sore to open," she said. "And my muscles around my crotch are aching. I need to take a hot bath three times a day!" She then laughed loudly; exactly like the big woman in that Italian film, Mama Roma, which Jian had watched in college. Laughing so that every part of her body shook, even her red curly hair, shaking as if electrocuted. Her laugh was coarse and threatening. It made Jian lose confidence. But he didn't dislike her. An old female lion, he thought to himself. But after that afternoon, strangely, each time Jian walked up and down the street where he had met her, she wasn't to be found.

Today, once again, Jian cruises along the street that is supposed to be Marie's haunt. Perhaps she is lying on a bed somewhere, with a client on top of her. Perhaps she is taking a hot bath after sex in a hotel room. Or perhaps she is taking a holiday. Do old French prostitutes take holidays? Jian wonders with disquiet. Or perhaps she is sick from some venereal infection and her lower body is right now overflowing with yeast. As the evening lamps illuminate rue Saint-Denis, Jian loses himself in the crowds. Those enchanting smiles under the lights, those elegant gestures and pleasant rendezvous in bars and restaurants. They remain intangible to him. His arms stretching out for attention and warmth reach nowhere to nobody.

Old bastard sky. I stared at the afternoon street, this street without Marie. I wanted to buy her a gift, for some reason, before seeing her again. And I walked up and down rue Saint-Denis, going in and out of one clothes shop after another. I felt foolish. A pathetic act. Nobody gives a damn about what I am doing anyway.

Hours passed. I hung around. Couldn't find anything useful to do. I ate the second apple as it was a leaden weight in my pocket. I had to tear through the tough skin with my teeth. I thought of that knife. The knife my mother used to cut herself. A long, slim knife that we used to peel the skin off sugar cane. It wasn't sharp. She didn't succeed at first. There were jagged scars around her wrists. She must have tried many times. My grandmother picked up the knife from the floor. The first thing she did was to wash the blood off. Then she hid it in our rice jar, as if the knife might fly around by itself and cut open everyone's heads. We never used that knife again. It sat in the kitchen and became very rusty. Layers of brown rust covered the whole blade. From then on we used our teeth to peel the sugar cane. I don't remember my grandmother eating sugar cane ever again.

The sun is at its zenith. Brasserie Le Clauzier. Mainly old men spend their afternoons here. Two bald men each occupy a table in the corner, reading papers and drinking wine. Then there is Jian, scribbling words in his diary and occasionally looking up at the old men to reflect on things. One of them is about eighty. Skinny and decayed, he looks like a handful of dried roots. Slowly, he sips his rosé and eats his beef bourguignon. The old man chews extremely slowly, his sunken mouth probably toothless. He seems to live in his old age with great patience. Jian imagines his own teeth falling out, his hair reduced to a few wisps: a dried-up skeleton like the one propped on this chair, wearing an old watch to witness each passing hour before death arrives.

The tunnel wind in the Métro at Belleville is very warm. The heat must be generated by the friction or pressure between the trains. Jian sits on the platform, upturns the straw hat he found the other day in the street, and opens his guitar case. His fingers are stiff. The guitar is out of tune. He tries to tune the cold strings. He tries to sing, not one of his own songs, but a song from a 1937 Chinese film, *Street Angel*, one of his favourite films. It is about a Shanghai street musician's encounter with two sisters. The sisters have been forced into prostitution and the street musician helps them and before long falls in love with one of the sisters. A few years ago, in a cinema in Beijing's Xiao Xitian area, Jian watched the film for at least the fifth or sixth time with Mu—holding hands together in the dark. They both remembered so well the songs from the film, and Jian even learned to play the main theme, "Song Girl at the Edge of the World":

> *To the ends of the earth*
> *To the edge of the sea*
> *I seek, oh, seek the soulmate who understands my song*
> *This little sister sings, and her man plays along*
> *You and I are of the same heart*
> *Aiya you and I are of one heart*
> *Towards the mountains of home, oh, I gaze to the north*
> *Tears, oh, tears wet my robe*
> *I long for my lover man even now.*

Jian feels a sympathy for the character: a street musician in "love" with a prostitute. But his heroine is his mother's age, and she's nowhere to be found.

The next day he sets himself up outside Pigalle Métro. A wild-haired African drummer occupies the platform; he doesn't sing, just madly hits his many drums, like he is caught in a powerful electrical current. As he seems to attract the crowds, Jian puts himself reasonably close to him.

Almost all street musicians like Pigalle—it's where tourists get off to visit Montmartre. Many are middle-aged American women and their families, and, with universal compassion for the artist, they generously throw a few euros into Jian's hat. As thanks, Jian sings Mongolian folk songs of the grasslands and horses, the bowmen and the yurts, although he can't hold a note for as long as those folk songs require. Most Westerners like the Mongolian style—the native tribal style somehow works better than rock 'n' roll down in a Métro station.

Over the next few days, Jian arrives at Pigalle station at ten in the morning every day and takes a lunch break to eat a half-chicken (which costs only two euros from Monoprix). Then he comes back to the Métro for two more hours' playing. But the afternoons feel lousy and long. Sleepy and weary, cradling his old guitar, he sees himself as a dirty street bum, a thief, a superfluous being, a nameless beggar at any Métro entrance. He feels he has no dignity left in him. So on the day the police arrive to check his street-performance certificate, Jian feels ready to leave, to move on, to move anywhere.

Rue Victor Masse, 27 July 2012

Au Jardin du Bonheur. The crippled madam gave me a big bowl of dumpling soup, pork and chive filling. Madame Wu of Au Jardin du Bonheur is about sixty-five; she cooks most of the food for her clients by herself, in her tiny but homely restaurant. She said I reminded her of her son (similar age and temperament, doesn't like to talk), who married a French girl and barely ever visited her again. I think she must be a bit discontented as a mother. She seems to be a very educated Beijingese with a

Buddha-like face (even received a college degree in agricultural science!—if she had remained in China she would probably be high up in the State Agriculture Department). But she is a woman, and a woman follows her man: she came to Europe with her husband and the dreams of a new life ended up in the same space—a kitchen. My mother didn't want her life to end up in a kitchen; instead she wanted culture; but what difference would it have made? Erik Satie didn't save her, nor did the Communists.

Try to live usefully . . . I sing outside Au Jardin du Bonheur to help Madame Wu attract customers. I sing slow songs. "What a Beautiful Jasmine Flower," she likes to hear that. Do jasmine flowers reflect a political issue or not? In China I would ask this question and somebody would argue with me. But here, how stupid the question is! And even if it were a valid question, who gives a damn whether the jasmine flower reflects a political issue or not? Pay us first and I will tell you whatever you want.

At night, as I lie with Chang Linyuan's health-insurance card under my pillow, I ask myself: is this going to be my life in the West? Old bastard sky! I'm becoming Frankenstein, or Frankenstein's monster. A large, stiff body, huge eyes staring into the world but seeing nothing, heavy legs moving without knowing their direction or purpose—a body without mind. A life without living. Fucking hell.

操他大爷的—Cao ta da ye de.

11 PARIS, JULY 2012

These girls, Jian thinks, are not girls. They are whales, or some other large beast. There are six of them, professional cabaret performers. The biggest woman is Madeleine, with huge breasts pendulously undulating inside her shirt. She is from San Francisco but has lived in Paris for many years. "I'm a lesbian," she tells Jian right away, and the conversation seems to end right there. The smallest of them is Anna, a French girl with a beautiful smile from the north, a town called Lille.

"You know, Jian, we're like porn artists. You understand what I mean by porn artists, right?" Madeleine tries to educate the naive Chinese man.

"You know, Jian, once you understand our style, you can make music for us, even improvise as we perform," Anna adds.

Jian gives them a quick rendition of one of his own songs, not "Long March into the Night" but another piece, one about Mongolia, mountains, yaks, wrestling and getting drunk on fermented roots. The girls laugh and clap their hands; they seem to like how he plays.

"What about French songs?" Anna asks.

He did learn a bit of Jacques Brel's famous "Amsterdam" when he was in the Lausanne refugee centre—"*Dans le port d'Amsterdam, / Y a des marins qui chantent*"—and he can even switch into English—"*They sing of the dreams that they bring from the wide open sea, / In the port of Amsterdam . . .*"—but only these four lines. Otherwise he plays "La Marseillaise" which he learned at school when he was a Young Pioneer, but this time he gives it a punk edge and adds some Chinese lyrics on top, so that it sounds half-parody, half-homage, electrified by twelve-bar blues-rock.

The girls laugh with appreciation. They like this Chinese man with his roaring-hoarse voice, an easy companion and a total mystery.

For his new job, the girls give him extra instruments to play with: two drums and an old violin. They say, "Practise!" Then they tell him to watch their live sex show that night to get ideas, and to think about how to play his music to fit in with their performance. Jian sits on a rickety cafe chair at the back of the room and watches. In the beginning, the girls wear a layer of leather, high-heeled boots, chains and belts. As the farce develops, their clothes are taken off by a male actor who plays a doctor professor-type character. Eventually the girls are naked, except for two shiny stars stuck on their nipples and a tiny G-string barely covering their crotch. In the final act the doctor asks one of the girls to lie on a table on which he lays out all sorts of medical instruments. Madeleine or Anna—it's usually one of them—then says, "Doctor, I believe there is a mouse in my pussy. You must get him out!" Then the girl on the table opens her legs wide towards the audience. Her vagina, shaved hair and pink lips, is exposed for everyone to view. The doctor now elegantly slips on his white gloves and enters his fingers into the girl's vagina to look for the hiding rodent. And finally a slightly moist cotton mouse is extracted from the reclining girl's lower body, and the German tourists crowd round the stage to look at the mouse, burst out laughing and applaud loudly. Jian laughs too, but stops when a line from Aldous Huxley pops into his head: "*An intellectual is a person who's found one thing that's more interesting than sex.*" He ponders for a few seconds, and wonders if he is still an intellectual.

In the dressing room after the show, Jian assures the girls that he can work with the performance. "No problem," he says, "I can either use a violin or a guitar, or a guitar with a drum, whatever you think will work."

"You sound very positive," Madeleine says, her left eyebrow raised quizzically, "like a real professional."

"I don't think I am a professional. But this job is similar to what I used to do in China, although I have never worked with women before," explains Jian, with a defensive sincerity.

"You never worked with women before? How come? I thought China had a bloody revolution only sixty years ago!" Madeleine laughs. "Listen, Jian. Just so you don't get the wrong idea, let me be straight with you: we are lesbians. We don't go with men, you understand?"

She points her long, plump finger, like a piece of marzipan, at Jian's nose. "We prefer women, and these sex shows are an artistic expression for us. We are not here to serve the male order. Do you understand, Jian?"

The Chinese man nods his head, narrowing his eyes, and silently slurps his bowl of beef noodle soup.

As Madeleine's words are popping in Jian's ears, his eyes cannot help but linger on Anna's scarlet lips and her wavy chestnut hair. She has such a petite body—the kind of figure, Jian admits to himself, that draws him. Normally Anna plays the nurse or an innocent schoolgirl, her short uniform tight around her compact bottom. Jian tries not to think about that right now. Although she has a soft, feminine face and a welcoming, kind expression, her eyes are sharp as knife blades. When she speaks to him she arches back her head, viewing him from above with hooded eyes to repeat in mellower tones what the more turbulent Madeleine has already impressed upon him. For a moment he feels he is in some kind of re-education camp.

"We are not prostitutes, Jian. We are performance artists, you get it, mon ami?"

Anna probably thinks he is nice but a bit limited, a country bump-kin lost in the big city, like she was ten years ago.

"We are artists. And we're serious about our careers. Madeleine is a well-known porn-film maker and acts in most of her films."

Then she hands him a glossy DVD. Jian takes one look at the cover and feels himself squirm: it is the face of Madeleine, her mouth drip-ping with thick, pearl-coloured liquid, against what can only be described as an erect male organ. The man above her is blindfolded and handcuffed. *Male Submission* is the title of the film. "Acted, directed and produced by Madeleine Magdalene," according to the credits.

"It's not designed for men, Jian. It's women taking control—women producing erotica for women. Men are just the props. Sorry."

Jian immediately sees himself blindfolded and tied to a chair, with Madeleine about to pounce on his manhood. It's the first sexual image that has entered his mind for quite a while.

Beyond anatomy, what is the difference between men and women? I watch Anna and Madeleine in their show, and all I can think of is Mu. Her girlish flat-chested body in a loose man's shirt. She uses her words and her voice to live. By Chinese standards, she is modern. But nothing like these white women with their heavy bodies. No comparison. Mu hasn't given up men, but these girls have. Is that the future of women? Maybe they are better off without men. My mother and her secret lipstick and her Erik Satie—men wouldn't let her be the woman she was. Yes, without men, the world might be a more peaceful place. Mao said a woman holds up half the sky. But I think it is more than half. The women of China took over the work of men, wore the same blue shirts, and worked in heavy industry. The gender revolution in China was not a sexual revolution. But for these white women of Pigalle, it's sexual through and through.

I've stopped masturbating. I can't do it any more. I am useless. Even my penis is useless. The only drop of sperm that ever worked is dead and buried. It's like my balls are in cold storage.

12 LONDON, AUGUST 2013

"It's like my balls are in cold storage." This is getting wild, Iona mumbles as she makes her way through Jian's diary. What's really going on between Jian and Mu? Their lives have taken completely different paths. It seems that before, their love was like an overgrown garden, full of weeds and thorns. And now their love is only a wasted land, a barren space; they no longer even mention each other's name, let alone speak of their love—it's lost in these endless, hardly meaningful human encounters. And it has lost its innocence. Iona still clearly remembers the first time she read about Mu in Jian's diary:

> . . . I looked down and she was looking up at me with her big black button eyes. Her eyes were the brightest eyes in that field of eyes before me. I thought I could see them glistening in the centre of the smoky haze . . .

It was an electric scene. It propelled her into the story. But now Iona feels let down, deeply disappointed even. She can't locate the source of the disappointment: whether it's about them or about her own inertia. Suddenly her own relationships with the men she randomly encounters seem hopeless; her love life is a cold, plastic pantomime of raw entanglements in the dark. The love between Mu and Jian seems almost non-physical, she thinks. It is an abstract love, young and innocent. She tries to imagine the way they would make love: childlike, sweet, dreaming, perhaps even laughing sometimes. And now what? Life has betrayed their love. Politics has sold their love to the devil.

Disheartened, Iona puts away the stack of photocopies of Jian's diary pages. She opens the original package, flipping through some other material and searching for something different. Then she finds a clean and elegant page of handwriting—Mu's diary. It doesn't have a date, but judging from the content it might be written not long ago, just before Jian left China in the winter of 2011, perhaps.

How can I ever persuade him to stop living like this? Doesn't he realise he is risking our lives with this manifesto? His grand idea is to hand out the manifesto at the concert next month in the Olympics Stadium. This will be his biggest concert. He and his band have been preparing for it for so long. He's in total denial: doesn't give a damn about the great danger he might face. The concert could be cancelled by the authorities just like that, and everyone will hate Jian, from his fans to his manager. Let alone his band members. But Jian seems to be oblivious of my worries. He is determined to distribute the manifesto at the concert. He says: "I have to do it, Mu!" I am at a loss for words. We have been back together for nearly a year, but some things never change. Does his obstinacy mean I should shut up and just give in to him? Should I just accept who he is and how he does things, and try to live with it? I feel I can no longer follow him, follow his way of thinking. Perhaps I have grown old and tired of his ways.

What a situation! Iona exclaims to herself. But then what a classic case. Jian is not Che Guevara, or Castro, or some other revolutionary hero, but he has all the characteristics of one when it comes to women. Revolutionaries are not good for wives or lovers, even if they have their special magnetism. The wives and lovers always end up sacrificing their lives for their men, for some big idea beyond reality and practicality. That's the fatal attraction. Maybe it's a kind of masochism. Or is it just love? The last idea runs like a stream through Iona's body. Entangled by these feelings, she gets up, and decides to take a walk.

13 PARIS, JULY 2012

After two weeks of working at the club, Jian moves in with the girls. He sleeps in a small box room in which the girls have placed a single mattress for a bed. Although his quarters are cramped and a little dark, everything else is more or less all right. Apart from one thing. The girls have the disturbing habit of walking around engaging in their daily tasks without a stitch of clothing on. Even during the day they are unclad. It's not that Jian has never seen a naked woman before. It's rather that, despite being a punk, an underground anarchist artist—or at least that's how he once thought of himself—he finds that some conservative idea of appropriate behaviour, a sense of natural modesty or some Confucian prudishness, is still there in his personality, and that leads to embarrassment. When he emerges from his dark bedroom and finds a full-frontal display of naked femininity before him, he has absolutely no idea where he is meant to put his eyes. The presence of sculptured flesh has a kind of gravitational pull on him—it's as if his eyes have a life of their own. They suddenly dart in the direction of a nipple, like fish darting towards a prawn in a pond. His brain—and his body—get completely hijacked.

Although Jian has been naked with Chinese girls and knows their bodies well, Western girls are another matter. Jian suspects that he doesn't feel comfortable under the naked gaze of Western girls. They have a physical power, whose source is some kind of aura. Their physicality is much more "physical" than the physicality of Chinese girls. Is it a matter of dimensions? Their breasts, for example, are larger, more developed, like globes of fruit, and they kind of demand attention. And the hourglass curve of the Western girl's body, the breast-waist-hip undulation, is more pronounced, whereas the body of a Chinese girl is more like that of a boy, more subtle, or even asexual, less of a statement. So is it just physical intimidation that leads him to feel embarrassed? It's more than that, of course. It's as if their bodies demand an answer from his body, a kind of hyper-masculine display, as if he must revert to some kind of alpha-male form, like Arnold Schwarzenegger, with rippling muscles and a large member between his legs.

And there is more. Jian thinks that maybe he also feels agitated, even defeated, because they are Westerners. The Westerner, the white Caucasian of Europe, is superior, and the Western woman is the untouchable one—she is the top prize in the world of sexual conquest. He is horrified by the thought, really disturbed that such a regressive idea is there in his mind, but he feels undone by this situation: these untouchable women's bodies emasculate him. Like out of some Fellini film—the giant woman crushes him between her breasts and draws him down between her legs to her sex, a sex he cannot possibly have the capacity to fill or satisfy; all he can do is be swallowed and lost, and then be eaten alive.

Anna is one of the extreme nudists in the apartment. The previous day they were walking down the street and, all of a sudden, she just lifted up her dress and flashed her silky transparent underwear at the passers-by. The only person interested was an old tramp at a pavement cafe, smoking and smiling to himself. It was like one of her performances, but with no music and bad lighting. Right now she has her top off while holding the noisy vacuum cleaner. Her breasts—there they are right in front of him, although he desperately tries not to look—hang down, not quite the Venus de Milo, but at least a goddess of hoovering. Hiding in the corner, peeling onions and chopping garlic, Jian shakes his head weakly. The body of a Western woman alienates him, robbing him of any romantic sentiment.

"We're leaving France next week, Jian." After a morning shower, Anna leans on Jian's door and dries herself with a towel, telling him the news.

"Leaving France? To go where?" asks Jian, with slight hope.

"Well, we're going to the east. Bulgaria, Serbia, Turkey, then to Russia. We've got an invitation from Russia to perform," Anna says, with a slightly excited tone. "You heard of places like Yalta, Varikono, or the Ural Mountains?"

"Ural Mountains?" Jian nods his head vaguely. "That does sound familiar. I think I've read about it in a war novel. So, I'll come with you then?"

"Sorry, we can't take you with us, Jian." Anna lights a cigarette. "We're only self-funded. Flight and accommodation aren't cheap. Plus, I think you will have problems at the border control."

"How long will you be away?" asks Jian weakly.

"Not sure. As long as we can, I hope! But you're welcome to stay here, Jian, looking after the flat. We won't charge you." Now she lowers her voice, hesitates and asks: "By the way, do you think we could borrow your guitar? We need a guitar to play the accompaniment. It's sort of essential for the tour."

Jian stares at Anna in silence.

Madeleine suddenly walks in, one hand holding her coffee, another hand with a bunch of performing leaflets. "Ah, my Chinese friend, it would be so very useful to have your guitar. We'll be stuck without music, and with your guitar Anna and I can play during the show."

A real instrument. Jian turns his head, gazing at his silent guitar in the dim light leaning against his bed. He has been carrying This

Machine Kills Capitalists for many years now. It's the most important possession he has ever had. He still remembers the day he bought it. He was about eighteen, still in his first year at college. That day he took a dozen crumpled and oil-stained yuan from under his mattress—his grandparents had left some savings for him when they died. At that time, music shops only sold traditional Chinese instruments like erhu, yangqin, drums, etc. Jian cycled and checked nearly every single instrument store. Eventually he managed to buy a beautifully made second-hand Fender. The seller told Jian that he had originally bought the guitar from an American agriculture expert he'd met in some northern province. Jian liked the guitar's background story, he especially liked the fact that the American travelling in China was a university professor in agronomy. Ever since the day Jian bought it, he has been true to that instrument, and it has been true to him. But what need has he of it now? The neck sticks up like a bayonet, urging him to action, but he is no longer a soldier. For the last few months it has had a fake existence—a mercenary's instrument to make a few coins on the pavement. No, he doesn't need it any more.

"Yes, Anna, you can have my guitar."

Jian kneels down, lifting his instrument, heavily and painfully.

Later in the night, Jian squats in the empty corner where his guitar used to lean, and thinks to himself: it seems like nothing can last, that everything escapes us in the end. Love, passion, trust. Perhaps even these things I have spent so long believing in and fighting for.

15 LONDON, SEPTEMBER 2013

Autumn in England is a temperamental season. It has this blue-golden daylight for about thirteen days, the grass is green and lush, the canal water is clear and flowing, then all of a sudden the temperature drops. You have to put on a heavy jumper and a long coat, and you might even need warm boots. Overnight, winter has arrived.

Iona strolls through Hyde Park in her wellingtons, walking upon fallen leaves and rotting chestnut shells. When she arrives at the offices of Applegate Books it is nearly evening, the unearthly premature darkness permeates everything like deep ink.

"You look tired, Jonathan. Are you OK?" This observation springs out from Iona's mouth the moment she sees him.

"Well, I'm still alive, just! Though I really do need to catch up on some sleep. I went to India for a week and just got back yesterday actually."

"How was India? You've got a tan." Iona tries to sound flattering.

"Ah, it turned out to be slightly less than good fun. It's . . . it's complicated. Family stuff, you know . . ." Jonathan doesn't seem to want to explain. "But . . . I'm now glad to be back at work."

Family stuff . . . Iona can't help being curious, but she asks nothing further.

"So, how's the translating coming along?" he asks as his mobile rings. Iona remembers the last time, the phone call he received and how he had to abandon her at the Hayward. She watches him checking his phone but not answering it.

"Yes—well, on the whole, but I'm still struggling to work out the whole story, to be honest," Iona answers, a little evasively. "It's very challenging. I've done nothing this complicated before."

"Right." Jonathan holds her gaze for longer than feels normal and she begins to feel her colour rise.

"You know . . . in the most recent diary entries I've read, Jian mentions his grandfather was a war hero who died on the Long March and received the highest medal from the CCP. I did a bit of research but I have no way of knowing who his grandfather really is, or finding out his father's name."

"Oh, brilliant! A war hero's descendant. What a great story! But perhaps it's no surprise then that a family like that might also produce rebels."

"Yes, I thought the same. You hinted in your email that you'd found out more about Jian's parents . . . I'd love to hear anything you've found out."

"Well, finally I've actually got some solid information," Jonathan says, leaning back in his chair and putting his hands behind his head. "I tracked down a person at the British Embassy in Beijing who seems to know the inside story. He asked me to be very discreet, not only because Jian's a dissident musician, but also to protect his own position at the embassy. It makes sense of course. Can't ever be too careful with things like this in China."

Iona studies Jonathan intently as the information spools out of him. She has a notebook open to a blank page in front of her on the table and a pen poised to write down vital facts, but for some reason, just listening to him is enough.

"Now, where to start? Let's begin with Jian's mother first . . . Is there any mention of his mother in the texts? What my contact at the embassy knew was largely hearsay—though it sounds pretty credible to me—but it would be great if we could back it up with information from the diaries and letters."

"Can't help you there, I'm afraid, Jian barely mentions her. Actually, hang on, there was a reference to a knife and Erik Satie. It all seemed shrouded in mystery but pretty bleak, I think. Suicide, perhaps? I didn't get much further. Do you know any more?"

Jonathan leans forward and looks very serious. "I'm afraid your suspicions are correct. It's a really tragic case. I'm not surprised he doesn't bring her up; it must be hard to think about. Her name was Ling Rui and her family was originally from Mongolia—she came from a rich half-Chinese, half-Mongol family in Ulan Bator, but she was born and raised in Beijing like Jian. We thought her background might explain Jian's adopted Mongolian name—Kublai. It seems Jian's mother was very well educated, which I think must have been very rare for a woman in sixties China. She worked as a secretary for the Culture Bureau of the Beijing Communist Party." Iona makes a note of this as Jonathan carries on talking. "It seems she wasn't a wholehearted believer, though: rich family background, good education, access to Western ideas—not the interests of a model party worker. I think Jian grew up largely with his maternal grandparents, and his father was a somewhat shadowy figure in the background who didn't live with them. There was that diary entry about the father nearly hitting Jian and locking him in a room overnight—"

"Yes, that awful moment with the steel ruler. I couldn't get that out of my head for days after I'd translated it."

"Well, let's say Jian's father was away, as far as we know. And one day, a group of Red Guards came to Ling Rui's office. It was a random check, I assume, though perhaps they had a tip-off, I don't really know how these things work. It seems they found a cassette of Erik Satie's piano pieces in a drawer of her desk. Apparently it was normally locked but just by chance on that day it wasn't. Along with the Satie, they found a tube of lipstick and a small cosmetic mirror. That's it. Satie and lipstick!"

Iona stares at him, horrified. "What do you mean? What happened?"

"I think they just saw blood. They went into paroxysms of righteous anger. Just the lipstick, let alone the piano music, would have been enough to slam her into re-education camp for ten years. Of course, no one really knew who or what Satie was, certainly not in the seventies in Beijing, but it was enough to see a photo of a Western man in tweeds. The guards would obviously just 'know' he was a counter-revolutionary. She was forced into the street. They got her up on a temporary stage on her hands and knees and, holding her head down, told her to confess her 'capitalist dog' lifestyle. Angry crowds bayed at her. My contact had to look hard—all the information's under strict lock and key, of course. But he found a horrible account of the event which is how we know all this. After the spectacle onstage she was officially labelled a—hang on, I've got this written down somewhere—yes, this is it: she was labelled 'a bourgeois hidden inside the Party Committee to poison the masses.' And I think it just got worse. Each day more punishment, more haranguing, more public humiliation and more beatings. The report says that on the fourth morning they were told she had died. It seems that Jian was the one who found his mother. He was only four. I can't even imagine what that would do to a four-year-old." Jonathan exhales heavily. "Apparently she was on the bathroom floor, lying in her own blood. She had cut her wrists. And Jian's father didn't even come back for the funeral!" Jonathan stops talking, sighs and leans back. Then he says, with a little venom and power in his voice, "It's pretty fucking tragic."

16 LONDON, SEPTEMBER 2013

Jonathan sips his coffee. For a moment, he seems to hesitate and search to find the right words.

"We've kept this pretty quiet." He looks into Iona's eyes again. "You must also keep it quiet, absolutely confidential, while our publication plan is coming together."

Still in shock from the news about how Jian's mother's died, Iona raises her upper body from the hard white triangular chair, a familiar tension rising from her shoulders to her neck.

"Kublai Jian is the son of a very high-ranking politician."

"Yes, yes, you said that already. Is there more?" Iona waits impatiently. The room is too hot, there are no windows through which to release her tension.

"I mean *very* high-ranking. This is huge, Iona. His father is the current prime minister, Hu Shulai."

"What? Hu Shulai!" Iona exclaims. Although she has had lengthy mental preparation for this news, it is still shocking to have confirmation that he is quite so important. In the Western media Hu is seen as a charismatic character, the most appealing in the Chinese Communist Party of recent years.

Jonathan nods his head, his eyes lighting with a well-groomed twinkle. "Kublai Jian's original name was Hu Xingjian. He cut off contact with his father after his father's second marriage, and changed his name to Kublai Jian. Apparently neither the son nor the father has mentioned each other's existence since then. It was a mutual hatred and denial too, from the information I have."

"Hu Xingjian . . ." Iona repeats that name, so alien, yet so familiar. The name sounds very insignificant to her, any man could have that name in the whole of China or even across the entire continent of East Asia. Kublai Jian is a totally different man from Hu Xingjian. Or perhaps Kublai Jian is the reincarnation of Hu Xingjian.

Iona drinks a mouthful of coffee. Her throat burns.

"It makes me wonder how that country is going to evolve," Jonathan says, "given that one of their most famous dissident artists is the son of their most powerful politician. And it's just unbelievable that their government doesn't want to do anything about it. It seems they've washed their hands of the whole thing."

"But how is that possible?" Iona speaks bitterly. "If he's the prime minster's son, he would be protected surely, even in the West."

"Not if he was perceived to be a problem for the current government. It's all about consolidating power. Not at all surprising in the light of recent Chinese history." Jonathan shrugs. "Think about their previous leader, Deng Xiaoping. His son was pushed out of a third-storey window by the Gang of Four and ended up with a broken back and life in a wheelchair. And there are many other cases. Mao sent his only non-dysfunctional son to the Korean War to be killed by Americans. It's a tradition. Think of the emperors and their offspring."

Iona feels her eyes pricking, as if a mote of sharp dust has got under the lid. The piercing lights are not helping either: bright white neon, as if she's been laid naked on an operating table and there's no place to hide. She covers her eyes to soothe the sharp pain.

"And how do you think Stalin's wife died? Killed herself after an argument with her husband." This is not news to Iona, but she'd not connected the dots before. Jonathan continued, "Jian's father renounced his wife and young son in the seventies by starting a new family. I guess that's why the son ended up such a bleak character."

When they have both finished their coffee and she stands to leave, Jonathan makes a suggestion.

"I've got something else for you. I'd love to know your thoughts. If you like, we can meet for a drink this Friday. I'm just completely caught up weekdays. You can imagine how it is."

Iona can't, but nods her head. "That would be great."

As she's leaving, Jonathan brings out a CD, a blank cover with the title handwritten in marker pen: *Yuan vs. Dollars.*

"Almost forgot to give this to you."

Iona smiles, putting the CD in her handbag.

As the ancient Chinese phrase says, 水落石出—*shui luo shi chu*: when the water rushes over the riverbed, the stones on the bottom become clear to the eye.

Iona sketches out Jian's family tree:

Jian's paternal grandfather, war hero Hu Dongshen, died in the Long March, 1934.

Jian – Original name Hu Kingjian. Changed his name to Kublai Jian when he was 10.

Father Hu Shulai
Current Chinese Prime Minister cut his relations with his family in 1982.

Mother Lin Rui
Former Secretary of BJ Culture Bureau. Committed Suicide in 1976.

Hu's 2nd wife Lin Mingyan works in BJ Sports censorship office. She had a daughter with Hu.

Iona is hungry for any information at all. Now she's started finding things out she wants to know everything, every little detail, every distant family member, in the hope that perhaps Jian might appear, might let her in a little, if only she knows all the facts.

She knows that Jian's father—Hu Shulai—was brought up by strangers in the 1930s. Jian's maternal grandparents, on the other hand, are barely mentioned, though she's pretty sure they're the ones Jian grew up with once his father had taken off. The information Jonathan gives here is a collection of random facts, rumours and titbits of a story, but she gathers that Ling Ting and Bolormaa Bagabandi, Jian's maternal grandparents, were born in the 1920s and were medical doctors from Ulan Bator. The notes say they died sometime in the 1980s in Beijing, which means, by Iona's working, Jian was alone throughout most of his teenager years.

Kublai Jian is, perhaps, the last remaining romantic pessimist on earth, Iona thinks to herself. His personal history, his family history, must have cut every illusion out of his heart. The family, the father, mother, grandparents, were all so driven by ideology and revolutionary sacrifice. No place for the love of a young boy in that. But it seems he did not become utterly cold inside. The boy's romantic soul continued to spin out its song. Iona sighs while she reads the latest diary entries from Jian.

> *No words from her.*
> *Pain in my stomach.*
> *I am cut by a sword.*
> *Her skin is still in the dark.*
> *Her moon-shaped face is lit.*
> *Her dark hair bleeding out.*

She turns to the next entry.

"I don't believe Communists can make people happier. It just doesn't happen. Look at history." That's Vasily Grossman's big statement in

his massive book. It takes him at least three hundred pages to say that, then another five hundred pages to prove it. The icy conclusion of an iceberg of argument, sunk in a history of devastation and madness. The great machine of power, grinding up people and dreams.

Each page has a short, mysterious, melancholy message. She feels weighed down by his words.

The Jewish physicist Viktor Shtrum, a poet-mathematician, struggles with the nightmare of politics on the one side and the dream of visionary truth on the other. Politics wins. He cannot just escape into his quantum mechanical world. Bullets speak the truth, not maths.

I think power will probably beat me as well. I've lost my quantum world. They talk of winners and losers. But there are only losers. Winning is merely the illusion of the winner. The heroic trap.

Iona thinks of poor, alone Jian, stuck in Paris in an empty flat, his buxom naked companions on the road—even his guitar has left him.

Dreamed of my father again. The same dream. The memory of him telling me the same old story, about my grandfather who died during the Long March. "Your grandfather had been eating grass and roots and cooking leather-belt soup for protein while he suffered from gunshot wounds. Starvation and war! So you better behave, you little piece of shit! Your life is built on top of millions of corpses! You understand? You little shit!" His voice in my dream was as coarse as if he were speaking from the grave.

On the next page Iona just finds a few cryptic lines.

Woman, the flower that traps too.
Her world is no longer my world.

Soon she will find another love.
She is a woman, after all.
Woman lives.

How much liberty does a translator have? The question has been playing on Iona's mind. One has to build or subtract to make a text less obscure. That's obvious. But Iona feels something else is going on. Like she herself owns these diaries. Or she now has a right to reshape them, or even a duty to do so. Or is it that the words have lodged in her mind and they are now reproducing themselves in a different way, like viruses in a new host, shaping their own structure? "*She is a woman, after all. Woman lives.*" Did Jian mean women survive better than men because women live beyond the mere political animal? And did he change his mind about politics from reading Grossman's book? How much despair was he in to write "*Bullets speak the truth, not maths*"?

Iona thinks of a little Zen story her mother used to read to her when she was a child: two young fish are swimming along in the water and they meet an older fish swimming the other way who nods to them and says: "Morning, how's the water?" And the two young fish swim on for a bit, and wonder: "What the hell is water?" Iona had always liked the story. Often she feels she can't see clearly what sort of world she is in, even though she has been witnessing it and feeling it vividly.

18 LONDON, SEPTEMBER 2013

These are perhaps the most important diary pages I have ever read from Jian, Iona thinks to herself. Away from her nightlife of pub visits and casual acquaintances, away from her nameless lovers, Iona has spent two sleepless nights trying to digest the contents, and to tidy up her translation.

15 November 2011. Beijing Olympics Stadium. 30,000 young people! Students from Qing Hua University, from People's University, from Beijing Foreign Language University, from Beijing Technological University . . . There were schoolteachers, young poets, young musicians, actors, workers, professors, magazine editors and newspaper journalists, even the secretaries and staff members of government bureaus . . . they all came to the stadium to listen to Yuan vs. Dollars. *Everyone, except my family. So no one witnessed that scene and that moment, the moment where I became the Number One Beijing punk star. But what do I care? My family is dead to me. Especially my father. He is doubly, triply dead. So he missed out on seeing his only son becoming someone significant, someone undeniable, a phenomenon. Well, they left me alone—I had no choice but to become a self-made force. When the lights came on in that massive place, all the eager and youthful eyes were shining and electrified, and then I saw the eyes of Mu. It was like the first time she came to one of my concerts—nearly two decades ago in fact! I remember that first concert, when someone cut off the power and the lights died and she jumped up onto the stage. And now tonight she was in the front row again, those eyes on me, reaching out to me, moist with tears, only more intimate and more intense than in the past.*

Then everyone was singing the song "Orphans of the Revolutionaries." The guys in the band were singing. But I could see, and hear, that the whole stadium, 30,000 young Beijingers, were singing too, beaming back my words, like a giant mirroring echo, a sound that lifted me up beyond the roof, and then seemed to reverberate out of my own mouth:

> *Orphans of orphans*
> *of revolution past,*
> *The fathers' dreams are buried*
> *The children are playing in the Orphans' House.*

And then in the midst of smoke and neon lights we began our usual closing song—"Long March into the Night." As the band played the final chords of the song I stepped to the front of the stage and hurled copies of the manifesto into the crowd. Hands reached out, grabbing at the pages, some people even started to read out loud the first lines. I threw the last bundle of manifestos at the audience and watched the white paper fly through the air like falling snow. Suddenly a swarm of police charged into the stadium. And from that point everything seemed to blur and become unreal: police snatched my manifesto out of the hands of the audience, they jumped onstage and I saw my bassist hit by an electric baton and drop, like a limp puppet, a sprawling body on the floor. The screams of the crowd gave me a chilled, sick feeling in my stomach. A dull thud shook me from the top of my head down through my spine, and a burning, sparking pain unleashed itself. My limbs exploded, and my face hit the ground. I found myself sucking on dust, and then blank darkness swallowed everything.

Iona is transfixed. Her insides twist and churn. Only a few months ago she was translating that other concert—that exciting concert when Jian was still only twenty—and now this one: how familiar and yet how very different.

A few hours later, past midnight, we found ourselves in a police station, bruised and aching. It was the Haidian District Branch, not far from our flat, a dirty place, with shabby yellow-green walls and windy corridors. We said nothing. The cops divided us up, taking us into separate rooms for interrogation, one by one. First, they took bassist Raohao, then guitarist Yanwu and then drummer Sunxin. I was the last to be interrogated. I was waiting, my hands in cuffs, with a dog-faced officer of the People's Police who was eating a pork bun, and staring at me, like I was a curious insect, or a carp fish dragged out of the river. Simply waiting. Then they came for me. All they did was put me in a room and take my ID card away. I was sure everyone else was being questioned or slapped about. I was secured to a shelf along the wall made of indestructible iron with a pair of handcuffs and just left there. My head was throbbing.

At dawn, they brought us into a larger main interrogation room. We were held apart and were not allowed to speak to each other. Then relatives of my band members came to visit. I recognised Yanwu's uncle, who used to come to all our concerts. Bail was put up; low chatter rumbled on; there were furtive looks, pointing, frowns. Policemen busied themselves with paperwork, and cigarette smoke from Red Tower filters filled the air. By noon, my three buddies were let out of the police station on bail. Then there was me, only me, always watched and always in handcuffs. Yet there still had been no interrogation. Then a policeman came with a food box and a bottle of water for me and unlocked my handcuffs. Inside the box there were three cold buns.

At some point in the afternoon, I heard Mu come to visit me. (I heard the special ringtone of her mobile echoing down the corridor—the ringtone was one of my songs—and her voice, angry and nearly crying, begging the police to let her in.) But they were refusing to let her visit me. I thought I heard a man's emotionless voice: "We can't let you see him, only family members are allowed." Then silence. Sometime later two police officers came to take me out, and shoved me into the back of an old army jeep with steel mesh on the windows. I was driven some-where—here, wherever this is. I can only imagine that this is a political prison, perhaps I'm somewhere in the eastern sector of He Bei Province, under the Shanhai Pass of the Great Wall. But I can't be sure. I saw nothing. The shutters were pulled down in the little box I was in at the back of the jeep. I could only catch brief glimpses. After hours on the road we stopped and they got me out of the jeep, roughly pulling my legs and tugging at my arms, and now finally I could see where we were. It looked like a hardcore, high-security operation. I know now this is the Shanhai Pass Confinement Camp. I've been thinking a lot about the famous Misty Poet, Hai Zi. I must have passed the railway track where he lay down to be cut open by that great locomotive, that railway track Mu and I once visited when we were students. He was Mu's favourite poet. I remember Mu lay down on the steel tracks and imagined the infinite nothingness of poetic death. I feared, as the jeep finally stopped, that no one would ever know where I was. All communications would be banned. All exits closed . . .

For Iona, it feels like the ruler raised in the air once again. The father's hand never landed on his son's head. It happened thirty years later. Then it hit the son with full force, delivered by the hands of a state police gang.

19 QING HUANG DAO 780 POLITICAL PRISON, CHINA, DECEMBER 2011

Kublai Jian was in Qing Huang Dao 780 Political Prison, the former Shanhaiguan Pass Confinement Camp. And indeed, he had passed over the railway track on the journey, the track on which, years before, Hai Zi had laid down his body and allowed himself to be decapitated.

Over the course of two weeks the guards left Jian in a cell and watched him, as he waited for his "trial." He wasn't handcuffed or beaten and he was isolated from other prisoners. They treated him in a controlled manner, cold, even slightly polite sometimes. Guards like automatons. Unlike the Beijing Haidian Police Station where he had been arrested, this place was very clean, scrubbed, as if even the sight of dirt, like freedom, was also withheld from the prisoners, so as to cut them off from all life. He was charged with engaging in "subversive anti-state activities." He was not surprised by this. Everyone got charged with some crime in the end. The reality of the arrest was harder than he expected, but then it flowed over him, since he felt all sense of control had left long ago. Perhaps his drive to perform and campaign had all been aimed at this in the end. Part of him now accepted it as a kind of fate. That all roads, however he travelled them, would lead here.

During that month, Jian "disappeared" from the public eye. No contact whatsoever was allowed. In fact, no one even knew where he was. The people who knew him had to live with that thorn in their sides: his absence. Some people in the capital were trying to help Jian. But they could do nothing. A group of fans tried to protest on the streets in Beijing, in front of public spaces like the Central Fine Arts

Exhibition Hall or Beijing Poly Plaza, or even Kempinski Hotel, playing his music and brandishing campaigning banners. But they were either ignored or intimidated by the authorities. It looked hopeless.

However, suddenly things began to happen, though just how and why wasn't clear. First, a warden in the prison received an important phone call from an undisclosed government telephone number. The order came from high up to transfer Jian from prison to a secret destination. Jian was immediately disappeared from Qing Huang Dao 780 Political Prison.

A Western fan of *Yuan vs. Dollars*, living in Beijing and working at the British Embassy, found out where Jian was being held. He had heard Jian's trial would be soon and wanted to help. But then, only a week later, he found out that the trial was indefinitely postponed. No reason given, no law cited. "Someone from the higher echelons of government made a phone call," the rumour said. Three weeks later, Jian was secretly driven to the south of China with a brand-new British tourist visa. On 29 December 2011, the day the snow became dirty and the frost broke, he left China via Hong Kong, with no resistance by the authorities.

When the plane took off from Hong Kong, Jian's eyes looked down at the blue water underneath him. The last few weeks had left him utterly exhausted, and utterly unable to collect his thoughts. He was just running, just living on his reflexes, which were about to fuse, and leave him in some stage beyond collapse. He had no idea what was ahead of him, or what he had left behind. The doors in Qing Huang Dao 780 Political Prison had been closed, slammed shut, cutting him off from the outside space, but also shutting him out from his past. But then those very doors had opened again. But who had walked out? Like the ghost of Misty Poet Hai Zi, Jian was now on a plane, his body being transported into the sky: a different kind of prison. His soul had been poured out and had seeped into the earth under the Great Wall, melting beneath the tracks leading into that dark tunnel. That day the events of 1989 seemed somehow alive again and his student self sat alongside the Kublai Jian of 2011, and thought about the long journey they'd taken together. It was the day he wrote his long letter to Mu.

Dearest Mu,

The sun is piercing, old bastard sky. I am feeling empty and bare. Nothing is in my soul, apart from the image of you.

I am writing to you from a place I cannot tell you about yet. Perhaps when I am safe I will be able to let you know where I am. I don't know exactly what the plan is and what my future might hold. One thing is for sure—I will try to stay free and alive, for you. And whatever happens, these ideas I have stuck by all my life— the beliefs that landed me here in the first place—I cannot let them go. I must live for them. I know we'll see each other again, my love, but how long until that day I cannot tell . . .

20 LONDON, SEPTEMBER 2013

From: Jonathan.Barker@applegate.co.uk
To: Iona1982@gmail.com
Subject: Read this!

Dear Iona

A million thanks for sending that powerful diary entry so quickly. What a find! It's incredible to read about Jian leaving China. I managed to get hold of my contact at the embassy in Beijing and he told me something even more shocking. He says that the rumour in Beijing is that Jian's own father had him removed from the country. The current Chinese prime minister himself!

I think it might be wise if you're a bit cagey, or better still, completely discreet, if you ever get asked about what you're working on. Sorry to seem paranoid, but you never know what might happen when you're dealing with China!

Apropos your question about the shape of the text, I feel even more excited now about the idea of really making this "book." The story is incredible and what it tells us about modern China, quite apart from being downright tragic—well, it just must be heard. Obviously I can tell you in more detail about my plans when we meet, but as a basic outline, this is what I'm thinking:

First off, I have mapped out the book as a dialogue led by Jian and Mu as two contrasting voices that reveal the political state in China and the struggle of individualism. Here is the basic vision

I have. Mu—how are we to see her in the future book? Well, for me, her voice provides the backbone, the continuity, supporting our access to Jian. She is our lens, providing the focus, the spot-light, even if a bit dim, through which the elusive Jian starts to appear. Mu and Jian in my mind are opposites, but connected. They are two facets of the great contemporary enigma: China. Jian is from the north, Mu from the south. Jian is Chinese aris-tocracy. Mu is the salt of the earth. Most of all: Jian is dark fire. I know it sounds perverse or even pretentious, but I've been thinking of the rockers of old, like Jim Morrison, but instead of dying in a cold bath in a Parisian one-star hotel, he lives and writes his manifesto against all odds. And, better still, he moves into another world, our world, the West, but undercover, kind of like Rimbaud disappearing into the Indonesian jungle after he gave up poetry. Mu is like Yoko Ono, the ex-peasant avant-garde, presenting an ideal of modern Chinese youth. And somehow they are joined, while also seeming to be opposed souls in their beliefs and their struggles.

As you can see, it's not all worked out yet, but that's how far I've got with the help of your pages. Does that seem to fit what you think of them? You're the closest to them by far, so I'd really value your thoughts. Let's meet up, if you can still do Friday. Say six at the George, 13 Addison Avenue—it's just round the corner from here.

Jonathan

Iona stands in front of her mirror wearing her fourth possible outfit for the evening. She plays with the hem of her long navy dress—it's terribly professional. With only minutes to go before she has to leave, she pulls off the navy and slips on the only low-cut dress in her wardrobe—a rich burgundy red—picks up her keys and leaves the flat.

The atmosphere at Iona's meeting with Jonathan couldn't be more different from the last couple of times. In a cosy pub near Applegate Books he is very casual and full of good humour. They start with red wine, each cradling a globe-like glass. He enthuses about his recent conversation with none other than Henry Kissinger, whose memoirs Jonathan is publishing. Fascinating man, apparently. Jonathan has worked up an appetite, and would Iona like a bite to eat? He's had a heavy week, he wants proper food not pub snacks. Let's go somewhere good, he says. On me, he says, or rather, on Applegate, and laughs. If she has no suggestions, he does. A great little place near Greek Street. Meanwhile, Iona is quietly wondering why he won't be going back home to his wife. But she says nothing.

An hour later, they are sitting in a beautifully lit French fish restaurant in Soho. They share a bottle, and the rendezvous stretches into a night-long daze of words and moods. Iona is a light drinker; Jonathan drinks deeply, but clearly knows how to pace himself. Soon the second bottle is finished, and then there's a pint at a pub round the corner.

On the way back to Angel, she can't even tell which direction Chapel Market is. The atmosphere of the night streets seems illuminated by her own anticipation, an almost feverish expectation that sweetens the air. They find her flat. And as soon as they get through the door and cross her rug, they fall on her bed without a word from their lips, as if an invisible sign has been given that they now both obey. He kisses her lightly on her lips. She is only half conscious with this man, a shadowy but irresistible force on her unmade bed. They make love. Jonathan seems to be very in control, of himself and of her body, and for a moment she feels a kind of perfect but painful beauty, the surrender and the desire for more surrender welling within her body. Her climax rolls out from her centre to her tips. She senses his breathless spasms—but not inside her. Warm foam on her thigh. They fall apart, panting, the cooler air reoccupying their steaming skin. A kind of half-sleep envelops them, blanking out any care, whether cares of the day, or cares of the night. And then in the peaceful half-light, he strokes her back and whispers that he must go home. It is a quarter past one, after all. Iona watches him from her bed, slipping into his clothes. The night is over, she thinks. "Take this," she murmurs, holding up a sock. He smiles, looking a little embarrassed. They now only have words for the simplest things. She puts on her pyjamas. Then he says something that brings them back to their professional relationship, abandoned sometime over the course of the evening.

"Let me know how you get on with the rest of the translation."

He kisses her forehead in the dark. He leaves like a boss after a long day, leaving his exhausted secretary with her computer and a few letters to finish. Is that how it is? Iona wonders. The door closes. Later, as she waits for the kettle to boil she watches the steam rise and fade, leaving its trace of condensation on the kitchen tiles. The room is still filled with the sound of their breathing, and perfumed with the ripe smell of sex. Somehow the Zen story from her childhood returns to her: the fish swims in the sea and asks, What the hell is water? Where is the sea?

The next morning Iona wakes up with a serious hangover. She tries to remember how she got from the pub near Applegate Books to her flat. She vaguely remembers the meal, their mutual seduction and the ensuing amorous meltdown into each other. And she can picture the moment she brought her hand to his while standing in the street trying to find a taxi. Perhaps that's when the idea of sleeping with him became a certainty—she reached for his hand in the dark street, and he took hers naturally.

She stands under the shower, letting the hot water cascade over her skin, assailed by chaotic thoughts. She makes a pot of tea, now her head is clearer. She puts on Jian's CD, *Yuan vs. Dollars*, while changing the bed sheets. The first song—"Long March into the Night," the one Jian keeps mentioning—sends its sonic wave into Iona's ears.

> *Hey little sister,*
> *Let me take you down the street,*
> *the long march is waiting,*
> *that's where we gonna meet.*
> *You don't need no San Francisco,*
> *nor Eiffel Tower for your home,*
> *no Champs-Élysées,*
> *no Golden Dome.*
> *You say money is poetry,*
> *I say your freedom is a brick in the wall.*
> *We got no coins in our pocket,*
> *we held no candles in our hands,*
> *on the long march to the light,*

on the long march to the night.
Hey little sister,
Let me take you down the street,
I'll show you a place,
a place where the Liars meet,
a place where Uncle Joe beats his people with a belt,
a place where the hands sign the contract.
The long march is waiting.
The long march is waiting.

She watches the tulips by the window tremble slightly in the blast of the music as she puts the dirty bedclothes into the washing machine. She comes back and listens to the same song for a second time. Then she turns it off. She feels, irrationally, a kind of resentment towards this intrusion of the real Jian, unedited by her own imagination. She can't take it, not this morning.

She sits at her desk and works on the next letter. The Chinese letter has a handwritten note in English clipped to its front page: "*The last letter Mu received from Jian.*" Once again she wonders whose handwriting it might be—perhaps Jonathan's, or his editor, Maria's. Or his assistant, Suzy's. Or even Mu's own—it's definitely as neat and composed as her diary entries. Who knows who else has been looking at these letters? Slowly, Iona reads.

A summer day, 2012

Mu,

> *We both know that there's been nothing, no word, between us for the last few months. I don't know where to write to you. So here is my last letter to our Beijing address, whether you read it or not. It's me being foolish, perhaps, breaking through the silence—no doubt that's what you'll think.*
>
> *Right now, where am I? I've just left Paris and I'm on a train towards the south. Paris was a strange place, the fancy*

scene around the Seine doesn't do anything for me. Even the women there! They were too First World for a Third World man. And I have finally made some contacts in Marseilles, through which I hope I'll be able get some work. There are jobs on ships here that don't require papers or much English. Maybe I could be a sailor, living on the blue sea rather than the dirty land.

I feel like I have been drifting up and down this European landscape over the last couple of months, like a cockroach running on the dirt. But Europe is a grim continent: they think everything starts from here, from themselves, from their land. Often you encounter some lonely cluster of stony homes in the middle of the countryside, and there'll be a woman doing some housework in her garden, a television glowing inside, and trees glimpsed through telegraph poles, the murmur of leaves the only sound. I picture myself living in houses like these, with that kind of life—is it life? For me it's dead, like the bottom of a well. If I were Woody Guthrie, I would sing: "This land is not my land, this land is not for you or for me." China is not here. You are not here. And my manifesto means nothing in this land and to these people. 乡愁—xiang chou—is the only emotion I have. I miss my land. There is no reason for me to put down my roots here, and there is no familiar earth under my feet. My roots have dried up and broken off.

The sunlight, too, feels remote, as if I'm moving far away from the source, as if the sun is trying to escape from me. The sun doesn't recognise me any more. My body's numb. It limps along like a strange loping animal, stiff, joints cracking, a cold-blooded lizard—yesterday's man in ragged but once fashionable clothes. That's how I feel on this train. I am no longer a soldier. There's no one waiting for me at my destination. The train will spew me out, like a cat pukes up a hairball. And where then . . . ?

Just the wind waiting to roll me along some small-town high street?

Every now and then, just for a second, I think I'm in China. It chills me and warms me at the same time: my country looms heavy, bigger even than my mind, but sometimes small too, like a point in memory. Each time I see a brown wheat field or an expanse of standing corn, I think of those intense yellow rapeseed fields of the Huabei Plains, and those wrinkle-faced peasants, shovels on their shoulders, walking like statues in the dirt, with glass-eyed buffalo following. Then the streets and their life appear in my mind, the smells and tastes, sashimi oil from hidden jars, the laughter of fighting kids, bicycle bells—even the deafening fireworks of the Spring Festival . . . These images and sounds flow as a river whose mirrored surface shimmers with sadness.

And you, my woman far away. Maybe you are beyond this crying and laughing. I've been thinking of your father. A strong man, cancer in his throat, going through the motions of life even as the anarchic cells invade each corner of his body-box. But which force is stronger? The evil cells or your father's spirit? I'm finding hope difficult at the moment, but I do hope your father survives.

My last words to you in this letter: whatever happens with your life and my life, I still have this love for you. So now I give it to you, wherever you are.

Your Jian

SEVEN | RETURN HOME

埏埴以为器，当其无，有器之用。
凿户牖以为室，当其无，有室之用。

yan zhi yi wei qi, dang qi wu, you qi zhi yong.
Zao hu yong yi wei shi, dang qi wu, you shi zhi
  yong.

We turn clay to make a vessel;
But it is upon the space where there is nothing
  that the usefulness of the vessel depends.
We pierce doors and windows to make a house;
And it is upon these spaces where there is
  nothing that the usefulness of the house
  depends.

TAO TE CHING, LAOZI (PHILOSOPHER, 604–531 BC)

1　LONDON, OCTOBER 2013

Iona stares at the photocopy of two black-and-white snapshots on her desk. Who are these people? One is an old Chinese lady in front of a house, sunlight coming from the low winter sky; the other is a little girl holding a balloon before a tree-planted yard. They must have been pasted in Mu's diary. They look old and faded.

Iona can't help but wonder whether the little girl with the balloon is a young Mu. She has no way of knowing. There is a TV aerial sticking out on the girl's left side, by the wall. Is that Mu's family house in the south? And the old woman smiling under two Chinese lanterns, could that be Mu's grandmother? Or Jian's grandmother, perhaps. The little tree in the clay pot looks like a bay tree or a small orange tree. She seems to remember seeing them everywhere in people's gardens when she visited southern China. Iona calls Jonathan's mobile.

"Hello?"

"Hi, it's me," Iona says, feeling a swell of confusion and awkwardness rising from that night, *their night*.

"Hi . . . Iona?" Jonathan is checking it's her; she feels her chest go tight at his lack of recognition. Then his voice softens and sounds slightly ambiguous. "Are you all right?"

"Yes, I'm fine. Do you have a moment?"

"I'm in my office. I've got—um, five minutes before my next meeting. Fire away."

"Did you manage to take a look at those photos—the two black-and-white photos?" Iona prompts him. "You didn't mention the photos. One is of an old lady standing in front of her house, well, I presume it's her house; the other one is of a little girl holding a balloon."

". . . the girl with a balloon . . ." He pauses, then two seconds later: "Yes, I do remember them, vaguely. What about them?"

"Well, do you know who they are? Would the little girl be Mu when she was a child? And I think the old lady could be Mu's or Jian's grandmother perhaps?"

"Iona, you might think I know more than you do from those documents, but I don't! Really I don't. I'm not the one who reads Chinese! I've looked through all the letters, diaries and photos, again and again, but without the language skills I'm at a complete loss. I'm just as excited as you are but I don't have any secret knowledge."

"Right, OK, sorry. Looking at the photos, there are clues that make me think they might have been taken in southern China—the architecture, the plants . . . that's why I think the little girl might be Mu . . . but it's all guesswork, really," Iona murmurs slowly.

A pause. Then Iona hears him say, "When can I see you again?"

2 BEIJING, JUNE 2012

A year and a few months ago, far away from Iona's evening desk, on a United Airlines flight from Boston to Beijing, Mu returns home. Beijing hasn't changed much since she's been away; the familiar scent and sights of the capital's polluted air—even thicker than before— still hangs in the sky like a noxious soup cloud. As she enters her one-bedroom flat on Beijing's Third Ring Road, she instantly throws herself on the dusty bed. She is overtaken by a deep sleep for three days, lying motionless, blank, dreamless, without dimension.

She wakes up and walks downstairs to her mailbox. It's been a while since she was home and there's the standard accumulation of glossy flyers and overdue bills—then she finds a lone letter. She looks at the stamp—a European stamp postmarked two months ago, and then redirected from Boston to Beijing. Mu can find no address, though, as she turns it over in her hands. It must have arrived when she was in Maine on her own—how odd that Bruce never mentioned it. She sits on the cold step in her pyjamas and opens the letter.

Dearest Mu,

I received your letter finally—the one about you going to America. America! Old Hell! I don't know how it made it to me, across seas and continents, but somehow it did. But that was two months ago, so who knows where you are now. I'm going to try this Boston address, but I don't hold out much hope—on tour means on the road, surely. What a surreal concept; my world is in stasis. I don't know what it is to explore any longer. I bury inside myself: that's all there is left.

I am still in an in-between state. I'm waiting for my asylum application to be granted. That is all. No news, no change—or at least that's how I feel after days in this grey box. I can't see what there is beyond this right now, I can't ever see you here with me, or us together in Beijing any more. Even my memories of our flat are hazy and dissolving. I hope you're having a good time, wherever you are. And I hope you can lead the life you've always wanted to live. America must be better than China, whatever I think of it.

You should start a new life, a brand-new life without me.
Good luck, Mu,
Jian

3 BEIJING, JUNE 2012

A week passes. She recovers. She thinks and plans in her pyjamas at the kitchen table each evening, sitting in front of a bowl of instant noodles. Now her flat is nearly empty. The pillows and sheets are packed in a box. Plates, cups and kitchen utensils are in another. Books and CDs are stuffed into two large suitcases. Mu's and Jian's clothes, divided into two separate bundles, lie like skins cast off their backs arranged in a dead geometry. All their belongings wait in the middle of the main room to be removed.

The living room is quiet. There's only the occasional sound of a water pipe, a twisting groan from under the toilet. Already the dust is settling on the bare floor, like the slow, thick flow of time. Mu sits on the edge of the empty mattress on which she and Jian used to spend their nights, lying together, sleeping, touching. She gazes at the remaining furnishings: the handmade lamp, the broken rattan chair, the old carpet from Pan Jianyuan market, the dried-out bamboo plants outside on the balcony. These things should be familiar to her; she and Jian lived here together only thirteen months ago. So why do they appear so alien? It's like her sense of belonging is something she cannot recognise any more. But then, she remembers, they were never theirs to begin with. They came with the flat—such an ugly, tasteless assortment of cheap cast-offs. It's so obvious: now that their meanings have been stripped from them, they no longer speak to her. And soon, after Mu leaves, new tenants will come, putting their own tablecloth on the table, wrapping their own bed sheets round the same mattress, and making these objects their own. What's this strange merging of life with the bare world of things? She tries to imagine the future of the flat without her and Jian. Nothing will remain of their presence as the new bodies move about, sit, sleep, breathe and dream.

Then there's the corner, beside their mattress, the corner where Little Shu's cot used to be. The cot was removed a few days after the baby died. The corner has been left empty and she has tried to sleep facing the other side of the room ever since. It is as if looking at the shadow of the cot that was once there is a bad omen for her future life.

One afternoon people from the removal company arrive. The workers, beefy young men with rough voices, carry her boxes and suitcases out in waves. With an indifferent efficiency it's all loaded onto the back of the truck. Doors are slammed shut, and she is squeezed into the front of the truck. Then they are off. They drive towards the storage depot as if they are on a journey to a cemetery. An hour later, she stands in an industrial space, watching her belongings—to which she no longer belongs—disappearing into a dark storage unit. It has a number: E33468. They should store her behind this number as well, she thinks. She'll exist in suspended animation till one day someone comes to release her.

4 ZHEJIANG PROVINCE, JUNE 2012

Our heroine's new station in life, it seems, has very little to do with Slam Poetry art-rock performances. Sabotage Sister evaporated somehow, along Highway 71, in the desert landscapes of western USA, or disappeared down a drain in a downtown Chicago side street, or in a polite Boston diner with its gleaming parking lot out back. When she returned to China, she stopped writing her diary for some months. She felt aged by the tour, as if she had suddenly gained twenty years; and she had put on some weight. She felt her body had grown so heavy that she could no longer do a somersault or stand on her head, things she used to practise at college. "Money is poetry, freedom is a brick on the wall." Jian's words strangely echo in her ears after the U.S. tour.

The afternoon on which Mu clears out of her flat and puts everything into storage, she walks back to the street where she and Jian used to live. She looks up at the flat once more. She lowers her gaze. She has kept the key, as well as the access to her mailbox. There is only one thing that makes her hesitate about when to return the key to the landlord: her hopes, perhaps foolish, that she might receive something from Jian. A final letter maybe, or many letters, or some sort of real farewell. She is not sure. Like a stray dog, she wanders about under her building for a while, carrying only her handbag. Ten minutes later, she stops at an old pancake stall to eat as she makes her final decision. Then she jumps in a taxi—direction: Beijing Railway Station. There she buys a one-way ticket for the earliest train she can get on, down to her southern province.

She stays with her parents for nearly a hundred days in the village where she grew up. Her father is at his end. The hospital in Shanghai

281

has given up on him and he's come home. The family is still trying to find ways to cure him with all kinds of traditional herbs. But cancer is cancer. Especially in its final stages. There is no mistaking it. For Mu, there is little to do, and she spends her time digging vegetables in the family plot. They used to grow beans and cucumbers when she was young, and her mother would take them to the market to sell. Now Mu resumes that labour. She spends several hours a day bending over, prostrating herself almost, to get small green things to send out shoots, or to prevent them from being eaten by slugs or hens. She is surprised that she still remembers how to grow them. Although a bit clumsy, she knows how to arrange the poles and to set strings to support the climbing plants. Maybe that's how life is, she thinks. Everything needs support.

In the heat, under the blue, encircled by the profile of egg-shaped hills, among flies and mosquitoes, her wordless companions, she sets about trying to re-create the small yam field which her mother had abandoned when her father fell ill. They don't need to grow their own yams any more—they can buy a kilo of yams in the market, in any season, for only eight yuan. But Mu tells herself: isn't this what village life is all about? It has been a strange time; her mind and body feel as if they have separated and left behind an empty skeleton. Those days in Beijing and in the U.S. are like a long-distant dream, evaporated in the southern China heat. The wind occasionally refreshes her sweating skin, but then she will be anguished again by the sound of her father coughing behind her as he tries to rearrange his aching limbs in his chair. Sometimes, with moist eyes, the father eyes his daughter who has returned so transformed and yet remains the same serious child. Mother too watches her spooling out the strings for the cucumber vines and beans. She doesn't ask much about her daughter's American experience; it is as if nothing is worthy of conversation now that the old man is in his final days.

5 ZHEJIANG PROVINCE, JUNE 2012

We know very well how families are in everyday patterns of life. No daughter or son can escape the family interrogation. It always begins subtly with a sigh, clearing of a throat, or rustling of the morning paper, a spike of activity in the kitchen. On this morning, the interrogation session begins while Mu's father is digesting his day's cocktail of medicinal syrup and tonics. Mother looks agitated, and is vigorously scrubbing a pot. Suddenly there is a clang of the pot being shoved onto the drying rack, and, without even turning round to her daughter, Mother gets straight down to business.

"Tell me, Mu, what are your plans for the future?"

"What future? You mean my work?"

"I don't see you getting interested in your career exactly . . . But no, I meant men! Your future with a man!" Her voice is slightly shrill.

"I just came back from America, Mother, give me a break." The daughter is instantly defiant.

"But do you not have a new boyfriend?"

Walking towards the garden, Mu pretends she hasn't heard, but her mother chases her.

"Don't tell me you are still with Jian, you told me you split up long ago."

"We are no longer together," mumbles Mu.

"That's good. You see, I have never liked him. He is not a reliable person in my eyes," her mother exclaims, conviction billowing in her breast. "I think it's good that you two have separated. But you must be quick, find someone urgently! We need to see grandchildren before it's too late!"

Mu's mother seems in her usual state of desperation whenever this subject comes up.

Her daughter gazes across the garden towards the hills in the distance, as if searching for a vision of her own future.

"A musician, or any artist, is not going to bring a woman a good life anyway, even if he is a handsome crane standing amid a flock of chickens. Family is family, not an endless concert for drug addicts." Then, with a pause and a depression of her brows, and stammering a little: "You need a husband with real substance—an upright man of bamboo quality, with a family house and good savings!"

"Do I? Men of bamboo quality often have no savings at all," Mu replies.

"You are getting old! A girl over thirty isn't worth much, no man will turn his head to look at you!"

Later that night Mu sits in her room, writing her diary, while her parents sleep across the hall.

"Family is family, not an endless concert for drug addicts."

What is a family? Isn't it a prison in the name of love and responsibility? As much as I love my father, I also love my freedom. If I must choose, I would prefer to live for my freedom than for my family. But my family won't let me.

Since baby Shu's death, my mother almost never mentioned Jian—it's as if it never happened. She didn't want to know about my life with Jian. Not our world, not Jian, not my son, not my pain. I still remember that cold loneliness—when we brought back Little Shu's urn from one of Beijing's crypts. I felt so alone when Jian and I rode the subway back to the flat, even though his hand was on my shoulder. Yes, what does it mean, a family? If Little Shu were alive, I would love him in a different way from how my mother "loves" me, then I would perhaps understand what a family really means.

6 ZHEJIANG PROVINCE, JUNE 2012

"How did Dad start painting in the first place, Mum?" Mu asks.

The daughter thinks about how difficult it is to uncover her father's story. He never speaks about his past. A very self-effacing person, her father has barely expressed his opinions on anything, whether in the house or outside. And now, the third-stage throat cancer has robbed him of his speech forever. Before it is too late, Mu thinks, I must understand everything about him.

"Well, I never really understood that either. He was just a rice farmer and all his family members had always worked on the land." Her mother has a wistful look on her face. "I remember he mentioned a painter's name, a painter from some Western country. But, you know, a peasant like me, I wouldn't recognise the names."

In the next room, the father hears the conversation between his daughter and his wife. He writes down two words, 梵高 (Van Gogh), on a piece of paper, and shows it to Mu as she comes in with his daily herbal drink. Then he begins to tell her his story, word by word, on a student notebook he found on Mu's dusty shelf.

From fragmentary details her father manages to write down when he has the strength, Mu tries to piece together his story. He writes that he grew up working in rice paddies and raising pigs. His hands were rough from using a hoe and his body sinewy from lifting and digging. He didn't ever think about culture or art—impossible for Mu to imagine now. He just thought about rain and heat, and how to make the plants produce fruits, how to raise pigs. Then one day, when he was about eighteen, he saw something he'd never seen before. It was a photograph of Van Gogh's painting *The Starry Night*. He did not under-stand what he was looking at, but the Dutch painter's brush, like a magical whirlpool, pulled him into another world, a world free from labour and poverty of expression. From that moment he wanted to become a painter, not just a man of fieldwork. He began to draw. To make use of his painting skills, the party told him to work in the draw-ing group; his title would be "artist-worker." From that day on, this artist-worker's job would be to paint smiling peasants in their straw hats in the rice fields under the bright sun; or a woman driver on a brand-new tractor, confidently resting her hands upon the wheel and gazing towards the horizon; or a group of strong fishermen spreading their nets upon the water while hundreds of fish lie captured on their boat. And a slogan would be written on top of every poster: "Our Destination is the Morning Sun. Our Leader is the Great Captain."

Then something terrible happened. One day, Mu's father painted a rice farmer's face on the back of an old poster. In the night, rain drenched the painting, and the farmer's smiling face became imprinted with the lines of the earlier drawing, that of a horse's arse. This faint yet manifest horse's arse branded Mu's father an anti-revolutionary, a "right-wing roader." At the age of twenty-three he became an enemy of the people, and was forced to confess his "anti-revolutionary con-spiracy." In his written confession, he told the party that he couldn't understand how he could be an enemy of the people since he was the son of the poorest of the poor. *"From the bottom of my heart, I love the people, the peasants, the proletariat. And I respect them as much as I respect the land that has raised me, and the soil which has borne us the food we eat. I cannot be an enemy of the proletariat."* On his bed, Mu's father writes these words painfully for his daughter, recalling a dark and cold night from his deeply forgotten past, some decades ago, when he was forced to write his confession in the camp, under the faint and flickering light of an oil lamp.

7 LONDON, OCTOBER 2013

Iona has in front of her a photocopy of a scrappy piece of paper, and on it the most beautiful handwriting she has ever seen. Although it is a second-hand or even a third-hand photocopy, she can still decipher the markings of the original writing paper—the back of a piece of herbal-medicine wrapping paper. In fact, she can still read the faint print of the ingredients for the herb medicines: 干枸杞 (dried gooseberry), 橘皮 (orange skins), 梨树膏 (pear-tree roots), 蛇粉 (snake powder), as well as some Chinese plants with names she doesn't recognise. The writing has its own particular calligraphy style, with very careful and elegant strokes. It reminds her of Mu's style. Perhaps it is her father's handwriting, she thinks.

Judging from what's written on the wrapping paper—走资派 (capitalist roader)—Iona is sure that the note was written by Mu's father. And the next diary entry from Mu proves her right.

I was never taught at school the history of those years of my father's generation. I feel like I must record his words. Perhaps one day I could show Jian these pages and he would understand another revolutionary and what he went through. My father, the young artist-worker, was sent away in the 1960s and punished with hard labour. Along with other "running dogs of capitalism," he was living in a buffalo shed in a remote mountain region. His daily work included cutting grass to feed pigs and cows, collecting cow shit for the yam fields, planting rice while up to his thighs in the muddy water, fertilising fruit trees, and so on. When the planting and harvest seasons had passed, he would join other workers to make bricks—carrying mud and clay, mixing it with water, hardening the clay in the oven, then cutting the bricks and distributing them to villagers. He told me he probably made about ten thousand bricks with his own hands. Each night after supper, the workers would be divided into groups to study Marx and Lenin under the sparsely distributed oil lamps. Day and night they worked and studied; no one had any time to idle or to contemplate the meaning of life, my father wrote. As the Great Leader said: "First make a big pie, then everyone can get a slice!" Every proletariat agreed on this sort of canon, even the punished ones—agreed with all their heart.

Sleeping alongside the buffalo, lonely but stoical, my father lived there for years. He hadn't met my mother yet; he had no friends at all; he was self-critical. But he discreetly painted the wheat fields Van Gogh's way—no people in the landscape, while nature appeared crazy and dreamlike. Of course he didn't show these paintings to anyone. It was a very dangerous thing to do, and it made me rejoice hearing about my father's little rebellion—trying to keep a part of him alive, even in the hardest circumstances. As my father was writing on his little scraps of medical paper about his hardship, I thought about Jian's father—a high-ranking official with anything and everything he ever needed; my father had nothing but a skeletal body and an earnest heart.

One day, he was working in a mine on the mountain, carrying heavy stones down towards the sea, to "gain farming land," as the authority had decreed, and his vision suddenly blurred. He couldn't see anything in his left eye. But fearing an accusation of being "bourgeois," he continued his work until the evening and only then reported to the team leader that he couldn't see. They took him to a local clinic and the doctor found that one of his retinas was broken. The next day the team leader compiled a report about the half-blind young man. Given that he was no longer suitable for hard labour, the camp decided he was ready to become "a good person." A month later, he was dispatched to a small village under Rocky Peach Town and became a teacher at the village school. There, he continued to paint every evening after a long day's work. My father didn't say this to me explicitly, but I know he deeply valued the experience of his youth, even those punishing years in the camp. He once said the youth of today have no value system. And his daughter's youth? I asked him. He didn't make any comment on that. He just looked at me and drank the bitter medicine my mother cooked for him.

8 ZHEJIANG PROVINCE, JULY 2012

"Was my father the first man you dated?" Mu asked her mother as they walked back from the village, carrying bags full of recommended herbal medicine.

"Dated?" Mu's mother answered impatiently. "He was the first man I ever *talked to* apart from your grandfather!"

As the young painter was being punished in the countryside, the young peasant woman was still a teenager. Along with her family, she grew yams on their distributed farming land. In the fallow season she worked in the local silk factory. In the factory, some hundreds of women would stand at the assembly line removing silk fibres from silk cocoons. The silkworms were collected every day from the farmers in the province. Millions of those white-shelled moths would be soaked in hot water to allow the silk to lift away from their shells. Then the assembly line would roll the silk into piles and then they would dry it. The working floor was always hot and wet. It was a very physical job. Mu's mother got mycosis and eczema all over her hands and feet. One day she could no longer bear the sharp pain of her fungus-ravaged hands and asked the management if she could do a different job. She was transferred to the factory's dance troupe, to become one of the "Mao's Thoughts" dancers—a Red Guard, singing and dancing and chanting slogans from the *Little Red Book* to promote the party's dogma.

Sometime in the late sixties, Mu's mother told her, the young Red Guard went out to the countryside with her team to sing for the peasants and the re-educated intellectual labourers, as the country was swept by a new revolution. And there she met her future husband. "So that was the time you two fell in love?" Mu asked her mother.

"What do you mean 'fell in love'? There was no such thing as 'falling in love' in that world." Unimpressed by her daughter's understanding of history, her mother went on. "Love is just a social condition."

"What do you mean?"

"Social conditions—one's obligations in life," her mother answered impatiently, without a second thought. "For example, in a family or in a society, man is the first order, woman is the second. So a woman should fulfil her obligations for her man. If a man needs help, the woman is obliged to help the man, even if the man is a monster."

Even if the man is a monster! My mother teaches me again what is "the second sex," and I can see the last two thousand years of our Confucian feudal education is much stronger and deeper than the last fifty years of Communist education. Since our conversation about how my parents met, I have steered clear of discussing "love" with my mother. I seldom mention Jian in front of them, or anything of my emotional life. I must keep my private emotions in the safe enclosure of my heart, and make sure I don't open it at all. If I opened it and exposed my possessions, they would be stolen and destroyed instantly!

Mu writes these words in her diary in the quiet night of her home town, with her sick father's occasional coughing in the room across the hall.

9 LONDON, OCTOBER 2013

Love! What a strange concept among those Chinese couples! Iona sighs, and stops reading.

How can love be so totally material and pragmatic for some people? Iona doesn't want to understand love like this. For her, everything else in life can be pragmatic, but not love. Love is something else. Maybe that's why she separated love from sex right from the start. And perhaps it is because her idea of love is beyond the pragmatic that, so far, she has only had a sex life and no love life, and fear has always won.

In the last few weeks, besides Kublai Jian, a man she has never met, there is only one other person whose presence, imagined or otherwise, has had an impact on her, who has affected her sense of embodiment and stability, both in the day and the night. It is Jonathan. Unable to sleep one night with an agitated torrent of images and feelings running through her, she realised it was to do with him. He was somehow the focus of these subtle storms in her mind and body at night, and those feelings of liquid anxiety percolating through her belly during the day. But how? They have only met six times! Yes, they did end up in bed together. And, yes, their lovemaking, she vividly recalls— though, for some reason, not in detail—was like a sweet fire passing through the sieve of their bodies. Yes, OK, but it was only one night. How many men had she had nights with, perhaps even similar nights? Nights of the same intensity and abandonment? That is, after all, what she, Iona, specialises in. She is used to nights with men. Add to this the fact that he is a decade older than her. Admittedly, he is not very like a father or an uncle. On the contrary, he was vigorous and hungry. And he was refined, and subtle, like no other she had known. A certain touch of the hand. Still, where is her sensible head? These thoughts about Jonathan can only be unwanted. He probably has a great family, a devoted wife with a tribe of children, and dogs, debts, everything. It's absurd; indeed, not her at all. When she thinks of love—but then why is she thinking of love?—she thinks of falling for someone younger. More like a comrade in arms, more like an earnest but sexy young scholar. To be attached to Jonathan could only be disaster: a one-sided case of a powerless younger woman giving everything up for nothing in return. Still, she cannot explain this longing.

Last night was unsettling, and strange. She rang Jonathan, but it went straight to voicemail. It was only eight thirty. He was probably having dinner with his wife and children, or with one of the prominent writers he publishes. His answerphone was the typical breezy, echoey voice-for-everyone-and-no-one. If a man was having dinner with his wife, he probably wouldn't take a call from another woman, she thinks. Unless he was with colleagues or friends—then he might take the call. After she'd put the phone down she had felt lonely, a sense of desertion. She sat for a while in the flat, not working on her translation; she contemplated the street lamp, some part of her waiting for her mobile to vibrate and light up. But nothing. Pointless to ring again. Other numbers lay inside her mobile that might have been pressed. Yes, there were others. But she made no effort to bring them to life. She went down to the pub on the corner of her street, sat at the bar alone, had a pint, chatted with a grumpy and tired barman. They played Memphis Slim songs, one after another: "*I'll just keep on singing . . .*"—the song made her brain muddy. As she drank the bitter beer, she gazed at her mobile. No sign from the other world. Then Memphis Slim sang "One Man's Mad." She watched two men hitting pool balls in the corner; they were in no hurry, no more so than the pace of the song was in any hurry. Such is the indifference of man. One moment you are drawn into a circle of warmth and promise, the next you are out.

She drank a second pint of beer and thought of her sex life. It seems that what she does to others has now been done to her. The cruel one. The heartless one. That's the face she likes to show. The face she showed to a perfectly decent bloke sitting beside her, looking at her attentively and waiting for her to say something. When her first pint was finished, he offered to buy her another. But she didn't even bother to raise her eyes. She nursed her gloomy aura to protect her isolation. She finished the last drop of her beer and left the pub at last orders. The man sat there and watched her leave. She walked back to her flat, closed the door behind her and climbed into bed. She slept. Next morning, her phone was still blank. If longing always brings disappointment and desire connects to a sense of emptiness, then love really is a melancholy affair, Iona thinks, in her solitude.

10 ZHEJIANG PROVINCE, JULY 2012

In those three months in the south, there is little change in Mu's daily routine, and apart from occasional visits from relatives or friends of Mu's parents, no one comes to visit. There is one interesting guest who drops by the family house every now and again, though. His name is Gu Chengde, a rich old man. According to Mu's parents, he is a shipbuilding tycoon whose business has been so successful he has offices all over the world. He doesn't seem to mind the modest hospitality of Mu's parents, though, despite arriving in his brand-new limousine driven by his private chauffeur and bringing rare fruits, herbs and gingseng to strengthen Mu's father's health.

"But, Mother, why would such a rich man want to visit Father?"

Mu's mother shrugs dismissively. "He's your father's childhood friend. They grew up in the same compound in their village. Unlike your father's useless interest in painting and communism, Mr. Gu has been doing 'useful things' like his shipbuilding business for the last twenty years." Mu's mother pours the newest tea leaves of the year into the pot and gestures to her daughter. "Mu, bring the tray into the front room for Mr. Gu. He is now one of the biggest international shipping businessmen in China."

"But Mother, how did he become quite so very rich?"

"I remember when he was nominated for China's New Entrepreneur Excellence Award. I saw him on TV, he went on to beat thousands of big names to win national recognition. He rose higher and higher, but he never forgot his roots. And he wanted to help your father, his childhood buddy."

As Mu's mother starts cooking for their guest, Mr. Gu apologises that he can't stay, he has to drive back to his Ningbo headquarters, for an evening meeting with clients. The mother hurriedly introduces Mu to the tycoon, and they shake hands formally. "Girl, if you have toured in America with your poetry, you must be a real talent! And your English must be good! You should come to work for us." Mr. Gu has a booming loud voice and shows off his two gold teeth as he speaks.

Mu says nothing, but smiles graciously.

"We need someone like you, with a good education and grasp of English."

Mu hangs back, checking for slugs on the cucumber leaves. Working in shipbuilding is not something she had ever considered.

"How kind of you, Mr. Gu!" Mu's mother answers quickly for her daughter. "Wouldn't that be fantastic? But I am not sure if our daughter wants to stay and work locally, she's got a big head!"

Now the millionaire is nearly offended. "I'm not talking about working in the province! I'm talking about getting her trained in our Beijing office, then posting her to our brand-new branch in London, you understand?"

"New branch in London?" Mu says, turning her head towards their guest.

Gu's chauffeur has now leaped out of the front seat and opened the car door for his boss to climb in.

"Yes, London branch!" he says, nodding, and leaning on the open car door, his generous paunch squashing against the glass. "Remember, we are running an international business!"

Mu's mother almost jumps when she hears his offer. As the shipping tycoon climbs into the smooth leather-upholstered back seat, he waves goodbye. Mu stands behind her mother, still holding the limp body of a slug she has just killed, and watches the shiny limousine disappearing along the winding country road. The landscape either side of the road is no longer the rice paddies she once knew, stretching flat and glowing green for miles. It is now a wasteland, littered with rubbish and industrial refuse. Plastic bags are everywhere, blowing in between the chopped tree roots and polluted streams.

11 ZHEJIANG PROVINCE, JULY 2012

In the early part of the night, rain drenches the windows in torrents. It's a steady downfall, on a tide of restless air. Then, in the second part of the night, Mu hears her father tossing and turning on the bed, and his strange, irregular breathing: short and fast, punctuated by groaning, his groans propelled by pain. He seems to be struggling to release something through coughing. But he cannot: something has clogged his throat and is choking him. Mu hears her mother getting up and asking him how he feels and giving him water to drink.

The night seems uncannily quiet outside. Only the sound of the rain can be heard; even the crickets on the plants have stopped their chirruping. Mu gets up and enters her parents' room. Her father's face is dark—redder than usual, slightly purple. His breathing is laboured, and rattling sounds come from behind his feverish tongue. He looks in pain. Her mother tries to turn his body on its side to help him breathe more easily. But his breathing grows heavier and heavier. After a few more minutes of agonised wheezing, mother and daughter begin to dress him.

Mu picks up the phone and calls an ambulance. A few moments later, the father struggles to write a note in pencil. His words are almost unrecognisable. But both mother and daughter understand instantly. 太痛了。让我走吧。*Too painful. Let me go.*

Tears like a fountain, coming up from the two women's throats, rising to their hollow eyes—but neither dares cry out in front of the dying man. As the ambulance's siren gets closer and closer, the father looks even paler, while his limbs have turned a darker colour than usual. His wife puts on his shoes. The daughter feels something dreadful is going to happen.

* * *

At two o'clock in the morning, the ambulance took us to the local hospital. We waited in the Emergency area only for a few minutes before two nurses put my father in a wheeled bed and placed him in a room with an oxygen tank and an angiogram recording his heartbeat. Buried in some place of great pain, he was only semi-conscious. A doctor came and asked my mother about all the past cancer treatment my father had received, then they gave him a morphine injection. He could hardly breathe. The doctor and nurse put a respirator on him, and inserted a nasal tube that fed into his lungs. His heartbeat was very weak and irregular. His mouth was half open, with very dry lips. At one point his eyes were moving and I called to him. "Dad? Dad, can you hear me?" He didn't respond, and although he was looking in my direction, his eyes froze for a few seconds. They ceased looking, ceased to be the eyes of a man, and right then my heart stopped beating. My mother whispered his name softly, asked him if he felt cold. But he made no response. His eyes were closing, as if he was falling asleep. His face looked green and grey. His lips looked dry and cracked. The nurse said he needed some liquid, but he probably couldn't swallow. She brought some small pieces of ice and placed the half-liquid, half-ice in his mouth.

Three hours of unconsciousness followed. We glazed, almost unconscious ourselves. The numbness was almost protection. Then suddenly he opened his eyes. My mother held his left hand and I held his right. We called his name. He seemed to be responding. His face showed strain and confusion, as if to ask, "Where am I?" I told him he was in hospital. He tried to take in my words, but his face had darkened. He closed his eyes again. His skin went cold, and felt moist, like some kind of cold sweat was coming out. Mother began to cry, but she suppressed her weeping. Her tears kept rolling down silently on the sheets that covered his body. We sat there and prayed he would wake up. But an hour later, as the morning light hit the window, his heart stopped beating.

The cremation has been arranged for three days after Father's death. Mother appears frail from long nights of grief. I stay close to her. But my throat is contracted and dry. My eyes produce no tears. When I look at myself in the mirror now I see a numbness clings to my face. I am a mute ghost in this old house. But when the moment comes and the coffin is pushed into the incinerator, and the ashes are collected, I suddenly feel an inexplicable relief.

In front of the crematorium, with the smoke still rising from the chimney, the relatives begin to part and go their separate ways. Mu walks home with her mother. Silently, they walk through their patch of field and open the door of the house. Rooting through the letter box, Mu is surprised to find a strange postcard addressed to her. The postcard seems to have come via a snaking path. It was originally from the singer Lutao in the U.S., and sent to his drummer, Dongdong, in Beijing. It simply says: *"I am in California. Sunny every day. Found a job!"* with a picture of a beach with palm trees, blonde girls in bikinis, and brown plastic-looking boys in swimming trunks diving into waves. Then under Lutao's scrawl is Dongdong's brief note, ending with the cryptic lines:

Mu! I'm working for a software gaming company now, given up on drums! You can only dig a garden for so long. Time to grasp the new spirit of the age!—Your little brother Dongdong.

In her southern home town, reading this readdressed, messily written postcard, Mu wonders how her ex-band member knew that she was digging in a garden. Was it just a lucky guess, or was it some sort of intuition? Or did he hear something? And what is "the new spirit of the age" anyway? Mu thinks to herself as she walks in her parents' vegetable garden. The beans are growing fast, the cucumber plants are flowering, but her father is gone.

"Grasp the new spirit of the age"—the phrase continues to play on Mu's mind. And then practical things start to happen. She takes a short trip to visit the shipbuilder Gu's company. It's a relief to get out of the house of mourning which she has been confined to, and she craves an escape. She didn't exactly know what she wanted from him, but it isn't long before she is enveloped by Gu's network of connections. Mr. Gu is indeed opening a London office. He needs a young employee with good English. Mu is the perfect choice. And for Mu, this is also the perfect chance to start anew. While her visa is being dealt with by the company, the future seems to become more and more real for her. It looks like this job is more concrete than her poetry, her American tour, even her past life with Jian.

One very warm morning, Mu says goodbye to her mother and takes a train back to Beijing. A small voice inside her whispers all through the journey that she will not be seeing this southern ancestral land-scape for some time: the watery rice paddies, the muddy buffalo following the farmers' children, the shimmering Yangtze River run-ning towards the east. She remains in the capital for a few months, every day going into the Beijing office to learn about the company and get the training she needs for the move to London. The company rents her a new flat in the expensive part of Beijing. She is indeed saying goodbye to her hutong life, the cheap rent and the dingy noodle bars. Yet on the first weekend free from her new work she takes the subway and visits her old flat, and she still has the key for the mailbox. As she opens her post, she finds a big package posted from France. In the package are old letters between Jian and herself dating back months, as well as Jian's own diary. Then she pulls out a letter written by Jian on the train from Paris to Marseilles. A goodbye letter, it seems, dated "A summer day, 2012." She cannot read the letter here, standing outside their old home. But nor will she be able to read it in her glistening new flat, decorated entirely with cold white tiles and white plastic surfaces. She enters a hutong and goes into a local noodle store, one she and Jian used to hang out at in the evenings. And then she reads the letter.

A summer day, 2012

Mu,

We both know that there's been nothing, no word, between us for the last few months. I don't know where to write to you. So here is my last letter to our Beijing address, whether you read it or not. It's me being foolish, perhaps, breaking through the silence—no doubt that's what you'll think . . .

The pain dilates slowly in her new office, with her new colleagues and new daily routine, as each day goes by. But for weeks, she doesn't know what to do with the documents. The package sits, like a talisman or a souvenir of the past. Every time she glances at it, sitting on the black marble counter in her hallway, she hears a little thud beat inside her. Then she picks up her keys, shuffles on her new high heels and walks out the door. In January 2013, she goes to an international literature festival where one of the days is dedicated to her favourite Russian novel, *Life and Fate*. She listens to an English publisher speak about publishing censored works of literature. And on that day, sitting on an uncomfortable chair at the back of a lecture theatre as a sandstorm outside whips up the capital, she knows exactly what she should do with this package.

She goes home and makes photocopies of all the material and, along with Jian's old diaries, she adds photocopies of her diaries that she has kept for years. She wraps everything in a large folder, goes to the festival site later that day and finds the English publisher who had spoken about *Life and Fate*. He seems confused to receive the package from her, but she insists. What can she possibly do from China?

A few months later, in the summer of 2013, she finishes her business training. On a very hot Beijing afternoon, she goes through her gate at Beijing International Airport. She travels with a bare minimum of possessions. It's an absolute goodbye to the once-innocent Misty Poet, a goodbye to the no-longer-confused, angry Sabotage Sister. In her brand-new suitcase even her sweater and her raincoat are newly bought. Within twelve hours she is transported across the world and emerges at London Heathrow Airport. She is exhausted, but when she gets through immigration she has a feeling that here, somehow, she will encounter "the new spirit of the age," whatever that turns out to be.

13 SCOTLAND, OCTOBER 2013

Iona is on a morning train winding its way towards Scotland. Sitting in the Quiet Coach, she surveys the sky, constantly changing its mood above her. One moment sunlight illuminates the carriage and her reflection in the glass against the rushing landscape, the next moment black clouds pitch the carriage into darkness and she disappears, leaving a world of shadow outside.

It is Wednesday and there are not many people on the train. Iona occupies three seats—on her left are the photocopies of Jian's and Mu's diaries, on her right is a large package, a birthday gift. Under the wrapping paper there's a Chinese vase, which she bought in Covent Garden the day before. It's her mother's sixtieth birthday tomorrow. Her mother likes porcelain objects and has a big collection at home. They are mostly those pseudo Qing-dynasty plates and cups, plus other pieces of oriental kitsch. So why not add another one? With that thought a shadow passes outside and also within. Has she become so mechanistic in her dealings with her parents? Once a needy child, she is now an occasional visitor, there through a sense of obligation only. Is she cold, like the oyster-shell sky of the London she has left behind? The dappled world of undulating fields and passing towns seems to answer: Yes. She looks away.

She tries to finish reading Mu's diary entry on the death of her father. Perhaps, witnessing one of your family members dying is a way of understanding death, as well as a way of overcoming the vanity of youth. Childhood is a kind of eternity, youth is the time of daybreak. And then . . . Iona imagines her mother's death. She thinks of the dying process taking hold of her mother's body. It has already begun: hair falling, flesh beginning to loosen from bones, the heart growing weaker, like a slithering lizard scratching inside a box. But her imagination is running out of control. It's only her mother's sixtieth. Suddenly, a downpour of light flushes into the train; she peers at her serious face in the window, frowning, with an unsettled look. She feels a needling disturbance, but she also feels she has never been so steady and accepting of her own sense of anxiety. It's like she can step back and look at herself, like watching a frightened animal. But as the shadow comes again, she wonders if her steadiness is just the coldness within her, rising up, like damp in a wall. Once the damp begins, you can't stop it. Like a frozen shoulder joint, movement impossible.

The train stops in each town on the way north. Stafford, Stoke-on-Trent, Kidsgrove, Crewe, Preston, Lancaster, Carlisle. She's not been anywhere; the names mean very little to her. She imagines Jian and Mu's figures appearing, from time to time, in the midst of the hazy green fields. But their shadows are swallowed by the dark tunnels into which the train plunges headlong. As the train passes Glasgow, a steward pushing a trolley stuffed with snacks and drinks stops beside Iona. She turns and stares stupidly at the sweets and crisps and drinks; at a loss as to what to choose, she buys a chocolate bar and turns back to Mu's diary.

In my peasant mother's eyes the shipping tycoon Gu is Chairman Mao's reincarnation, perhaps even more useful than Mao himself. Now, as I write, a London address is before me. And that address will be my new home—as a lodger in a flat in east London. Goodbye to my old life. Goodbye, China.

When Iona gets off the ferry, the afternoon light is already waning. She carries her bag and her Chinese vase across the evening moorland. The earth is wet and spongy and her shoes sink into the muddy ooze. Her trousers get spattered. It must have been raining yesterday. She gazes at the clouds. The landscape seems already paralysed by the autumn chill. The grass is grey-brown, the island static, suspended in a gloomy blue-grey. In the near distance she can see a few cows in front of her parents' stone house, silhouetted against the grey sky. Then she sees the old pine tree in front of the house.

It's a black mountain pine, producing plenty of cones each year. She used to climb this tree when she was a moody little girl. And she would sit on the branches for a long time on summer afternoons; through the foliage she could see the sea, and in the distance the small island which bears her name: the Isle of Iona. And then she would speak to herself, to the little Iona inside her: "I want to see the world, I want to know everything about the world!"

Iona's mother has prepared a familiar family dinner. Steamed broccoli, roast potatoes and roast beef. Her father is not at home. "He went to the Beak," her mother says lightly. The Beak is Swan's Beak, their local pub down the valley. It has been going strong for decades, a local haunt, and her father has frequented it since long before Iona was born.

"Is Nell not coming tomorrow?" asks Iona, noticing the kitchen is dim in the minutes before the last of the twilight fades to dark.

"She's just too exhausted with the twins . . . and Volodymyr can't get time off work this week . . ." Her mother looks a little despondent. "I'll miss having the boys this year." She staggers to her feet and seems about to trip, but steadies herself.

Iona notices her mother's hand shakes a bit when she tries to open a bottle of whisky. She feels panicky—early symptoms of Parkinson's disease? She says nothing.

The wind penetrates the windowpanes and agitates dust on the slate floor. It is only late October but it is freezing cold, though the heating is on and the fire is lit. Iona takes off her muddy shoes and sits beside the fire, adding more wood.

"Have you been to see the doctor recently, Mum?" Iona asks.

"I went last week. He said my arthritis is stable—no worse, no better. I just need to learn to live with it . . . and he gave me some sleeping pills."

"Sleeping pills? Is that all he gave you?"

"Well, you know how it is; there's not much to be done about my legs."

Her mother takes another sip of whisky, her hands steadier now.

"Maybe you shouldn't drink so much," Iona says with a frown.

"It's good for my joints and my blood," her mother insists, as she always has done.

As usual, they don't wait for the old man before starting supper. The three of them will have a big birthday breakfast tomorrow anyway. The two women sit at the kitchen table thoughtfully, the silence punctuated by windy shivers and the sounds of their eating. Iona adds some salt to her plate. The broccoli is hard, zesty, but too simple for her. She begins to feel they are goats feeding on roots on a rocky clifftop.

"Hmm, I steamed the broccoli, but it is still rather firm," her mother mumbles apologetically. More silence and more chewing follows. The beef has been carved from a plate with a bloody pool of gravy. It has a real country heartiness, but there is no garlic, no spice, something Iona craves.

Outside, the highland world is quiet but for the wind and the occasional animal cry. As she watches her mother eat, a sad tenderness colours Iona's heart. Iona remembers flavours from her childhood— strong, pungent, full of spice—and the energetic mother of those years that this unhappy woman before her once was. When she was very young, her mother read her and her sister *The Little Mermaid*. She had cried when she learned that the mermaid had to cut off her exquisite tail to become a human so she could love a prince from the human world. And in the end the prince marries a human princess, leaving the little mermaid with her anguished heart and bleeding body, alone. Some years later, when Iona had her first period—the painful twist, like a screw inside her, bringing her to womanhood—she remembered the story again.

"Seeing any nice boys?" her mother asks, liberally sprinkling salt on the potatoes. They are a rich golden brown, crisp and buttery.

"Not really . . . I have met someone, but he's a lot older . . . so, I don't know."

"Well, as long as he's not your father's age . . ." Her mother looks at her quizzically.

"No, not that old, Mum!" Iona feels anxious, a pause, she adds, "But I think he might be married."

"Then you must get over him."

"It's not like taking an aspirin, you know." Iona doesn't even know what she feels for Jonathan exactly, but she won't be told how to behave.

"Tell me, Iona, what is it?"

"What do you mean?"

"You know what I'm talking about. What is it you're after?"

"I don't know . . ." Iona tries to think of a word. "I feel like I'm looking for something—a certain aliveness."

"Aliveness," her mother murmurs, then sighs. It is not the first time the older woman has heard this curious term on her daughter's lips. "That might have meant something to me once. At the moment, I'm just happy enough getting from one day to the next."

"Oh, things aren't that bad, are they?"

One, two, three, four, five, Iona counts, as she eats each potato. The rain is starting outside, carried by the sea wind. Her father is still not back from the pub. Iona remembers that when she was here having dinner with her mother last time, she also had a plate of crispy roast potatoes. Next day, right after her morning porridge, she took the first morning ferry and got the train back to London.

"Mum . . ." Iona wipes her mouth and suddenly has a totally spontaneous idea—something grows from her guilt with this old farm and this old family. "You know what? Let me take you and Dad on holiday."

"What?" Her mother's eyes are wide open; she turns her head aside, thinking she might be mishearing words. "What? A holiday?"

"Yes, a holiday, Mum, you deserve a holiday, I want to arrange that for you and Dad . . ."

Her mother hasn't left the island for a long time. "Really? Well, I don't know, darling."

"You could go somewhere warm and sunny." Iona thinks, and improvises suggestions. "Crete, Mallorca, Cyprus . . . We can ask Dad when he comes back."

Her mother smiles gently, as if listening to a radio programme she likes. It seems she doesn't really mind whether it happens or not; just imagining being on holiday with her daughter is in itself a wonderful gift on her sixtieth birthday.

EIGHT | LAST DAYS IN CRETE

种瓜得瓜，种豆得豆。

zhong gua de gua, zhong dou de dou.

Sow melon, reap melon; sow beans, reap beans.

DONG ZHOU LIE GUO ZHI, FENG MENGLONG
(PLAYWRIGHT, MING DYNASTY, 1574–1646)

1   LONDON, NOVEMBER 2013

Above Chapel Market, Iona is nearing the end of her translation. There are two more pages to go of Jian's diary.

I was ten years old. One day the school took us on a day trip to the seaside town of Qinghuang Island. It was the first time in my life that I had seen the sea. Blue. Blue was the colour I loved, just like this blue in front of me now, but I no longer care about this blue on this foreign ship with a foreign language I have never encountered before. That day my school friends and I played volleyball on the beach with the tide coming and going beneath our feet; we swam among the waves; we rolled in the sand; we found blue crabs under the rocks and we made a bonfire from driftwood; we cooked our catch of crabs and sang songs under the evening moon. I was with my "da jia"—my "big family"—all the Young Pioneer boys and girls, not even teenagers yet, laughing and crying together with joy. But the sea here, today, is different. It is totally desolate, devoid of the people I once knew, devoid of their laughter and cries.

Now I think that was probably one of the happiest days of my life. I felt so free. I remember the soothing wind, the boundless sky, the daring seagulls wheeling overhead and then diving into the water and plucking fish from the waves . . . Nature was so great that day. Nature was much greater than my family, than my Beijing life, than everything I was taught and forced to learn. I wish I had remained forever in that moment. I belonged to it like the sand belongs to the beach, like the seagulls belong to the sea.

And this morning I woke up with a single image in my head. I dreamed of the bluest sea I will ever see.

Iona turns to the next page of Jian's diary. She is on the last page, there are no more photocopies in his file. On the white sheet, there are only two lines, scribbled with big characters. But the characters are sprawling out every which way and so messily written that they are nearly unrecognisable.

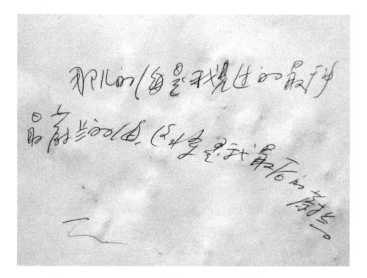

It takes her a while to make out each character and she has to hold the page at odd angles to try and decipher the words. Eventually she has a rough translation of Jian's two final sentences:

The sea there is the bluest and purest. It's the last blue I will see.

There are no more words from Jian for her to translate, at least not from the files in front of her. Iona double-checks the whole package Jonathan gave her. There are a few unfinished poems from Mu that she hasn't got to yet, but this is the last fragment in Jian's scrawl. No dates, no location either. She returns to the page, murmurs and repeats these two mysterious lines out loud in Chinese and then in English. There is something so simple, so enigmatic about this small fragment. The meaning is elusive. She tries to translate it a different way, unsure exactly what he meant.

The sea there is the bluest and purest. And this is the last blue I can see.

Then she changes the tense. Since Chinese has no tense indication with verbs it can be hard to determine the meaning.

The sea there was the bluest and purest. It was the last blue I have ever seen.

And finally, she plays with the tense one last time.

There, that sea, the bluest and purest sea. It will be the last blue I shall ever see.

Iona stares at the original Chinese characters, those two sprawling lines, for a long while. After a few minutes suddenly a sensation of cold, a shivering, takes hold of her, welling up from somewhere. She feels anxious. Standing up from her chair, she moves to the window. Did he? Is he? Was he? Will he?

What does that mean exactly, *the last blue*? She scrolls back on her screen to the page before that she's just translated, and stares at one of the lines: "*I no longer care about this blue on this foreign ship with a foreign language I have never encountered before.*" So he is, or was, on a ship somewhere in the middle of the sea, surrounded by a language he doesn't understand. Surely not English or French? Iona thinks hard. It could be Italian, Spanish, even Greek! She feels herself straining to find any thread, any clue from all the lines, all the words she has translated, that might elucidate such a cryptic fragment. Suddenly she remembers a diary entry early on, somewhere Jian and Mu mentioned the name of an island they might go to. She scrolls up on her computer and finds the page she translated several months ago.

13 October 1993

I met that girl again from the volleyball match . . .

Iona scans down the screen until she finds the right place. The cursor blinks at her impatiently as she reads.

"I'm looking at these small islands in the middle of the sea." She pointed at an expanse of turquoise blue in the centre of the world map. "Wouldn't it be amazing if one day we could visit these islands?"

Her slightly bent index finger pointed out a few yellow dots in the blue sea. She pronounced their names haltingly as she placed her finger on each island. "Easter Island, Pitcairn, Majorca, Corsica, Sardinia, Crete."

"Where would you go, if you could choose just one island?" she asked me.

"I don't know," I shrugged. "How are we to know anything if we have never been outside of China?"

"Come on . . . just imagine. Imagine that one day you wake up and find yourself on a quiet and beautiful island in the middle of a very blue sea. Where would it be?" She nudged me.

Then she covered my eyes with her palms, lifted my hand and let my finger land at random on the map. Then she removed her palms from my eyes and in an excited voice said: "Here it is, Crete." A Greek island in the middle of the Mediterranean. That's where my finger had found its place.

2   LONDON, NOVEMBER 2013

Iona calls Jonathan's mobile, but it goes straight to voicemail. She tries a second time. The same seductive, offhand tone. Then she digs out his office number. The receptionist asks her if she'll hold. A few seconds later, she hears the voice of the Applegate secretary with her indifferent tone, which now seems entirely offensive. "I'm sorry, Jonathan is in a meeting, do you want to leave a message for him?" Iona leaves her number and asks that he return her call.

She comes back again to the lines: "*'Here it is, Crete.' A Greek island in the middle of the Mediterranean. That's where my finger had found its place.*" Is she making too great a leap, too big an assumption, that over the space of twenty years, he might still have that same wish? But there is something in the naive urgency of Jian's voice as a young man, and the melancholy of his words now, that convince Iona she isn't going crazy. And then the ambiguous scribbles on Jian's last diary page, like a lift shaft through which she has fallen. The two lines are translated on her computer with four different tenses. The right version for this translation depends on which timeline Iona puts into Kublai Jian's story in her narrative; and perhaps it finally depends on what is a true Kublai Jian story, when exactly this story begins—and when it ends! Months have passed since the date of Jian's last diary entry. Where is he now? Did Jian just stop recording thought? Or is there a continuation of the story, fragments of another diary? What if there is something else they haven't discovered?

Restlessly, Iona tries Jonathan's mobile again. This time it's not the recorded baritone she knows so well, but another voice, Jonathan's brisk "Hello," which now seems strange.

"It's me, Iona."

"Hi, Iona. Sorry, not great timing. I can only talk briefly. I'm just about to go into another meeting."

Although resonant, his voice is nevertheless reserved and distant. He is in office mood.

"Of course. I've got just one question actually: Do you know where Kublai Jian is now?" Iona asks bluntly.

"Where? If I knew where he was, things would be a lot easier, wouldn't they, and we wouldn't have to go around digging up random pieces of information from cautious embassy clerks. What's your point, Iona?"

"Do you think he's still alive?" Iona is growing a little desperate.

"Alive? God, Iona, I don't know—I haven't thought about it. I imagine he might still be detained somewhere . . . perhaps . . ."

"Do you think I could find him? I mean, a Greek island is small enough surely for a lone Chinese man to stick out?"

"A Greek island? Sorry, Iona, I think you've lost me there. Surely he was last in France—why would he suddenly be on a Greek island?"

"In the final section of the diary, there's a hint of where he might be headed. He was on a ship somewhere."

"Right, OK . . . but . . . Really, Iona, I have no idea what you're talking about. And, I mean, how could you possibly find him?" Jonathan pauses, thinking. Then he asks: "So does this mean you have finished the translation?"

"Nearly . . ." Then she hears him telling his secretary or assistant that he will skip the beginning of the next meeting. "Listen, Iona, we've just managed to find out Mu's address in London. It seems she's now working for a UK branch of some sort of Chinese shipping company, based in east London."

"Really?" Iona is instantly excited. "So she is in London after all. Can you send over her address? Why didn't you tell me earlier—this is such great news!"

There is silence at the other end of the phone and Iona starts to say something, but Jonathan interrupts.

"Yes it is, but—well the reason we stopped our background research is because . . . Well, I don't know if I should tell you this." Jonathan slows down and it feels to her that he is choosing his words with great care. "I got a phone call from China last week—from the office of the Ministry of State Security. The man on the phone told me that I shouldn't publish anything linked to Kublai Jian, and in fact that I mustn't use his diaries or letters in translation form or even just as reference material in any way whatsoever, and must certainly never release any of the material to the public."

"Mustn't?" Iona repeats, exasperated. She pulls at her hair in frustration.

"Yes, mustn't. Mustn't translate. Mustn't publish. Practically mustn't even talk about Kublai Jian. Hang on, let me read you what he sent me. I received an email from the Minister after our phone conversation, and—um, here it is, yes, 'Our Chinese politician's son should not become the subject of media attention. We demand a mutual respect between Western media and domestic Chinese politics. If you insist on publishing these documents, we are afraid you will face certain consequences. We cannot guarantee that any future business plans you may have in China will not be adversely affected if you fail to comply with our wishes.' That's it."

There's a pause. Iona tries to get her head around this new piece of information. Then Jonathan's voice becomes weary.

"As you can imagine, I've been thinking this over for a while. When you get phone calls from the Chinese government you have to take them seriously. Clearly, they don't want news about Kublai Jian's exile to become public knowledge, nor his relationship with his father. And then again last week, we received another phone call, this time from the Chinese Embassy here. They seem to know all about it and were very adamant about warning me."

Iona hears Jonathan breathing. She says nothing.

"And that was far from being the end of the story. Yesterday we found that someone has hacked into our archives and had gone through all our electronic files . . . All your emails have been deleted and the files with your translation corrupted or deleted, too. It's a good thing you have your own copy!"

Jonathan's voice becomes subdued, as if he is not particularly keen to discuss this on the phone.

"I might be paranoid. But you never know. It's scary, Iona, I can't be too careful. If the Chinese government is watching what I'm doing . . . maybe even what you're doing—well . . . I've got to take this call really seriously. I've kept quiet about the book with everyone, except you."

Iona waits. "So what does this mean? What are you going to do with my translation?"

Jonathan speaks slowly, with an uncertain tone. "I am thinking of shelving the project. At least for now."

"Shelving it?" Iona is devastated.

"At least for a little while. Let the heat of their interest in us blow over. In a couple of years they'll have forgotten all about it. I need to be careful, Iona. I'm responsible for the future of my company, the job security of my employees," Jonathan says in a resigned voice. "And then, just to top it all off, this morning my assistant tried to get me a visa to go to China, thinking it might be a good idea to find out a bit more on the ground, as it were. I was planning on telling you about it. But the Embassy have refused my visa application outright. No explanation, just a few words from an official source: 'We have been informed that for political reasons we are not able to issue you the visa until we receive further instruction.' So that's it, the door to China closed for me."

"But . . ." is all Iona can say. Her urgency and energy seem to have dwindled to nothing. Outside, the pale winter sun has made its exit, leaving only layers of dull British clouds hanging in bloated forms. The Atlantic wind sweeps the streets, carrying dead sycamore leaves, ushering them into drains and front gardens. People on bikes and in cars rush onward, to homes, to warmly lit pubs, or to what might be oblivion, anywhere to escape the forecast storm.

3 LONDON, NOVEMBER 2013

Iona gets off at Shoreditch High Street station, galvanised by a single purpose and turns up Bethnal Green Road. She feels thirsty, in her throat, but also in her mind. On this busy and crowded street in the east end of London, she is forced to slow down and join the stream of jostling bodies. The haphazard stalls lining the side of the road brim with clothes and people buying and selling. There are cheap home products, pots and pans, trinkets and toys. The bargain hunters are veiled Bangladeshi or Indian women. It feels for a moment as if she has been transported to some Dhaka side street, and that she herself is a local wife, searching for ingredients for tonight's curry among the tindoras and gongura leaves spread out on metal platters. Iona keeps walking and turns into one of the side streets, until she arrives at a four-floor brown-brick council block, one of London's 1970s monuments to immigrant workers.

Iona checks the sign on the front of the building. The fenced gardens and public corridors, the balconies with their newly-washed laundry strung on clothes lines, dark red-brick festooned with sari fabric and windows clogged with potted plants and domestic relics. In the courtyard, a group of black kids are kicking a football around with boisterous yelps. As she climbs up and up the concrete stairs she feels a panic rising. Number 35. Iona watches her hand knock on the green door. Her knock is timid, awkward and she even has a strange feeling of criminality. She waits, it's quiet inside. She waits patiently, secretly hoping no one will ever open this door. What is she supposed to say if a Chinese woman were to open it? How would she introduce herself? Would she ask her if she still writes poetry, if she still thinks of a Beijing dissident and their life together in the subterranean bars of the

Chao Yang district? Or would that be too intrusive, too like a ghost knocking from the past? Perhaps she might find a surprising scene: inside the door, both Jian and Mu there, living together. Would Mu even ask her in? But of course Iona knows that she's totally unknown to them, she does not exist in their lives, in the way that they do in hers. She is at best a voyeur. She has fed on their life's meaning, but it has left her feeling empty, famished, and now, here, standing alone in a corner of London in which she is an interloper, a trespasser.

Iona knocks again. She listens inside and holds her breath. She finally hears footsteps, and a cat miaows in some corner of the flat on the other side of the door. A middle-aged man with a moustache opens the door, accompanying the pungent odour of Middle Eastern food. He looks Turkish or Lebanese, like many of the locals here.

"Yes?" He stares at her, leaning on the half-opened door.

"Hi . . . I am . . . I am looking for a Chinese woman at this address," Iona says nervously. "Her name is Mu, Deng Mu."

"A Chinese woman?" The man's voice softens a little; he lets the door open a little wider. "Who are you?"

Who am I? Iona mutters the same question at the back of her throat.

"I am . . . her friend. My name is Iona."

"She has just gone back to China. Didn't she tell you?" The man puts his full weight against the open door and it makes an ominous creak.

"Right . . . I didn't know."

"She left two days ago."

"So she does live here? Deng Mu?"

"Yes, the Chinese woman with long black hair, works for a shipping company in China—do you mean her? She's just with us temporarily—our lodger."

The cat miaows again somewhere in the kitchen. Then the animal saunters out, a black cat with sparkling green eyes, and weaves itself in between its owner's legs.

"Do you know when she'll be back?"

The foreign man shakes his head.

"Right. Thanks . . ." A pause. Iona asks with uneasiness: "Has she ever talked about another friend—a Chinese man. I thought she might be living with him."

The foreign man scans Iona up and down with increased suspicion. Still holding the door ajar, he nevertheless seems friendly. "No. There's no one else here. Just me and my wife."

A woman's voice in the flat calls the foreign man in a language Iona doesn't recognise.

He turns his head and shouts back an incomprehensible sentence. Iona feels it's the moment to leave.

"Thanks, I'll contact her when she's back."

The foreign man nods his head, closing the door. Iona waves her hands, squeezing out a polite smile.

Now standing in the courtyard among chained bicycles and rubbish bins, Iona looks up once again at the third floor, the green door and the windows of flat number 35. She notices there is a wilted plant sitting by the window. A strange emptiness fills her. The world seems to fade out around her, leaving her bare and alone on a deserted square.

As she walks back down the concrete steps, more slowly and with none of the adrenaline-rush excitement she had on the way up, she thinks of Jonathan. She tries to turn away from him, this married man, but she cannot remove his image, or expunge the feeling that fills her body like dye staining a still pool. "I'm thinking of shelving the project." That's how he refused her, in his way, both on a professional and a personal level. Now she is not even useful for the project. This is what it's like to be expelled from the kingdom once and for all, she thinks. Though this will never be acknowledged except by her, with a mute bitterness too vague to be given words. He is probably oblivious to her now, back at home after work, making dinner with his wife of twenty years, his kids jumping around his knees, adoring their father-idol and asking him for all the things a daddy is supposed to do and give; and he is probably discreetly planning to publish someone else's biography, Gaddafi's, Castro's or Putin's, or some other big shot. Such a picture of domestic perfection and professional success appears before Iona in the twilight, with the damp beginning to send its cold fingers crawling over her shivering skin.

Iona sits on a bench in the courtyard of Thistle House for a while, until an African family comes by, two small kids showering each other with playful blows. When the kids spot her, they stare at her as if they know she is some sort of spy, someone who doesn't belong to this building or this dark-skinned community. Iona turns and leaves the courtyard. On the way back, she passes an old Chinese man. Thin and short, he is carrying a Tesco shopping bag in each hand; she turns her head, watching his bent frame disappear into a side street, against the hard glow of the street lamps, turned on early on this winter afternoon.

4 CRETE, NOVEMBER 2013

*Why are there no songs in my head any more? Like Rimbaud
in Africa who gave up poetry for gun running. Like the Misty
Poet Hai Zi who decided to leave the world behind, lying on a
railway track. And I've lost the need for music. Or maybe it's
that the music doesn't need me any more.*

*A phrase from Dante came to me earlier: "Abandon all hope,
ye who enter here." Am I entering Hell? Is this blue sea Hell, the
Circles of Hell under this white sun?*

The diary Jian is writing now he will never post to Mu. Nor will
Jonathan or Iona read these words until it is much too late.

As he scribbles on the white page, sunlight burns his eyes. The
sunny hours feel longer here than Jian's days in England and France.
Time stretches and slows down, like the shadows of the poplar trees
lingering forever on sun-bleached walls and facades. Like some aged
horse, the bus travels slowly from Iraklio to Rethymno. There are very
few passengers. A sense of self-abandonment wraps around the single
Chinese man, it dissipates into the thin air of this island, becoming
the very air he breathes into his lungs. No one is in a hurry on the
bus; it is as if the bus itself knows there's nothing to hurry for, nothing
waiting at the end of the line. Just another evening, another night,
another day. Just the shadows projecting shapes from a slightly different angle of the sun.

As far as Jian can see, this Greek island is no poorer or richer than
anywhere else he has been. Dark-skinned old men walk around under
the low winter sun, or sit and contemplate. One wonders how much
influence the outside world has on the locals. Picking olives from the

same olive tree, walking the same hills their ancestors walked—does the outside world really affect their day-to-day life? Jian still remembers those lines from Confucius's *Book of Odes*: "We get up at sunrise, at sunset we rest. We dig wells and drink, we plough the fields and eat, what is the might of the emperor to us?" If the old sayings are right, does that mean all his struggles are pointless, even foolish?

Jian tries to think clearly, but he is too tired to think. He closes his eyes, drifting into sleep. In his folded arms lies the third volume of *Life and Fate*; he is on the very last section. The book has grown mouldy, the cover has crumbled and fallen off, and the Chinese title has become unrecognisable.

5 CRETE, NOVEMBER 2013

Crete is in the middle of the Mediterranean, but for Jian it feels like a forgotten island adrift from the world. He remembers being stuck in the detention centre, reading about Napoleon and the island of St. Helena. The memory disturbs him and he tries to stop himself thinking. Here, too, the weather is extreme. Rainstorms arrive after a hot morning, raindrops like a vast wet curtain sweeping through the island, blasting the yachts and the pine trees and every living creature on the land. Occasionally, children swim in the bay with water-wings on their arms, but they are called back by their parents when the rain starts. Cars drive away from the beach, ferries leave. Nature knows well how to scare the humans away.

Living on a boat is not a long-term plan, but so far this is all he has found. It looks like the boat has been abandoned: spiderwebs criss-cross the ceiling of the cabin and knot in every corner. Reeds grow wild all around. It's a very old sailing boat, all broken down. Inside, the living space has a narrow built-in bed and resembles the sleeper compartment of a train. Lying on the bed, hearing the sea lapping right beside the boat, Jian feels fine and safe. There's little chance that some-one will come to arrest him or accuse him of stealing their property, but he's not planning on staying long anyway.

Hidden inside the boat, beside the ravaged pages of his Russian novel, is Jian's journal. It is his sole companion.

So many people died in Volumes One and Two that when we come to Volume Three the dead are no longer mentioned—the Russian soldiers, German soldiers, the people of Stalingrad, the Jews in the gas chambers, the sons and the daughters and the mothers and

the commissars, let alone everyone starving on the collective farms.
I wonder how many Chinese men and women have read this book;
it would be devastating for the Chinese: the true sorrow is that the
hero loses his faith. In the end he cannot believe in either commu-
nism or nationalism; the people in the book are left alone without
belief and without their loved ones. Do ideologies die as people
die? I hope so, for the sake of peace.

So hear me, this is my confession: ideology is a slaughter-
house. And I have been living in this slaughterhouse from the
very beginning.

In years to come the old Greeks on this island will be gone,
just as the old Chinese will disappear, the old French, the old
English, and the old Germans . . . all of them will die out.
Humans will be no longer. Only the sea will ta ma de *senselessly*
stay.

Jian falls asleep. For hours he doesn't move, not even to wave away the
last of the summer mosquitoes or scratch himself. It is as if he were
already dead. The storm lingers, wrapping itself around the island, the
forest, the town. Jian wakes up, shivering with cold, completely soaked,
the boat filled with water. Later he finds some plastic sheeting to cover
the boat, and he bails out the water with a bucket.

In the middle of the night, the rain and wind subside. There is no
cry from the seagulls, no human voices from the shore, not even a dog
barking. Every living being seems to have been scared off by nature's
ire. Under a moon slipping into the west, Jian thinks of those Communist officials in *Life and Fate*—how familiar they appear to him! He
sees his father as being in the mould of the true Stalinist. He sees how
the man has always held on to some cruel weapon or other, snatching
power, terminating those who have threatened him, even his wife and
his son, in order to build his empire.

In a nearby village, an old couple seem to be the only people who can be bothered to talk to Jian. Perhaps it's because he mentioned that he used to live in Grantham and the couple are English. Slough is the town where they were both born, but is not the place they have planned to die. There is Hugh, who is about eighty, and his wife, Rosemary, a few years younger. They moved to Greece fifteen years ago when they retired. They weren't rich, but they had enough money to buy a modest house with a big garden. Hugh was in the RAF for nearly twenty years, he says. He tells Jian that he used to smuggle diamonds and gold from Angola when he served as a pilot. It was Angola, the gold country, which burnt his skin, but also seared its way into his heart. Hugh says he made a lot of money, but then lost everything a few years later: risky investments with dubious bankers and investors. Still, his face now seems serene, if somewhat wizened. A wry smile crackles under the mahogany-coloured skin and lined cheeks. Rosemary likes to offer the Chinese man her lemon cheesecake, or fruit cakes made with fruits from the garden. She is proud of their little plot. But in Jian's eyes, her pride is too light—built as it is on almost nothing: just the ownership of a lone English-speaking house on an isolated Greek island.

Still, life goes on, at least for some people. Each morning Hugh walks his two dogs, and then swims in the afternoon, even in winter when it is not too windy, his brown body like a naked Don Quixote's. His wife moves her old skeleton about, white beneath paper-brown skin, tending her courgettes and tomatoes. Then she'll gaze onto the beach from the garden, listening to the BBC in the shade. "The sea is too rough for me now," Rosemary says to Jian, "but I used to be a good swimmer, I used to swim in the river and the boys would stand by the bank, impressed by their old mum." Rosemary has this typical educated Englishwoman's composure; she looks like a white colonial landowner in Kenya, spry and graceful but sharp as a knife, ruling her sun-baked farmhouse.

"You don't miss your country?" Jian asks in his humble English.

"No, Jian. Thank the Lord, Hugh and I don't need to stay in miserable cold England any more," Rosemary says, her eyebrows moving very slightly. "What about you? Do you miss China?"

"Yes—" He stops there. There is too much to say.

"Then you should go back." Hearing no response, she continues. "Are you visiting Europe for a short time, or are you planning on staying?"

"I don't really know," Jian answers, with some difficulty.

He gazes at Rosemary's garden, thinks of the effort she puts into this small vegetable patch—every day watering it under the hard relentless sun, maintaining the well-structured grape vines, the tomato plants and red peppers, weeding the herb patch, repairing the shed, painting the stone walls. Does gardening make her feel rooted to this place? That this might be home? He thinks of the peasant farms on the outskirts of Beijing. The labour is much harder there, but the great care that is taken, mixing human intention with earth and water, is the same. The idea of working on their soil brings forth fruit from the ground; the idea also roots the people to their land.

"You remind me of my youngest son, Matt. He's a musician. His career has taken him to many exciting places. Now he's gone to Japan, the farthest place he could go! Well, you're still young, Jian, you've got plenty of time to wander around and find what you have to find. I would do the same if I were young." Rosemary pours Jian some tea. "Would you like another piece of cake? It's rather good, even though I say so myself."

Jian shakes his head gently. His throat is knotted. His head is heavy.

328

The English lady enters her kitchen and fetches something. Moments later, she hands Jian a small plastic bag. "Chocolate shortbread. I baked it yesterday."

Jian wants to embrace Rosemary. But his body is stiff, as if the wind had frozen his limbs in one position. His brain is telling his arms to move to her, but despite all his efforts only his fingertips manage to touch her sleeve. Ever so lightly, he pinches the soft fabric of the old lady's blouse. No words come. Rosemary is looking at him sympathetically, barely breathing. Pausing as if time itself had thickened, pouring more slowly through their veins.

Later he finds himself walking slowly back to his boat. It's quite a long walk, especially as he has chosen to pick his way along the heavy, waterlogged beach. As his sandals move through white sand and lapping water, he realises that a melody from an old song is looping in his mind. It's one of his. He wonders why it has come to him now, out of nowhere, like a homing pigeon flying to its master, who has long thought it dead, or has forgotten it entirely. They're lines he wrote long ago, in college. Lines he wrote for someone called Mu. "Yellow Dust on Your Black Hair"—that was the title and the first line. It's like a dream; almost a dream of a dream. He sees the character of her name: 木, and a face somehow merging with the character, covering it, like the gossamer threads of a spiderweb. The lyrics of the song seem to speak to the moon-shaped face, and through the character 木 he seems to clasp the face close to him.

He looks up at the cliffs, the headland falling into the sea. A small pine and some daisies cling to the top of the cliff. The wind is trying to uproot them, but the pine and the daisies cling on. Maybe it's time to let this homing bird fly away, Jian thinks . . . And just as it comes, it leaves. Now there is only the sound of the ocean swell, and the bubbling cadence of pebbles. Then nothing.

No salt tears join the salt-sea's wave. No knotted heart finds its place in the knotted cliffs. No inner cry. Nothing.

7 CRETE, NOVEMBER 2013

The sand is covering Jian's ankles. It's so dry that it seems to him the world is transforming itself into a desert. And that will be the end of civilisation. Everything will return to sandy wastes and salty seas. Barrenness eternal. The world just one great salty ocean, its only life the wind-dragged waves and roving clouds.

He pauses in the middle of the road and lifts a broken sandal, rubbing away the small stones from between his toes. He makes his way forward, step by step, but something still hurts. A spine has pierced the rough skin of his big toe. He looks down and sees a small crushed cactus, its cylindrical trunk bristling with spines—like a tiny landmine waiting to destroy its enemies. He kneels down and tries to pluck the barb from his toe. The little bastard doesn't want to come. Maybe it wants to sprout anew inside me, he thinks, colonise me. Damn these thorns! Swearing, Jian walks through the little cactus patch tentatively. He knows that the power of the sea is stronger than the power of the desert plants. The sea will wash them away in the end—roots, spines, seeds, as well as all other land-dwelling life. All will be washed away, all. Then the sharks and whales, the jellyfish and squid, the sea slugs and the sea urchins will feed on the land-dwelling creatures that float now in the body of the sea. All will be consumed in that boundless blue water. Nobody, nothing, will escape the final reckoning, the whirl-pool sucking in and dissolving all the forms of nature.

He continues to walk, slowly, towards Hugh and Rosemary's house. It seems such a long way today, as if the house had been pushed further along the desert road each day by an enormous powerful hand. Maybe he is just exhausted, he tells himself, from hunger, from lack of water, or from the dry, unforgiving heat. His steps are heavy and his head groggy. The Mediterranean afternoon is an endlessly static afterglow stretched forever on the deserted beach like a burning rainbow. Apart from the occasional dog barking, there is not a single soul around to disturb his solitude.

In the early evening, Jian arrives at his neighbours' house. Hugh is out with the dogs. Rosemary is descaling a big sea bream she has just got from the village market. In the living room the TV is on. The BBC is reporting the news from Parliament; and now, how Manchester is going to build the world's biggest stadium. The familiar sound of English television enters Jian's ears and moves into deeper parts of his brain. The old couple don't seem particularly reflective. They look like they've signed a good contract with their shared fate, and now all they have do is take time and enjoy each moment as it comes.

"One day you'll get married and have children. Then you'll understand," says Rosemary. "Hugh and I have been married for nearly fifty years, and we've been up and down all the way through, but we coped with it all. Now the kids look after themselves. Our children and grandchildren are coming to stay for Christmas. You come over too if you like. All right?"

Jian listens in silence. Children and grandchildren and Christmas, these subjects sound so remote. He can't picture himself sitting at an old polished dinner table wiping his grandson's dripping mouth while his wife washes dishes in the background or hoovers the carpet in the living room where Christmas songs are playing. He is Chinese, he doesn't even worship Laozi or Confucius! Plus his ancestors are the Mongols. What does Christmas mean to a Mongol Chinese? He would worship green grass under the blue sky if he had to worship something. No, Jian can't put himself inside this Christmas picture.

Rosemary slows down. "But here I am, still alive and walking on this warm beach! Life is a blessing."

Life is a blessing? Jian wonders.

The old lady washes her scale-covered hands. Although wrinkled and skinny, her hands are muscular, like her face. "I don't suppose you know what war is like, Jian, you're too young. Now Hugh and I can live the way we want. It's a pay-off, I would say."

Rosemary walks to the front garden, checking if her husband is back from the beach with the dogs.

"What about you, Jian, do you have someone you'd like to be with for Christmas?" Rosemary looks into his eyes. "She's in China, I suppose?"

Jian nods his head, and then shakes it. "We separated a while ago," he answers in a hoarse and effortful voice. He has almost forgotten how to speak.

"Oh, dear . . ." Rosemary doesn't press him.

"She was called Mu." A pause, and Jian adds: "It means tree."

He looks at the sea in the distance, the ever-lasting blue energy. He doesn't really want to talk; he has barely talked in the last few months. Now Mu's moon-shaped face appears, and his toe hurts again. He kneels down, poking his damaged toe out of the top of his sandal, and tries once more to pluck out the spine.

Rosemary fetches her glasses and a pair of tweezers. She bends her frail body down to Jian's toes. Her hair is close to his face, grey yet soft, thinning in the middle but well combed, dignified, and with the fragrance of lavender. He wants to touch her hair, yet he refrains. The smell of Rosemary's hair sends him a warm and inexplicable sadness, and to a memory he has kept so long, kept only for himself, that of a black-haired girl, her hair and body smelling of the gardenia-scented soap she liked to use. That familiar yet so far away silky skin, the small and bony hands which belonged to her. Mu. The sound of her name and the image of her moon face make Jian lose his words in front of this English lady.

8 CRETE, NOVEMBER 2013

The strangest dream I've ever had. This morning I dreamed I was Pangu, the first creature in the universe. I, Pangu, had been in a cosmic egg for 20,000 years, then one day I broke out of my shell, I looked around and set about the task of creating the world: I separated yin from yang with a swing of my giant axe. I wanted to separate the earth from the sky. But the earth and sky had been stuck together for so many thousands of years that it was very difficult to separate them. I took a deep breath, and stood between them and pushed up the sky. The old bastard sky! So heavy and tough! This task took me some thousand years, the sky each day growing ten feet higher, the earth ten feet wider, and I ten feet taller. I stood there pushing the bastard sky for so long that the animals started to gather together to help me. The four most prominent animals—turtle, phoenix, qilin and dragon—helped to raise the sky with their powerful backs and tails and claws. After several thousand more years, the animals had evaporated into invisible spirits, and I was exhausted. I lay down to rest. Days and nights passed and my breath became the wind, my voice the thunder, my left eye the sun and my right eye the moon; my body became the mountains; my blood formed rivers; my muscles the fertile lands; my beard the stars and the Milky Way; my fur the bushes and forests; my bones the valuable minerals; my sweat fell as rain; and the fleas on my fur became fish and the animals of the land. I, Pangu, became this universe. Then I disappeared, in an ethereal but immense form.

* * *

A small figure walks upon the sand dunes. Everything around him is still, but he walks aimlessly with no clear direction in sight, on and on. At one point he enters a village he has never been to before. He passes each house, looking over the white, low stone walls at their gardens. The walls are decayed and the paint on the windowpanes is faded and peeling. Then he is back on the bumpy country road again; occasionally he encounters an old widow dressed in black, staggering towards the village market. They must be going there to buy bread and onions, he muses. People try to get by, until the last day comes.

It is dark now. Someone by the shore is playing a ukulele, broken tunes with something of a Japanese mood. When the wind comes, the music is taken and dissolves into the ether. The moon is full. The waves lick the rocks at the water's edge.

At midnight, after a whole day's wandering, Jian returns to his boat. He finds an orange on his narrow bed. A blood orange—Tarocco or Sanguinello, as they call it. It is fresh, and still almost warm from the heat of the day's sun. Has someone been here? Did someone leave him the fruit on purpose? Or was it Pangu who visited him? He can't think any more. Slowly, he peels the orange and the red juice spills from the flesh. He drinks the juice, leaving the pith and peel beside his bed.

> *The last page of* Life and Fate. *I should have stopped reading on the previous page, then I could have gone back and started again. I wish there was never a "last page." But this is it. I've lived with the Shaposhnikov family for centuries, and I know everybody's story by heart, Viktor's, Krymov's, Karimov's, Chernetsov's, Abarchuk's, David's, Mostovskoy's, Lyudmila's . . . endless pages of human struggle and defeat. "There was a deeper sadness in this silence than in the silence of autumn. In it you*

could hear both a lament for the dead and the furious joy of life itself," Jian reads. Yes, the spring will come if you ever get through the long winter, he thinks. But Grossman knows only too well that death runs faster than humans, death snatches our hope long before spring arrives.

9 CRETE, NOVEMBER 2013

When the plane touches down at Heraklion International Airport in Crete, Iona feels exhausted. She booked the early-morning flight and her head aches from lack of sleep. This was not a planned trip, she bought the ticket on the spur of the moment in a travel agency the day before, the cheapest she could get. She's brought almost no luggage with her. Apart from her daily necessary things in her backpack, she has only a jacket, jeans, two T-shirts and Vasily Grossman's novel. She feels liberated.

The airport feels a little desolate; it is winter, not a good season for tourism. She buys a local map from an old Greek woman at the tourist office. Holding the map awkwardly, she impulsively jumps on a tourist bus waiting in front of the airport. She has no accommodation booked and no plans. Under the clear Mediterranean sunlight, she moves along the dry, mountainous landscape.

She gets off the bus with two young backpackers at the second stop. It is on the way to the Iraklio area. There are a few shops along the street ahead and a hotel named Kazantzakis Inn. She walks into the hotel lobby and asks the price of a room.

The afternoon idles away through Iona's tired and lonesome eyes. Although sunny, it is very windy and not warm at all. Winter seems to be the same old cold everywhere in the northern hemisphere, even on this sunlit Greek island. She wanders about by the harbour, on the beach, and in those small streets where they sell different editions of Nikos Kazantzakis's famous novel *Zorba the Greek*. Everywhere she goes, she imagines Jian might have once sat: here and there, in that cafe, on this low wall, hungry and weary, scribbling words in his diary.

Or even—perhaps, he is still here somewhere on the island. Iona feels she should conduct her investigation properly: stay for a good few weeks; travel to the west coast of the island; talk to locals; walk along the rocks by the seashore. Then she may find her Jian.

When evening arrives, Iona drops her tired body on a chair at an empty beach bar. On the counter a TV is showing footage of a national football game and two sluggish waiters loaf around, half asleep. She sits outside on the terrace, slowly drinking a bottle of beer called Mythos. It doesn't taste bad, better than most English ale she's drunk in pubs at home. Her empty eyes scan the empty streets under the evening street lights, looking for a Chinese figure. The sky is dark above her, black and golden clouds drift by. Gradually stars invade the boundless space.

The next morning Iona wakes early in her small hotel room, rested and eager. Pulling back the curtain, she opens the window, breathing in the salty sea. Ah, this is Crete; as Jian said, the sea here is the purest and bluest! As the sunlight burns into her retina, she feels fresh and energised. She comes down to the lobby where the hotel serves breakfast with her hair still wet from her shower. She picks up a bilingual local newspaper called *Expat Crete*, and drinks a glass of orange juice as she casually reads. Well, even if I gain nothing on this island, even if I find nothing, still, I will have just given myself a special holiday. She tells herself: why not just enjoy it? She flips the newspaper pages as she sips her coffee. The paper is not very exciting, mainly notices about forthcoming local festivities, hotel adverts and the mention of cruise trips and island-hopping for Christmas. Then on page 3, she spots this:

```
Crete West Coast Police report:
   At 5:18 p.m. on 15 November, a local fisher-
man in Rethymno and his grandson discovered
a body washed up on the shore near their
```

fishing hut. The man, who likely drowned, may have been dead for up to twenty-four hours, the autopsy yesterday confirmed.

The victim is an Asian male said to be in his late thirties. Police are yet to release the name of the dead man. The fisherman told our reporter: "I found a green army bag behind a bush while I was drying my net on the rocks." Police confirm that the bag contained a ten-euro note, a Chinese passport, a French health insurance card and a diary written in Chinese. The fisherman added, "At first I thought maybe someone had gone for a swim and hidden his belongings in the bushes. But there were no clothes or shoes around. Later that evening I saw a body being washed onto the shore."

The fisherman, who is first-aid trained, claimed that he and his grandson pulled the body out of the water and that chest compressions were performed. Medical staff confirmed the man was dead on arrival. Further details will be released by police once family have been found and informed.

What? Iona reads the first line again: *At 5:18 p.m. on 15 November?* Yesterday afternoon. Yesterday afternoon when she was sitting in this lonely terrace cafe by the sea, looking at the snow-capped mountains while drinking a Mythos beer. *The victim is an Asian male.* He was drowned only some hours before Iona wandered around the island, or probably he was sinking down while she switched off the lamp in Kazantzakis Inn. She scans the article again: . . . *a ten-euro note, a*

Chinese passport, a French health insurance card and a diary written in Chinese . . .

It cannot be! Oh fuck. Iona puts down her piece of toast, pushes away the pot of mango and strawberry jam, her plate, her coffee. Grabbing the newspaper, she stands up and rushes out of the hotel.

10 CRETE, NOVEMBER 2013

Two and an half hours later, Iona jumps off a bus in Rethymno, and finds herself at the Crete West Coast Police Station.

"What's your relation to the victim?" the female police officer asks her in English with a heavy Greek accent.

Her young male colleague squints at Iona from time to time as he takes notes.

"Well, I'm his friend. But—look. Um, first—has the body been identified?, I need to know. Can I have a look at his passport?—then I can be sure if he's someone I know . . ." Iona mutters, still holding the torn page of the newspaper she took from her hotel this morning.

There are no systems or rules here, it seems. The officer behind the desk is completely uninterested in Iona backing up her claims to be the victim's friend. Instead she opens her desk drawer, and throws an old passport onto the table in front of her. A People's Republic of China Passport. Oh God, Iona thinks.

She opens it at the identification details section:

Surname: Jian
Given name: Kublai
Birth date: 10 November 1972
Birth place: Beijing, China

Then the face of a Chinese man, a man whom Iona has imagined hundreds of times—Kublai Jian with his eyes uncovered. There is something indefinable in those dark eyes under his straight, thick eyebrows.

"So, is he someone you know?" the female officer asks, taking back the passport.

"Yes. I am his . . . his translator, you could say . . ." Iona feels her heart beating fast, and she is shaky and sweating. She needs a glass of water, or perhaps something to eat, to calm her down.

"You are his translator . . . Yeah. OK, right . . . and where do you live?" The officer's tone is monotonous. She has a form and a pen poised to take down details. She tilts her head to the side, waiting.

"I live in London, and I'm working on the translations—" Iona is about to say more but realises that it just doesn't matter. This police-woman doesn't care who Jian was and what her connection to him is. It's all procedure. Iona says, "He is, or was, a musician."

"Right . . ." The officer writes something on the form and looks up again. "Do you know if he used any other name? Like a Western name?"

Iona shakes her head. "I'm not sure, but he might have a French health insurance card with a different name . . ." She hears her own voice trembling slightly.

"Yes, we've got that. A—" she takes the plastic card out and reads the name badly in Greek-accented Chinese—"Mr. Chang Linyuan . . . Yes, that was also found in his bag."

"I think Chang was a chef Kublai Jian met in France."

"We can lead you to the morgue to check the body, but before that you have to fill in all your personal details here."

In the morgue, Iona's eyes rest on a seawater-washed body. His face is pale, swollen, although it still retains the traces of youth, and a vague sense of some original character. His eyes are closed, those eyes Iona has never seen, and now, as if they completed their final statement, the secret is sealed forever. A certain horror creeps from the corpse lying there on the slab to Iona's body.

"So is this the man you say you know? A Kublai Jian?" the female officer asks.

A few seconds of silence, then Iona breathes out. "Actually I have never met him. I only know his writing, and I am not certain this is him."

"What do you mean?" The police officer is not happy with Iona's answer. Her face becomes rigid. "When we were upstairs you told me you were this man's friend, you were his translator."

"Yes, but I have only been translating the documents about him, I have never actually met him in person."

The cool gaze of the policewoman chills Iona. Neither of them says a word. There is only sickly heavy air hanging around them.

Back upstairs Iona is handed a diary and a letter. A letter with familiar scrawly handwriting. This time, it is not a photocopy, but an original.

Under the gaze of two police officers and a secretary, Iona silently reads the first four lines of the letter. Then she stops. She can't bring herself to believe what she is reading.

To the ones in this world who will eventually read my words:
And to Mu:
The sea here is the bluest and purest I have ever seen. It's the last blue I will see. They say planet Earth is a blue planet when you see it from space. So I want to go out with the blue.

Iona takes a deep breath, and reads a few more lines.

And the air, too. As much as I like to breathe the fragrance of the gum trees and the dried sunflowers, it's not going to win me back. It's not an argument that can convince me to stay. It's just a smell in my nostrils. So what? There is something in my head that I can't swing out of, and now that thing in my head has spread to the whole world. It saturates it all. So there is no space left for me.

I have sung my songs and there's no longer a place for me to sing them, either in the East or the West. There never was a punk culture in China. Punk isn't an illusion. It's the masses who suffer from the illusion. They cannot escape to see through the veil of commodification and the advertising slogan. I do not regret, or think I was wrong in, the manifesto I wrote. But maybe there was never a manifesto in the end: it is me, becoming what I wrote.

You are in my mind every day. I am talking to you every day of my life, but our life in this world has ended. I am already with those who have taken the other path. My dead mother, my deceased grandparents, and our baby boy Little Shu. Whether the end is now or in the future, since time has stopped flowing forward, it's all the same. I don't have dreams of living in an afterlife. I am not for life. I know I have disappointed you, my dearest.

Time is flowing backwards here. Leaves are leaping from the ground and attaching themselves to the trees, and waves are going back out to sea. The wind is dropping sand from the sky onto the beach; but I am not growing younger . . .

Best to draw a line in the sand. No more than this.

Don't forget, my love for you is beyond this life.

Jian

11 LONDON, NOVEMBER 2013

When the plane lands Iona switches on her mobile and rings Jonathan. As she waits for the line to be connected, she realises it is Friday night, nearly eight o'clock.

"Listen, Jonathan, I know the timing is shitty, but is there any way I can see you this evening?"

"This evening? I'm busy right now, Iona. We're actually having a little celebration in our office for—"

"It can't wait, Jonathan. It's really urgent. Please, it's about the work—about Kublai Jian."

Iona can hear background noise from the other end of the phone. "Well, if it is about work, how about you come into the office on Monday morning and we can talk about it then?"

"No, I need to see you. How about tomorrow morning?"

"Tomorrow morning? You mean Saturday? OK, if you want. But you know, as I said, Iona, I'm not going to publish this book for a while—"

"Yes. I heard. So, where can we meet?" Iona keeps it brief.

"How about lunch? I can cook something simple at my house, if you don't mind coming to Shepherd's Bush."

For a second, Iona thinks she has misheard. Go to his house? What about his wife and children? But she hasn't misheard, for then he says, "I'll text you the address. Say around one o'clock?"

Iona is surprised, confused perhaps, but she answers a weak "Yes." The phone is hot against her ear. She doesn't really know how she should feel. The London sky is dark and starless, the concrete pavement frosty under her sore feet. It must be reaching near-freezing.

12 LONDON, NOVEMBER 2013

Saturday morning. Waking up from a series of feverish dreams with the faces of men she's slept with—even the face of a peaceful, dead Jian—Iona opens her eyes. She looks at the clock; it is already ten thirty.

In the shower she lets the warm water run through her hair and down her body. She dimly remembers an episode of her dream—first there was an urgent doorbell, twice, very impatient; then, as she opened the door, two Chinese policemen stood before her with inscrutable faces. They pushed her away, entered the room and walked straight to her desk, where they snatched her computer, along with all the Chinese documents laid beside it. Then suddenly, in that inexplicable way that things happen in dreams, the figures disappeared, leaving her alone and confused standing by the open door, looking back at her empty desk. When she realised what was happening, she tried to run downstairs, but her body was so heavy she couldn't lift her legs—her dream had chained them together, she had no strength and she struggled, forcing her legs to move until she was exhausted. And then she had woken up.

When she opened her eyes, the first thing she did was sit up instantly and stagger towards her desk. And there was her computer and all the Chinese files. They were there like a pile of fossils, untouched, secretive, but safe. In her pyjamas she had sat down at her desk for a moment, just laying her hand on the pile of papers for a few minutes. A verification. A prayer. Until she was properly awake.

Two hours later, Iona comes out of Shepherd's Bush Tube station, crosses the main road and checks the map on her phone. She walks down the street scanning the house numbers. It doesn't take her long to find Jonathan's place. It is a typical Victorian family house, with wisteria growing up the side of the heavy door and a broken child's bicycle in the front garden. As she presses the doorbell, a dog starts barking inside; then Jonathan opens the door. He is wearing a T-shirt and low-slung jeans, and has a cooking spoon in his hand. They kiss on both cheeks. Iona feels slightly disappointed.

"Come on in. Are you hungry? I've just finished making some soup."

She shoves herself, curious and yet unprepared, into a house she has imagined for a long while. There is a strong smell of roasted onions coming from the kitchen. As she takes off her winter coat and scarf, she doesn't hear the expected noise of children, and nor does a woman emerge to greet her. The house is quiet and spacious, but very messy. Newspapers and books are piled everywhere, as well as some manuscripts. Iona spots the early pages of her translation which she sent to Applegate Books all those months ago. Well, here we are, we are on the same page now, she mutters to herself. At the back of the kitchen, the garden is wild and the grass untrimmed, a leafy old apple tree standing in the middle. In a corner of the garden lies a pile of sun-bleached children's toys.

"Make yourself comfortable. Do you want some soup? And I couldn't resist getting some fish, too," Jonathan says. "I remember you saying you liked sea bass."

He seems to be in a good mood and glad that she's there. He does not know why she is suddenly here for an urgent Saturday visit, but equally he does not ask, and she is glad of that. Iona feels nervous and unsettled. For a brief moment she thinks perhaps she won't tell him anything. They can have a nice lunch together, perhaps go upstairs to bed, or sit and talk about books. She doesn't know where to start, to ask about where his family is, or to tell him she has just been to Crete, and found Kublai Jian's dead body in the basement of a police station with a suicide letter.

But there he is: Jonathan, a man whose life is about constructing stories; the man who has sent her on a heavy emotional journey in the last few months. He is not at all just someone; he is a particular one, with a clear mind and firm presence.

"Where is your . . . family?" asks Iona hesitantly.

He turns his head from the stove and the hot steam rising from the pot of soup. He looks at her intently then turns back to his cooking. "They don't live here any more. Let me get the cooking done and then we can talk."

She stands behind him, watching him cooking, and waits. But she is not watching him at all, in fact her eyes see nothing of this reality. All she can see is a frozen body on a slab in the basement of Crete West Coast Police Station.

"Kublai Jian is dead," she blurts out.

"What?"

"He died three days ago. I went to Crete, and I went to the local police station on the island to see the body."

"You went to Crete? You saw his body? What? Stop, hang on. Iona, what are you talking about?"

"I just got back last night." Iona's voice is taut, frustrated. "I was too late . . . if I'd only gone to look for him two days earlier, or even a week earlier, a month earlier . . . I could have talked to him. I could have saved him! I knew he was in Crete. I figured out from his diary that Crete might be where he would go if he—if he felt that awful he—but I didn't get there on time! I was too late! It's so stupid of me!"

Iona's control crumbles and she bursts out a flood of words and tears all at once. She feels extremely angry with herself.

Jonathan still doesn't say anything. He stirs the soup very slowly.

Iona takes a battered piece of paper out of her pocket. Jian's final letter to the world, a photocopy she brought back from Crete West Coast Police Station.

An hour passes. A deep sense of lassitude and loss have taken over them both, making them numb and speechless.

13 LONDON, NOVEMBER 2013

They sit down to eat the soup, barely lukewarm now. Green lentil soup and steamed sea bass to follow. Jonathan puts a bottle of white wine in front of Iona, while he opens a can of beer for himself. He breaks the silence.

"You were asking about my family before, well, I can tell you now . . . if you still want to know."

Iona nods her head.

"A year ago, my wife took my two boys to India," he starts slowly. "It was supposed to be a holiday, but then it stretched into months; later she returned with the boys but only stayed in London for two months. Then she went to India again, taking the children with her. She hasn't been back since."

"What about the children?"

"She's put them in an international school in Delhi and is asking for a divorce."

A pause. Iona puts down her spoon.

"And I can do nothing in India, apart from be a tourist. I need to be here with my work, and my company."

"I'm sorry to hear that . . ." Iona says in a low voice. "You did mention you were in India a while ago."

"Yes, and it turned out to be a disaster." He finishes his soup, pushes his bowl to one side, and continues talking, his voice a little subdued. "She didn't let on that she had been in love with her yoga teacher for the last two years. The holiday was a ruse; he'd moved out there and she couldn't resist following. You could say I had a bit of a rude awakening. When I arrived in Delhi I was standing in the doorway with my suitcase still in my hands when suddenly her boyfriend came out of her bedroom and started playing with my children in their sitting room like a big happy family."

Jonathan falls silent. Iona watches him picking out bones from his sea bass with a fork.

"Is he Indian?" Iona asks.

"No, he's a hippy from America, actually. Used to teach here, then moved to Delhi." Jonathan's voice becomes calmer. "I left and checked into a hotel. It was a new place, run by a Dutch couple. I holed up in the bedroom, put the air conditioning on, and read most of your translation. I thought: here I am, in a tacky Indian hotel, reading an exiled Chinese man's story, unable to see my wife and my children. How absurd is that." He sounds resigned, calm almost.

Iona takes a bite of the fish, it's overcooked and cooling fast. She puts her knife and fork down, gazes into the dull eye of the fish on her plate, trying to comb out a tangle of thoughts. "Sorry, Jonathan, I don't know what to say," she mumbles.

"That's OK. It's mainly my fault, I realise . . ." Jonathan's voice becomes clearer as he finishes his beer. "Her dissatisfaction with me is understandable. I care too much about my work, never give enough attention to her and the children. Right now I feel like I care more about Kublai Jian's family than my own."

It is a chilly Saturday afternoon. The winter air penetrates the door and streaks of condensation slip down the windowpanes. Iona looks out to the garden, the branches of the apple tree shiver and bend in the wind. But there is something unusual in today's air. She looks more closely. Yes, it is snowing. Jonathan follows her eyes and watches the snow for a beat. They walk out of the kitchen, and stand in the middle of the garden, gazing at the gently falling flakes.

Iona reaches out her hand to the snow. Suddenly she no longer feels anxious, either with herself or with Jonathan.

They return inside and pick over the remainder of their lunch.

"I had a dream last night," Iona says, looking at her food, and then looks up. "It was horrible. I dreamed two Chinese policemen entered my flat and confiscated all the documents and my computer. Then I woke up. I wondered why I wanted to come here today—just to tell you Kublai Jian is dead, or something more? And then I found the answer on the way to your house." Iona looks into Jonathan's eyes. "You must publish this book, Jonathan, as soon as you can. I don't think we should worry about pressure from China."

Jonathan folds his arms, sits back and listens to her attentively.

"This is Britain after all!" Iona raises her voice, flicks her hair back dramatically. "It's also my book, Jonathan. I've been working on this for months now. It's got into me. You might not know what it is to struggle to translate and bring out something from another world into our world. It's hard, and it takes it out of you, your energy, your days and nights. I've been getting deeper and deeper into these two people and their story. They've laid it all before me, like they're ready to open themselves up to the world. And I have been a part of that opening up."

Jonathan looks confused.

"Opening up—to China. Mu and Jian have such an incredible and tough story. It cuts across so much of what we take for granted. Don't pretend you don't understand. Don't pretend you don't believe in this too, Jonathan . . . And maybe it's about responsibility also. It's a cliché, but we owe it to them to tell their story, to show their love, and their destruction too . . ." Iona's eyes glitter. "Maybe also to report on Jian's death. We can show what his choice was and how he decided to die, and that's important. I thought, here it is, I'm going to live with them, live through them, until the day this story comes out into the light. And there's no way I'm going to let anyone hush it up. We must publish it. And soon!"

Jonathan smiles and says her name. "Iona."

She suddenly feels she has known this man for a very long time. She is so familiar with his frown, his smile, his discreetly greying hair about the temples, and she feels that she probably knows his awkwardness and his weaknesses too. She recognises what he is, and is comfortable with that; but it's subtle, as if it comes from some recess in the back of her mind.

As their eyes meet, a phone rings somewhere in the house. Jonathan turns round; it's the phone in the living room. He lets it ring until it stops and the room becomes quiet again.

They grin. Her dimple is deep. The air in the winter house becomes sweeter, thicker; it collects between Jonathan and Iona and links them. She knows there is something precious in this moment, something to do with love, in this space, right now. She feels like crying. This feeling is so fragile, so discreet, and yet it seems mutually acknowledged without either of them saying another word. For a while, in this space, all they hear is the wind shaking the windows, and the soft hush of snow falling on the apple tree in the garden.

NINE | WOMEN WITHOUT MEN

海底捞月。

Hai di lao yue.

It's not likely to fish the moon out from the bottom of the sea.

SONGS OF YONG JIA ZHENG DAO, SHI YUAN JUE
    (WRITER, TANG DYNASTY, EIGHTH CENTURY)

1

Buckingham Palace
London, SW1A 1AA

Mr. Kublai Jian
Lincolnshire Psychiatric Hospital
2 Brocklehurst Crescent
Grantham NG31

Dear Mr. Kublai Jian,

I am pleased to inform you that I have received your letter regarding your situation at the Lincolnshire Psychiatric Hospital. We are indeed highly sensitive to your plight, and are most sympathetic towards your personal predicament. However, your demand concerns a sphere of action beyond the remit of the obligation of one's duty as monarch. Regrettably, no legal or diplomatic assistance can be extended to you under the circumstances. We are cognisant that your case will be duly processed by the UK's Home Office Immigration Department.

Be aware that as monarch, and head of the Church of England, we are serenely beyond prejudice against, or partiality towards, your person, and you can rest assured that fairness and impartiality will prevail, as is proper for our situation. We are told that the population of the UK has reached 62 million, 18 per cent of whom comprise ethnic groups, with 22 million non-white British citizens. We are truly living in a multicultural society. Therefore, one believes you will manage to gain solid ground through the legal process.

Finally, we enclose your CD, Yuan vs. Dollars, *as per your request that it be returned. We listened with some degree of interest to this assemblage of undoubtedly authentic ethnic expression. Indeed, we were amused. We believe your musical career will continue to flourish despite your current difficulties. We wish you a swift resolution of your present setbacks.*

Yours truly,

Elizabeth R

2

Deng Mu
35 Thistle House, Tudor Lane
London E2 7SF

Iona Kirkpatrick
9B Chapel Market
London N1

Dear Iona,

This is Deng Mu, a Chinese poet. We have never met. But I think you know my story.

I'm writing to you as I found out that you are translating the writings between Jian and me for future publication. I hope you are managing well with them.

Jian posted me his diary and letters, just before I left China for the UK. And only very recently I heard he is "dead" from a newspaper. It said he drowned himself on a Greek island. But so far there is barely a proof my eyes can see and believe. From what I knew about Jian, he was a very vigorous person, and I would never imagine he would choose to die in such a way. In my memory he doesn't believe in killing oneself. I really find it hard to believe what I've heard is true.

Before he posted me his writings, the last letter I received from Jian was about a year and a few months ago, he wrote to me when he was in France. He said he didn't like the Western life, he dreaded the solitude, or rather being totally cut off from his past. He missed China badly, it haunted him. He said he was taking the train down to Marseilles, where he would work on a ship with someone he knew there. And I've heard nothing since. He's never had a stable address, especially after he left the asylum centre. On my side, I've moved around a lot, too. I left China to go to America, then ended up here in the UK. It seems that my life and his life are destined to drift apart.

But recently, about two weeks ago, I saw a man who really looked like Jian in east London. I was at Old Street station and I was going down to the Tube on the escalator, and I saw a Chinese man coming up on the other side of the escalator. He was wearing this old black leather jacket like Jian used to wear in Beijing, his startling black hair was long and covered his shoulders but it was very much Jian's hair. He was small-framed like Jian was. The only feature I couldn't catch were his eyes, and that trademark scar under his left eye which he had when he was a child. Before I reached the bottom and could run back up he had already disappeared from the top of the escalator and off into the night. I've been back a few times at the same hour but I haven't had any luck. I have been thinking of this for days now, and I still think it might have been him.

One more thing—as you know, Jian and I always argued about politics and how it fits into life. Jian's answer was to write; he was constantly writing a new manifesto. In the end, he was forced out of China thanks to the manifesto he distributed at his last concert. This one was not like the ones before.

Jian was obsessed with trying to understand power, and the power of men. He grew up with very little love but plenty of rigid ideology around him. He was too caught up in that sphere of ideas and ideologies. Men often lose themselves in these things. I know we come from different backgrounds, but you might have discovered this too. If we always have to engage in ideological struggle like Jian, to try to gain political power, where is the place for life? And in the end it kills us. Over all these years I have come to believe the opposite of Jian. We die, governments change, ideologies evolve, borders disappear, rivers merge, islands sink, trees rot, bones dissolve, even nature expires one day. But the universe exists, with stars or without stars, with air or without air, infinitely and unimaginably beyond man. I know that the infinite world is there beyond trivial ideologies or politics. And we only have one life to live. I know this is a long discussion, and maybe it will even sound silly to some people, but it was a never-ending discussion between me and Jian. Anyway, I leave these pages of the manifesto to you. As always, his handwriting is messy, like the drawings of a drunk calligrapher, but I'll let you judge the discussion for yourself.

Finally, one last thought: I was wondering if you might be able to attend my first poetry performance in this country. It will be held next Friday, at Foyles on Charing Cross Road. The reading will start at 7:30 p.m., please say you are on the guest list of Deng Mu. I sincerely hope you can make it—it would mean a lot to me.

Your new friend,
Mu

TRANSLATION OF THE MANIFESTO

DREAM:

I had a dream. I dreamed I was a great nation. I was a state. My power stretched over the land and its peoples. I felt power running through my veins, and felt it strong in my heart. I was China.

Then I woke up. I wondered: was I a man waking from a dream of being China, or was China dreaming of being a man?

If I am a man dreaming I am China, I want to rule the world. To be a great state, with power over the people like small animals beneath me.

If China dreams of being a man, then I am just that man living out the myth of a great state. My thoughts and desires are not my own, but are taken from the state. China rules my heart.

POWER AND MYTH:

The state needs myth: it creates a mythical vision for the people to live by and live for. This is China. China is the great myth-maker.

GUNS AND POWER:

Why does China need myth? Is it not enough that a state has guns? If there are guns, can't the guns be used to control the people? Mao said: Power flows out of the barrel of a gun. Gun is power. But the rule of the gun is not the greatest power. There are only so many bullets, and people will always resist. If the state kills its people, it will have no one to grow rice, build cars and create luxury.

The state needs to control its soldiers and its people. Myth is necessary to control the soldiers who fire the bullets. With a great myth the people control themselves. China's myth used to be that of Tian Zi—the emperors. Now it is the myth of the great democratic middle-class society who consume this and consume that with commercial freedom.

INVISIBLE:

I am a drop in the ocean, in an ocean I cannot see.
I am a brick in a wall I cannot feel.
I am a citizen of a state, but of a state that is everywhere.
I am a citizen of China, but China is everywhere.
Our leaders hid themselves after the revolution, and became secret manipulators. They held up images of past great leaders. They forced themselves into our dreams.
The real state hides itself, to hide how it works. When the citizen dreams, they know nothing of who makes their dreams.

COCK / GUITAR / ARTIST:

Who really has the power in this invisible state? The artist looks down at his cock, and his cock looks at his guitar. Then his guitar looks at him. They all look at each other. Who is playing whom? Each said: "I am!"

ART AND THE ART OF POLITICS:

Now the artist must deal with politics. That's why art is always a political thing. What is a political thing? The political is power *exercising itself at the moment of revolution. It is when we create the impossible. That is art.*

Art is the politics of perpetual revolution. Art is the purest revolution, and so the purest political form there is.

A great artist is a revolutionary.

Revolution = art, and art = perfect freedom. Right now, we have no revolution, no real art and no freedom.

INCONCEIVABLE REVOLUTION:

Revolution happens when we strip off the invisibility cloak and show the emperor.

Revolution happens when the water in which the citizens swim is frozen. The ice breaks and shatters and the fish are cast out onto the dry land, gasping for air.

REVOLUTION:

Revolution is impossible. This is the first fact about revolution. Revolution is when politics happens. The only real political act is revolutionary. Otherwise, it's just the day-to-day grind of the state, the day-to-day buying and selling. In a democracy the people think there is politics. But it is just theatre.

Revolution is impossible because the people live in prison by choice. They consume the state's myth as their daily comfort.

REVOLUTION IN CHINA:

In China the impossible happened more than once. The youth of Tiananmen Square realised the impossible for hundreds of years.

But it did not last. The impossible vision faded into concrete reality and China became a state again.

PERPETUAL REVOLUTION:

The perpetual revolution is the revolution that even revolutionises itself. Perpetual revolution is complete freedom. Art is complete freedom. And love is complete freedom.

A DEBATE: THE REALIST VS. THE REVOLUTIONARY:

You, my realist, say this: "What you say is unrealistic. It is of no interest since it is unreal and unrealisable. I can only feel and respond to what is around me. And love, which must be there in the end, lives in a reality separate from revolution."

The revolutionary answers: "My friend, you accept this world of everyday imperfection and appearance, of compromises and small steps. And you talk of 'love.' You speak as if there is no love in me. But that is not true. Our love has been dragged onto a political battlefield. And often it just doesn't look like love, it looks like a battle."

The realist responds: "But love only lives in the work of imperfection."

"Love should live in the perfect revolution," says the revolutionary. "It's a process. It's not something we arrive at, but an imperative. It is an arrow. It always moves beyond itself."

BREAK THE SPELL:

I am China. We are China. The people. Not the state.

3 LONDON, DECEMBER 2013

Iona raises her head from the Chinese files. The translation is finished. Somehow she never imagined she would arrive at this point. It feels like the first time in her life that she has managed to finish something significant, totally and completely. It's the end of something, and the beginning of something else.

In the street below the winter light illuminates London in a hazy half-glow. She sees people rushing along the pavement, sellers packing up, buyers leaving. She hears the sound of trucks driving away for the day with their unsold goods; the Turkish shop downstairs turning on the TV, and the evening-ready clack of high heels on the street below. Life is roaring with full force, even though the evening swallows the city whole. But perhaps all this is not natural, inevitable. One cannot take it for granted. Perhaps it is not determined by any law of human life. It is a matter of history and luck. Iona finds herself murmuring: "*I am China. We are China . . .*" She repeats, in a hypnotic mood. "*The people. Not the state.*"

The number 38 bus on this Friday evening is crowded with people jostling each other in the sardine-can interior, fiddling with their iPhones and iPods, or just staring blankly ahead. Outside, the sky is pierced by a rosta of burning red clouds. Against the horizon are dark trees and curious towers, whose shapes are reflected in the windows of the bus. They zigzag through London's narrow streets. As the light gets darker and glows redder, everyone on the bus becomes restless. Spanish-speaking, Swahili-speaking, French, German, Swedish, Japanese, Vietnamese, Greek, Turkish, Portuguese, Russian, the voices flood into Iona's ears, like a dark but mysteriously busy underworld she can't understand.

Right now she is eager to hear only one voice, the voice she has imagined for so long, the voice from so many letters and diaries.

The bus halts abruptly. It's already a quarter to eight. She hurries up Charing Cross Road, wishes she could have left her flat an hour earlier, as her ears ring with a Chinese-sounding voice: "*The reading will start at 7.30 p.m., please say you are on the guest list of Deng Mu. I sincerely hope you can make it—it would mean a lot to me.*"

Iona pushes the glass door of the bookshop and enters the hallway. She runs up the staircase that leads to the reading area. A woman's voice projected through a microphone seeps into her ears. At first she can't figure out whether the words are Chinese or English. But as she climbs further up the twisting staircase, the voice gets clearer. It's English, spoken with an oriental accent. The words finish, then there is the sound of applause.

And there she is, stepping off the stage: a Chinese woman, slim, bony body, long black hair hanging like a veil on her shoulders. Her energy feels young but her eyes betray some gentle signs of age and experience. Still, they shine in the dark, lighting her moon-shaped face. Holding loose sheets of paper are small hands, the very ones Jian wrote about. Have I missed her reading already? A shudder of disappointment grips Iona. It can't be over yet! A second reader takes to the stage as Iona moves quickly, piercing the crowd, towards the dark figure now whispering with a member of the audience. It is as if her attention were reaching out to the poet with some invisible connection. The moon-shaped-face woman turns to her, before they have exchanged any words, as if with a certain recognition.

"Excuse me . . . I'm Iona, the translator of your own and Jian's writings."

The Chinese woman grips her hand; she seems to be matching Iona's name to her physical presence. "I'm really happy you've come." There's more applause and Mu stands up. "I have another reading to do now. Stay and listen. You will understand it better than anyone here."

She returns to the stage area, her eyes illuminated by the spotlight. Then the room is filled with the resonance of her voice.

"Now I want to begin with the work of a poet whose spirit means a lot to me. The poem is 'America' by Allen Ginsberg, but I have changed the word 'America' to 'China.' I want to dedicate this poem to a man whom I was very close to. His name was Kublai Jian. He was a poet, too."

China

China I've given you all and now I'm nothing.
China two dollars and twenty-seven cents.
I can't stand my own mind.
China when will we end the human war?
Go fuck yourself with your atom bomb
I don't feel good don't bother me.
I won't write my poem till I'm in my right mind.

China when will you be angelic?
When will you take off your clothes?
When will you look at yourself through the grave?
When will you be worthy of your million Trotskyites?
China why are your libraries full of tears?
China when will you send your eggs to India?
I'm sick of your insane demands.

When can I go into the supermarket and buy what I need
    with my good looks?
China after all it is you and I who are perfect not the next
    world.
Your machinery is too much for me.
You made me want to be a saint.
There must be some other way to settle this argument.

Burroughs is in Tangiers I don't think he'll come back it's
      sinister.
Are you being sinister or is this some form of practical
      joke?
I'm trying to come to the point.
I refuse to give up my obsession.
China stop pushing I know what I'm doing.
China the plum blossoms are falling.

I haven't read the newspapers for months, every day
      somebody goes on trial for murder.
China I feel sentimental about the Wobblies.
China I used to be a communist when I was a kid and I'm
      not sorry.
I smoke marijuana every chance I get.
I sit in my house for days and stare at the roses in the
      closet.
When I go to Chinatown I get drunk and never get laid.
My mind is made up there's going to be trouble.
You should have seen me reading Marx.
My psychoanalyst thinks I'm perfectly right.
I won't say the Lord's Prayer.
I have mystical visions and cosmic vibrations.
China I still haven't told you what you did to Uncle Max
      after he came over from Russia.

China I'm addressing you.
Are you going to let our emotional life be run by Time
      Magazine?
I'm obsessed by Time Magazine.
I read it every week.
Its cover stares at me every time I slink past the corner
      candystore.

I read it in the basement of the Berkeley Public Library.

It's always telling me about responsibility. Businessmen are
    serious, movie producers are serious. Everybody's serious
    but me.

It occurs to me that I am China.

I am talking to myself again.

POSTSCRIPT

On a snowy London afternoon two years later, a lone Chinese woman walks into a bookshop. On a front centre desk, there are copies of a new book with a scarlet-red cover. She picks one up and flicks through the first few pages. Her eyes begin to glisten, her moon-shaped face is illuminated with surprise.

She reads: "*This book is dedicated to Jian and Mu, who will meet again in these pages.*"

At the same hour of that day, in another part of the town, another black-haired woman, clutching a copy of the same book in her right hand, walks into her favourite garden. The snow has just stopped; blackbirds come out searching for food. And her lone bench is visible between the pine trees and withered honeysuckle plants.

It's as if she is sleepwalking, or in a daydream. She is surprised to find herself where she is. It's like she has gone back in time, but the world has moved on. The garden is unchanged, although a thin layer of new snow covers the earth. She looks at her feet; they are planted firmly on the crisp short grass. How incredible, she thinks: it didn't drift away or disappear; she looks at her hands, yes, the same bony hand grasps the new book she has spent an intense time of her life working on. And the garden, it is still at the junction of the same two streets, with the same paint-peeling gate, the same flyers on the noticeboard, the same pine trees standing on the right and the dead rose bushes on the left; and the two chestnut trees are exactly where they have always been. Nothing has moved. It seems obvious, yet unbelievable at the same time. Not even the dried-up maple leaves on the ground have changed their composition. Iona walks further, passing a group of children playing hide-and-seek among the bushes.

Around the trees there is laughter, screaming, and a mother's calls. The scent of the pine needles is intoxicating. She drinks in the flavour of their smell and reaches up to touch the low-hanging pine cones, green even in the middle of winter. She walks towards her bench. The bench is still here. But there is an elderly man sitting on it. A man in a winter jacket and a fur hat, smoking a cigarette. It looks as if he is something that has just sprouted out of the ground and taken human shape. This again surprises her. She sits beside the old man, and he squints at her from under his winter hat.

The afternoon sun shines on the pines and warms the people on the bench. A helicopter passes above their heads, its panicked whirr disrupting the calm. The young woman and the old man both gaze at the giant pine in front of them.

She realises there is a child underneath the tree, a little girl in a white coat. The girl jumps, trying to grab the low branches. She fails, jumps again. Finally she grasps hold of a branch and clambers onto it. Unsteadily but persistently, she climbs into the heart of the tree.

Iona gazes at the little girl climbing the pine, holding the branches, and moving higher and higher. She watches for a long time, until the girl disappears. From the treetop, high up in the branches, the little girl looks out across the park. She has never been this high and it's slightly scary. She sees the two people down on the park bench, an old man and a dark-haired young woman. Through the foliage she thinks she can spy the sea, the lapping waves, the soaring gulls and, in the distance, a dark island she has never visited. They call it the Isle of Iona.

APPENDIX: CHRONOLOGY

The abdication of Puyi, the last Emperor of China: 1912
First World War: 1914–18
Chinese Communist Party founded: 1921
Civil war between the Nationalist and Communist parties: 1927–50
The Long March of the Red Army: 1933–35
Hu Shulai (Jian's father) born: 1935
Hu Dongsheng (Jian's grandfather) dies: 1935 (during the Long March)
Chinese War of Resistance against Japan: 1937–45
Second World War: 1939–45
Mao Zedong proclaims the People's Republic of China: 1949
War to Resist U.S. Aggression and Aid Korea: 1950–53
China's first Five Year Plan: 1953–57
Anti-Rightist Movement: 1957–59
Great Leap Forward: 1958–60
Great Chinese Famine: 1958–61
Cultural Revolution: 1966–76
Apollo 11 lands on the moon: 1969
President Richard Nixon visits China: 1972
Kublai Jian born: 1972
Deng Mu born: 1975
Mao Zedong dies: 1976
Jian's mother dies: 1976
Introduction of one-child policy: 1979
Deng Xiaoping begins China's economic reform: 1978
"Misty Poets" form in Beijing with the magazine *Today*: 1978
Shenzhen becomes China's first Special Economic Zone: 1980
Tiananmen Square Student Demonstration for democracy: 1989
Jian graduates from university: 1997
China holds its first Olympic Games: 2008
China launches spacecraft *Shengzhou 9* with three astronauts: 2012
650 million peasants remain in rural China: 2014

ACKNOWLEDGEMENTS

The last few years have seemed to be the hardest years I have gone through in my adult life. First, my father passed away, then my mother. Both suffered badly from terminal cancer. Then I spent a period wandering around Europe trying to decide where to make my home. In the autumn of 2012 I returned from Berlin to London, madly looking for a new flat. Then in 2013 my own child was born—a brand new Hackney citizen only knowing too well the sound of sirens and the drone of traffic along Mare Street. Eventually, I managed to finish this novel, the most demanding and slowest project I've worked on so far.

I am so very fortunate to have found a home with my most loyal publishers: Chatto & Windus in the UK, Nan Talese in the U.S. and Claudia Vidoni in Germany, and to have found editors and agents who have become my friends, who support me in my personal life as well as in my work: Julet Brooke, Clara Farmer, Rebecca Carter, Claire Paterson. I have also found great support in Ruth Warburton, Kate Bland, Anne Rademacher, Kirsty Godon, Martin Ouvry, Owen Sheers, Suzanne Dean and Ruth Little, as well all the people who are behind me on the publishing side of things. And a heartful thanks to *Granta*, who found me before I turned forty.

A deep gratitude also to Stephen Barker and Philippe Ciompi, your absolute support, patience and love is written in the pages of this book.

Last but not the least, to my dear readers across the continent, from Germany to China, from Canada to Australia, from Spain to Argentina. Perhaps you are one of the most important reasons why I continue to write.